Penny Parkes lives in the Cotswolds. She has appeared at literary festivals around the country and has written for the *Telegraph* as well as extensively in her local media. You can find her on Twitter and Instagram as @CotswoldPenny.

Also by Penny Parkes

Home

The Larkford series:

Out of Practice
Practice Makes Perfect
Best Practice
Snowed in at The Practice

eBook only:

Swept Away (eBook short story)

PENNY PARKES

Maybe Tomorrow

SIMON &
SCHUSTER

London · New York · Sydney · Toronto · New Delhi

First published in Great Britain by Simon & Schuster UK Ltd, 2023

Copyright © Wibble Creative Ltd, 2023

The right of Penny Parkes to be identified as author
of this work has been asserted in accordance with the
Copyright, Designs and Patents Act, 1988.

1 3 5 7 9 10 8 6 4 2

Simon & Schuster UK Ltd
1st Floor
222 Gray's Inn Road
London WC1X 8HB

Simon & Schuster Australia, Sydney
Simon & Schuster India, New Delhi

www.simonandschuster.co.uk
www.simonandschuster.com.au
www.simonandschuster.co.in

A CIP catalogue record for this book
is available from the British Library

Paperback ISBN: 978-1-4711-8015-6
eBook ISBN: 978-1-4711-8014-9
Audio ISBN: 978-1-4711-8193-1

Typeset in Bembo by M Rules
Printed and Bound in the UK using 100% Renewable
Electricity at CPI Group (UK) Ltd

MIX
Paper | Supporting
responsible forestry
FSC® C171272

For my Rosie –
Through love, laughter and tears
Thank you for holding my hand
Love you, darling girl, always
Px

Chapter 1

The first casualty of hard times had been spontaneity and even that had been a whispering death by a thousand paper cuts. Jamie pushed aside thoughts of day trips to the beach, or even a simple evening at her favourite tapas bar on the corner; her priorities these days were so much simpler.

In theory at least.

As she arranged the bottles of olive oil in a perfect phalanx, labels all facing front, she allowed herself to enjoy the pleasing symmetry. There was no harm in taking a certain pride in her work, no matter how far she had strayed off course.

Jamie mentally ran through the contents of her fridge at home as she worked, planning out their meals for the rest of the week. Bo's packed lunches, in particular, were a triumph of creativity, a bittersweet pride in her ability to make something out of nothing. And not one single gnarly potato would go uneaten.

There was simply no room in her life for waste or extravagance. She glanced at the bottle of olive oil in her hand and sighed – £37.99.

Obscene, really. And more than her entire weekly shop for two.

But if she was lucky – and if his ever-fluctuating mood allowed – there was always a chance that Nick Harrison might yet allow her to buy the out-of-date stock at the end of her shift.

Discounted.

But still.

It probably wouldn't even occur to him to *give* the stuff away.

She smiled at Daniel, one of her favourite colleagues, as he waltzed along the aisle, sweeping arcs with the heavy, cumbersome mop. Finding his own satisfying distraction in the soothing, rhythmic pattern.

They were none of them here for the mental stimulation or career opportunities, after all. But in the small, suburban town of Harnley, a pay cheque was a pay cheque and not to be sneezed at. As more and more of the small shops along their High Street closed their doors, a quiet pall had settled over their once-vibrant community, the haves and the have-nots never so clearly delineated – in her lifetime at least. 2020 had put paid to their energetic, bustling street of independent shops; 2021 had all but broken them. And to think they had once been so very proud not to have a single chain store, not one single franchise, among them.

Yet Harrison's had survived, their clientele still wanting the niceties that their trust funds, well-endowed pensions or comfortably secure public sector jobs allowed.

It was just a shame that Nick Harrison was such an entitled arsehole. He'd even had the gall to rebuff Daniel's suggestion that they have a basket by the door to collect contributions for the local food bank, on the basis that his customers didn't want to be reminded of 'things like that'. Not when they'd just shelled out nearly forty quid for a bottle of olive oil without a second thought, presumably.

It left a bitter taste in Jamie's mouth.

The very notion of the food bank at the community centre made her uncomfortable too – but not for the same reasons. Every week was a balancing act, robbing Peter to pay Paul. Staying awake late at night, trying to prioritise where her meagre salary should go. And which of her creditors might shout loudest if she fobbed them off again. Trying not to think of the escalating, debilitating interest.

Turning to the food bank still felt like an admission of defeat, though. An admission that she couldn't take care of her own son. Of herself.

All her years studying, training and building a satisfying career for herself, and yet still she couldn't make ends meet. It was hard not to feel like an abject failure, in the grand scheme of things. But truly, she reminded herself, as she always did: she was one of the lucky ones. She had Bo. And she had this job, even with its lousy hours and minimum wage. And she had her health.

Never something to be taken for granted.

She instinctively checked her pocket for Bo's folded prescription and glanced at her watch. As always, she'd be cutting it fine – the sweaty dash to the pharmacy from Harrison's a familiar part of her routine these days.

'Are we keeping you from something more important, *Ms* Matson?'

Nick Harrison should wear a bell around his bloody neck, Jamie thought crossly, as she fixed a smile on her face. 'Of course not.'

Of course, he wouldn't call her Jamie. And she bitterly regretted the instinctive way she'd corrected him at her first interview. Only a man like Nick Harrison could imbue her chosen '*Ms*' with quite so much judgement and disdain. A faux respect afforded to her, when Daniel was Daniel, and Neil was Neil.

'Perhaps you could up the tempo a tad then, Ms Matson. I need the new grissini displayed for our promotion tomorrow.'

Jamie blinked hard. 'But that's next week—'

'I changed my mind. Make sure it's done before you leave. It's not my problem if you can't manage your time properly.' He swept away, leaving Jamie flushed with anger and not a small amount of panic. There was no way to get to the pharmacy before it closed unless she left on the dot.

'I'll help,' said Daniel, stashing his mop against the jars of roasted red peppers. 'Many hands and all that . . .'

'I owe you one,' Jamie said gratefully, as they carted armfuls of the delicate breadsticks in artfully rustic Italian flavours across the store to a more accessible vantage point.

'Don't be daft. I think we can spare a little solidarity for each other, don't you?' he grinned.

4

He looked exhausted, worn down by life, yet still his grace and good humour always made Jamie smile. 'I just don't think that Nick's realised yet that he's nailing the whole team building thing. I mean, there's nothing like a common enemy to bond the troops, is there?'

They deftly arranged the display, many hands making light work of the balancing act required. 'Is Bo on the mend at all, Jamie?' Daniel asked quietly, his English nearly on a par with Jamie's since he'd acquired his beloved dictionary of idioms; only the gentle lilt of his Syrian accent remained as a giveaway. 'Is there any news on seeing that consultant, because you know I'll cover your shift if I can. Just say the word.'

'Thank you,' Jamie said with feeling.

Bo's worsening asthma was a constant in her thoughts, a low, demanding hum in the back of her mind whatever she was doing. And the waiting – the endless waiting, yet again, to see the consultant while they juggled his meds and dealt with the increasingly frequent dashes to A&E for the nebuliser, stretched Jamie's nerves to breaking point.

Yet another thing that Nick Harrison could hold against her: '*More* time off, Ms Matson?' with that raised eyebrow that had the power to invoke such rage in Jamie, as though Bo's hospital appointments were a jolly luxury. Just for shits and giggles, to make the very most of a day away from arranging the fancy fayre on Harrison's shelves.

'You are sweet to help me, Daniel. Truly,' Jamie said with a grateful smile, as they stepped back and admired the display they'd assembled in record time.

'Do you know what, Jamie, I think it's high time you had a bit more help. You do so much, and with such grace.' He gave her a wink. 'Now bugger off before the Silent Assassin comes back with another pointless closing-time task to assert his superiority over us mere mortals.'

He gave her a nudge. 'Seriously. Shoo . . .'

Jamie didn't need telling twice. She glanced out the window and saw that the rain had passed; abandoning her coat in her locker for the night was a small price to pay to get out the door on time for once.

As the electric door swooshed shut behind her, she heard Nick Harrison's voice, calling out, calling her back, but she feigned deafness and broke into a jog. The new inhaler for Bo her priority, no matter how much sway, how much power Nick Harrison held over her.

She'd pay for this tomorrow. She knew that. He'd find some way to undermine, to admonish. And she would fall on her sword, as always, apologising for the sheer audacity of leaving on time.

Within the mini empire he'd built up – Harnley's answer to Wholefoods – Nick Harrison considered himself quite the deity, and his daily power plays had become just a sad part of doing business when you were all out of options. He seemed to be oblivious to the incongruence of offering minimum wage, minimum respect to his employees, yet always – always – demanding maximum commitment.

She ran on, past the cosy Brazilian café she had so loved, its vividly coloured windows now boarded up and disconsolate.

She closed her eyes, not wanting to see the gaudy discount store that had replaced the independent bookstore she and Bo had so adored. God, how she longed for those Saturday mornings browsing the shelves with Bo and chatting with Sara, a fountain of all knowledge and so very sadly missed. Yet another loss. And one among so many, but that didn't make the pain any less.

And then, of course – as every day when she walked this route – there was the empty shell of her own hopes and ambitions. *The Big Trip* lettering already fading to a silvered, flaking memorial to the energetic and exciting team, *her* team, which had organised travel to the furthest corners of the world.

A team she and Anik had chosen together, nurtured together and that she had always felt fortunate to be a part of. Boldly striking out, daring to dream.

Not offering holidays – never 'holidays'.

These were *adventures*, for single parents who wanted to travel, yet longed for a cushion of security. Adventures that took every ounce of her logistical skills to organise, and her psychological intuition to plan. And yes – she had been amazing at her job.

Successful, but also fulfilled.

And how rare was it to find a job that didn't actually feel like work?

The question was, of course, purely rhetorical. Because it was already obvious to Jamie that, in this newly shaped world, it had been a once in a lifetime opportunity. And she tried to be glad that at least she'd had the chance to experience such a rush. All those trips, all those wonderful, appreciative clients . . .

Being appreciated was like a drug, Jamie had long-since decided. And it had been a very, very long time since her last fix.

She swallowed hard, the hot flush of discomfort bringing a now all-too-familiar wave of disappointment. And yes, if she were honest, a little shame. An uncomfortable taste of bitterness, striking through the grief of losing Anik so suddenly, so abruptly, before any of them had really known what was happening, and how their lives would never be the same again.

Borders closed, lives lost and their precious business quietly folding. Without fanfare or drama – just another statistic – and nothing compared to the loss of her very best friend in the whole damn world.

It just wasn't supposed to be this way, she thought, as she queued to collect Bo's prescription. And not for the first time.

Yet somehow, looking around her, knowing she wasn't the only one struggling, didn't take the sting out of it. Not one little bit.

Chapter 2

'Oh love, catch your breath. You're fine.' Rea leaned forward and dropped her voice. 'His Nibs has me doing a stocktake this evening so there's no rush and you look done in.'

Rea's kindness was very nearly Jamie's undoing. She handed over the green paper with a tired smile. 'Well, maybe this new inhaler will be the charm and we can finally get some sleep?' Her natural optimism had been taking a battering of late.

Even Bo – normally animated and affectionate, with her at least, if not with the world at large – was becoming more and more withdrawn and quiet. His sketchbook his constant companion these days, in lieu of the few sparse playdates he'd entertained before. Yet another thing to worry about and doubtless the reason she'd been summoned to sit on the tiny chairs by Bo's earnest and well-meaning form tutor, Mrs Taylor, next week.

Rea frowned as she read the details and typed into the pharmacy's computer. 'Grab a seat, sweetheart. We might have to order some of this in.' Rea tutted at the computer and then did what she always did: 'Harris? Harris, can you check on the shelf for me?'

Her ever-tolerant husband poked his head through the curtained doorway. 'And this, my love, is why we need to do yet another stocktake, and you really, truly need to master this software.' He gave Jamie an apologetic smile, took the green script and disappeared, rubbing his wife's shoulder reassuringly as he passed.

Rea shook her head. 'This blasted computer will be the death of me.' She came round and sat down beside Jamie. 'How is the lad, though?' Rea knew better than most on this small High Street the juggles and struggles that went on behind the scenes in Jamie and Bo's tiny flat. 'You seem to be in here every five minutes, and if you don't mind me saying, you do look so tired.'

Jamie shrugged. 'I keep thinking it'll get better when the weather improves. When it's not so cold and damp, you know?'

Rea sighed. 'And there's still no news from your landlord about sorting that out? Because Harris and I were saying only the other day, that kind of damp and mould is almost certainly breaking all *sorts* of regulations . . .'

'Rea, you're so kind,' Jamie put aside the niggle of unease that her living situation had been a topic of marital debate, 'but I think we both know that Kieran Jones doesn't really care about regulations.'

There was an awkward pause, a moment of shared understanding. The economy would flourish, and pigs would fly, before Jamie's tight-fisted landlord provided more than the very basic care and attention to his properties. His tenants, on the other hand . . .

'Is he still hassling you?' Rea said crossly, dropping her voice to an angry burr.

'Well, he's still threatening that rent review. And he always wants to talk about it "over drinks" ...'

'Creep,' Rea said with feeling. 'I swear to God, Jamie, nobody would blame you for reporting the guy.'

'To whom? Who would genuinely give a shit? I'm employed, and we have a roof over our heads. Bo gets his treatment on the NHS. We're provided for, aren't we? Box ticked as far as the powers that be are concerned.'

They were both silent for a moment, thinking of friends who couldn't honestly say the same right now.

'Doesn't mean it isn't hard though, Jamie. Doesn't mean a bit of help sometimes wouldn't, well, you know, help ...'

It seemed to be the story of Jamie's life the last two years. Falling into the gap – out of sight, out of mind – and barely scraping by.

She blew out her cheeks as she exhaled. 'I did phone that number you gave me – the careers support thingummy? – but I don't qualify. I'm not unemployed.' She shrugged. 'And obviously I'm grateful to have a job, you know. But I can hardly get my life back on track with a part-time minimum wage.' She shook her head sadly. 'They told me I'd be better off signing on.'

Jamie felt that hot flush of rage and impotence that was never far from the surface these days. It went against every fibre of her being to take something for nothing. Her pride furiously protesting.

'Maybe they're right though, love?' Rea said gently. 'All those nights at the hospital with Bo, all the struggling with childcare and bills. You might get a bit more support if you weren't actually working? Might be worth talking to someone, at least?' She turned around and pulled a flyer from the noticeboard behind the till. 'The Citizens Advice Bureau' picked out in a jaunty, optimistic font.

Jamie shook her head. 'There'll be people who need their time more than me, Rea, I promise you. I'm just having a bad day. Or maybe a bad week . . .' She tugged her bag onto her lap and pulled out her phone to check the time, an easy and familiar evasive manoeuvre. 'Thanks though. Seriously, I do appreciate it.'

That particular role reversal was just too great for Jamie to contemplate. The memories of how capable, resourceful and yes, altruistic, she had felt manning the phone lines at the CAB of a Sunday morning still felt all too vivid. Making a difference, however small, in whatever way she could.

No desire to become a painful 'do-gooder', but equally knowing that her conscience demanded she volunteer her time and her experience, to actually *be* a good person. All those lessons she herself had learned the hard way growing up were not to be wasted.

Before 2020.

When everything had changed.

When suddenly she was the one in need of advice again, rather than having what she now understood to be the luxury of dishing it out.

Redundant – on so many levels.

'I'm here, I'm here! Don't close—' The door slammed back against the wall as a young woman burst in, dishevelled and out of breath. Her dark curly hair pinged out like a halo around her face, and her cheeks were flushed from running.

Jamie stiffened for a second, caught off guard seeing her out of context.

Rea shook her head and smiled benevolently. 'Stand down, Bonnie. We're still open. Catch your breath.'

'Argh, sodding stitch.' The girl – Bonnie apparently – bent double, clutching at her side. 'How can I be so unfit when I'm on the go all day?'

'That'll be the booze and the fags, Ms Fuller,' Harris said drily, with an affectionate smile, as he emerged from behind the curtain, a small white bag in his hand.

Bonnie laughed, a breathless but incredibly rich sound that took Jamie by surprise. After all, when was the last time she had heard an adult laugh? Properly laugh. Without inhibition or guilt, or politeness?

She found herself smiling, warmed by the sound.

'You girls,' Rea fussed, 'always rushing, always trying to fit too much in . . .'

Bonnie caught Jamie's eye with amused solidarity; after all, it was rarely a choice to be running around like headless chickens.

She gave a small shiver, glancing out of the window at the grey mizzle that had now descended over Harnley High Street. 'Don't suppose you've bottled any sunshine back there, have you, Harris? Can you pop some in with my meds? I'm so sick of this never-ending grey ...' She turned and smiled at Jamie. 'Am I right? My body's just not designed to drop below twenty degrees.'

Bonnie let out a heartfelt sigh, as she wrapped the layers of her eclectic – and almost certainly vintage – outfit tighter around herself. Her slender body now completely out of proportion with the proud statement of her hair. She sat down, flopping like a rag doll, into the chair beside Jamie. 'Seriously, wouldn't you give anything to be getting on a plane to somewhere warm and fabulous right now?'

'Ah go on, Jamie, show the girl your photos. Give her a boost and let us all live vicariously.'

Rea had always been obsessed with the brochures and window displays at *The Big Trip*, but never once had Jamie been able to tempt her onto a flight away from Harnley. 'It's not natural, to be up in the air like that,' Rea had always said, brooking no argument. If she couldn't get there in Harris's Volvo estate, they weren't going.

But still, she liked to look, to flick through the album of Jamie's Greatest Trips on her iPhone. It was, indeed, a semi-regular event.

'Oh—' groaned Bonnie in appreciative longing, as Jamie flicked open the album, landing on her favourite crystal-clear lakeshore in the Rockies. 'And you actually went here? I mean, this is for real *your* photo?'

Jamie nodded, a bit choked up by Bonnie's reaction. 'Back in another lifetime ...'

She looked away as Bonnie flicked through the album, unable to deal with the slight claustrophobia that increasingly washed over her these days. Just knowing that her globe-trotting days were over, that her entire existence had taken place within just a few square miles these last few years, was enough to make her feel that incipient prickle of confinement.

'Jamie? Here you go then,' Harris said, holding out the pharmacy bag. 'I've only got the one in stock, but I'll order the second and it'll be here in a few days.'

Rea tutted. 'I'll drop it over to you at Harrison's when it comes in, love. You haven't got time to be traipsing back and forth.' She shook her head at her husband, as though he were personally to blame, before Jamie could say thank you.

'If only we had a better ordering system that would reorder low-stock items automatically,' Harris said, returning her hard stare. 'Oh wait, we do.'

'Don't you start . . .' Rea huffed.

Jamie couldn't help it; a small hiccup of laughter escaped her, and she looked away, trying to swallow it down, only to find that Bonnie was similarly afflicted.

'You two are like some adorable sketch show, you know?' Bonnie said with a grin. 'All that bickering, but you love each other really.'

'That we do,' Harris said, as Rea leaned into his side. 'That we do.'

'Do you two actually know each other?' Rea said. 'Jamie, this is Bonnie. Bonnie, meet Jamie.'

Bonnie frowned for a minute. 'You know, you do look kind of familiar, actually . . .'

'I work at Hamilton's,' Jamie offered.

Bonnie snorted. 'Yeah, like I could afford to shop there! I get most of my food from the—' She paused for a second, as the penny dropped.

Don't say it. Don't say it. Don't say it . . . Jamie begged with her eyes, a pleading look of desperation. And yes, a certain embarrassment at her own ridiculous need to still save face.

'—from the Lidl,' Bonnie finished. Another soft smile of solidarity. 'And you know I can't resist the crazy stuff, Rea. I got me a cracking slow cooker for a tenner from the Lidl the other week. That and some snow shoes, because you never know, right?'

There was a small flurry of paperwork and handing over of bags. Jamie tried not to stare at the size of the carrier bag stuffed with prescriptions that Bonnie collected.

It was none of her business, she told herself, even as she swallowed the thought that maybe Bonnie, too, might be in need of more help and support than she was actually getting.

They stepped out into the drizzle, almost in tandem.

'Thank you,' Jamie said quietly.

'Not a problem, truly.' Bonnie said with feeling. 'I guess I'm past the stage where I care if people know I'm relying on the food bank. Desperate times and all that . . .'

'I think I'm still a work in progress on that front,' Jamie admitted.

'Yeah, well, looking at the life you used to have, I imagine it's more of an adjustment,' Bonnie said magnanimously. 'Was it every bit as wonderful as it looks, in the mountains and lakes and stuff?'

Jamie nodded. 'Oh God, Bonnie, it really truly was.'

'Well then, at least you know what you're aiming for, right?' Bonnie stopped suddenly. 'My plans are a bit more local.'

They stood outside the old Churro kiosk, the faint smell of hot sugar and warm dough still noticeable on a dry day. Inside, a banner had been erected.

OPENING SOON   CRAP BUT CHEAP
HAIRCUTS WHILE YOU WAIT!

Bonnie grinned. 'I've got three months' free rent and rates from the council to give it a go as an entrepreneur.' She picked up a lock of Jamie's sodden hair. 'Pop in one day and I'll give you a trim.'

Chapter 3

Jamie tucked her hair back behind her ears, instinctively trying to look just a little more respectable as she approached the school gates. It had been a gradual evolution for sure, but Jamie was increasingly aware that she teetered closer to the brink of becoming a source of embarrassment to her son with each passing school year. Long gone were the days when he would run towards her, talking nineteen to the dozen, proudly waving his artwork and leaping into her arms.

Instead, there was the awkward shuffle, both of them concealing their true feelings in their own way. For Jamie, it was just as often a question of relief as delight.

Another day navigated. Another bullet dodged.

Perhaps, if they were lucky, another day without bruises and incident forms to sign.

Another day without Robbie Clark asserting himself as the bane of Bo's everyday existence.

Bo's day would be 'fine'.

Even if all evidence suggested otherwise.

For Bo, it would be three streets — at least — before he would lean into Jamie's shoulder, bumping against her in lieu of taking her hand. Any hope of a hug would have to wait until they were at home – and then his slight, gangly body would fold into her arms and she got to hear about the reality of just how 'fine' his day had been.

The last whispers of daylight caught, reflecting in the many windows of Bo's school building – so many young lives tangled together simply by virtue of their postcode. And so few of them still here at the tail end of the day – the tiny minority thrown together for Breakfast Club and After School Club, rather than being ferried around town to soccer practice or ballet class . . .

A tiny, *tired*, minority whose school day extended far longer than it should into their young lives.

Tugging at her hair again and smoothing down her bobbly jumper, shivering against the chill, Jamie pressed the buzzer and waited for Clare to let her in. Clare – the incredibly patient, overly enthusiastic, wonderfully kind woman who ran the After School Club with no nonsense but plenty of fun and affection. Almost as though she knew that these young kids would so much rather be anywhere else but here – had earned the right, really, to loaf on their own sofas, or let off steam after a long day of phonics and fronted, fecking adverbials.

Who sweetly ignored 'activity guidelines' in favour of letting her charges follow their feet into a book or into the art corner.

Instead, it was Andrew Davies who pulled open the door with an apologetic smile.

Jamie's heart sank instantly. 'Evening, Headmaster,' she said.

'He's fine,' Mr Davies said immediately, holding up his hand reassuringly, only too aware that it was all that parents ever really wanted to hear. 'I just wanted a quick word, if I may?'

He stepped outside, the door swinging closed with a hush behind him. The lack of clipboard in his hand persuaded Jamie to breathe a little easier, but she couldn't help wishing they could have this conversation inside. Whatever it was, it would be so much easier to concentrate if she wasn't utterly freezing.

'I'm sure you're aware that Bo hasn't been having an easy time of late? Thankfully we've been there to intervene on a few occasions when things might have got more, well, physical – but that's for us to worry about. What I need your thoughts on, Ms Matson, is how we can best support Bo in finding his feet here. Socially that is, I have no real concerns academically. But then, we both know where the kids' priorities lie at this age.'

He paused, as though waiting for her to respond. But what could she possibly add?

They both knew it was the twirling.

It was always the twirling, or the humming to himself as he worked, or just simply Bo's apparent inability to communicate with his peers, to understand their teasing and boisterousness. His daily confusion was only comforted by the endless hours he spent sketching, but even his unerring eye could cause ripples – there was nothing tactful about Bo's pencil.

Clever and insightful? Absolutely.

But it was hardly the currency of friendship among ten-year-old boys. As Bo knew to his cost.

And so Jamie – and apparently Andrew Davies – was watching her funny, artistic son dilute himself day by day, just to stay under the radar of idiots like Robbie Clark. The sporty, untouchable cult of popularity seemed to start earlier and earlier, Jamie thought. What chance did these kids have to explore who they were, who they *actually* were, without the weight of social opinion pinning them down?

And without the common currency of sport, Bo was left on the sidelines in every sense. Any hint of athleticism eclipsed by the inhalers in his pocket.

'We've been talking to the children today about their application options for secondary school and they'll be coming home with information packs in the next day or two. I'm sure I don't need to tell you how quickly all that comes round,' the headmaster said earnestly. 'And I know,' again with the reassuring hand in the air, 'it's not always possible to get your first choice. In fact, it's incredibly unlikely. But I wanted to let you know that I'd consider writing a statement of support, if you'd like?'

Jamie nodded, caught off guard. The very thought of Bo's impending move to secondary school and the dearth of decent options on their doorstep was yet another topic that haunted the wee small hours of her sleepless nights. Impotence and sheer frustration stymieing her every consideration of the rational, proactive steps she needed to take. Sooner rather than later, apparently.

'If you're looking at Stoneleigh and, let's be honest, it's the only option with a decent arts programme, then every little helps.' Mr Davies looked serious. 'I know the head there and she's a formidable woman, so it would need to be a very specific letter, Ms Matson. I would need to disclose quite a lot about Bo, about his circumstances, and his particular, er, challenges ...' He paused, his professional respect making this conversation awkward for both of them. 'So I need to know that you're happy with that?'

Jamie blinked. It was something she'd considered, of course. The spectre of the necessary steps they might need to take for Bo looming long into their lives of late. With each passing year, the truth of his unique view of the world becoming increasingly difficult to brush off as simply 'artistic'.

Still, the very idea of a formal letter – of what it might include – made Jamie feel vaguely nauseated with guilt for a moment. She wasn't a bad parent; she knew that.

And yet still the labels stuck.

Asthmatic child.

Social integration issues.

Single mum.

Free school lunches.

Minimum wage worker.

And those were just the monikers they couldn't avoid. Helpful and supportive, or pejorative and judgemental, simply depending on who was using them.

And *how*.

It wasn't supposed to be like this.

She'd worked hard all her life. And yes, she'd made the decision to have Bo by herself, his father just a fleeting summer fling, but in many ways that only meant she'd been *more* prepared for life as single parent, rather than having it thrust upon her by a cheating husband, having been worn down in a war of attrition over whose needs were more important.

She'd been prepared, or so she thought, for everything life could throw at them.

And Bo had always been the priority. Always.

Shelving her last vestiges of pride, Jamie nodded. 'Thank you,' she said. 'And please don't spare our feelings – write what you need to write. The thought of Bo ending up at Kingsway is just too awful . . .'

Two thousand kids. The vast playing field that thrilled other prospective parents, but left her cold. No music, no art, no drama. Anonymous blocks of buildings and still the long bus ride to get there.

'And if there's anything – anything – that Bo and I need to do to improve his chances for Stoneleigh too . . .'

Mr Davies nodded. 'Bo mentioned something about buses being a problem?' He hesitated, clearly choosing his words with care. 'Is that, I mean, is that a medical issue or more of a—'

How could the poor bloke finish that sentence without sounding critical? Jamie stepped in to save him searching for a polite descriptor.

'It's the smells,' she interrupted. 'The perfumes and body sprays – the wet, musty coats when it's raining. They all set off his asthma. It's a nightmare really.'

Too many times they'd had to step off, mid-journey, the air catching in his lungs, stealing his breath. And, for sure, there was a touch of anxiety in the mix too – a self-fulfilling prophecy, as so many asthmatics discovered. The very fear of an attack, in the face of a previous catalyst, enough to trigger a response.

Not to mention the concern that so many shared, after the last few years – the legacy of feeling off balance in crowded places. So many people. On the Tube, in a queue, even a crowded restaurant. So many breaths ... She could hardly blame him.

'We walk everywhere we can, and sometimes it really is unavoidable. But for him to do that journey twice a day? We'd never be out of A&E.'

Mr Davies nodded. 'Can you get that in writing, from your GP maybe? I can add it to his file. I know it seems like an impersonal lottery, but we do have some leeway with special cases, Ms Matson. And, in my opinion, Bo is a wonderful boy with a bright future ahead of him. We just need to be clear on what he needs. His *particular* needs.'

Jamie blinked.

In her small world, it was increasingly rare for anyone to share that opinion of Bo.

'Thank you,' she said, 'you have no idea how much that means to me.'

Mr Davies just nodded again. 'Come on in and get Bo. I know he's tired, so we can talk another time about the importance of those special assessments and the like. Denial isn't always the best parenting strategy, Ms Matson.' He frowned. 'Oh, and I've got a flyer somewhere about a weekend art club he might be interested in ...'

Oh, Mr Davies – so close, Jamie thought. If there was room in the budget for an art club, didn't he think that Bo might also have had some new school shoes that weren't a size too small, or even a new Big Coat for the winter that extended beyond his wrists.

And as for these 'assessments' – well, she knew full well what he was alluding to.

She just wasn't ready, or maybe Bo wasn't ready, to address the elephant in the room.

Yet another label marking him out as somehow 'other'.

But all of those worries fell away the moment she turned the corner and saw Bo – her Bo – sweeping a paint brush over a large painting, whorls and swirls of colour that had no form or meaning, and yet still spoke so vividly. Singing away, he was in a world of his own as he daubed with an instinctive flare that she herself could never hope to replicate.

'He really is a very special boy,' Mr Davies said quietly beside her as they watched. Bo yet to notice their arrival, so absorbed in his own little world, the last child to be collected.

Special.

Jamie glanced at the man beside her sharply, trying to read between the lines. Trying to interpret which of the very many meanings of that word he had intended. Whether this was his non-too-subtle segue into *that* conversation, yet again.

'Mum!'

Jamie couldn't help but smile though, as Bo abandoned his brush and launched towards her, tugging at her sleeve with indigo hands. 'Come and see this. I'm being a little bit Monet, a little bit me!'

'A little bit *fabulous*,' Jamie agreed, her whole day lightened by the sheer exuberance on his freckled face.

Chapter 4

It was one way to spend a Saturday morning, Jamie supposed. Although she couldn't pretend the constant conflict in her head, swinging between thwarted pride and sheer relief, was exactly relaxing.

Bo tugged on her hand as they walked the pavements, leaping across puddles that shimmered with iridescent oily rainbows in the morning sun.

Get there early. Get in. Get out.

It had become a familiar routine and yet this morning nothing had gone to plan. The chaos and the dust from next door's building project had eclipsed any chance of Bo having a decent night's sleep. In fact, sitting with him as they ran the shower in the small hours – ever hopeful that their tiny steamy bathroom might yet be enough to evade another midnight dash for the nebuliser – Jamie had been mentally counting the coins in her purse to feed the meter.

And so now, with hair still wet from her own, cold, shower, she was reframing their day – the library was an easy and welcome respite, of course. Warmth and comfort for free was not to be taken for granted.

But before that: food. Food for the week ahead and hopefully enough to supplement the meagre supplies still sitting in her larder. Exactly one can of kidney beans, one packet of rice noodles and the lurking packet of dried chickpeas that nobody seemed to know what the hell to do with.

And it wasn't as though she came to the food bank every week. Sometimes just knowing it was there took the pressure off a little, but there were also weeks – like this one – when seemingly every bill came due, the interest on that stupid emergency credit card alone enough to break her, and there was simply not enough left over.

Not even to go hunting for snarks – rootling through the end-of-date discounted items in their local supermarket. Even if Bo was still young enough to see it as a game, it dented Jamie's sense of self every single time. Making it 'fun' helped a bit.

But not a lot.

'Jamie!'

She turned, one hand on the door handle of the community centre. No way of disguising their intended destination.

'Morning!' Bonnie's exuberance spoke of too much caffeine, or perhaps a surfeit of sleep. Or perhaps simply her youth. She jogged towards them, loud turquoise bag banging against her side, arms held wide. 'And this must be Bo . . .'

'Hi,' said Bo quietly, taking a small step closer to his mother's side, yet at the same time apparently fascinated by this peacock-like apparition in their otherwise bland morning.

'Right then, Master Bo – do you want to play food bank

bingo with me?' Bonnie's dark eyes twinkled. 'You get points for the following: I don't normally come here. Is there a choice? Do I really have to queue? You mean, you come here *every* week? Who actually eats this stuff?'

Bonnie grinned. 'Am I right? All these entitled sods who think they're the first people to have ever fallen on hard times. As if coming here is beneath them somehow.' She shook her head and her hair flew outwards. 'I mean, you can blame Brexit, you can blame Covid, or the government or whatever – but when it comes down to it, if you're hungry and you've got no cash, then you're out of options. So at least be polite and grateful about it, am I right?'

Bo smiled shyly. 'You are *absolutely* right.' He looked up at Jamie enquiringly, checking if it were okay to engage with this exuberant woman, who apparently knew his mum.

'D'you mind . . .' A middle-aged man in a tailored jacket pushed past them and went into the community hall, the tell-tale yellow voucher clasped tightly in his whitened grip.

Bonnie raised an eyebrow and looked at Bo. 'My bag of Jelly Tots that he doesn't say thank you – what do you say?'

Bo laughed. A proper laugh too, not the polite ones he normally offered up when talking to anyone other than Jamie. 'I think that would be a bad bet.'

'And I think you're right. But you can have my Jelly Tots anyway.'

They turned, the three of them making their own small group, and walked into the main hall. There was no rush, as the queue snaked ahead of them towards the front where the volunteers did their best to hand over the food parcels and still manage some conversation and conviviality.

Jamie blinked. It was never this busy at 7am and somehow, despite the inevitable wait ahead of them, it felt easier, more wholesome, than skulking in at first light. And it wasn't just the number of people here waiting either, it was the sheer diversity – a snapshot, with almost everyone who lived in Harnley represented.

It was easy to spot the first timers though, the ones staring at their feet, or folding and refolding their voucher, mortified to find themselves here. And of course, like the chap who had barged past them moments before, it was the clothes that told the tale – his smart tailored jacket spoke of a fall from grace, from a world where it was acceptable to spend the equivalent of a month's rent on a single item of clothing.

'I wonder,' Bonnie said quietly, as though reading her mind, 'whether they knew just how many people in the middle would be coming here when they set it up? I mean, it's a different world here these days, not just the indigent and unemployed anymore, is it?' she huffed. 'Case in point, for God's sake: there's Kath from the hospital over there. I mean, she's like a staff nurse or something, but her husband's an absolute chancer so who knows.'

Jamie glanced up to see who Bonnie was waving at now. Shocked to see one of the lovely A&E nurses in the parallel queue. 'Hi,' Bonnie smiled, giving a small wave as Kath looked over, exhausted and still in her uniform after the night shift.

'Morning,' Kath said, shaking her head at Bonnie's bound-less enthusiasm. 'I swear to God, Bonnie Fuller, I'll have what you're having—'

Bonnie snorted with laughter, nodding towards the identical crates of food parcels lined up at the front of the hall. 'I'd bet on it!'

Kath laughed, her innate good nature eclipsing the exhaustion for a moment. 'And how are you doing this morning, young Bo? I missed you last night – not one single patient I could talk to about Minecraft. Not one.'

Bo grinned. 'I built a new fortress but I burned it down. Not on purpose. I'm not a monster!'

She looked up at Jamie. 'And how about you, Jamie? If you don't mind me saying, you look like a proper night's sleep would make the world of difference.'

'What's that then?' Jamie said, knowing that of all the people here, Kath would understand just how unlikely that would be.

'I was reading,' Bonnie interrupted, 'about how siestas are better for you anyway.'

'Were you now?' Kath smiled. 'And would that be on top of your full eight hours?'

Jamie watched the easy familiarity between the two women as they bantered back and forth, Bo smiling too, as they teased each other. This was a whole new experience. And somehow the solidarity in waiting for their pre-selected groceries outshone the frustration that this whole process was even necessary.

'Morning, ladies, gents.' Father Bill held out a tray of hot drinks and orange squash towards their little group, as he made his way along the queue, checking in with his flock. He winked at Bo, as he crouched down lower. 'This hot chocolate here is made with soya milk and no dairy, just in case you fancied one.'

Jamie swallowed hard, blindsided by his consideration for her son.

'Can I, Mum? Can I have it?'

Before Jamie could express any concern, Bill held out his phone towards her, a photograph on the screen. 'That's the ingredients if you wanted to check first?'

Never one to ascribe to any religious fealty, Jamie found herself blown away, week after week, by the small yet meaningful ways that Father Bill welcomed and included everyone who had need to be here. His cosy maroon cardigan clashed with his pink cheeks, and he had clearly never met a body spray he didn't like, but the man had a heart of gold.

'Thank you, Bill. That's perfect – go ahead, Bo. What a treat!' And a treat it truly was – dairy-free fun was hardly the stuff of spontaneous snacking – and she knew that Bo missed out more often than not.

'I've popped the rest of the jar in your parcel, over there, okay? Seemed like hot chocolate weather this week . . .' Bill gave Jamie an understanding smile, before wending his way towards some new arrivals who didn't yet know the form.

'That man is almost enough to make me believe in God,' Bonnie said quietly.

'Almost,' Kath said sadly under her breath. 'But if he exists, he wasn't in A&E last night. It was brutal.'

How was it possible, Jamie so desperately wanted to ask, for someone like Kath – with her highly skilled job, her dependable, important job – to be standing next to her, here, in this queue. Waiting on the benevolence of strangers.

When did life stop making sense, Jamie wondered? When did hard work and being a good person stop being enough?

Bonnie rummaged in her handbag and pulled out a hot pink canvas roll. 'Haven't you got that staff appraisal with Tanya the Tyrant coming up, Kath? Do you want me to give your fringe a trim while we're waiting? Have you looking all presentable and polished?'

And to Jamie's astonishment, there, in the queue, Bonnie whipped out her hairdressing scissors and comb and set to work.

'Don't look so surprised, Jamie,' Bill said as he walked back past her, his tray now empty. 'There's a whole world that goes on here that you've been missing with your early morning dash. And we're hoping to set up a cosy café zone so people can catch up properly and chat, maybe even get the kids together, if you'd be interested?'

Jamie nodded, even as the very thought made her feel uncomfortable. What did she really have in common with half the people here? After all, wasn't she just another one of those people in the middle that were dipping into the system temporarily, possibly even taking resources away from others that really needed them?

Somehow, on some level, it was still utterly incomprehensible to her that she actually *was* one of those people in need right now.

A brash, loud woman pushed past them all on her way to the door, not looking up as she rummaged through the bag of provisions she'd just collected. Her vowels and accent marking her out as different just as much as the smart leather handbag swinging from her arm. 'For God's sake, there's some chicken to roast in here, but have they included any stuffing or gravy? Of course not. Honestly! I'm not sure anyone's put *any* thought into this at all. I mean, seriously, who even uses evaporated milk these days?'

There was an awkward silence as she looked up and saw Bill standing in front of her. Not to mention Bonnie, Kath and Jamie looking aghast at her ingratitude and snobbery. After all, she would hardly qualify to be here if she wasn't in need . . .

'And that's bingo!' said Bo, his reedy voice echoing clear and loud, as he smiled shyly at Bonnie. 'I get the Jelly Tots, right?'

Chapter 5

'You know,' Father Bill leaned down towards Bo, 'everyone who comes here has their own story. And we try to cut everyone some slack because lots of people here have had a really tricky time.' He paused, clearly wondering whether this tactful understatement was actually necessary for Bo.

After all, he was hardly your average ten-year-old.

'Like us,' Bo offered with a frown. 'But that doesn't make it okay to be so rude, when you're all working so hard to help.'

'Out of the mouths of babes,' Father Bill said with a wry smile, straightening up. 'But then, it's also possible to be grateful for our help and still embarrassed for needing it at the same time, Bo.'

Jamie looked away, unable to meet his gaze. As always, Bill had the unerring knack of getting right to the heart of the matter. And she knew she wasn't the only one here experiencing that strange duality. Kath, she noticed, had coloured instantly, her neck flushing a dull hot red.

It was probably the disbelief that registered more than anything, Jamie decided. That half the people in this queue had jobs, worked long hours, and yet still were unable to meet that most basic need of having food on the table three times a day.

As if tuned in to her train of thought, Jamie's stomach rumbled loudly.

Father Bill didn't miss a trick though, as he silently proffered his tartan biscuit tin in her direction.

'Thank you,' she said quietly, taking a large digestive over a pink wafer, thinking only of filling the void since lunchtime yesterday.

'Right then,' Bonnie said, combing Kath's bob into place so it swung like a neat curtain onto her shoulders. 'Who's next?' She held up her scissors and twirled around. 'Anyone got a job interview this week and need a little tidy-up?'

'Seriously?' A young red-headed girl beside them in the queue turned around. Her eyes were wide and almost Disneyesque in disbelief. 'You would do that?'

'I would and I will,' Bonnie said with a grin. 'Tell us about the job – do you need to look sophisticated and fabulous? Because I could really do something statementy with this if you'd let me . . .'

Apparently not one for holding back, Bonnie had pulled the girl's mane free of its clip and watched it tumble over her narrow shoulders. Her shabby-chic vintage dress hovered on the line between style statement and necessity, right down to the rather battered leather brogues on her feet.

The girl snorted. 'I was aiming for reliable and slightly dull actually—' She gave a small sheepish smile. 'I'm Amy, by the way.'

36

There was a flurry of introductions and Jamie couldn't help but wonder why someone like Amy wanted to hide herself away.

Jamie couldn't help herself, it seemed. It soothed her anxiety to try and put the pieces together, to try and understand what had brought people here.

'Why dull?' Bo asked, intrigued. 'Why would anybody *want* to be dull?' He reached out, his hand hovering inches from Amy's thick, tumbling red locks, clearly longing to touch. 'And with hair that red, how is that even *possible*?' He sounded wistful, almost as though he were jealous.

Amy smiled, probably closer to Bo in age than any of the women standing around her. 'With hair this red, everybody assumes you're going to be trouble. That you have a filthy temper, or you're all about the partying. So, sometimes it's easier to play it down a bit.'

Bo nodded, his expression serious. 'Like me at school? Mum thinks I should dial down the twirling and the humming and stuff, then maybe I wouldn't get picked on so often.'

Jamie mouthed incredulously. Had she said that? Had she actually articulated that thought to her young impressionable son? 'Bo—' she began, before he cut her off.

'I know you haven't *said* that, Mum, but we both know that you've been thinking it really loudly.'

Bonnie snorted with laughter. 'Christ, these kids don't miss a trick, do they?' She combed through Amy's hair as they all stepped forward in unison, the queue getting longer behind them even as they got closer to the front, an ouroboros of need.

'Is it an office job?' Kath asked. 'Because you're more than welcome to borrow my seriously boring black suit . . .' She hesitated. 'I don't even wear black to funerals anymore.'

Bonnie nodded her agreement. 'Say it loud and celebrate the life that was lived, I say. I have the most amazing turquoise jacket that's waved off many a good friend.'

A mantle of silent understanding hung in the air around them for a moment. Not many people had escaped the losses and heartbreak of the last few years.

'I like that,' Bo said with feeling. 'Mum says we should celebrate a little bit every day, just because we're here and we can. I mean, not here-here. But, you know—'

Kath smiled. 'I do know, Bo. I really do. And you are absolutely right. My Grandma used to say that you only get each day once, so you have to do at least one thing, every day, to make it count.'

Bo gave his mum a knowing look. 'So maybe my humming isn't something I should give up. Actually. If it makes me feel better.'

Amy laughed. 'Well, I can't see how humming would hurt. But all-night concerts and turning up late, hungover, hasn't exactly been the best career path for me.' She shrugged, somehow looking incredibly young and incredibly jaded at the same time. 'So, I'm going for dull and dependable desk jockey from now on.'

Bonnie grinned. 'Shall I apply for the same job too? You know, to make you look even better by comparison?'

Jamie laughed, and then stopped for a second. When was the last time she had felt like this? A part of something? She glanced around at Kath, and Amy, and Bonnie – not one of these women were natural allies – and yet she felt an immediate solidarity with them that she couldn't quite define.

Forever on the periphery of life these days, Jamie so often found herself looking at the women at the school gates, gathered together in cliques: the career mums, the stay-at-home-and-go-to-Pilates mums, the tiger mums with their insistence on a full extracurricular schedule for their little darlings . . .

And not once had she felt as though she fit.

'I can take a look at your CV if you like. I have a certain way with words,' she offered tentatively, not wanting to patronise in any way, but falling short of any other discernible skill she could contribute.

'It's true,' Bo piped up. 'The letters she sends to my school are really something. They talk about them in the staffroom . . .'

Bonnie snorted again. 'Oh Jamie, you are so screwed.' She paused for a moment, looking around. 'You know, if Father Bill does sort out that café zone, he might really be on to something here. I'd walk past every one of you in the street and have no idea we were in the same boat.'

'Ah, but not all boats are created equal, are they?' Kath said quietly. 'Sometimes a fresh perspective is worth a lot.'

Amy nodded. 'I've lost count of the number of jobs I've applied for recently, so I'm clearly getting something wrong. I mean, if you guys really didn't mind helping . . .' She shifted awkwardly from foot to foot. 'And it's not even like I'm that picky. You can't really afford to be when you've only got two GCSEs and a bus pass to your name.'

They were all silent for a moment. Only the week before, the *Harnley Standard* had reported over four hundred applications for jobs at the out-of-town supermarket, half of which were from graduates.

Chances are they were no longer talking about 'career advancement' and 'networking' – it was more a case of finding a living wage.

Suddenly Jamie's job at Harrison's didn't seem quite so bad.

Building *The Big Trip* with Anik from an idea sketched out on a paper napkin, through the early starts, the late nights and buoyed by their shared passion and determination, had been everything Jamie had ever dreamed of. And even if that dream had died, at least she'd had that experience, that joy of throwing herself wholeheartedly into her work.

Even if she had no idea how to get her life back on track and reclaim some measure of independence – starting with the ability to choose and pay for her own groceries!

Even if her degree certificate still hung on the loo wall at home, mocking her with her First in Psychology as she scrabbled around to rebuild her working life from the ground up. About as useful as a chocolate teapot right now. Unless . . .

'Seriously, Amy, I'd be really happy to take a look, maybe

rephrase things here and there. Maybe we can make your application more, well, persuasive?'

Amy nodded enthusiastically, causing Bonnie to yelp. 'If you don't want a fringe, you should really keep still, while I tackle these split ends.'

Father Bill walked past, patrolling his flock and handed Bo a dustpan and brush with a wink. 'Keep an eye on that one for me, Bo,' he said, nodding towards Bonnie. 'She leaves a trail of destruction in her path.'

Kath swished her newly neatened bob defiantly. 'I wouldn't say that, Bill. You'd be amazed at the boost a little TLC can provide.'

Bonnie tucked her scissors back into their pouch. 'Pop by and see me on the High Street, Amy. I can give you a proper trim – and maybe you'd let me take some photos for the window?' She held out a neat printed card from the machine in the arcade: *Crap But Cheap* in swirling italic font.

'Should we maybe talk about your branding while we're at it?' Jamie said hesitantly, wondering why it was always so much easier to view other people's choices with 20:20 vision.

Bonnie shook her head, glossy afro curls flying. 'Nah, I know my market. Nobody wants to spend a fortune these days – half my clientele will be there looking for the churro guy anyway.' She handed cards to Kath and Jamie too. 'Under-promise and over-deliver, that's my thing. And it hasn't let me down yet.'

Chapter 6

Jamie stepped out into the midday sunshine with Bo at her side, tiptoeing as always between the cracks on the pavement, concentrating hard. The plastic handles of her two carrier bags strained under the weight of a week's worth of groceries, packed like Jenga by the willing volunteers at the food bank. Every care and attention considered, and a large Dairy-Free sticker on the side of each bag.

As promised, Bill's jar of vegan hot chocolate powder nestled at the top of one bag, promising long evenings with popcorn and cosy drinks for Bo as he watched and rewatched his favourite black and white films on repeat.

Jamie tilted her head back and let the sun warm her face; after a pretty brutal week, she felt surprisingly enthused about the weekend ahead. Time just to be, to breathe. To leave worry about her bank balance and dead-end career for another day.

'You know,' said Bo beside her, the last vestiges of his hot chocolate still colouring his top lip. 'I don't think I realised how many other people, nice people, did their shopping at the food bank too.' He laughed self-consciously. 'Well, not shopping, but you know what I mean?'

'Me too,' Jamie agreed. 'In fact, maybe standing in a queue with them is actually better than dashing in the door first thing? What do you think?'

'Duh! If I get to sleep in as well, it's a no-brainer, Mum, really.' Bo paused, his face wrinkling in thought. 'And I think it will be really easy to choose my three good things today.'

Bo took his three good things very seriously, to the point that Jamie almost regretted introducing them. But hundreds of psychologists said it helped, training the mind to seek out the positives rather than dwelling on the negatives – and so they persevered. Even if some days the only things they could come up with stretched the definition a little.

I have clean pants every day, was a classic they both resorted to from time to time. Still, never something to be taken for granted!

Along with Bo's favourite: fresh sheets on his bed.

Jamie's was easy – she had Bo.

Even as her son pooh-poohed this one, forcing her to look beyond, to dig a bit deeper, Jamie stayed resolute. Without Bo in her life, nothing else made sense. The compromises, the sacrifices ... The quirky little guy twirling beside her put everything into perspective.

Even the sheer paraphernalia of inhalers and spacers in her handbag, banging against her thigh with every step she took, was just part and parcel of helping Bo to be Bo: healthy and happy and content to be himself, at least two days a week, without the spectre of Robbie Clark's flailing fists.

'Shall we watch *Sabrina* again tonight? We could eat on our laps in front of the TV?'

'Deal,' Bo said, his face lighting up. 'And then we could start on my collage for Arts Day? I want to do something really soft and flowy and different.' He hesitated. 'They said we could do anything, Mum.'

Jamie's pulse quickened instinctively, her protective instincts screaming against her desire to always, always encourage Bo to be himself.

'Sure,' she said, making a mental note to tuck her one and only smart dress out of reach of his scissors and thread. 'I actually wondered if you wanted to show one of your portraits? Maybe a fabulous black and white one? Super cool, super casual.'

He raised an eyebrow, seeing right through her clumsy ploy to steer him away from his instinctive desire for soft and silky fabrics.

'Like the Brie Larson one,' Jamie said with a smile. 'It's just stunning, Bo.'

'It's my favourite,' Bo said, nodding. 'But I wanted something more swooshy, to be honest, Mum – something you can touch, you know? Something that *feels* nice.'

His gaze was open, trusting and incredibly sweet. His sentiments with her, at least, so rarely diluted, that she daren't even hope how much longer that might last.

Being Bo's friend, his only confidante perhaps, was an honour she never took for granted.

And yet she knew that its shelf life was limited. Once he

found his feet, found his tribe or his voice, she would doubtless be relegated – exactly as she should be. And yet . . .

'Then let's stop by Oxfam for some fabric,' Jamie suggested lightly, as they walked along, side by side.

Side by side, she was quickly learning, being the best possible way to have the most nuanced conversations with her growing son these days. And if he chose to sit down and talk to her face to face, that was his call, but Jamie just wanted them to keep talking, keep communicating, however confusing it was for both of them at times.

She leaned against him fleetingly as they walked, listening to Bo chatter on and on about his plans for Arts Day. The one day of the school year, apparently, that her son was actually invested in. Her input wasn't needed. He knew his own mind, for the most part. And Jamie had no desire to always be the voice of caution, of holding back and reticence.

Maybe she could talk to Mr Davies, just quietly, and get the lay of the land?

They stopped at the traffic lights, waiting to cross, and Jamie's eye fell on the display in the estate agent's window . . . She couldn't help but stare; her obsession with the local property market only increasing as her own options dwindled.

Quietly edged further and further afield by an ongoing wave of gentrification, Jamie's own options had become increasingly limited over the last few years. The bane of being dependent on a buoyant rental market was the frequency with which she found herself priced out of the market. And that was just renting . . .

Who *were* these people who could afford half a million to buy a semi-detached 'villa'? Who were these people who could shell out three or four grand each month in rent, should they want to keep their options open, while keeping up appearances?

God knows, even the bland and insipid couple on her favourite property show last night had a budget of six hundred thousand.

How?

Seriously – there was nothing rhetorical about Jamie's confusion. She wanted answers. Needed answers.

And she refused to believe that, as a graduate, as a hardworking single mother who was prepared to compromise on everything except her child's well-being, that there was nothing out there for her. No prospects. No hope, really, of turning the corner and making life just a little easier.

Not much. She wasn't asking for a handout. She was prepared to put in the graft.

She just needed a small sign.

She just longed to go home at the end of the day to a home that was clean and warm and dry. Without bankrupting herself in the process.

Without the prospect of more and more debt, just to get by, with fewer and fewer possibilities to ever pay it down.'Can we live in a proper house one day, Mum? I really like the idea of going upstairs to bed.' Bo looked up at her with a soft smile. 'And having a bath as well as a shower . . .' He stared at the window display beside her. 'Can you even imagine?'

And that was part of the problem because Jamie could more than imagine; she could remember.

Not only her own beautiful en-suite in their last rental, but also the nights in beautiful hotel rooms, as she'd led *The Big Trip* groups on their travels to some of the most inspiring spots on the globe. Watching single parents and their children revel in the experience, knowing that her team's hard work and support had made it possible. Revelling herself in a taste of luxury.

She so rarely allowed these thoughts headspace anymore – what could she seriously hope to gain by the comparison? Not just of her lifestyle, but of the hopes and dreams she had so carefully nurtured for herself and Bo.

And while Bo may not remember the vast bathtub he had practically learned to swim in, the photos were still pinned to their kitchen noticeboard – his wide gappy smile and flotilla of yellow ducks emerging from the foam. Making Jamie smile with nostalgia for an easier time, a more optimistic time, filled with promise and possibility.

'One day—' Bo began again with a cheeky grin, looking up to catch his mother's eye. It was a much loved and familiar refrain.

The sillier the suggestions, the better.

'I'm going to have a pet llama called Pickles and he'll be housetrained and sleep on my bed,' Bo said firmly.

'One day,' Jamie countered, 'I'm going to . . .' She paused, the lack of sleep and long week catching up with her. The only suggestions that sprang to mind were the things she really, truly longed for, both for herself and her son.

A meaningful career that paid the bills.

Flexibility.

Spontaneity.

Security.

'One day,' she began again, 'I'm going to dye my hair bright pink and only wear evening dresses. All the time.'

Bo's face lit up. 'One day,' he said with a wide grin, 'I'm going to draw dresses from the softest, silkiest silk and everyone who's anyone will want to wear them.' He hesitated, deep in thought, 'Obviously you'll get first choice, Mum, if you're still wearing evening dresses every day.' His burst of cheeky laughter was uninhibited and joyful. 'But I really don't think pink hair would actually work with your skin tone.'

'One day,' Jamie said, sticking out her tongue, 'I'm going to cook a Thai feast, with oodles of noodles and sticky ribs and teeny tiny crab cakes that make your tongue tingle with chilli . . .'

'Like sherbet?' Bo asked, confused. 'And this is a good thing?'

'This, my love, is very definitely a good thing. Because then, when – one day – we can get on a plane to Ko Samui, you won't be asking for fish and chips like a daft English numptee. You can have huge bowls of delicious pad thai from a shack on the beach.'

Bo frowned and shook his head. 'How will I know if it's safe for me to eat? Is this one of those "one days" where I don't wheeze like Darth Vader anymore and I can actually eat dairy?'

'Nope. Although that would be amazing, wouldn't it?' She ruffled his hair. 'This would be because they don't really use dairy in Thai cooking. Italy, France ... well you're right, that's a bit trickier. But as long as you're okay with a coconut and a peanut, then Thailand will be your friend, my love.'

'Show me?' he said, snuggling into her side and tapping on her mobile phone screen. 'Just quickly so we don't use all the minutes. Show me a beach in Thailand so I can think about it later when I want to fall asleep.'

Chapter 7

Hours later, replete from their jacket potato fiesta, splurging with both beans *and* little sausages on top, Jamie tucked Bo into bed, layering on a second thick duvet against the chill. Hesitating for a moment, as she heard the breath grind tiredly into his lungs, and wondering whether to crank up the fickle night storage heater tonight, or save enough for the meter for a few more nights to come over the week ahead.

Everything was a balancing act.

It had taken all her powers of persuasion to convince Nick Harrison to pay her weekly instead of monthly; he bore no truck with advances. And it was four full days until the next instalment of her child benefit would drop.

Yet again, she considered the option of unemployment, universal credit and stepping back from her stoic, proactive approach to getting their lives back on track.

Still, her stupid, stubborn pride prevailed.

But at what cost.

She lay down beside Bo; her body heat was free and, most days, he didn't object.

'One day, Mum,' Bo whispered in the dark, his small

gangly body cocooned and cosy, 'I'm going to go to school with my hair all long and nobody will give me detention for it.'

His fingers instinctively reached for her hair, habitually seeking comfort by curling her locks round and round in a perfect spiral. Whether it was hair, like Amy's earlier, or silky fabrics, Bo's comfort had always been tactile.

'And it wouldn't have to be a one-day-dream. Like, I could actually have my hair longer at school. Like in the holidays . . .' He sighed and there was a wobble in his voice that spoke of unshed tears and frustration.

'I know, Bobo. I know.'

'The girls are allowed long hair, but Mr Davies says boys' hair can't touch their collar. And that's not really fair, is it?' The injustice was one they had revisited time and time again.

'It's really not,' Jamie agreed. 'But the school have their uniform code and—'

Jamie broke off – there was no logic in that code. And certainly no room for manoeuvre. Even if it was obvious, to Jamie at least, that Bo was more settled, happier, more able to concentrate when his own hair offered that same kind of self-soothing opportunity. Not something he could get from the crackling acrylic sweatshirt that every child wore to Harnley Primary. Even with every label removed and lashings of fabric softener.

And the small jelly cat keyring on his pencil case had been a complete disaster as a compromise; catnip to the bullies and fools.

Long hair in the school holidays had been the compromise they always adopted, and it was increasingly clear, to Jamie at least, that Bo needed more and more by way of a soothing environment with every passing month. That he didn't feel the need, necessarily, to fit in the way the other boys did. His needs seemed more urgent, more a part of who he was.

But it wasn't always her place to point this out; this was his journey of self-discovery. She could only make sure she was there, ready with support, guidance and uncon-ditional acceptance. And occasionally – increasingly – a shoulder to cry on when everything became confusing and overwhelming.

But would having some kind of formal assessment change anything for the better?

Her personal loathing of labels aside, she could only be grateful that Bo had been born into a generation with a positive bounty of descriptors. One day, he might choose to embrace them.

The daily minefield of getting it right weighed heavily.

And Jamie so badly wanted to inform herself; to be whatever the Mum-equivalent of 'woke' might be, but the goalposts just kept moving.

The English language kept evolving – as indeed it should – but for someone like Jamie, with no free time to read the papers, go to the movies, even listen to radio – she could only wish there was a crib sheet somewhere she could refer to. One that was regularly updated to avoid the crushing, stifling embarrassment of getting it wrong.

Anything to escape that hot mortifying sensation of being badly out of touch, of sounding less than tolerant through a simple lack of vocabulary.

Because the very last thing she wanted to do was make Bo uncomfortable around her, lest perhaps he decide not to confide, not to share . . .

'Creative' was Bo's descriptor of choice right now, and he was comfortable with that, so Jamie chose to simply focus every ounce of her energy on loving and supporting her wonderful boy. Being his champion, being his voice when his was drowned out in a crowd.

She swallowed hard, listening to his wheezing settle as he snuggled in beside her.

She just never wanted him to feel alone.

She wanted him to be able to twirl, and hum, and seek comfort in his tactile yearnings – soft fabric, silky hair, and smooth, polished surfaces. She wanted him to have space to think, to draw, to avoid the plague of noises and discomforts that tormented him.

She wanted his world to be cushioned for him, no matter how unrealistic that desire.

She didn't see what others saw – she knew that.

And she didn't see Bo's reality reflected in the media, however hard she looked. Any child on the spectrum that she saw in films, in books, on TV – they bore so little resemblance to her Bo. Of course, sometimes they too sought comfort in art and textures and sounds that could be replicated over and over, but there was no sign of Bo's sweet, empathetic soul.

So she waited, angry at times that she found herself ana-lysing him, rather than enjoying his endearing quirks – sadly aware that her idea of endearing might be annoying to others, those without the willingness to see the whole picture.

It was just a small part of who he was – her beloved boy.

And so she'd simply decided: no more labels required until Bo was old enough – aware enough – to choose them for himself.

Whatever Andrew Davies might believe.

Jamie remained firm that she had Bo's best interests at heart. Resolved. Determined to let Bo have the agency in his childhood, of which she herself had been so sorely deprived.

It was galling to realise that, no matter how challenging the lockdowns had been, in a way it had made *their* life easier. Simpler. Home schooling had brought them closer together, and given Jamie a clearer understanding of the environment Bo needed in order to be his best self, to achieve without cost to his sense of self. Of course, the constant mantel of fear and uncertainty had been the price they'd had to pay, and living in a bubble was hardly a long-term solution. But those weeks closeted together had given Jamie a new insight into how her son's mind actually worked, evolving and growing with each passing year.

She squeezed him into a hug, dropping gentle kisses on the top of his head.

'Mu-um ...' He wriggled, still young enough not to be enraged by such obvious displays of affection and yet just beginning to shy away.

'Anyway,' Bo said, his attention span rarely longer than a few moments, 'did you look at the form for that art club? Maybe we could go tomorrow and have a look? It's on Sundays, isn't it?' He'd talked of little else since Mr Davies's suggestion and Jamie could cheerfully have strung the well-intentioned headmaster up for even suggesting it.

Of *course*, Bo would love it. He had a valid point. And no doubt it was a kind thought.

But now Jamie could add that particular guilt to her roster as well.

'Let's see,' Jamie hedged. Four pounds a session. Maybe she could find it from somewhere? 'I'll give them a call next week and find out the form, okay. But I can't make any promises, Bo. They might not even have any spaces.'

He yawned, reaching beside his pillow for his soft, stuffed monkey, well worn and well loved. 'I'll make it work.'

And he was probably right because, somehow, Bo always managed to. His resilience, his determination and, yes, his bravery in the face of some pretty constant bullying was almost inspirational.

Actually inspirational – in the very literal sense – if you really stopped and thought about it, Jamie realised.

For both of them, their struggles were very rarely of the overt, black-eye-inducing scuffle variety. It was the background noise, the everyday hum, the low-level, energy-sapping kind of bullying that coloured much of their time. For Bo, it was the boys at school who were so clearly discomforted by his artistic flair and refusal to buy into the hype of popularity. There was zero scope for individuality in their local school and so conformity had been the byword since Bo had gone up to the junior school, and even at six, his ability to blend into a crowd had been sorely tested.

Four years later, it was only getting harder.

For Jamie, it was both her boss and her landlord. Two small-minded men abusing their modicum of power over her to their own advantage. In fact, Jamie often wondered whether they simply enjoyed seeing her squirm – flustered and longing to bite back – but hamstrung by her financial limitations and maternal obligations.

All out of choices.

With Bo fast asleep and snuggled in, Jamie slipped away and back to the kitchen, pulling the door quietly closed behind her. She eyed the persistent mould in the corner as though it had personally aggrieved her. Which it had in a way.

An hour with the bleach only last night and yet, again, the wall bloomed its own small colony.

Boiling the kettle and reaching for the generic bottle of bleach – 39p with a voucher – she prepared herself for battle.

'You're seriously pissing me off, do you know that? What's it going to take for you to just fuck off and die?'

The vehemence, the inherent rage in this whispered curse, took even Jamie herself by surprise.

It wasn't just that; every time she looked at it, she could almost see the tiny spores floating in the air, irritating Bo's lungs, setting up camp and inflaming his airways.

It was the sense of invasion into this, their home.

It may not be much.

It may not be fancy.

But she alone held the front door keys and she paid the rent.

This was their refuge, their safest space, and Bo deserved fresh air to breathe as he slept.

Jamie picked up her mobile and tapped out a text to Kieran Jones. In the grand scheme of things, surely it would be an investment to send round the Rentokil man, rather than have his property crumble into absolute disrepair?

She held her breath as three small dots appeared on the screen below her message. Perhaps her landlord might finally do the right thing by them, and without it involving a convoluted quickstep of him insisting they meet over a drink to discuss, and Jamie – politely, firmly, repeatedly – declining the offer.

Three dots scrolling and then gone.

Nothing.

No reply.

Jamie closed her eyes and counted slowly to ten, as the kettle clicked off.

Hot water, bleach and elbow grease. It would have to do for now.

Chapter 8

Jamie opened her eyes, the pale morning sunlight streaming through the windows onto her face. For just a second, one brief moment, the gentle warmth made her smile, revelling in the loose limbs and pliant mood of having, finally, blissfully slept as she stretched out on the wonky sofa bed.

And that thought alone made her heart pound furiously in her chest, a flood of adrenaline forcing clarity.

Jamie stood up, far too quickly, sheer panic driving her body, fighting the wave of nauseated dizziness. Dashing through to Bo's room, she held her breath for what scene might be awaiting her. Bracing herself for the worst; she genuinely couldn't remember the last time Bo had slept through the night.

His bed was empty, the covers pushed back and rumpled. Slept in. Yet empty.

His inhalers lay, ordered neatly, just as she had left them on his bedside table.

She swallowed hard, her brain refusing to stand down just yet, even as relief hit her firmly in the chest.

'Bo? Bo? You up?' Her voice cracked, betraying her

fears, her panic. The background hum of trepidation that one day – one night – Bo's inhalers might not be quite enough.

'Mum! I'm in the kitchen – I made pancakes!' His high, reedy voice conveyed all his excited delight. 'For you!'

Jamie stepped back across the hallway and returned to their open-plan living room/kitchen/dining room/study/laundry room, sidestepping a basket of whites that had been awaiting her attention and folding for several days.

In the 'L' of the room, the scene of devastation was somehow exactly what Jamie needed to prove to her brain that all was indeed well with her son. Almond milk splattered across the worktop, puffs of flour scattered the splashbacks, his face lit up with pride at the wonky puddles of batter smoking in the pan. 'Just because.'

Jamie stepped forward and wrapped her arms around Bo's slender waist as he non-too expertly flipped the scotch pancakes over, the edges already curling upwards. 'Well, this is a very lovely surprise.' She paused, not wanting to always be the voice of practicality. 'And you, you slept okay?'

He grinned. 'Like a baby. But you know, without all the screaming and pooping myself.' His laughter, easy laughter from clear, easy lungs, was like balm to Jamie's soul.

'Well then, clever Dr Monkfish.'

Bo laughed again. 'You really shouldn't call him that, Mum. Because next time we see him, you'll do it by mistake.'

Jamie nodded. 'Okay. Clever Dr Monkton – who does

look like a grumpy fish whatever you may say – has obviously hit on something with this new inhaler.'

'Maybe I don't even need to see the consultant now, Mum?' Bo's voice was high, hopeful.

'We'll see,' Jamie answered, despite already knowing the answer to that one. You didn't sit on an NHS waiting list for months to see the lead consultant only to turn down an appointment after one good night's sleep. 'Now then, once we've demolished a stack of these beauties—'

'—with golden syrup,' Bo pointed out proudly, nodding towards their food cupboard, which looked happily well stocked for the next few days at least.

'With golden syrup,' Jamie agreed. 'What do you say we go for a nice long walk in the park and enjoy the sunshine?'

Bo hesitated, distracted for a moment, biting his lip as he slid the pancakes onto a plate. 'Can we watch a movie later too? With popcorn?'

'Sounds like the perfect Sunday,' Jamie agreed, already trying to plan a route through Harnley that didn't pass the football ground where so many of his year-group would be practising this morning, or past the old theatre, where that art group would be happening, or indeed past the bakery filled with pastries and patisseries that would make her own mouth water.

A route that could encompass all the wonderful attractions of their small town without tormenting themselves unnecessarily.

'This might take me a while,' Bo said, concentrating hard as he poured four more small circles of batter into the pan. 'And you don't need to help me.'

Bo-speak for bugger-off-and-stop-hovering.

Jamie grinned, reassured that he'd put the oven gloves on before he popped the plateful of pancakes into the oven to keep warm. 'Okay then, chef. I'll grab a quick shower and stay out of the way.' She paused. 'I'm really incredibly proud of you, Bo. This is very thoughtful.'

'Well, if you think this is impressive, just wait until you see what I can do with a chickpea!' He grinned conspiratorially. It had become a running joke between them: they never knew what to make with the bloody chickpeas in their weekly food parcel. 'Bonnie told me about a cake! Just call me Jamie Oliver, really.' He waved his hand in her direction, his absolute focus on the pan in front of him, flour in his hair and chuffed to bits with himself. 'Er, shower?'

Jamie smiled, biting her lip to quell the urge to laugh, to tousle his hair, to scoop this adorable soul up into her arms and dance him around the kitchen as she had done when he was small. Instead, she breathed into the moment, enjoying the relief.

It was quite literally amazing the difference a good night's sleep had made to the mood in their world.

It wasn't entirely clear to Jamie whether her priorities were skewed or whether it was simply a product of circumstance, but she knew that Bo's health trumped everything, with sleep coming a close second – beating even a lottery win into perspective.

She unfolded her towel from the hall radiator and slipped into the bathroom, one ear open for kitchen carnage. It was just so much harder loosening the apron strings than she had ever really realised, and at times she was embarrassed by memories of how she had judged her own mother's constant clucking and cossetting.

Stepping under the streaming water, Jamie adeptly washed and rinsed her hair. She had the whole procedure down to a fine art now – hot water was a scarce commodity, but the feel of freshly washed hair had to be one of the cheapest pick-me-ups that she had found. That and freshly shaved legs.

Such decadence, she snorted with wry amusement at the very thought.

How times had changed.

Wrapping herself in a towel and using a flannel to give the whole bathroom a quick once-over while it was steamy, Jamie allowed herself a moment to breathe.

She was doing okay, she thought contentedly, as she towelled her hair roughly dry, taking her time.

She had this.

Her gorgeous son was cooking her breakfast and she already knew what was for supper. Was he even perhaps now old enough to watch *Some Like It Hot*, she wondered, convinced that half of the plotline would go straight over his head, but equally knowing just how much he would adore the black and white classic.

Smoothing her hair down, Jamie heard raised voices from next door. She stilled, wondering if it was the TV, before recognising Bo's voice, panicked and confused.

'What the hell?' Jamie wrapped the towel around her even more tightly, goosebumps prickling her damp flesh.

Kieran Jones stood in the middle of the room, swinging a set of keys around his fingers and looking smug. 'I hammered on the door. Nobody answered.'

'I'm not allowed to answer the door! I told you that!' Bo shouted, properly angry, his breath coming in short sharp bursts of frustration.

'And I told *you*, I smelled burning. Landlord's discretion,' Kieran said, his eyes ranging all over Jamie's body in a way that made her want to vomit, or throw something at his stupid, smug face.

'Get. Out,' she said. 'Now.'

The fury in her voice made even Kieran baulk a little.

'Leave my son alone and get out.' She glanced over at Bo, checking his breathing, as always. She tucked the towel even tighter around her and caught her own breath at the realisation she would have to squeeze past Kieran to get to Bo, to his inhalers.

Kieran stood his ground a beat longer than was surely necessary, presumably to try and maintain his upper hand.

'You know, if you heated this place properly, you wouldn't have such a problem with the mould. In fact, I should probably be charging you to fix it – after all, you've hardly maintained this place. Put the bloody heating on, why don't you? And—' He stepped forward and leaned over her until she could smell the garlic on his breath.

Jamie froze, panicked, her thin, wet bath towel offering little protection.

'—by the state of this place, I don't think you'll have a leg to stand on when I hold onto your security deposit when you leave.' He nodded towards the batter-splattered kitchen.

'And – as I have told you before – we are not leaving. You, however, are leaving *right now* or I'm going to call the police.' Jamie's voice shook with fury and alarm at just how vulnerable she and Bo truly were.

She wasn't, of course, and never had been, the only person with keys to their small sanctuary.

Kieran shrugged, taking one last intrusive and lascivious eyeful of her state of undress. He stepped back, pausing as he got to the front door. 'My money says you *are* leaving, though, Jamie.' He pulled a letter from his back pocket and skimmed it across the room, watching it skid to a halt at Jamie's bare feet.

'You're quite right of course – the whole property is in need of a bit of sprucing up. A little maintenance.' He smiled and for a fleeting moment, Jamie frowned down at the letter, allowing herself to hope.

'Because then, darlin', I can get top whack for it, not the pittance tenants like you can pull together,' Kieran continued, clearly thrilled with his attempts at misdirection. 'So that there's your two weeks' notice. You can accept the rent review or you can get out. Your choice.'

He winked at Bo and then left.

The vacuum of panic in the room pulled the air and brutally served to highlight the very cruelty of their situation.

Choice, yet again, a luxury they could no longer afford.

Chapter 9

The rest of Sunday had passed in a blur, walking the line between fury, righteous indignation and panic, all the while with her most reassuring expression plastered on her face.

But Bo wasn't stupid.

He was, however, more pragmatic than his mother.

'So, we move house, Mum. You hate it here anyway. You said – well, I've actually lost count of how many times you've said it was supposed to be temporary. We weren't *supposed* to still be living here, were we? In your plan?'

Ah yes, the plan . . .

The naivety – or possibly sheer, foolhardy arrogance – of her plan still had the ability to bring her out in a cold sweat.

Downsizing to save on spiralling rents, taking what little she had saved and investing in *The Big Trip* with Anik.

Elevated with one simple signature from employee to partner – a whole new world of potential. A whole new level of responsibility and commitment.

The memory of handing over the keys of her last rental – the tiny terraced house with the bathtub upstairs – was etched into her mind. It was *supposed* to have been that take-a-chance, investing-in-herself moment she would one day look back on with pride.

She had decorated all four rooms of that house with love and hard graft, and her cuticles and lower back had never quite recovered. She hadn't been building a house, though, had she? She'd been building a home, a nest for her and Bo.

How had she *dared*, she wondered now, to jeopardise their security, to gamble with their safety on a misbegotten quest for a better life, and the promise of future prosperity. Had everyone simply been bolder then? More convinced of their own invulnerability?

Reckless.

There was no avoiding the verdict.

No hindsight required.

She had gambled, and they had both lost.

No wonder she could barely manage to walk past the empty shopfront on the High Street without feeling a physical wrench at what might have been. Mourning for the lifestyle that she and Bo had lost still felt somehow trivial, even now, compared to the loss of her best friend and business partner, Anik. The ultimate loss, really, throwing any grief for the blissfully challenging career she had adored into the shade.

Jamie shook her head. 'It's not what I wanted for us, Bo. But things have changed a bit the last few years.'

'So it really doesn't matter if it changes a bit more and it's not as though it's going to take us long to pack . . .' His face turned up to hers, wide-eyed and trusting, eager to reassure, open to anything his mum might suggest. He gave her a wobbly smile. 'As long as I can bring all my art stuff, I'll be fine anywhere.'

She leaned down and kissed his forehead. 'So what did you have in mind, Bobo? Shall we pack it all in and move to the Outer Hebrides? Or find a tiny cottage on the wild and windswept moors?'

Bo shook his head. 'Mum, be serious. We're not moving to the middle of nowhere. But maybe we could find somewhere quieter on the edge of town? Not on this horrid road with all the buses?'

And all the fumes, Jamie thought.

And so, they walked, chatting as they went, in loops around Harrison's and Bo's school, along to the very end of the High Street where the roads were leafier and the houses weren't divided into bedsits; wandering into the catchment area for Stoneleigh and wondering whether they might one day look back at this abrupt turn of events as an opportunity.

But the window displays in the estate agents were hardly reassuring. You could almost see the prices go up and up and up, the closer you got to Stoneleigh and the promise of a decent education on the state's dime.

'Are we definitely doing this, Mum? Definitely moving?' Bo said, fidgeting beside her as she scanned yet another window of rentals, each photographed with judicious lighting and maximum creative licence.

Jamie thought of the formal rent notice at home, shoved behind the bags of pasta, out of sight, but hardly out of mind.

There was simply no way she could afford the hike. Nearly double their current rate – the intention was clear.

Kieran had his beady eye on gentrification, and Jamie and Bo didn't make the cut.

'We are definitely moving,' Jamie said. 'What about this one?'

She pointed to a one-bedroom flat in their price range – not so much a kitchen as a kitchenette, but with room for a sofa bed for her, if they eschewed a table.

It looked sad and neglected; you could almost smell stale takeaways and must.

'Well—' Bo hesitated, trying to be supportive, yet clearly conflicted. 'Is that the kind of thing we'd be looking for then? Like that?' No garden, third floor, no sign even that the windows would fully open. It was hardly the stuff of dreams.

'Okay, then, maybe you'd better tell me more about those Outer Hebrides,' he said, leaning into her side and taking her hand.

'Or that one . . .' Jamie felt her pulse ricochet for a moment. A tiny photo, a tiny postcard really, in the bottom corner of the window. Two up, two down. The right part of town and a tiny square of green. 'Tenants will be thoroughly vetted, affordable rent on application according to circumstances.'

And who on earth were the Waverly Trust?

Jamie pulled out her phone, desperately hoping she had enough minutes left. 'Hi,' she said to the automated voice-mail, 'I'm calling about the house on Miles Street. It's me and my son – he's ten. Very quiet. No pets. No smoking.

We could move in straightaway and I have references. I work at Harrison's in town. Could you call me back as soon as possible, please. I'm on—' She reeled off the digits of her phone number and offered up a little prayer, just as her credit ran out.

Could they possibly be that lucky?

She squinted at the card on display once more, taking in the neat window boxes of geraniums and the polished silver fox door knocker. This house was cherished. This house was perfect.

This house was less than one hundred metres from the gates of Stoneleigh.

Jamie swallowed a wave of emotion, the tears prickling her eyes; maybe, just maybe, someone up there was looking out for them?

She leaned against Bo, his very presence her constant comfort. 'Cross your fingers, Bo,' she murmured, smiling as he did just that, entwining his slender pale fingers with complete concentration and commitment.

The little house on Miles Street felt like a sign. A good omen.

And Jamie hadn't been able to resist casually walking past on their way back home, looping casually into the smarter end of town. No fuss; no need to get Bo's hopes up. But the bright yellow front door looked so cheery, so confidently self-assured. Four small sash windows looked out onto the quiet cul-de-sac, rows of terraced redbrick cottages leading up to a large wrought-iron gate bearing the legend 'The Old

School House', beyond which trees obscured the view along the gravel drive, only a single ornate chimney pot visible through the foliage.

The very thought that they could live somewhere like that had filled her with a buoyant wave of optimism that carried her through the rest of her day. Even as she'd checked and double-checked her phone over and over again.

Just knowing that there were possibilities on her horizon had given her such a boost, yet by the next morning, with Bo exhausted from a disturbed night, Jamie was blindsided by the critical voice in her head. Loudly chastising her for all the months of inertia, for dwelling on the maxim of better the devil you know, keeping them stuck in this God-awful flat.

As though even her own subconscious was unwilling to accept the truth – there had been scant headspace for planning ahead, for hopes and ambitions, when she was so firmly stuck in the day-to-day grind of survival, juggling the immediate and unavoidable. Every scrap of attitude reserved for supporting Bo, running on fumes at the end of each day.

Even her memories of studying Maslow and his oh-so-accurate hierarchy of needs weren't as helpful as one might imagine. Knowing that the human brain would always prioritise food and security over creativity and self-fulfilment didn't really appease the self-reproach that she simply should have done better.

Hustling to get out the door on time, the weight of parental guilt on her shoulders had rarely felt heavier.

How ironic that, this time, the trigger had been the merest hint of possibility.

Jamie discreetly checked her phone yet again, slipping it out of her pocket to reassure herself that it wasn't on silent, hope dwindling with every passing hour as she methodically, robotically restocked the shelves with fancy pasta at Harrison's. Not even taking pleasure in aligning the labels with precision as she usually did.

She had no credits, so phoning again wasn't really an option. Whoever had come up with the £10 minimum top-up really didn't know their customers very well, she thought with a sigh of frustration.

Hope was a slippery emotion, just as likely to torment as uplift and the last twelve hours had twisted Jamie's stomach.

Focusing on the promise of that yellow, cheerful front door was the best she could do, as though she could manifest a tenancy just by wanting it the most. And so, she had big plans to dash to the estate agent on her lunchbreak. Have the conversation in person. It was doable – just – even if she would doubtless arrive looking sweaty and harassed and hardly ideal tenant material.

'Jamie? Jamie love? Oh, you were miles away.' Rea from the pharmacy stood beside her holding a white paper bag, and smiling. 'I didn't forget – I said I'd save you a trip. All signed and accounted for.'

'That's incredibly kind,' Jamie said. 'Thank you.'

'How is the lad? Any progress?' Rea asked, one of the few

people who were genuinely interested in the answer, rather than any possible knock-ons and inconveniences.

Jamie looked around and knocked her hand against the wooden display cabinet. 'I think maybe. He's had a few decent nights, but last night was awful again. There's just no predicting it and he'll be exhausted at school today. Still, I think maybe we're on the right track with all these new meds. At some point he has to be allergy-proof, right?'

Jamie looked to Rea for reassurance more often than was probably fair. The little pharmacy on the corner so much more accessible than the vast medical centre in town, where you rarely saw the same GP twice and you either booked weeks ahead or ran the gamut of triage at 8am. Rea and Harris had been her lifeline and a mine of information at times.

'I think it's a good thing he's going to see that immunologist chap,' Rea said, nodding. 'And all credit to you for pushing for it. Not many mums advocate as well for their kids as you do. And, d'you know, it really irks me that the dad rushing into A&E with his kid is seen as heroic, but the mums are always dismissed as being overly anxious and overreacting. So you keep going, Jamie. Calm, collected and informed. That's the way forward. Bo's lucky to have you.'

Instinctively, overwhelmed by this unexpected praise, and truly touched, Jamie leaned forward and hugged her. 'Thank you, Rea.'

She'd lost count of the times doctors had raised an eyebrow or even rolled their eyes as she'd carried Bo into the hospital.

But she knew – she was at the proverbial coalface – she knew how small the window was when things went south.

Did they honestly expect her to wait at home until it became a high-risk emergency?

Maybe.

But she'd rather look stupid than be wrong.

'Oh, and before I forget, Bonnie said could you swing by *Crap But Cheap*. She's a sweet girl, our Bonnie – it's nice to see her reaching out and making friends. Would do you both good. But, Jamie, don't buy into the hype of all that exuberant energy, will you? She's—' Rea broke off, looking as though there was so much more she wanted to say, yet discretion prevailed. 'Anyway, she's got the information from Amy for you? I presume that makes more sense to you?'

Jamie nodded. 'I promised I'd take a look at her friend's CV and her job applications – you know, just in case a fresh pair of eyes can help get a few more interviews. It's a numbers game really, these days.'

'Well, there you are then, paying it forward. It's what I used to love the most about our little High Street, you know, Jamie. We all looked out for each other.' She rubbed Jamie's arm and nodded. 'And you're a sweet girl too, helping out. Even when you clearly haven't got time. It's nice to see that spirit of yours coming back. Maybe it's the first green shoots of recovery, you know?'

'And, it's useful to know you're so well versed when it comes to job applications, Ms Matson.' Nick Harrison made them both jump, silently turning the corner of the international foods aisle in front of them. 'Just don't expect a glowing reference from me if you're always gossiping on shift. Save that for your own time.'

'I was just delivering her son's medication, Nick,' Rea said tiredly, shaking her head. 'Don't make it into something it's not.' She passed the white paper bag to Jamie.

'I hope that's legal,' Nick Harrison said with a smirk. Making no attempt to hide the intimidating undertone.

'Oh, and Jamie? You can make up over lunch all the time you've spent gossiping.' He gave a tight, forced smile and walked away, brooking no argument.

'Twat,' said Rea with feeling.

But Jamie had no words, just a plummeting sense of loss, thinking only of the little house with the yellow front door.

Chapter 10

Another morning, another shift, and still no word about the house on Miles Street. No hope of pushing open that happy yellow door and being at home; safe and warm, cossetted from the world.

She'd raided the last of her emergency fund to top up the credit on her phone, leaving yet another message at the estate agent's first thing. But still nothing.

It was a pipe dream anyway – how on earth she would scrape together the security deposit, let alone the first few months' rent was beyond her.

And Nick Harrison's increasingly foul mood nixed any thoughts of asking for an advance.

She would simply have to bite the bullet and apply for emergency housing.

She had two weeks – well, technically thirteen days now. Not long to get her act together and the responsibility weighed heavily. Bo, on the other hand, was increasingly excited by the prospect of living somewhere new. Somewhere without mould and car fumes, and the building work next door that seemed to be lasting an eternity and covered everything they owned in a fine film of dust.

But then Bo was still under the impression they would be moving somewhere nicer.

And Jamie couldn't make any promises at this point.

She'd scoured the property listings on the internet – as Bo concentrated intently on arranging his waffles like a Roman mosaic – but it was hard to know where to even begin.

And it wasn't as though she could just pick up the phone and call on a friend.

Her own fault, as much as anything, she knew that, but somehow life had worn her down, way past the point where the rewards of a social life outweighed the effort. Or the cost.

Little by little, she'd simply given up trying to communicate the realities of her life to her university friends.

They just didn't get it.

Or perhaps, she thought darkly, they just shied away from the suggestion that one of their tight-knit group could have fallen so low. All her grand ambitions seemingly shelved.

As though her fall from grace, her poverty, might somehow be contagious.

But, really, who was to say who had ultimately dropped the ball?

Jamie had surely been equally complicit in stepping away, as she struggled to juggle even the necessities of her own life? Of Bo's life. She sighed, knowing all too well how easy it was to become utterly self-absorbed when life did not go to plan.

And so, she searched the internet and hoped.

The number for the local council was saved on her phone, alongside a search for what constituted 'legally homeless' and what might trigger an obligation for them to help.

Two days, she thought.

She'd give it two days and then she would swallow what was left of her pride and call.

Jamie quietly left the shop floor, leaving Nick Harrison standing sentry by the tills with his hands behind his back, for all the world as though he saw himself as Harnley's answer to Prince Charles. As though Harrison's might one day be spoken of in the same breath as Duchy Organics.

She locked the loo door behind her and fished her phone out of her pocket. A single voicemail. Quickly checking the missed call wasn't from school and cursing, yet again, Nick Harrison's abhorrence of mobile phones on the shop floor, she sat on the loo and pressed her phone to her ear, multi-tasking.

He was kind of weird about how many loo breaks you were allowed too, so call this one an investment wee.

And God help you on the days you had a gnarly period to contend with.

There was no way around it. Cheap sanitary towels were just shite. Four pairs of pants and a prayer the only effective supplement.

She exhaled slowly as she listened to the estate agent's nasal voice, a facsimile of apologetic, claiming he hadn't received her earlier message. Only the follow-up this morning.

She was too late – a tenancy had already been agreed with, er, another applicant. His hesitation spoke volumes, the words 'more efficient' hung in the ether, yet he still welcomed her application for any other properties on his list if she could see fit to call in office hours *this time*.

Jamie dropped her head into her hands and breathed out slowly.

That house had felt so right – admittedly she'd only stood on the pavement outside – but it had felt as though there was a connection. *She'd* felt a connection to the place, a gut instinct.

But her gut had clearly been wrong.

Again.

Chapter 11

'Psst. Over here!'

Jamie looked around and saw Bonnie hiding behind the tapenade display, with a box of rosemary salted crackers balanced on her head. 'Jamie! Psst, I'm incognito,' she grinned.

'Jesus, Bonnie. I'm already in *so* much trouble today. Please don't . . .' Jamie was on the verge of tears.

Bonnie looked instantly cowed, taking down the box and reading the label like a normal, respectable customer might. Still, all the while, whispering through the pyramid of olive tapenades in their black, green and aubergine jars from the adjacent aisle.

'We're going to have a tiny party to launch *Crap But Cheap*. Like, at six o'clock tonight. And you must bring Bo. I'm doing nibbles, so don't bring anything else, I have it covered.'

'But I—'

Jamie realised she was talking to thin air – Bonnie was gone, the rosemary crackers abandoned, and thankfully no sign of Nick Harrison. A clean getaway.

Once the relief had passed, Jamie realised there was another, unfamiliar emotion left behind – anticipation.

And, oh how she'd missed it. Even the prospect of some dodgy canapes in the tiny churro kiosk was somehow appealing.

No expectation to be anything other than herself.

No pressure to spend more than she could afford, just to fit in, to avoid making other people feel awkward.

She smiled as she rearranged the porcini and morels. Rather than sighing over the memories of rich morel risottos in a sunlit piazza in Florence, as she normally might, she thought instead of what she could contribute to the celebration that evening.

A celebration of spontaneity and authenticity. Not to mention generosity itself.

With Bo on the guest list as an insistence rather than an afterthought, with none of the all-too-familiar stigma that came from having a child who *coughed*. A lot. Even now, it was telling to watch how people shied away. Just in case . . . And how much it hurt Bo's feelings.

Someone like Bonnie would never have been on Jamie's radar before, if she allowed herself that moment of honesty. Their paths would barely have crossed, and she was embarrassed to admit that, even if they had, Jamie might well have been tempted to look down her nose a bit at the adult woman, the curvaceous adult woman, wearing lime green dungarees.

But wearing them with such boldness and impudence, they could surely only elicit a smile, even from the most jaded and judgemental of folk.

'Who the hell was that lunatic woman?' Nick Harrison stormed over towards Jamie. 'Is she a friend of yours?'

Well, that killed that theory.

'She's opening a hair salon on the High Street,' Jamie told him, not one word a lie. 'Do you think you'd allow her to put flyers on our noticeboard, help to spread the word?'

'God, they always want something, don't they?' Nick shook his head and walked away, muttering under his breath.

Who exactly did he mean with his all-encompassing 'they', Jamie wondered.

Were 'they' the same people who had made her own heart sink when they sat down in front of her at *The Big Trip* and asked about static caravans in Pembrokeshire?

Dear God – she must have been unbearable! – she thought with a shiver of embarrassed recognition.

And she bloody loved Pembrokeshire too; it just hadn't fit in with the aesthetic and business model she and Anik had been trying to build.

Maybe her situation now was actually the comeuppance she deserved. God forbid, she'd have ended up like the kind of entitled entrepreneur who was now her boss.

Daniel, meanwhile, whistled cheerily as he tackled the floors, sweeping up a sunburst of *tipo '00'* fine white pasta flour – £8.99's worth of mess dropped to the floor.

Jamie frowned and looked further along the aisle, a trail of chaos strewn behind him. 'What the hell?'

Daniel rolled his eyes. 'We had a visit from little Merritt and his super chill mummy again . . .'

That kid was a liability. And yet Nick Harrison – two-faced sycophant that he was – turned a blind eye because Lara was a stay-at-home mum with an Instagram account, or as she liked to call herself – an 'influencer'. And so, not a word was said, as Merritt regularly barged his way around the store, pulling items off the shelves and often as not, making abrasive fire engine noises as he did so.

The boy was six – not a toddler.

And yet he had no concept of boundaries, and Jamie would wager that the velvet knickerbockers he wore to prep school signalled the vanishingly small likelihood of any in his future either.

'That kid's a bottle of Gaviscon just waiting to happen, isn't he?' Jamie sighed. 'I'll get the mop and we can tag team this, before anyone slips on all this mess.'

'I'm already on the case with the liquid spills – no broken glass, thank God – and put the sign up,' Daniel said, and grimaced. 'But that balsamic stink is going to linger. He's got excellent taste, I'll give him that – top of the range product every time. Although you'll be pleased to know that you won the pool – by my count there's fifty-two quid's worth of damage. So you, Jamie Matson,' he put on his silly TV quiz-show voice, 'are now the proud winner of all £2.50 in the pot. You just have to decide – will you save, or will you splurge?'

Jamie grinned, buoyed as so often by their daft but uplifting humour. It didn't take much, yet somehow their shared jokes made all the difference to the daily grind.

'Or will either of you perhaps stop mucking about and get on with your jobs? Look at the state of this aisle – do you have no pride in your work?' Nick Harrison shook his head as he stormed away, leaving Jamie and Daniel silenced for a moment, trying to swallow down their shocked laughter at his puce fury.

'You know,' Daniel said, 'I've come to the conclusion recently that if our man, Nick there, took a few Valium from time to time, then none of his staff would need to.'

'I've come to the conclusion,' said Jamie, with a tired smile of appreciation for her empathetic colleague, and wrapping her hand in a swathe of the elephant loo roll they used for spills, 'that I'm going to go insane if I stay in this job for another year of my life. I mean, as much as I like paying my bills – and I do – it's the side order of ritual humiliation that's really wearing me down.'

Silently, each lost in their thoughts and mindful of the lurking, humourless presence of their boss, they cleaned up the mess. Jamie wondered whether Daniel was caught up in the metaphor too: the privileged leaving a trail of destruction in their path, oblivious to the needs and challenges of those left behind to deal with it.

And it was hardly as though she and Daniel were without useful skills.

They just weren't the skills destined to survive the recent cull.

Daniel's beautiful restaurant now stood empty, the rave

reviews from all the major broadsheets stacked, still in their frames, in a dusty corner of his studio flat. The premises along the High Street, right next to *The Big Trip*, boarded up in the same graffitied chipboard.

His had been a story of triumph over adversity already. He had, quite literally, arrived in Dover with nothing except his older sister, the clothes they stood up in and his culinary talents. And they had been the lucky ones.

His tiny restaurant had flourished due to his skill, his flair and his willingness to build from nothing. One long family-style table, then two, then six. Slowly, slowly building his clientele and his reputation.

But there had been no safety net for Daniel's business either. Hospitality had been hit almost as hard as travel.

And so, together, Daniel and Jamie stacked shelves and scrubbed floors and loos, and put up with Nick Harrison throwing his weight around, simply because they needed to. And because, yet again and in so many ways, they were still lucky; luckier than some.

Keeping the faith that they could start all over again was the bond that also kept them sane. Well, perhaps sane was stretching things a little.

'Excuse me?' A slightly tremulous but polite voice cut into Jamie's thoughts. 'Might I have a moment of your time?'

Jamie smiled at the rather stylish but distinctly vintage customer standing a few feet away. Her silvered hair was swept into a single fat plait over one shoulder, and she wore rather incongruously trendy trainers with her thick

American Tan tights and long linen dress, under which she had layered several tops of varying weight, colour and sleeve length. It was the kind of outfit that Bo had put together when he was three; this well-spoken woman either assertively, two-fingers-up, stylish or conversely in the early throes of some kind of Alzheimer's situation. It really was hard to read.

'Of course,' Jamie said, wiping her hands and stepping away from the mess, yet still carrying a cloud of acrid vinegar with her. 'I'm so sorry about the smell.'

'Not a problem at all, although I guess it's much harder when you're up close and personal with it.' She rummaged in her handbag. 'Would you like a puff of L'Arpège to outsmart the little beggar?'

Jamie couldn't help but smile at her genuine concern. There was something incredibly appealing about this customer – and clearly, despite her attire, she knew her own mind absolutely. 'I'm fine thank you, but I appreciate the offer, not to mention the style.' Jamie led her further away from the scene of devastation. 'Now, what can I help you find?'

She waited expectantly for a moment, half expecting a list to emerge from the handbag too – the early Lulu Guinness handbag, if she wasn't mistaken. Just because Jamie carried her belongings in a Bag For Life now, didn't mean she hadn't once been appreciative of all things *Vogue*. Even if only on the page, rather than in person.

The customer frowned as she noticed Nick Harrison

watching their every move. 'I'd like to talk to you about *linguine*,' she said loudly, as though for his benefit.

'Okay then,' Jamie said, gesturing towards the far corner where there were more different shapes of pasta than feasibly useful.

'I don't really,' the customer confided, once they were ensconced in the realms of orecchiette, farfalle and rigatoni. 'I just needed to know you were okay. You are Jamie Matson, aren't you?'

Jamie jerked, blinked hard, thrown completely off balance by the intensity of the woman's gaze, the softening folds on her face doing nothing to offset those cornflower eyes that seemingly missed nothing.

'I am,' Jamie said, 'but . . .'

The woman nodded and held out her hand, 'I'm Ruth. Ruth Waverly, and to be honest, my love, I just needed to see for myself that you were okay.'

Waverly. As in The Waverly Trust.

Jamie stood fractionally straighter, held her breath, in case this was some kind of curious tenancy appraisal, in case the prospective tenant had fallen through and . . .

'I'm so sorry I couldn't get back to you after your message. Your phone cut out, you see, leaving me a few digits short.' She gave a wry smile. 'In the literal sense, rather than what my darling husband might imply. And I'm so sorry but the cottage is already let. I just couldn't let *you* know that.'

'Right, well, yes.' Jamie allowed herself to breathe again, to feel the disappointment. 'Thank you, I guess. I did manage to speak to the agent in the end. You really didn't need to come all the way down here just to—'

'Well, that's where you're wrong, Jamie. Because I'm afraid your message rather stayed with me. You just sounded so very – well, not just worried, but hopeful too. Dare I say it, a little bit desperate? As though our cottage was the answer you were looking for.' She shrugged apologetically. 'I couldn't get you out of my mind, I'm afraid. And then we were just walking past this morning and there it was, Harrison's. Like a sign,' she smiled. 'Well, actually a sign, you know, but then the opportunity seemed too good to pass up – as I said, I really just needed to see for myself that you were okay. You and your Bo. I hope that doesn't make me one of those stalking people now?'

Jamie blinked hard. There was no ulterior motive here; Ruth Waverly's visit seemed to be entirely driven by her genuine concern and Jamie was moved once more by the kindness of strangers.

She shook her head. 'You're so very kind and, honestly, the cottage would have been the perfect solution – Bo and I do need to find somewhere new to live. But I'm looking into other options,' she hesitated, 'you certainly don't need to be worrying.'

She hated to think of this elderly lady lying awake at night with this preying on her mind, just as much as she was touched by her concern.

Ruth nodded, considering. 'You might want to let me be the judge of that.' Her eyes flickered towards the hovering spectre of Nick Harrison that had appeared at the end of the aisle. 'There's just so much choice – but which of these can I put in my *soup*?' she said loudly, plucking a packet of orzo from the shelf, unable to disguise her shock at the price sticker.

'These might actually be what you're looking for,' Jamie put forward an alternative brand that was currently on sale, even knowing that Nick Harrison would chastise her for it later.

Ruth clasped the packet tightly, waiting for him to move on. 'I do need to go, actually, my Henry is over in the café opposite. He thinks I'm a right soft touch with all this – or more likely going soft in the head, but bless him, he humours me either way.'

She gave Jamie's hand a gentle squeeze. 'If you're ever stuck, Jamie – and I do remember what that's like with small children – you have my number. Do use it. No judgement here.'

Jamie breathed out slowly as Ruth walked away, on a waft of L'Arpège and genuine kindness. She could only hope that Ruth wouldn't come to regret her incredibly expensive Tuscan orzo soup.

Chapter 12

'You came!' Bonnie was visibly touched, ushering Jamie and Bo inside, even though there was barely room to manoeuvre in the tiny kiosk.

In an ironic nod to the previous tenant and possibly because the very walls of the place were imbued with the scent of warm sugar and batter anyway, Bonnie had laid out platters of churros and vast jugs of lurid punch.

She tugged on Bo's arm, pulling him into the throng, 'And these are for you!' Individual bottles of lemonade sat in a bowl of ice. 'And I made sure that Billy made all the churros dairy-free so you can fill your boots!' She grinned, clearly very pleased with herself.

Bo glanced up at his mum, confusion writ large on his face. 'But I'm wearing trainers.'

Jamie smiled, leaning down to Bo, whispering quietly. 'It means you can eat as many as you like . . .'

Bo threw his arms around Bonnie and hugged her, taking all of them a little by surprise. Bo didn't really hug people, well *anyone* actually, except Jamie. With Jamie, at home, it was like having a pet koala sometimes.

'Oh, you—' Bonnie said, clearly thrown, but definitely delighted. 'They're only churros, you daft sod.'

Bo laughed, visibly shocked. 'You swore.'

'Well, you're short,' Bonnie retorted, tousling his hair. 'And you definitely need a haircut.'

Bo pulled away, indignant. 'I absolutely do not. What's wrong with long hair?'

Bonnie crouched down beside him and tugged gently at the locks at his neck where they curled forward with just a hint of mullet. 'There is absolutely nothing wrong with long hair, but you need some shape there and a bit of style – you can't just let it get longer and longer, or you'll look like an English sheepdog.' She turned him gently by the shoulders so they were both looking into the floor-length mirror she'd only just had installed. 'See? Here? And here . . .' She bent and tucked his hair with her fingers until it fell just so.

'Oh!' Bo said, all his furious indignation evaporating in a moment. 'Like that – that's how I've been wanting it! Mum? Mum, can you see? Bonnie gets it.'

Jamie nodded. 'She absolutely does. And maybe you could be one of her very first customers when this place is officially open?'

'Can I? Can I be your very first customer?' Bo asked, eyes wide with excitement, his fingers instinctively reaching for his hair, wanting to touch, but not wanting to disturb Bonnie's clever tweaks.

'You'll be needing a waiting list soon, Bonnie,' Amy

said, stepping into the fray and holding out a bottle of sparkling cider. 'Congratulations, B. What's it like to be so in demand?'

Bonnie hugged her. 'A bit confusing actually. I'm kind of conflicted between praying it lasts and wondering if I should have done this years ago instead of letting myself get beaten down by all those superior arseholes in suits.'

Amy's face instantly dropped and Bonnie cringed. 'Shit, I'm so sorry, Amy. How did the interview go?'

'Do you even need to ask?' Amy said with a heartfelt sigh. 'There were like thirty people interviewing and they said they'd had over two hundred applications. Can you imagine? Two hundred people actively wanting to answer their stupid phones.' She choked on the word 'stupid' – they all knew exactly how much Amy had wanted to do exactly that.

'Do you know,' Jamie said quietly, looking around at the vibrant and welcoming world Bonnie had created, making her own luck, relying on her own skill, 'I'm not sure the job market has all the answers we need right now.'

'Nope, but it does have all the, you know, *actual* jobs,' Amy countered. 'And now I'm the Eeyore at the party. Let's celebrate Bonnie and her bold ballsiness tonight and then tomorrow it's back to the drawing board.'

'Can we have a big whiteboard and make a plan? I can pinch the coloured markers from work,' Kath said, squeezing into the group. 'Call it a rainbow of thanks,' she said wryly, 'in lieu of the pay rise we all so sorely need.' She wore a fleece over her NHS uniform and the mask imprints across her face and red raw hands told of yet another exhausting shift in A&E.

'You need this,' Bonnie said, passing her a large paper cup of punch and giving her a hug.

'I'll get your suit dry-cleaned,' Amy said, dropping her voice to a whisper.

'No need,' Kath replied with a sympathetic smile, 'Just hold onto it for next time.'

'Oh God!' Amy blew out her cheeks. 'I can't even think about there being a next time. Even though I know it's inevitable.'

'Yes, but before the next time, I'm going to attack this mop of unruliness and Jamie's going to savagely edit your CV,' Bonnie said firmly. 'We're allowed to be ruthless in our pursuit of a decent career. Paying the bills is really the bare minimum we should be expecting from our daily grind. Whatever happened to fulfilment and, dare I suggest it, enjoyment?'

There was an awkward silence.

'Do you actually watch the news, Bonnie my love?' Kath asked eventually, shaking her head with a wry smile.

'I try to avoid it wherever possible,' Bonnie confessed. 'It's all *seriously* depressing . . .'

Her look of consternation was enough to lift the mood once more, and whenever Jamie glanced over at her son, he seemed to be happily engrossed in either a churro or someone else's conversation. Eavesdropping being apparently 'far better than Google' for all the stuff he actually wanted to know and preferring, as he always had, the company of adults to his peers.

Jamie breathed out slowly, the scent of warm sugar and vanilla helping her to find her balance. She would put all thoughts of their imminent homelessness aside for the next hour, she decided, and celebrate Bonnie's bold leap into self-employment.

Bonnie clambered onto the single chair in front of the mirror once the party was in full swing, clutching hold of Jamie as the chair rotated, making her whoop as she lurched. 'Well, *that* got your attention,' she laughed as the tightly packed group of well-wishers fell silent. 'I'd like to welcome you all to this not-so-grand opening of my very own little enterprise. *Crap But Cheap* has a three-month pass on this High Street. Three months to prove it can work and that haircuts don't need to cost the earth to be absolutely fabulous.' She raised her plastic cup, 'And so, I'd like to propose two toasts. The first to the life-changing promise of a decent haircut – trust me with your hair and I'll give you back your self-esteem! And secondly, to you – to all of you – for turning up tonight and making this evening incredibly special. Rather than just incredibly daunting . . .'

She clambered down to rapturous applause and cheers, and before the moment got the better of her. Jamie watched the full gamut of emotions pass across her face. Bonnie was really adept at putting on a show, it was true, but there was no doubt she was actually a tiny bit terrified of what she was taking on.

'Any words of wisdom, ladies?' Bonnie said, looking

around the cluster of women, all of them overqualified and underappreciated in their own lives and careers. Well, apart from Amy, who still didn't seem to grasp that her two GCSEs really might not be enough to catapult her through the hierarchy of local business.

'Do your accounts every week. Like literally every week. Because once you start letting those receipts pile up, then it becomes a mammoth task, so you leave it a few weeks longer, and then . . .' Jamie threw up her hands. 'Then, it's a bloody nightmare, to be honest.'

'But you don't do that, Mum. You put all your receipts in that shoe box and never look at them again,' Bo chimed in, helpful as ever.

Kath snorted with laughter. 'I have a box exactly like that too, Bo. But Bonnie is starting something brand new, so she can start with all the good habits the rest of us have given up on.'

Bo gave Bonnie a wicked smile. 'So you'll need to eat all your vegetables and drink lots of water too then, if you want to be *really* successful.'

'And get eight full hours' sleep,' Amy added, joining in with Bo.

'You'll need to start doing yoga at sunrise. Obviously. And you can kiss goodbye to that lethal concoction,' Kath said, plucking Bonnie's cup of punch from her fingers.

Bonnie wrinkled her nose and pinched it back. 'You're all rotters. And besides, you've forgotten the most important reason to be nice to me right now?'

'Dodgy haircuts on the cheap?' Kath asked innocently.

Bonnie poked her in the side. 'Shush you. You're forgetting that I'm a business owner now, don't you know? A *respectable* local businesswoman . . .'

'Well, I wouldn't go that far,' said Kath, and Jamie couldn't help but laugh at their back-and-forth banter. The kind of ribbing that spoke of friendship and respect and, yes, even love.

The kind of bond she had really truly been missing in her life.

Bonnie rolled her eyes. 'As I was saying to *Amy*, who is lovely and doesn't tease me. Much. I could write you a *really* fabulous reference?'

Amy shook her head vigorously, her red mane flying. 'I couldn't do that. It's dishonest, isn't it? I mean, I've never worked for you, have I? And I can hardly say I met you in the queue at the food bank, can I?'

Bonnie handed her cup to Jamie and turned around, unhooking a dustpan off the wall. 'Hmm. Well, firstly, there's nothing wrong with making friends in the queue at the food bank and secondly, Ames, could you just scoop up that churro behind you, on the floor, before someone slips on it?'

'Of course, hang on.' Amy bent down and rescued the flattened churro before it became a hazard.

'Excellent work,' said Bonnie, retrieving the dustpan and flicking the churro into the bin. 'Amy is reliable, confident and follows direction well. She would be an asset to any team,' Bonnie said with a grin, while Amy mouthed speechlessly.

'If you don't think all those posh twats who call on friends-of-daddy for a reference aren't doing exactly the same thing, then you're wrong,' Jamie said to her quietly. 'The sheer nepotism in the job market at the higher echelons would make you wince, Amy. Not to mention all the internships for godchildren and fellow alumni's offspring. Put it this way: I wouldn't lose any sleep over a tiny favour from a friend.'

A moment's silence fell over the group, each of them no doubt realising that, when it came to cronyism, they were woefully ill-connected.

'Maybe a *character* reference would be truly appreciated then, Bonnie, if you really don't mind?' Amy said, wobbling on the fence of her convictions.

'And from me,' Kath said. 'And if you pop into the kids' ward on a Tuesday afternoon and read them stories, you could put that on your CV as volunteering too.'

'Can I do that?' Bo asked. 'I mean, I know I'm a kid as well and I don't have a CV, but I can do all the voices?'

Kath glanced at Jamie for her approval.

Jamie nodded. 'I can't deny it – he can do all the voices.'

'Fine by me,' Kath said. 'I'll talk to Sheila tomorrow about both of you reprobates. She organises all that. Maybe it would be fun to come in together after school finishes?'

Amy sighed. 'Speaking of, do any of you think I should go back to school. I mean we all know what the elephant in the room is here?'

'The kiosk,' Bonnie corrected. 'Technically. And it kind of depends what you want to do. I did an apprenticeship to move into hairdressing because, to be honest, Amy, it turned out that being a hairdresser is all I'd ever wanted to do, so I'm not convinced any more fancy qualifications were really going to make any difference to my life.'

'What do you want to do, Amy?' Jamie asked, intrigued. 'All things being equal.'

Amy's face crumpled. 'Well that's half the bloody problem isn't it – I have absolutely no idea.'

Chapter 13

'Oh Amy, love,' Kath soothed the sobbing, hiccupping girl.

Bonnie, to her credit, didn't look even vaguely fazed that her evening of celebration had descended into tears before even the last guest had arrived.

'Do you think blokes cry when they don't get the job they applied for?' Amy asked, mascara streaking down her pale cheeks.

'Nah, they probably just punch something, or go out and get wasted,' Bonnie said dismissively. She really had no love lost for the opposite sex.

Jamie thought of Daniel, his eyes red and sore, emerging from the staff bathroom at Harrison's yesterday after yet another rejection. His hard work and experience rarely enough to even get him the interview, but one of a dozen shortlisted this time, still never yet making the final cut.

'You know, whatever anyone's background,' Jamie said gently, taking Amy's hand, 'it's always bloody hard when the big stuff is out of our control. And you can only do so much, and work on the things within your orbit. The rest is just a question of timing, of being in the right place at the right time.' She sighed, thinking of how she had missed out on the little house with the yellow front door. 'That and a pinch of luck – and I have no idea how to increase *those* odds.'

'I've got a Ouija board somewhere,' Bonnie offered. 'We can call on higher powers.'

Kath shook her head. 'You mad sod. We're not waking the dead; I've just spent half my day easing them into the afterlife with just the right amount of morphine to keep it legal, but still take the edge off.' She shook her head. 'I swear to God we're kinder to our animals in this country than we are to our people. So, no Ouija boards, okay? But maybe get Father Bill to offer up a prayer or two?'

Amy sniffed her tears away and then looked mortified at the echoing rattling sound, just as Bo looked equally impressed.

'If you want to go back to school,' Bo said, 'you can always come with me. It would be nice to have someone to talk to.' He caught himself, 'Someone fun, I mean.'

Kath and Bonnie both caught Jamie's eye, compassionate looks over the top of her son's tousled head. His words so heartfelt, so wrenching. Being lonely at school – when all the adults around you insisted on perpetuating the myth of your school days being the best days of your life – was brutal.

'But,' Bo continued, as so often oblivious to the reactions he was eliciting around him, 'we have to move house soon, so maybe I can go to Stoneleigh next year. They have an art department and a photography studio and everything. So really, it wouldn't matter if I'm always off games then, would it?' His focus was firmly on Amy, perhaps realising that her experience of school might also have missed the cookie-cutter parable by a country mile.

'That's exciting – moving house?' Amy said. 'We moved around a lot when I was your age. My dad was in the army. And sometimes having a new bedroom, and sorting out all your stuff, reinventing yourself – well, that was kind of cool. And art's the only subject I ever loved at school too. The only one that ever made sense to me, really – no reading required, see? Dyslexia doesn't matter with a paintbrush in your hand. So who knows, Bo – maybe at your new school, you'll be the star of that art department and everything else will just fall into place?'

Bo looked hopeful, glancing up at his mum as if to say, 'See, I told you . . .'

'Let's find somewhere to live first, maybe, and then we can give serious thought to Bo 2.0?' Jamie said gently. 'Although, for my money, no reinvention is required. Let's focus on getting you into the right school where you can just be yourself, exactly as you are, eh Bo?'

'Sorry,' said Amy, all flummoxed. 'I didn't mean to imply—'

'You're fine,' Jamie interrupted her reassuringly. 'We have this conversation about three times a week.'

'Well, so would you if you had to go somewhere you hated, and where nobody appreciated the things you were good at, always judging you by all the things you don't care about and that you just can't do!' Bo's outburst was filled with pent-up crossness and frustration, which unfortunately had the side-effect of making him look utterly adorable, his fringe flopping into his eyes and his slight shoulders worked up around his ears.

'Oh Bo, you dear sweet child,' Kath said, trying not to laugh. 'You've just described the everyday experience of almost everyone here.'

He blinked, looking confused. 'But you're all grown-ups – you all get to choose.'

Bonnie shook her head, her tight curls bouncing with feeling. 'Don't believe the hype, little man. Choice is a luxury.'

'Mum?' he looked up at her, his face crunched in consternation. 'You said it got better when you were a grown-up and could choose – you *said*.'

Jamie crouched down, not so much so they were eye-to-eye, as her boy now towered over her as she knelt, but she didn't want to talk down to him in any way, literal or metaphorical. 'I *chose* to have you, Bo, and it was the best decision I've ever made. I *chose* to go to university and be a part of *The Big Trip*. But yes, just recently, a lot of the things I've chosen have been because of need and circumstance, rather than a sudden and overwhelming desire to know everything there is to know about balsamic vinegar.' She gave him a squeeze. 'And, look Bo, you know we're not exactly choosing to move house right now, but it might yet end up being the absolute best thing for us.'

He nodded, seemingly reassured, but Jamie knew from

past experience that he would cogitate over this and analyse her every word, until a few days from now, an entirely salient question would surface and put her on the spot.

'Okay,' he said. 'Can I have another churro, Bonnie, please?'

'Of course,' Bonnie said, 'but only if you grab me one.'

Jamie glanced at her watch. It was coming up to seven and while no doubt this little gathering was only just getting started, it was still a school night. 'Ten more minutes, Bo, and then we need to make a move.'

He didn't react, ignoring her as he wove through the packed group to get to the churro platter, but she knew he'd heard because his ears went pink, as they did every time he was pissed off with her.

Bonnie gave a shudder. 'God, who'd be a kid again?'

'You see,' Amy countered, 'why would I knowingly walk back into all that again? All that angst and coursework?'

'There's evening classes,' Kath suggested. 'But d'you know, I think Jamie has a point here – don't go leaping into getting qualifications just for the sake of it. Have a proper think about what you actually might want, even do some work experience, because you might find that an apprenticeship or something vocational is actually more helpful.'

Jamie nodded. 'It makes me feel physically sick when I think how much money I spent getting my degree. And has it made one tick of difference? Would all that money make the world of difference, though, if it were in my bank account right now? Hell, yes.'

'The moving house thing?' Bonnie asked. 'I presume that's

what Rea in the pharmacy was going on about the other day. Creepy landlord guy?'

'Sort of,' Jamie nodded. 'But we're not leaving because he's creepy, although God knows we should have. He's put the rent up. A lot. Like a lot, a lot. Absolutely no chance I can meet that, and he's keeping my security deposit too, arsehole that he is. Probably knows I haven't the energy to fight him in small claims. But it does leave me a bit stuck. Bo's super excited about the idea of a fresh start, but that's just the theory. Obviously he doesn't realise just how hard it is to find another deposit, the first few months' rent etc. I honestly have no idea how to even make this work.'

'My sofa is your sofa, if push comes to shove,' Bonnie said reassuringly.

'I can store your stuff in my room for a bit,' Amy said. 'I'm in a house share with my cousins, so I can't really offer you the sofa but, if you need time to save a bit of money . . .'

'I could always chuck my kids onto the sofa bed for a bit, if you and Bo want their room for a month, like Amy said, just to scrape together the necessary,' Kath offered. 'And they're staying with my sister for a few weeks at half-term, and Craig'll be off on the rigs then too, so . . .'

Jamie was truly touched. Blown away actually.

These women – these women whom she hardly really knew – already more generous, more kind and understanding than her oldest friends, the contacts stored in her phone under Favourites and yet so rarely called, as their experiences of life had diverged.

And as always, Jamie marvelled at these people with extended families – imagine having cousins, or an aunt to casually invite the kids to stay! What would that even *be* like? To have a wider safety net in case you fell, and a bigger table to celebrate life's milestone moments?

She couldn't begin to comprehend.

'Thank you,' she said simply, in the end. They all knew that she was hoping against hope it wouldn't come to that. And yet, for once, Jamie didn't bat away any offer of support.

She no longer had that luxury.

But tonight had also reminded her that, in this roller-coaster existence, the ups were just as significant as the downs, if not more so. To be savoured and appreciated, tucked away for a rainy day.

'Right,' said Kath, 'now we've covered evictions and existential crises, can I skip straight past my imploding marriage and ask: has anyone got any advice for my review on Friday with Tanya the tyrant – aka my supervisor? Do I go polite, personable and deferential? Or confrontational and demanding? As a point of note, neither have been successful in the past.'

'Is there anyone in the department she actually *does* like? Actually respect? Because if it were me, I would just do whatever they're doing,' Bonnie suggested.

'Mimic them?' Kath asked, frowning.

Jamie nodded. 'If there's someone she genuinely likes or respects it could actually work. Or, you know, you could mirror her own speech and body language – from the snippets I've heard, it kind of sounds like she thinks she's the only person in the department actually pulling their weight. That's what they teach to sales people with NLP.'

'There, you see,' Bonnie shook her head, 'that degree of yours is *kind of* useful.'

'Why did you choose psychology anyway? Are you sure you didn't learn to read people's minds and stuff?' Amy asked, clearly intrigued.

Jamie laughed. 'Sadly, no. But I think on some level I thought that if I understood how people think, then it would help me no matter I wanted to do.' Even that fleeting memory of her old self – energised, proactive and logical – lit a tiny spark of optimism that maybe one day she would feel that way again. 'You know,' she added, 'even if it's sales or advertising, there's still an element of persuasive psychology in there somewhere.'

'Makes sense,' Bonnie agreed. 'I wish *I* understood how people think – they damn well confuse me most of the time.'

Amy nodded. 'God, me too! Maybe Jamie should write all this down – like *The Guidebook to Getting What You Want*.'

Jamie baulked instinctively. 'You mean *How To Manipulate People and Bend Them To Your Will*? I don't think so . . .'

'Although *I* would definitely read that,' Bonnie said with feeling, as Kath and Amy nodded too. 'Shelve those pesky scruples of yours, woman. This could be life-changing.'

'Nope, it's not for me,' Jamie said firmly. 'I have this whole free-will thing going on.'

Bonnie raised one perfectly shaped eyebrow, 'And how's that working out for you?'

Chapter 14

'Mum? Mum ...' Bo's voice was shredded wafer-thin, dragged through his angry, inflamed airways.

Even fast asleep, Jamie's subconscious was tightly attuned to her son and she stumbled across the flat in the half-darkness.

Sitting on his bed, arms curled around his knees, inhaler and spacer clasped in one hand, tears rolled silently down Bo's face as he struggled to breathe.

'How many puffs, Bobo?' Jamie asked, her adrenalin kicking in like a double espresso and the last vestiges of sleep gone in an instant.

'Two,' he rasped. 'And two earlier.'

There was no point chastising him for not calling her earlier – that could wait for the post-match analysis later. For now, he just needed help. His lips were turning that terrifying shade of blue and with panic flaring in his eyes, there was no doubt that he was struggling to stay upright, to stay awake.

Jamie flicked on her phone, checking the times for an Uber to the hospital versus the 999 call. Being a frequent flyer made the decision harder, not easier, but one look at Bo's face told her that this wasn't one of those nights where a cuddle in the steamy bathroom would do the trick.

It was all a question of far too much experience.

She sat down beside Bo and wrapped her arms around him; keeping him calm and reassured the very first and most effective step. 'Definitely time for a road trip,' she whispered as she pressed those all-too-familiar three buttons on her phone. 'Ambulance please,' she said quietly.

There was no need to pack a bag – it was there ready and waiting.

And in all likelihood, they would be home again before dawn.

This was not their first rodeo.

Bo leaned into her side, breath rasping and his forehead now cold and clammy. 'Thanks, Mum,' he managed.

Did it ever get any easier, Jamie wondered hours later, sitting on the hard plastic chair beside Bo's bed in A&E, the nebuliser doing its work and the colour slowly returning to his face.

The paramedics had been amazing, sweeping in, taking the weight of responsibility from her own shoulders for the short but speedy dash to the local hospital, but the blue sirens only ever served to emphasize the urgency to Jamie, rather than reassure.

It was one thing being the patient; it was a whole different ballgame being the parent. She glanced around the bays in

A&E, the kids cordoned off from the main melee by a series of brightly coloured curtains. The bright lights, the noise, the very intensity of the place was exhausting, and she wondered how on earth Kath coped with it night after night, only to then go home and know that all her hard work still wasn't enough to make ends meet. How on God's green earth was that right?

Hollowed out with exhaustion, with worry and fear, Jamie sat still, even as waves of vertigo occasionally overwhelmed her. She held Bo's small soft hand in her own as he dozed, the nebuliser puffing away, allowing the medication to get to the heart of the problem. They were in the right place at least, and Jamie willed herself to relax just a little, even as her heart rate refused to listen to reason.

How often did they need to make this nocturnal trip, only to be sent home again with nothing more than the advice to keep on top of his triggers and medication? The medication she could do. The triggers were a different question altogether – because to manage those, she would need to know, categorically, what they actually were.

She watched Bo's eyelids flicker, wondering what was going on behind those beautiful lashes. Was he frightened? Or perhaps relieved that a day off school was on the cards, assuming they yet again refused to admit him.

She breathed out slowly, the logistics of the next few days beyond her.

No school meant no work.

No shifts at Harrison's meant no money, and also a further fraying of the final straw with her unfeeling boss.

It was always, always, about priorities.

And Jamie was under no illusion that her decision to constantly put Bo first meant that other parts of her life had been neglected.

But how could she possibly choose otherwise?

She bit her lip, wondering whether – just for once – Nick Harrison might allow Bo to snuggle in the staff room with a book for the day. Hardly ideal care after a night in A&E, but nothing about this situation was ideal.

'How are we doing in here?' Dana, the nurse assigned to Bo's care, noted down the readings from his Pulsox, thankfully edging back into the nineties now, the nebuliser and the steroids doing their work. 'Can I tempt you with a warm drink, Bo? Mum?' Bo shook his head, but Jamie hesitated. Dana wasn't here to be her waitress.

'I'll pop along to the drinks machine in a mo – once he's okay to be left,' she said. 'But thank you . . .'

Dana shook her head. 'Stay there and I'll fetch you something from our break room. Right now, I'm not entirely sure who to be more worried about, if you don't mind me saying.' She dropped her voice. 'When did you last eat anything?'

Jamie blinked, suddenly tearful in the face of this unexpected kindness and consideration. Could it have been breakfast? She'd been too distracted by the conversation to grab one of the churros at the party, and it was a no-brainer to prioritise Bo's supper over her own. Even if these days he was highly sceptical of her insistence that she wasn't hungry.

Dana nodded, understanding dawning. 'Stay there, Mum.'

She was back moments later with a mug of hot sweet tea and a plate of digestives. 'You missed out on the chocolate ones – like locusts in there – but you're welcome to these.' She smiled at Bo. 'Have to look after the carers, don't we?' She made a few more notes on his chart and moved on to the next cubicle, disappearing behind the curtain with an exclamation of familiarity, 'And what have you been up to this time, young lady?' Jamie heard her say with a welcoming smile in her voice.

One o'clock in the morning and Dana was here, taking care of business, taking care of her patients with more empathy and affection than might reasonably be expected. And Jamie couldn't have been more grateful.

Chapter 15

Jamie awoke with a start and a moment's panic as she looked around, her neck cricking with a rush of hot burning pain as she tried to sit up in the plastic chair where she had slumped. Hello hospital neck, my old friend.

Bo was sitting up on his trolley, tucking into a piece of toast, for all the world as though he'd had a full eight hours' sleep. His gingham pyjamas were now buttoned closed and all the monitors and sensors squared away.

'Morning, sleepyhead,' said a familiar voice.

Jamie blinked, her mind still focused on the transformation in her son and swept into a blur by a tsunami of relief.

'Have you been here all night, Kath?' Jamie managed.

'I came on late, but I've been over there most of the night,' Kath nodded towards the resuc room on the far side of A&E. 'Big crash on the motorway in the wee small hours. But everyone's okay so I'm calling it a good shift. You, on the other hand, look wrecked.'

'I can't believe I fell asleep,' Jamie said, rubbing at her neck.

'And you snored,' Bo said matter-of-factly. 'Really badly.'

He reached over and squeezed her hand, as always, sweetly affectionate after one of 'their nights'.

'Anyway,' Kath said, 'I'm clocking off in a bit if you want a lift home? Looks like this one's on the mend.'

'Until next time,' Jamie muttered under her breath, the rollercoaster all too familiar, all too exhausting and all too predictable.

Kath nodded. 'They've added to Bo's notes overnight though, so maybe that will speed up the referral. Fingers crossed.'

Jamie nodded. Her son's health, his ability to breathe, didn't seem to be something she should be crossing her fingers about. 'Is there anything at all I can do on that front? It's been months.'

Kath shook her head. 'Short of going private, or maybe being admitted . . .'

'Am I going to school today, Mum?' Bo asked.

Kath shook her head. 'Not today, Bo. Rest and cuddles and maybe some fresh air later if you feel up to it.'

Jamie nodded, the relief swirling in her stomach with the acidic roar of the logistics required to make that happen.

She stood up and kissed Bo on his forehead, his fringe falling back into place and framing his gorgeous little face. 'Sit tight, Batman, I just need to make a few calls.'

She walked outside into the early morning sunshine and took a breath before she dialled. 'Nick? Hi, it's Jamie Matson calling. I need to talk to you about my shift today.'

She knew he'd heard. She knew he understood that a

night in A&E was hardly a night at the movies and yet he was unmoved.

'Look, Ms Matson, I understand that you've had an eventful night, but this is hardly unprecedented, is it? And it's not my responsibility to sort out your childcare issues. In fact, a *responsible* parent might have provided for this very eventuality.' He paused, took a self-righteous breath. 'Given the frequency.'

Jamie was stunned into silence. Checking in with herself that she'd spoken the words aloud. Had shared with her boss the exact nature of the situation.

'I don't want to let you down, so I was hoping Bo could rest quietly in the staff room today, so I could still work—'

His exhalation drowned out her words. 'We are not a creche, we are a place of business. And I am not a charity. So, let me put this in simple terms that even you can understand, Ms Matson. You have a choice – find a way to come to work today, on time, without your ailing offspring, or don't come back at all.'

The click echoed down the line as he hung up, and Jamie felt herself flush red hot with impotent rage.

'Twat,' she said to the phone in her hand, tears threatening. Empathy apparently not an option, in addition to her minimum wage. A few other choice epithets sprang to mind, but Jamie knew all too well the futility of her frustration.

Her neck screamed with every movement, and she would wager that a shower and a toothbrush might be right up there with a lottery win.

Jamie felt the energy desert her. How had she allowed her

world to shrink so small that there was simply nobody left to reach out to – not without feeling beholden or hypocritical? She guessed she'd made her own bed, with every invitation declined through lack of funds, every chatty call going through to voicemail while she worked . . .

It was a simple fact of life, but it felt just wretched to acknowledge.

Wretched and utterly exhausting.

She walked back in to find Kath perched on the end of Bo's bed, a fleece now covering her uniform and marking her out as off-duty. They were talking about waffles and Jamie's stomach growled at the very thought.

'He's all signed off and good to go,' Kath said. 'And I had a quiet word with the registrar about fast-tracking the referral, so keep your fingers and toes crossed, Bo.' She yawned. 'Let me give you a lift home?'

Jamie hesitated, still not sure what to do. 'I think I'm going to have to take Bo to work with me and sneak him in. My boss is being – well, true to form, I suppose. I'm already on thin ice.'

'But Mum . . .' began Bo, his new-found energy visibly deflating at the very thought.

Kath, however, simply nodded; nothing seemed to faze her. 'Well then, Master Bo, if you can cope with being king of the remote control while I have a nap, and then helping me sort out some clothes for my girls and Amy later, it looks like you're with me today. We'll need waffles for breakfast, though, obviously.'

'Obviously,' said Bo, a huge smile spreading across his face. Anything other than being smuggled into his mum's workplace yet again.

'I can't ask you to do that,' Jamie said, her words choked.

'You didn't,' Kath replied with a gentle smile. 'I offered.'

Chapter 16

Feeling stale and exhausted, yet buoyed by Kath's incredibly generous gesture, Jamie stepped down from the Number 62 bus that stopped right outside Harrison's with ten minutes to spare.

Slipping in through the stock entrance, she ducked into the staff room in search of deodorant and, if she was incredibly lucky, a clean jumper to pull over her jaded T-shirt. For one moment, she didn't care about the ozone layer, or the sodding CFCs – she just wanted the burst of an aerosol, the illusion of fresh presentability. And not the raddled appearance of a mother who'd spent the night living on her nerves in A&E.

Reaching under her T-shirt, she rolled the ice-cold deodorant under her arms and considered the turn of events, for really, could Bo actually be in safer hands than with Kath right now? Short of being where Jamie firmly believed he should be: in a bed on the paediatric ward awaiting a sensible conversation with the immunologist.

'Nice of you to show up.' Nick Harrison stepped into the room, the concept of personal space entirely alien to him. He tapped his watch as though she were tardy.

Jamie instinctively glanced up to the clock on the wall. Still five minutes in hand.

His gaze narrowed. 'It's not your punctuality that's in doubt, Ms Matson – it's your commitment.' He turned and left, presumably because at least on some level he knew he didn't have a leg to stand on.

Her dignity, her privacy, her priorities – all bought for the price of the minimum wage.

She breathed out slowly, determined to take these scant minutes now to centre herself. And, of course, to remind herself that not all jobs were like this. Even the badly paid ones. With the fond nostalgia of rose-coloured glasses, she thought of her first job after *The Big Trip* had folded. Easy company, convivial conversation and the feeling of her work being appreciated. Running the hotel laundry through the rolling cylinders, taking pride in the crisp, neat finish and the comforting aroma of freshly laundered sheets.

Pride in her work and in her ability to provide for her son, no matter how badly the world economy was tilting on its axis.

Knowing – or possibly just hoping – that one day her hard work and perseverance would get them back on track. Buying into the myth.

And until then, she would focus on the part of this job that she did enjoy – helping the customers, guiding their choices and, often as not, making small talk, very likely being the only person they might speak to that day. And that, in itself, was no small thing, she realised. The one good thing perhaps about this whole sorry situation. Jamie walked out onto the shop floor, methodically arranging the wicker baskets by the entrance and tweaking the displays. No matter how many times she mentioned to Nick Harrison that people sometimes needed a trolley even for a small amount, he refused to listen.

It was all about about the aesthetic.

Across the road, she could see Bonnie, vibrant against the drizzle in some extremely mustard-coloured dungarees, cleaning the large panes of glass of her tiny kiosk's shopfront. Her folded wooden sign stood outside on the pavement and a large pair of plastic scissors was suspended above the door – surely a crime against health and safety, if not the local by-laws – but she had certainly achieved her goal. *Crap But Cheap* looked fun and accessible. Inviting even, Jamie thought, as she tucked her own shapeless ponytail over her shoulder.

Working deftly through her morning routine on autopilot, Jamie ran through her options for the day, from what Bo would eat later, to whether there was time to follow up with the grumpy rental agent over by Miles Park.

She may not be a desirable tenant in terms of financial range, but she was stable, reliable and quiet. Surely that had to count for something?

'Morning, J,' Daniel said, having climbed down from the extendable ladder at the back of the store, now negotiating its exit without destroying any of their fragile displays. 'That's those two light bulbs sorted.' He rolled his eyes. 'They'll be gone again in a week though, unless El Capitan actually spends the money on the right bulbs. For an affluent man, he's a proper cheapskate.'

'Isn't that where the affluence comes from?' Jamie said quietly. 'You know some of the biggest debtors here are the people with money coming out of their ears. Cheque's always in the post, you know?'

Daniel nodded. 'I suppose it's easier to get ahead when you're climbing on the backs of everyone around you.'

The ladder squared away without incident, they worked side by side for a moment, waiting for their first customer of the day. 'Daniel, can I ask?' Jamie said, glancing around to make sure their lurking boss was safely in his office. 'Your interview the other day? Do you get *any* sense of what people are looking for?' She hesitated. 'My friend missed out again this week too.'

Daniel nodded. 'I'd like to tell myself that it's a level playing field, but I just don't think it's true. I think if there's a personal connection, that will *always* carry more weight than an extra few years' experience, or maybe a different qualification. It's like rolling a dice half the time, and the only thing that keeps me going is the cold hard fact that you have to be in it to win it. I'm not going to have my dream job just land in my lap while I'm stacking farfalle and fois gras, am I?' He paused. 'In fact, I'm thinking I need to consider retraining. There's a dozen chefs for every position out there. I'm too old to be a sous chef, and too skilled to work short order. Falling between two stools, that's me.'

'You're not alone in that,' Jamie said sympathetically. 'I

spent half the night re-reading all the blurb about how to become a social worker. I've got half the qualifications I'd need already, but the other half is beyond me right now.'

Daniel sighed, looking up as three smart women in quilted gilets walked in, deep in conversation. 'I think it's time we both concede that there's no such thing as a job for life anymore. Or even a career.'

There were posters everywhere in the library. Retraining. Reshaping. And that poor, much maligned ballerina lacing up her pointes and surely never once dreaming of a career in cyber.

But as much as Daniel may have had a point, Jamie couldn't help but wonder how many jobseekers might retrain, only to find there were no positions available in their new field either, unless you happened to know the right people.

'Excuse me?' One of the women pulled away from her companions, impatiently waving her list, as though she'd been ignored.

'Good morning,' said Jamie, stepping forward and into happy-helper mode. 'How can I help you?'

'I need to find all this for a dinner party and I don't even know where to begin.' She shot one of her friends a look. 'But I gather you carry all the delicacies and whatnot.' She handed Jamie the list, the perfect stylised handwriting worthy of a wedding invitation rather than such a mundane endeavour, then immediately turned back to her friends – was Jamie expected to do her shopping for her now?

And yet, Jamie knew that's exactly what she would do.

Would always do, if asked. Because why do a job badly, however mundane, when you could go the extra mile? Perhaps it was coded in her DNA somehow, that if a job was worth doing, it was worth doing well? Although she couldn't deny that life might be so much easier at times without that particular drive and disposition. Or perhaps simply less exhausting.

'Shall I just—?' Jamie began, only for the woman to flap her away, as though she were interrupting.

Okay then. In all honesty probably quicker than leading the woman around the store, aisle by aisle, to find her quails eggs, truffle oil, black quinoa and squid ink – although surely one negated the need for the other. Daniel would know, but she was damned if she was going to throw him under the bus.

Gently placing all the items into the wicker basket, Jamie ran a running total in her head. When she hit three hundred pounds, she began to wish that she worked on commission.

She put the basket at her feet as she tried to calculate portion sizes – all she could think was that the long tubes of bucatini her customer had requested would be a bastard to cook for sixteen. But then, maybe she had someone to do that for her too?

The carefully curated pasta corner was a refuge from the comings and goings in the store, but even so, Jamie's neck prickled uncomfortably as she heard the familiar refrain.

'Sweetie, Merritt, be nice for Mummy. Just a sec, Merritt. I'm on the phone, my love.'

A flicker of guilt for leaving Daniel to deal with the short straw, and then Jamie returned to the list, stacking four boxes of the pricey bucatini into the top of the basket.

'That looks like quite the party.'

Jamie looked up to see a rather dapper and slender gentleman eyeing the contents of her basket. There was a hint of Bill Nighy in his stylish cravat and the wave of his hand, eyes twinkling with mischief. 'Although judging by the prices in here, you'll need a second mortgage for that little lot.'

He reached forward and plucked a single packet of orzo from the shelf beside her. 'My dear wife has decided that only this particular orzo will do. I may be black-balled for life for even suggesting we just break up some spaghetti.'

Jamie laughed. 'Well I wouldn't say that too loudly in here either. And sadly, no party for me,' she held up the endless list, 'I just work here.'

'I'd forever be ravenous,' the gentleman decreed, waving his hand at the display, the liver spots on his skin giving away his advancing years, despite the neat tailoring that held him straight. 'But is it a nice place to work? Surrounded by such bounty?'

'Erm,' Jamie flustered. Nobody had ever actually asked her that before. Not least a customer.

There was a resounding crash from a few aisles over and then Daniel's firm but soothing voice handling the situation. Merritt. Again.

'It's all right, you can take the Fifth.' His smile crinkled the corners of his eyes and he weighed the small, dense packet of orzo in his hand. 'I'm only on a mission to tempt my wife's appetite to be honest. All of this stuff is far too rich for her these days. But her outing here the other day, finding this – finally, something she wants to eat. Well, it's been a boost for morale.'

Jamie nodded, touched by his obvious dedication. 'She's just wonderful, your wife. Ruth, isn't it?'

He focused on Jamie more intently then, as though a switch had been flicked, 'Which would make you Jamie? And I'm Henry, so that's all the introductions out of the way.' He smiled. 'You made her day, you know, helping her so sweetly when she came in here. I only wish every day was as positive. She won't complain, but I know she's struggling, off her food, and a little company and conversation was just what she needed this week—' He broke off, as though he realised he was oversharing.

From where Jamie was standing, his wife wasn't the only one desperate for company and conversation.

'I can have a think about some really palatable options for her, if she wants to pop in again. It must be rubbish being off your food. I will confess to not being the greatest cook myself, but Daniel over there is a serious chef. Maybe we can help, if you'd like,' Jamie offered.

He smiled gently. 'I think we both know that's going above and beyond. But I won't pretend I wouldn't appreciate the input.' He sighed. 'I've always felt that the best antidote to ageing is the company of young people, but I hadn't really factored in that the majority of young people would look at me, and my Ruth, and find themselves instantly bored rigid.'

'Hardly,' Jamie said, shaking her head. 'It's the opposite for me.' She leaned in and dropped her voice. 'If I have to listen to one more "influencer" talking about their social media brand while they shop for truffles, I may truly slip into a coma. Get Ruth to pop in and I can bore her senseless instead with my in-depth knowledge of Italian delicacies.'

'You're a good girl, Jamie. I can see why Ruthie liked you.' He straightened up and turned to leave, his walnut cane tapping against the polished floor.

In a sudden whirl, Merritt came barrelling around the corner of the aisle, knocking three bottles of expensive wine flying and charging into Henry with a thump. The cane skittered out of reach, and Henry folded over, gasping for breath. Broken glass was scattered around them, and clearly somebody was bleeding, but in the sudden chaos it was hard to see who.

Jamie reached out and caught hold of Merritt's elbow, halting him in his tracks, as he rained tagliatelle down from the shelves upon Henry, still bent double, edging towards the glass jars of Pesto Alle Genovese. 'Enough!' she said firmly.

Merritt froze, blinking slowly, stunned and then made one last lunge, a glass jar toppling, almost in slow motion and smashing on the floor beside Henry.

Jamie tightened her grip. 'Enough now, Merritt.'

And then he began to scream.

Chapter 17

It was hard to imagine how such a small boy could produce such a blood-curdling sound, but young Merritt was giving his all.

As his mother belatedly caught up with her son, he ramped up the volume even more. 'She did this! Mummy! And she *hit* me!'

There was a stunned silence for a moment, hanging over all of them, Merritt taking the opportunity to free himself from Jamie's clasp on his elbow, cradling his arm as though she'd snapped it in two.

'Oh, it hurts. Mummy. It really hurts.'

Jamie was mute with shock. She blinked and took in the scene of devastation around them, the blood on Henry's temple, running freely down his face now, his walnut cane on the floor, snapped in two by Merritt's careless trainers trampling over it. The heavy sickly scent of basil from the pesto oozing across the floor.

Henry pulled in a deep breath and righted himself before Jamie could say anything. 'Madam, we haven't met, but I'm afraid your son is lying to you,' he said.

He was trying to help, Jamie knew that, but his words were like a red rag to a bull. Merritt's mother rounded on him. 'How *dare* you?'

Daniel and Nick Hamilton arrived on the scene just in time for Merritt to double down on his accusations. He cradled his elbow and squeezed out a few tears. 'She hit me,' he wailed. 'Mummy!'

'Simply not true,' Henry said again, asserting himself, even as he shook, and the blood began to congeal in his abundantly bushy eyebrows.

Nick Harrison frowned, slowly taking in the ruined stock, the bleeding elderly gentleman and the distress of one of his best customers. He turned to Jamie and barely missed a beat, 'You're fired. And you can forget about this week's pay cheque, *Ms* Matson. Just be grateful I'm not charging you the balance for all this damage.'

He paused, clearly weighing up the importance of the gentleman in the vintage cravat and deeming him secondary.

Passing trade.

He turned to Merritt and his mother, placing his arm around the woman's shoulders as he guided them away from the carnage. He glanced back at Daniel, 'Make sure this mess is dealt with.'

There was a stunned reverberation in the air once they'd gone.

A dazed disbelief, and not only at the behaviour of a spoiled six-year-old boy.

'Arsehole,' said Daniel with feeling. 'I'd quit in solidarity,

J – you know I would – but I really need this job . . .' He looked pained, as his principles collided once more with his reality.

'This isn't right,' Henry began again, furiously, before listing suddenly to one side, without the support of his cane.

'Can I get you out of here?' Jamie said, catching him before he fell. 'Away from all of this?'

Henry nodded, the colour drained from his face. 'If it wouldn't be too much trouble?'

Daniel helped them both around the worst of the debris. 'Head over to the Bean, J. I'll bring your things over in my break, okay? It's just the stuff in your locker, right?'

Jamie nodded, sickened. How could the day get any worse?

Not only the loss of her job, but her entire week's pay – the money she'd already *earned* – snatched away to add insult to injury.

It was only once she and Henry were settled in a booth at The Coffee Bean and she'd ordered hot sweet tea for them both that she realised there were tears streaming down her face.

'I'm so sorry,' she hiccupped to Henry. 'I think it's all caught up with me.'

She wiped her eyes with a paper napkin, the warp and weft raw on her tender skin.

'I'm not surprised,' Henry said gently, reaching into the breast pocket of his jacket and pulling out a perfectly pressed handkerchief, 'but please take this.'

His chivalry and kindness stood in marked contrast to

the treatment she'd just received in her place of work and Jamie couldn't help but wonder how things had changed. Or indeed whether they actually had.

For every man like Henry, there would be another with arrogance or misogyny blurring his boundaries of decency.

For every man like Daniel, there would be a grasping, ambitious bloke, who believed that 'banter' was an excuse for demeaning abuse.

Something had to change, Jamie thought tiredly.

Something had to give, in this twenty-first century, in this civilised country, where nurses queued at food banks, and social-media followers equalled supremacy.

If only she had the energy to rise up, to rally a mutiny of the overworked and underpaid.

Jamie felt her teeth chattering, although The Coffee Bean was overheated as always.

'It's the shock,' Henry said, adding another spoonful of sugar to her untouched mug of tea and nudging it towards her.

Jamie nodded. 'It's been a difficult week – and I think this might qualify as the final straw.'

'I think it would certainly qualify,' he said, reaching into his pocket and pulling out a smart iPhone, tapping away at the screen with surprising efficiency. 'I'm just letting Ruth know where I am. She worries.'

'And she'll be disappointed about her soup too,' Jamie said, as always finding it easier to focus on irrelevant minutiae.

'I'd eat dog biscuits before I'd shop in there again,' Henry said with feeling. 'I'm utterly disgusted by what I've just witnessed. There must be someone we can report this to? Are you in a union? This kind of injustice really sticks in my craw.'

Jamie stilled, knowing that there really was no higher power to which she could turn. Just another example of her own impotence, her own vulnerability.

And, although part of her increasingly inferior status was undoubtedly because she was a woman, Jamie had to be frank with herself and admit that it had never been this bad when she was a woman of means, of education and standing in her community.

Losing her job, losing her agency in every sense of the word, had thrown her into a whole new perspective – not just life as a female, with her keys clutched between her fingers walking home at night, but life as a female scraping by financially, dependent on others for her very subsistence.

It was a whole new level of invisible.

Kieran Jones.

Nick Harrison.

The kind of men who could see that all too clearly and took absolute advantage.

And, as always, Jamie felt disgusted with herself for not speaking up, speaking out and fighting back.

For fear of losing her job.

For fear of losing her home.

Or perhaps simply fear of knowing that she had no back-up and a child to consider.

In the twenty-first century.

She shook her head. 'I'm not going to report it, Henry.' She paused. 'But that doesn't mean I won't leverage the threat to get the money I'm owed.'

'Well, that's something at least.' He watched her shrewdly for a moment. 'I think I may be about to overstep, but I would like you to consider something for me, Jamie.' He sat back, his hands folded across his tailored waistcoat. 'You are, as of now, without a job. And Ruth – as I may have mentioned – is in need of a little care and company.

'Jamie,' he continued, considering his words carefully, 'I have no idea of your qualifications, or indeed your situation – but I believe I've been granted some insight into your moral code and your decency and I'd like to offer you a job. With us. Helping out – a flexible role, if you will.'

His fingers fluttered over his split eyebrow for a moment, clean now, but angry and obviously painful. He looked uncomfortable. 'There is, of course, no obligation on your part to even consider it, Jamie. But the offer is there ...'

Jamie hesitated; always a huge believer in serendipity, she found herself wary now, of leaping from the frying pan into the fire. After all, she knew nothing about this man. Other than the fact that his wife seemed just lovely, and his manners were impeccable.

And perhaps that was enough?

More than she might know about an anonymous advert at the job centre, certainly.

'That's incredibly kind,' she said, 'but in all honesty, I have no idea of my plans. This week has been ... Well, this week has thrown everything into disarray.' And then the tears began to flow in earnest; whether it was the fact that Henry was actually listening to her, or that she felt safe enough to share, here, cocooned from reality, with the condensation fugging up the windows of The Coffee Bean and Matilda humming soulfully in the galley kitchen behind them . . .

But once she started talking, it seemed as though Jamie's filters slipped away and the whole sorry mess fell between them on the Formica tabletop – the long, long night in A&E and the endless waiting for a referral and the desperation that morning in choosing between Bo's needs and Nick Harrison's ultimatum.

Well, she'd clearly made the wrong call there, hadn't she? Prioritising her job, a job that had proven without doubt just how expendable she was.

And of course, the imminent eviction hanging over her head and the implied alternatives that Kieran Jones would consider to the hefty rent review . . .

Henry took a sharp intake of breath at that one, she noticed.

But she also knew she was far from alone. The only difference being, since the lockdowns, women like her were actually talking about it.

It was the women who were silently shamed into accepting that bargain with the devil that she worried about, though. The ones who genuinely believed that they didn't have a choice. Caught in the spiral of impotence that threatened Jamie's existence right now.

Henry Waverly had that rare ability to actively listen, not just mark time until it was his turn to speak. He nodded occasionally, taking in every word.

When Jamie fell silent, purged and exhausted, he didn't leap in with solutions or advice – or worse, a critique of her life choices – he simply sipped his tea for a few minutes, deep in thought.

'My wife is an excellent judge of character, Jamie.' He spoke quietly but with resolve. 'It's unerring and sometimes, if I'm honest, a touch annoying at times.' Another sip. 'But these days, she's about as subtle as a brick and she was very upset not to offer you the cottage, you know. Even talked about ripping up the tenancy agreement we'd just signed, all on the strength of your voicemail.'

He waved to Matilda for the bill and gathered himself together, slipping a well-worn leather wallet from his jacket pocket.

'Let me be clear on this, in case any confusion over my motivation might cloud your judgement – you would be doing me, doing Ruth, the most enormous favour by even considering what I'm about to suggest. I'd like to offer you a job.' He held up his hand to fend off any possible interruption until he'd said his piece. 'And I know perfectly well you are capable of so much more, but even as a temporary measure until you're back on your feet, I would like to think there was some mutual benefit here.

'You see, Jamie, my lovely wife refuses to admit she's in need of any help. Certainly more help than I can give her.

But I cannot impose someone in a floral tabard on her; she deserves so much more. Someone like you, Jamie. Because if Ruth thinks we're helping you . . .'

'A mercy mission,' Jamie said with a quiet smile of sudden understanding.

'Exactly,' Henry said.

He placed a crisp five-pound note on the table and then held out his card. Embossed. Tasteful.

'Come for tea this afternoon and we can all talk about it together. Bring Bo and see if he likes the cut of our jib.'

'Bo?' Jamie said, wondering whether letting a ten-year-old make her job decisions was a sensible precedent to set.

'Well, he can have a look at the flat in the annexe, take a few breaths and all that.' Henry shrugged. 'If Bo's not happy, then there's no way on God's earth that you will be, Jamie.'

'I—'

Henry smiled, clearly very pleased with himself, playing his ace. 'Did I not mention that the job came with accommodation: a private annexe, if you'd like? Only small, but dry and clean.' He paused. 'And safe.'

'I don't believe you did mention that, Henry,' Jamie said, with a wobbly smile, fighting a wave of emotion and struggling to identify the feeling. It took her a moment, with Ruth's twinkling smile suddenly clear in her mind's eye, to realise it was hope.

Chapter 18

Jamie sat on Kath's sofa, at ease for the first time in hours, with Bo dozing on her lap and mindless television burbling in the background.

The baskets of clean laundry, waiting to be folded, stacked in the corner, somehow made it easier to relax. Ditto the slithering heap of crumpled magazines on the floor by her feet and the wilted tulips, gasping their last breath in a vase on the mantelpiece – their vivid redness a shot of colour in an otherwise vanilla sitting room.

There were no touches of individuality, or so much as a hint of interior design – this room was the heart of a busy family home, where functionality would always win out over fashion. And IKEA would always be an easy and affordable go-to, even at the risk of looking like a spread from page 42 of the catalogue, rather than *Country Homes and Interiors*.

Kath came back from the kitchen, balancing a plate of flapjacks on top of the mugs of tea she had decreed were necessary for any conversation like this.

'You must be exhausted,' she said, nudging a clear space among the schoolbooks and clutter on the large coffee table, around which her three-piece-suite was centred. 'I've had four or five hours sleep, haven't I, Bo? And I still feel like death on a stick.'

'I had a nap too,' Bo nodded. 'I didn't mean to, but honestly, Mum, there's only so much fun in watching these people looking around fancy houses and moaning about which direction the garden is facing.' He shook his head in mild disbelief but nevertheless carried on watching.

Jamie bit into one of the deliciously chewy flapjacks and realised just how ravenous she was. 'Oh my God, these are amazing.'

Kath nodded. 'They're addictive though, I'll warn you. Izzy makes them by the trayful and calls them breakfast bars. It's one of those battles that'll have to wait for another day.'

'I've had three,' Bo confessed quietly. 'Does that mean there won't be any breakfast for tomorrow?'

'There's plenty left, Bo. And I told you to help yourself, anyway, didn't I?' She turned to Jamie. 'He's been good as gold, actually, hardly knew he was here. Nothing like my noisy buggers. And,' she glanced over at a Post-it covered in scribbled numbers that was stuck to the mantelpiece, 'his peak flow and Pulsox have been strong and steady all day, haven't they, mate?'

Bo nodded, 'I could probably have gone to school, but this was *so* much nicer.'

Kath smiled. 'For me too, Bo. You probably don't realise that all the nurses worry about their patients once they get sent home. We like knowing you're okay.'

Bo looked bashful for a moment, as though it hadn't even occurred to him that that would be the case and then turned his attention back to the screen, where a dowdy couple in beige were stating their need for a mammoth kitchen table for all their 'entertaining needs'.

'Can you imagine,' Jamie murmured to Kath, 'how much one of their "kitchen suppers" for twelve would cost?'

'I think the more salient flaw might be these two having ten party-loving friends who want to be entertained,' Kath laughed. She glanced at Bo, as though assessing the need to filter her words. 'Now listen, this job you've been offered? What does it actually entail – I mean, I'm sure you've already clocked this, but being a carer means a lot more than making a cup of tea and having a bit of a chat, a wander round the garden and then a game of bridge. This might be proper full-on nursing – all the slog and none of the training or support.'

Jamie nodded. 'I know. And I'm also self-aware enough to realise that I am not cut out to be the endlessly patient and understanding angel they might need. But I have met Ruth and, honestly, she seemed totally together. Smartly dressed, eyeliner on, totally compos mentis.' She frowned. 'But obviously Henry has a much clearer insight into what needs doing, if he's been the one doing it.'

'Tricky with the invisible stuff, though. Harder to see the needs when the patient looks fine. Harder to be empathetic too, even for a trained nurse. The doctors are a nightmare with it, to be honest.' Kath sighed crossly. 'Especially when it comes to women. They just assume it's hormones or anxiety and start dishing out pills. I swear to God, if doctors actually listened to their female patients for five minutes more, we could balance the NHS budget in one cycle.'

Jamie blinked, remembering all too vividly the excruciating pelvic pain she'd had for years after Bo was born, and the fob-off she'd received from her GP. And just as vividly she remembered tearing up the green prescription for antidepressants he'd foisted upon her as a parting gift.

One session with a decent chiropractor and the problem had been rectified.

And at no point had Jamie felt depressed or anxious; she had, however, been extremely pissed off at being in constant pain and unheard, being told it was all in her head.

She thought of Ruth, and the glorious Lulu Guinness handbag clasped under her arm. Eyeliner could hide a multitude of sins, but until they actually had a conversation . . .

'And you say that Henry would know,' Kath continued, 'but I'd suggest that actually *Ruth* might be the authority on her own needs and requirements.' She shrugged. 'Unless there's dementia involved, why wouldn't the patient know best?'

Jamie felt that hot flush of embarrassment, much as she did when she mis-spoke with Bo or any of his friends. 'I think we might have to just get a feel for what they want when we go over there.' She glanced at her watch, not wanting to be late. This opportunity was either a complete waste of everyone's time or exactly what she and Bo needed right now. Somewhere to live and a flexible job that would work around Bo's health. Not to mention a seemingly sane and sensible boss.

But looks could be deceptive.

Jamie checked her watch, wondering how much preparation was really required for this curious interview. Or was it literally just afternoon tea and a chat? Either way, it felt prudent to give Bo an idea of what lay ahead.

'Arsehole,' Kath breathed suddenly, after a flurry of text alerts had lit up her phone, her good mood seemingly evaporating with each successive chime. 'Absolute *arsehole*.' Tension radiated from her slender body, as she turned away and started tapping at the screen.

'Everything okay?' Jamie ventured, not quite knowing how far their friendship extended just yet. It was obvious, of course, that things were far from okay; it was just a question of how much Kath wanted to share. 'Can I do anything?'

Kath shook her head and turned back, shoving the phone deep down the side of the sofa, as though it was the phone itself that had offended, or possibly betrayed her, if the winded look on her face was anything to go by. She gave a tight, ironic laugh. 'I forget that you haven't been introduced to my wonderful husband yet. And trust me when I say that you're not missing much.' Another laugh, confusing and incongruous, as the tears hovered unshed in her eyes.

'Kath . . .' Jamie reached out only to see Kath shrink into herself a little more.

Kath shook her head tightly. 'Don't worry, he's a few hundred miles away on a rig in the North Sea. Two weeks on, two weeks off. But he still has broadband and apparently thinks it's okay to spend the last of my wages on fancy AirPods.' Her voice cracked. 'There's like five quid left in my account and all my direct debits are bouncing.' She forced the breath into her lungs only to expel it again with a single refrain, 'Arsehole.'

'Absolute arsehole,' Jamie echoed, her heartfelt sympathy and support in every syllable. 'Can you phone him? Get him to return them if he doesn't realise—'

Kath shook her head. 'Oh, Jamie love, this is nothing new. And his timing is spot on, almost every month. Like, if he's not here when the shit hits the fan, it's not his problem, you know?'

Jamie blinked in shock. It hadn't even occurred to her that the timing of this extravagant purchase might be deliberate.

'What Craig wants, he finds a way to get, if you know what I mean,' Kath sighed. 'God, they're all such big kids aren't they, men? Boys and their toys.' She gave a wry smile. 'And to think that only the other night I was watching you struggle with Bo at the hospital, all by yourself, and feeling sad there was no partner in your life to support you.'

Jamie reached out and took her hand. 'Well, if it makes you feel any better, hearing about the realities of married life surely does help with the what-ifs and maybes. I mean, at 3am, it's hard not to second-guess every decision you've ever made. The bold ones in particular.'

Kath nodded, leaning in against Jamie's shoulder, the tension slowly easing from her body. 'I guess we're all just stuck in the same patterns, over and over, aren't we? And denial *is* a wonderful comfort.'

She pulled back, a frown creasing her tired face. 'Look, don't hate me, Jamie, but I know all about the 3am wobbles. I've been there. And there's really no right answer when it comes to our kids; we just have to make the best judgement call we can at the time. But the thing is – well, I've learned to my cost that bureaucracy carries on like a fecking bull-dozer, with or without us on board. So, when it comes to Bo, when it comes to those school deadlines . . .' She looked incredibly awkward. 'Don't miss out because you're waiting for a miracle, Jamie. If you want a place at Stoneleigh for Bo, it really is time for action, not introspection.'

Jamie felt the heat rush up her chest, prickling her neck and catching her breath, shocked to find that her ostrich approach to the big decisions in life was so transparent to everyone around her. Apparently. 'I know. I do. It's just . . .'

Kath nodded. 'It really is. But it's also like that joke about the battle cruiser and the lighthouse both insisting the other change course. Some things are never going to change, so somehow, we have to make the inevitable work in our favour.'

'Are we still talking about school deadlines?' Jamie said gently. 'Or have we slipped in to accepting the things we cannot change?'

'More like trying to find the courage to change the things we can, I think,' Kath replied thoughtfully.

Jamie nodded. 'Well, if it helps, I'm still working on having the wisdom to know the difference,' she said, 'and trying not to freak out about getting it wrong. Inertia feels easier sometimes, you know?'

'That I do.' Exhausted, Kath leaned her head against Jamie's shoulder once more, both taking comfort in knowing they were not alone in their frustrations and fears.

'Only me.' Bonnie's echoing voice preceded a slam of the front door a short while later. 'Got your texts. Sounds like you've all been having a bit of a day.' She plonked herself down in the armchair opposite Jamie, a carrier bag of odds and sods spilling over as she dumped it on the floor. 'And since I've had the square root of fuck all clients all day, I thought I'd swing by. Do you need anything?'

'Nothing a fortnight in Bermuda wouldn't fix,' Kath yawned. 'And a government that gave a shit about the NHS, if you're offering?'

'Outside my remit,' Bonnie said sadly. 'But I can do moral support and hair dos – you might be lucky and get some decent advice and empathy, but I can't guarantee it.'

Bo rolled over under the duvet on the sofa, nearly booting Jamie off the end with his increasingly lanky legs. 'What's empathy?'

'It's kind of like sympathy but better,' Bonnie said, looking to Jamie for her agreement. 'It's like putting yourself in someone else's shoes when they're having a horrible time and agreeing "that sounds hard", rather than just pitying them.'

'And that feels different?' Bo said, clearly wanting to understand.

'To the person on the receiving end, it does,' Kath agreed. 'Nobody likes feeling pitied, but everybody likes feeling heard and understood.'

Bo just nodded and turned back to the television, but Jamie knew they'd be discussing this again later. She knew, too, how much of a difference that one small shift might make to Bo, if only his classmates understood.

And then she realised that she wasn't just thinking about his asthma, all those days missing school, missing sport.

She was thinking about who he was to the world. What they saw when they looked at her gorgeous boy – was he creative and artistic to them? Or aloof and incomprehensible?

Was he 'soft'? Or awkward? Or genuinely very kind?

However much he clearly confused his classmates, Jamie knew all too well how confusing it was for Bo, inside his own head, inside his own body.

Or at least, she thought she did. Kath's words about Ruth echoed in her mind, as she allowed herself to admit the truth. For all the conversations, for the empathy upon which she prided herself, there was no way that she could possibly have the full measure of Bo's everyday experience. And even though they talked – a lot – she could only ever hear what he chose to share, or indeed actually noticed. And she could fill in the blanks, of course, but only from her own experiences.

She laid a gentle hand on Bo's legs resting beside her, somehow hoping as always to convey her unconditional love and absolute belief in him, by osmosis if necessary.

'Jamie's got a job interview in a mo,' Kath said.

Bonnie stilled. 'You don't waste any time, do you? Jammy sod.'

'I haven't got any time to waste,' Jamie replied, taken aback.

Bonnie opened her mouth and closed it again. 'Shit. *Obviously*, I meant to sound more pleased for you than that. I didn't mean to sound like a jealous cow.'

Jamie shook her head. 'Bonnie, don't worry about it – the vile feelings I get every day when I see friends of mine thriving and flaunting their good fortune online could fill the entire pages of this book,' she said, plucking Izzy's *Introduction To Psychology GCSE* from the stack on the coffee table and waving it around. 'It's not something I'm particularly proud of, but I've come to accept that a little subliminal resentment is just a part of life.'

'Mu-um,' Bo protested, pushing it aside, 'I'm watching.'

Jamie put the book back down and Bonnie gave her a tentative smile. 'Yeah, I know what you mean, and I don't know why I reacted like that, Jamie. God knows, you deserve a few decent breaks ... I think maybe a little envy got to me. Again.'

'Look,' Jamie said, 'if it helps – and I truly hope it doesn't make me a horrible person – but I find it really hard not to feel a bit envious of friends having an easier time. Even if you suspect, deep down, that their entire life of comfort and privilege is built on sand.'

Kath shook her head at the pair of them. 'Look, either way, let's not get into competitive mode. You've got your salon, Bon, and, yes, it might take some time for word to spread but it's yours. I've got my oh-so glamorous career and Jamie needs a bloody miracle right now, as far as I can see. So let's not judge if she happens to get one.'

Bonnie nodded. 'I can do your hair if you like,' she offered with a smile.

Much as Jamie's beloved grandmother had always plied her with food, the only currency for love and friendship that she understood, Bonnie played to her strengths.

Jamie smiled. 'I'm not sure whether wishing for miracles extends to my hair, but it would be great actually.'

Bonnie reached into her bag and pulled out the tools of her trade. 'Amy got another interview too,' she said, 'and I was a crap friend to her as well. It's just really hard to keep getting enthusiastic every single time, you know? When it's just one disappointment after another.' She shrugged as she bossed Jamie into position. 'And I really thought my little kiosk might be the solution, cutting out the middle-man.'

'And it might well be, Bonnie, but not in the first *week* . . . It might just take time for word of your brilliance to spread,' Jamie said as she freely submitted to Bonnie working her fingers through her tangled locks. 'I could write you a press release later, if you like. Send it round to all the local papers. Maybe get you on Radio Harnley?'

'Now *that's* an idea,' Kath said enthusiastically. 'Make your own luck, Bonnie. At least so you can explain your ethos about the whole *Crap But Cheap* thing. So people don't think they're actually going to get a crappy haircut.'

Kath and Jamie deliberately avoided each other's eye;

Bonnie was not for turning on this particular topic of contention. Stubborn didn't come close.

Bonnie said nothing for a moment, apparently concentrating hard on finding Jamie's parting.

'I think you're right, Kath,' she said eventually. 'It's not just about making our own opportunities, is it? Or helping each other with clothes, and dodgy references and the odd bit of childcare. None of those fancy charities are interested in people like us, either, are they? The *under*employed.

'I mean, take Jamie here – woefully overqualified, no doubt, for whatever this new job is, destined to be underpaid and underappreciated. No offence. But there's no system to help her get back on track until she throws in the towel completely.'

'We're going to have to help ourselves,' Jamie said.

'Or reinvent ourselves,' Bonnie said thoughtfully. 'Hold off on that press release. I've got some thinking to do, and you've got a few more pressing issues than job fulfilment on your mind. But I can't help thinking that we need to come together . . .'

'It takes a village,' Jamie mused.

'I'm not moving to the bloody countryside for anyone,' Bonnie shuddered. 'All that mud! I just meant we could all help each other get where we individually want to go.'

'That too,' Jamie said, a little emotional at feeling heard and understood.

Empathy indeed.

Chapter 19

Jamie walked along the pavement, feeling uncomfortable in the tailored jacket that Kath had foisted upon her.

'They already know what I look like,' Jamie had protested, but she was helpless in the face of Bonnie and Kath's conviction that an interview was an interview, no matter that on both occasions Jamie had previously crossed paths with her prospective employers, she'd been wearing her well-worn Harrison's polo shirt.

Bo's questions petered out as they got closer to the small road where they'd seen the little house with the yellow door and Jamie once again checked the directions she'd been given. There was only so many times she could say, 'I don't know,' to her son without adding to the surreal sense of stepping into the unknown that they were both experiencing.

Stepping away from the main throughfare of Harnley and the pulsing, noisy artery that linked their small world together – the flat, the High Street and Bo's school all within a stone's throw of each other along the busy road – was like being in a different town. Passing the community centre that seemingly straddled the divide, and into the smaller residential streets, was a lesson in questionable town planning at the very least. The have and have-nots separated by geography, as much as prosperity. Stoneleigh's imposing clock tower stood sentinel on the horizon; something to aim for at least.

Hesitating in the street, Jamie breathed out slowly, wondering if this whole enterprise was a mistake, as far out of her oxymoronic comfort zone as it was possible to imagine right now. Yet no matter the job situation they were walking into, and the fear of something new and unknown, it was still a job, with a pay cheque and accommodation to boot – and it didn't have to be forever.

'Did they seem *nice* though?' Bo whispered one last question to his mum, slipping his hand into hers as they arrived in the quiet enclave of Miles Street, listening to the birdsong from the trees beyond the gates at the end.

'Yes,' said Jamie truthfully. 'They did actually. Slightly eccentric maybe, Bo, but they seemed rather kind.' She nodded, almost as though she were in agreement with herself. They *had* seemed kind, and thoughtful, she reminded herself. And, of course, generous. But there were still alarm bells ringing, as though this opportunity might yet be too good to be true.

Fool me once and all that.

But – she looked down at Bo's hopeful face – it was also all too easy to forget that good people did still exist in this world. It took a conscious effort, indeed, not to paint Ruth and Henry with the same suspicions of prejudice and ulterior motives, with which she was far more intimately familiar.

Her mother's innate suspicion of 'other people' and their motives had coloured her entire childhood, a legacy Jamie had always worked hard to eclipse.

Was being suspicious of a kind gesture just a part of her reality now too, she wondered, thinking through the offer that Henry had made, looking for the flaw. Hearing Bonnie and Kath's tentative concerns, advocating a measured approach before she signed up to anything.

But the small voice of hope in her head was louder and more persistent; and she longed to trust her gut feelings when it came to Ruth and Henry Waverly, rather than sullying the potential of a fresh start with cynicism and misgivings.

She gave Bo's hand a gentle squeeze. 'Let's just see what it's like? We can get a feel for the house, for them, and we don't have to agree to anything today, okay?'

She refused, point-blank, with each step closer, to slip into the mindset of her mother's generation. For how she had loathed those ever-hovering nerves, quashing her spirit and her fearless adventuring. Shaping her world. How she had bitterly resented the seeds of doubt and uncertainty those well-meaning words and warnings had sown – so many experiences ultimately tarnished.

She would not do that to Bo.

'So, Henry was telling me that this house used to be a school. A boarding school, actually.'

'Cool,' said Bo, whose only experience of such things was through the pages of a book. He pushed open the tall wrought-iron gates where The Old School House was picked out in swirling metal curlicue. The drive swept away between the foliage, away from Miles Street and the house with the yellow door, away into a garden oasis in the heart of their busy town, the traffic noise absorbed by the trees surrounding them.

'They bought it years ago when the school closed down and turned it into their family home,' Jamie said, wondering at the kind of circumstances that might allow such a vast undertaking.

An undertaking, apparently, that was far from finished. What she had presumed to be their lawn, was in fact a small football pitch. And beyond that, some tangled, ageing bowling nets, small heaps of cricket balls moldering at the crease.

'This place is insane,' Bo said in awe.

'Isn't it just ...' Jamie murmured, looking up at the imposing Victorian building in front of them. The brickwork had mellowed with time, but the façade was none the less commanding, taking centre stage in this leafy plot and hardly the cosy townhouse that Jamie had envisaged for Henry and Ruth.

It was eccentric and demanded attention and yet filled her with both intrigue and a sense of reprieve, of being able to take a deep breath and consider her options. Slowly. Without the mad angst of pace that had become her new normal.

Bo tilted his head back to catch the sun that filtered through the foliage, twirling around as he so often did just to take it all in. 'This place is brilliant.'

'Oh, you're here! Henry, they're here already ...' Ruth stepped out from a pair of glazed double doors, eschewing the grander front door which towered over all of them. She caught Jamie's gaze and laughed. 'Oh darling, we haven't been able to open that monstrosity in years.'

She crunched across the gravel in her sheepskin slippers, a tea towel flung over one shoulder. 'I'm just so thrilled you've come for tea,' she said, a smile lighting up her face and casting back the years. She dropped her voice. 'And that you're even thinking about helping us out for a while. Poor Hen – he just won't admit that he needs a little more help than he used to.' She tapped the side of her forehead, leaving a smudge of flour on her temple. 'He's still got most of his marbles, bless him, but not necessarily all on the same day, if you know what I mean.'

As Henry emerged from the house to join them, Ruth straightened up and gave Jamie a conspiratorial wink, even as Bo tugged at his mother's hand for clarification.

'Later,' whispered Jamie, trying not to smile at the misdirection these two, undoubtedly elderly, but equally wily characters were working to create. Neither of them ready to admit, it seemed, that an extra pair of hands was needed on *their* account.

'What do you make of the place?' Henry said, striding over. 'Isn't she a gem?' He crouched down, knees clicking and protesting, and pointed up to the roofline. 'What do you make of my dragon, then, Bo? I call her Gerty.'

Bo's eyes lit up at the sight of the gargoyle, her body carved from pale stone and her wings and tail tipped with ageing copper.

'You have a dragon,' he breathed. No longer ten in that

151

moment, but perhaps seven or eight when his obsession with fantasy had been at its strongest.

'And see how the sunlight is catching the very tip of her tail, Bo? That means she's happy. Not fond of a storm, my Gerty.'

Ruth rolled her eyes fondly. 'Mad old sod that he is, I swear Henry spends more time worrying about Gerty than anything else when it's raining hard. All that water spewing out ...' She wiped her hands on the tea towel and flicked it over her shoulder again for no particular reason that Jamie could discern. She had the distinct feeling that Ruth was weighing up their reactions, and probably seeing straight through any polite reserve that they might offer.

'Now then,' Henry said, taking command of the situation, 'would you like the five-shilling tour first and then we can have some tea?' He looked nervous just for a second, as though he were trying desperately hard to please and impress, while at the same time trying to convey a welcoming sense of take-us-as-you-find-us.

But before Jamie could say a word to put him at ease, Bo tugged at her hand. 'Can we look around first, Mum, please?' He looked up again, his face so young and filled with enthusiasm, the greyness and exhaustion seemingly falling away in his excitement.

'Let's start with our bit, so you can get the lay of the land, and save your abode for last, shall we?' Henry said, turning back to the house, clearly assuming they would simply follow.

*

And follow they did, like a line of ducklings. Henry's confidence in his route through the house was encouraging actually; there was no dithering or confusion, but there was no shortage of eccentricity.

A framed map of East Berlin with checkpoints and annotations in fading ink.

A large stuffed emu in the corner of the sitting room, its imposing stare mitigated somewhat by what appeared to be an Olympic medal hanging around its neck.

And that was before one reached the hallway through to the kitchen – row upon row of tiny pegs, all at waist height, each peg bearing a succulent growing in a small terracotta pot.

'We never did quite finish our renovation project,' Ruth said with a shrug. 'There's all sorts of nonsense round this house left over from the prep school.'

Henry nodded. 'I swear the downstairs loo is barely a foot off the ground – it's a bugger for my knees I can tell you.'

Jamie had noticed that every door they passed had a small glass portal, with an empty brass frame below, just big enough for a nameplate, presumably. Instead, there were small curling Post-its tucked into the spaces, bearing such legends as 'Bins out on FRIDAY' and 'Defrost the milk'.

'We were so full of good intentions when we bought this place – couldn't believe our luck!' Ruth said, still looking slightly in awe. 'So many big plans, but we never quite got around to it, did we, Hen? There's always something shouting louder for one's attention as a parent, isn't there?'

Henry shook his head. 'More like just fixing the roof and the electricity ate up the whole budget. No wonder we got it for a song.' He shook his head fondly. 'Been a bloody money pit this place.' He patted the wall affectionately, barely seeming to notice the plasterwork that flaked from above with each small impact.

Jamie glanced to gauge Bo's reaction, concerned really, that this was all just a step too far from their reality. She needn't have worried; he was entranced by the luscious pile on the vast velvet curtains that hung either side of the front door – tentatively stroking the luminous bottle green fabric and watching the colours change.

This house was certainly one of a kind – not so much an interior design scheme, as a collection of *objets* and experiences. The furnishings were tired, yes, but not tattered, more well loved and well used. And there were so, so many photographs, paintings and sketches on the walls, it was actually hard to see the original colour underneath. It was one way to put off redecorating.

Camping trips, canal boat holidays, gap-toothed school portraits and one very smart graduation photo – there was nothing flash or gratuitous about any of these pictures and yet they painted a picture of a rich and full family life.

Indeed, every room they passed through was a testament to a life of travel and family and exploration. Not just in the photos but in the knick-knacks: wooden eggs, blown-glass vases, vials of sand, petrified wood twists and the occasional polished pebble.

And Jamie couldn't help but feel a lurch of connection, or was it longing? Just to be a part of something like this, even if it was as the hired help. She smiled to herself, convinced that they would never be short of conversational prompts in this house, convinced she could make this work.

She glanced around the hallway once more and tried to imagine living here, working here. It was certainly small wonder that they struggled with the dusting.

Chapter 20

The annexe that Ruth proudly showed them had clearly once been matron's domain, now cleaved off into a neat and functional unit on the far reaches of the ground floor. The bedrooms still bore the marks on the wooden floor where they'd been sectioned into small dormitories and there were two bathrooms, one in miniature, plus the by-now-obligatory rows of pegs and random framed chalkboards everywhere.

'Obviously we never quite got around to finishing everything in here, either,' Henry laughed. 'Bit of a bugger's muddle, I'm afraid, but it's all spotless and dry – no worries about damp or anything like that.' He was earnestly reassuring, gesturing to the freshly painted walls and the beautifully restored huge sash windows that allowed the light to pour in to illuminate the whole space. 'And all yours, if you'd like it.'

Quirky and vintage, yes, Jamie thought, but also blessedly clean and quiet, the crisp white bedlinen and bizarre assortment of china on the dresser making it feel like an upmarket, shabby chic B&B. It was far beyond what she'd been expecting.

'And I'm sure we can sort out a TV and whatnot for you, Bo – get you signed up to the interweb and all that,' Henry said reassuringly, looking down at Bo with a hopeful expression.

It was the strangest interview that Jamie had ever experienced – as though she were the one to be courted and persuaded.

It was flattering, actually, if somewhat perplexing.

Bo, it seemed, needed no persuading, following Henry back out into the garden via their own back door. Chattering away, the two of them stood in the arc of sunlight like bookends, separated only by the decades between them.

'Your Bo is a lovely boy,' Ruth said quietly beside her. 'And Henry has so missed having our Theo at home.' She paused. 'Although actually I think Bo might appreciate Henry's interests more than Theo ever did – bit of a clash of personalities really. Theo was all about rugby and building vast dens that never stayed up in a strong wind, while Henry's always been rather content with a decent campfire and anything creative – pottery, woodturning, his record player and the ukulele. Oh God, the summer of the ukulele is responsible for most of my grey hair!' Ruth shook her head affectionately.

'Shall we leave them to it and have a cup of tea?' she said, as Henry showed Bo how to reach up to refill the various birdfeeders dotted all around the walled garden. 'We can keep an eye on them from the kitchen door.'

Her consideration that Jamie might not want to leave her

son alone with a strange man touched Jamie enormously. She knew she was overprotective of her son, but then, didn't she have every reason to be? And not just because of nights like last night, plugged into the nebuliser, but because Bo seemed to have no filter as yet. No sense of how much of himself to share with the world, or whom to share that with. No filter on his opinions either, no matter how tactless or astute.

And therein lay the kicker because Jamie never, ever wanted him to have to filter himself, sensor himself, just to be safe or fit in. But the world didn't want to comply with that dream, did it?

And so, it was just another worry to carry in the back of her mind, tucked away among the endless decisions and responsibilities she carried alone as a single parent. Deliberately. Determinedly. Protecting her son at all costs.

'Ruth,' Jamie said as she followed her back through the rabbit warren of corridors towards the kitchen, 'do you have a specific role in mind here for me? Is it some housework or cooking or are there personal care issues you might need help with?'

She mentally thanked Kath for her briefing earlier. Personal care sounded so much better and more professional that asking whether either of them got stuck on the loo, or needed hoicking out of the bath on occasion.

Ruth paused in the doorway to the kitchen, considering the question.

'What would you feel comfortable doing?' she asked. 'We're both quite able to deal with our,' she smiled at Jamie's tactful expression, 'personal care. So I imagine it might be a case of mucking in with whatever needs doing . . . You know, playing it by ear a little – so if you're in the mood to batch cook some meals one day, or take a punt at getting us more organised on another . . .' She held out her hands. 'I think if you're going to live here too, especially fitting life around Bo, then it's going to have to be organic.'

She stepped away and then paused. 'But you'll have to step in and play backgammon with Henry – I've played enough for seven lifetimes by this point.'

'But I've never—' Jamie began, before Ruth waved her off.

'He'll teach you then. And Bo too, maybe. He'll like that.'

She talked about him, Jamie noticed, as though he were a much adored pet, to be humoured and indulged occasionally. And it was obvious to Jamie – in the middle of whatever chaotic arrangement they were cooking up – that both of them felt that Jamie would be here to help the other one.

Their own independence and the keeping of their marbles both high on their own list of priorities.

Strangest job interview ever.

She followed Ruth into the kitchen, eyes widening at the scene of semi-organised chaos that confronted her. Jamie quailed for a moment, stepping up to the huge arched window over the sink to catch a glimpse of Bo while she composed herself to take a proper inventory of the situation.

It was the *stacks* that confounded her. There was no filth or unwashed dishes; it was the stacks of magazines on the table, of clean dishes and mugs on the draining board, of saucepans in a stainless steel Leaning Tower of Pisa by the Aga. Nothing was put away. The shelves of the dresser were bare and yet every surface was covered.

So maybe they weren't actually disorganised, even if she herself couldn't grasp the systems that were at play here?

Ruth watched her carefully. 'We're not crazy hoarders, Jamie, in case that's what you're thinking. We both just have a bit of trouble reaching up to get things down, so once they're in circulation, we tend to just keep them handy.' She nodded upwards at the fancy wrought-iron rack hanging over the Aga, rows of saucepan hooks hanging empty.

'That makes sense, I suppose,' Jamie said, considering the logic and still wondering how they even found the space to sit down to eat at the vast scrubbed pine kitchen table. Wondering why there was a brand-new dishwasher, still covered in the display stickers from the shop, and yet a tumult of washing-up was stacked drying on the draining board.

'Oh, don't mind that blasted machine,' Ruth said, following her gaze. 'Theo seems to think we can't manage, and gets these gadgets and gizmos delivered. Hardly a week goes by without the Curry's van turning up.' She shook her head. 'We think it's because he feels guilty about being in the States all the time and he's a good boy for thinking of us, but we don't need more *stuff* – we'd just like to see him occasionally, you know?' There was an undertone of hurt laced through her words and Jamie could see just how much she missed her son. A fancy dishwasher a poor substitute for a hug.

Ruth gave herself a shake and stepped forward to place

the large shiny red kettle on the hotplate of the Aga to make tea. 'It just doesn't seem to occur to him that we managed perfectly well without mobile phones and whatnots for most of our lives.'

'But I do rather like my mobile phone, though, Dotty, my love,' Henry said, ambling in through the back door, 'I rather like listening to the cricket on it,' he confided to Bo. 'And I've downsaved some rather jolly music too.' He rummaged in his cardigan pocket and pulled out his very smart iPhone, tapping at the screen until the flagstones fairly reverberated with seventies hits.

'Henry!' Ruth shouted, waving her hands around until he took the hint and lowered the volume.

'What was that?' Bo asked, leaning in to see the screen enthusiastically, rather taken apparently by the harmonies of the Mamas and Papas. He was nothing if not a touch eccentric as ten-year-old boys went.

'I wasn't sure what Bo might like to nibble on, so I got a selection,' Ruth said, balancing a plate full of individually wrapped treats on the edge of the tray, where what looked like the best china was already arranged for tea. Jamie stepped forward and took the weight. 'Shall I put this somewhere for you?'

'The sitting room's easiest,' Henry nodded. 'On the ottoman please, Jamie.'

Bo trotted after her, waiting until they were out of earshot. 'Mum? This place is amazing. Can we really live here? With Henry and Ruth?'

'Would you like to?' Jamie asked, balancing the tray carefully.

Bo nodded. 'I like the flat and I love the garden.' He paused. 'And I'm not sure, but I think Stoneleigh is literally, like, two streets away – so that's another really good thing, isn't it? Like, I'd be a shoe-in for a place next year?' He hesitated. 'But what do *you* think, Mum? I know being a – what is it – a carer? Cleaner? Cook? – it probably isn't what you were hoping for.'

The fact that he'd even considered her feelings about this potential move was incredibly touching. But likewise, his obliviousness at just how little her own career ambitions tallied into this decision was probably for the best – she was a single mum, without a job, and shortly without anywhere to live. She'd probably sign up to unblock the Waverly's drains if it gave her son a chance of some stability.

But he didn't need to know that.

'I think we can make it work here, don't you?' Jamie said, ignoring Bonnie and Kath's advice that whatever was on offer, she should ask to sleep on it.

Even in the short time they'd been here, there was more colour in Bo's cheeks and more sparkle in his eyes than she'd seen in a long time. And you couldn't put a price on that.

'Ruth will be along in a moment with the teapot,' Henry said, announcing his arrival as though he knew perfectly well that he and his wife were under discussion. 'And now, Jamie,' he said, steering her over to the double doors and dropping his voice, 'I'm not sure how these things are done when one hasn't exactly advertised a position, but I had a quick check in the local paper to see what the going rate is—' He passed over a folded piece of writing paper that he'd been holding tightly in his hand. 'Do you think this might be appropriate remuneration for you?'

He seemed to hold his breath as Jamie unfolded the note, clearly hopeful of a positive response, just as Jamie's own hopes took a dive. She frowned at the number, written in beautiful swirling handwriting, but disappointing none-theless. She began doing sums in her head, heart sinking, because even taking out rent, it was really more pin money than a monthly stipend. And it didn't come close to covering even the minimum payment on her credit cards.

'I'm not trying to negotiate, if this is what you can afford, Henry, but for me and Bo,' she paused, hesitant to turn down such an opportunity, 'it's just that there are certain costs I can't avoid.'

She was rather shocked by just how disappointed she actually felt. Even knowing there was probably some young, single person who would leap at this package, she knew that she couldn't accept. Couldn't knowingly, willingly, sink deeper and deeper into debt, even if the trade-off was a safe place for her and Bo to land.

Henry looked equally crestfallen, as he took in her response.

'I just don't think that Bo and I can manage on this for the whole month, Henry. To be honest.'

His face lit up, confusing her no end. 'Oh no,

Jamie – Ruthie and I were thinking it might be, er, well, helpful to you, if we paid you each week.'

He leaned forward and tapped on the paper in her hand. 'That's for the week, dear girl, not the month.'

Jamie blinked, a little overcome. From scraps to relative riches with a tweak of perspective. And with it the prospect, one day maybe, of not owing anybody anything; a pipe dream, perhaps, but one that Jamie clung to with conviction.

'Can we stay then, Mum?' Bo asked, having quietly walked over to join their clandestine negotiations.

She looked at him questioningly, waiting for the nod of approval, feeling only relief when he grinned enthusiastically.

'We'd be delighted to accept, then, Henry. If you and Ruth are quite sure you can cope with rather more chaos in your lives.' She gave Bo a gentle nudge.

'Oh, how very fabulous,' Ruth exclaimed, joining them in the sitting room and catching the tail end of the conversation.

'I think a celebration is in order,' Henry announced.

And Jamie stood back and watched them clasping each other's hands, a look of relief passing between them, and wondered what she'd actually signed up for.

Chapter 21

'Listen, I know you're kind of out of options at the moment, and I don't want to be a downer, but did they even talk about the hours you'd be working? Or what they *actually* needed you to do?' Bonnie didn't really look that conflicted at being the one to rain on the celebrational parade the next morning.

Jamie swivelled from side to side in the barber's chair, strangely lost without an early clock-in at Harrison's, and Bonnie's kiosk once again their logical meeting point.

Amy's head was tipped back in the basin a few feet away, her voice projected too loudly above the running water. 'Any idiot can work for free, is what my Gran always used to say.'

'And even the best pay cheque gets smaller if you're work-ing all hours God sends,' Kath agreed, leaning against the wall and looking exhausted. 'If I actually worked only the hours I'm contracted to work, it's not such a shit deal. The problem is, I can't just walk away at the end of my shift if there's nobody to cover a patient in distress, can I?'

'I could,' Bonnie said firmly. 'I need my eight hours, or I'm just no use to anyone.'

Jamie shook her head. Bonnie may talk a big game, but

she was a softie at heart too. 'I think we've all lost sight of what nine-to-five actually looks like. Even Bo. He was totally confused this morning when I didn't need to drop him at Breakfast Club, even more so when I said I'd see him at 3.30!'

Kath nodded. 'Mine were the same at that age. And I genuinely looked into ditching nursing altogether at one point. The hours were shit, the money was worse ... But then,' she shrugged, 'sometimes you gotta do what you gotta do.'

Amy sat up, her hair sodden, as Bonnie cursed and did her best to capture the drips. 'Bloody hell, woman, would you keep still ...'

'No, I mean, I have to ask,' Amy said. 'Kath, how did you know what you wanted to do? I mean, it's a pretty lousy job, right. But you still *know*, I mean really know, that it's the one for you.'

Jamie turned, also a little invested in the answer.

'How does anyone know anything? Like with a relationship, or a friendship, or where you want to live? You just have to follow your instincts, don't you really?' Kath said simply.

There was a quiet lull in conversation as each of them considered their own situation.

'The only times in life I've come really unstuck are when I haven't listened to my gut,' Jamie said reflectively, fiddling with the combs and brushes laid out in front of her. 'I mean, I think my subconscious has like twenty IQ points on me, is all I'm saying.'

Amy fidgeted again, causing Bonnie to exhale in

frustration. 'My gut says I don't want any of these stupid jobs, but my bank manager says I do.'

'How about we get you one of these "stupid jobs" so you can pay your bills while you consider your options, then?' Kath said. 'Because you know we think you're capable of so much more than answering phones for minimum wage for the rest of your life.'A sharp tap on the door made them all jump and Jamie instinctively felt her heart race at the sight of an official-looking man in a suit, despite the fact that he clearly wasn't looking for her.

'Shit, it's Paul from the council,' Bonnie said, swaddling Amy's hair into a elaborate wrap. 'Give me a sec. He's the guy in charge of new business and rates deals or something, so everyone be nice.'

'I have to confess, Bonnie, I'm very impressed at how quickly you've got yourself up and running. The local councillors had their doubts about this scheme, but you've rather proven that early support to an entrepreneur can go a long way in a fluctuating economy.' He nodded, as though confirming his own opinion. 'Look at you, with a queue of eager customers already in just the first week.'

Jamie and Kath just nodded enthusiastically; no need to disillusion the bean-counter, especially if it was his department making Bonnie's venture viable.

'And maybe soon, bigger premises and employees – that's how to rebuild the economy. You support the growth, and the growth takes care of the rest.'

He nodded, brow furrowed, taking everything in. 'I hope you're taking advantage of the promotion and advertising rates available to you – it's all in your welcome pack.'

Bonnie nodded. 'I've just been taking some advice about PR demographics actually – you only get one chance to make a first impression and all that.' She glanced gratefully at Jamie, trying not to laugh. Was it obvious that the word 'demographic' had never passed her lips before?

Paul nodded, deep in thought, making a few notes in his leather folder. 'You know, that shelf ideally needs another support,' he said after a moment. 'If you don't mind me saying.' He stepped over to the barber's chair and the slim shelf in front of it. 'It's the height, you see. You probably only want it for a cup of coffee and a magazine? But you see, people will lever themselves up on things . . .' He gave the shelf a waggle. 'And I'm not sure this chap would survive that.'

'Okay,' said Bonnie, looking a bit perplexed, perhaps not realising that a health and safety assessment would be part of Paul's remit.

He clocked her expression and smiled reassuringly. 'Not an official statement, that, Bonnie.' He tapped his chest. 'Amateur carpenter, I'm afraid. But I would still get it looked at.'

He sighed, and for a moment, Jamie was taken aback at the wistful expression on his face.

'Such a great business idea, you've got here, Bonnie. And credit to you for being bold enough to take the plunge. Not everybody does,' Paul said, nodding again.

'Thanks,' Bonnie said awkwardly. 'I guess it's easier if you're starting from nothing, with nothing to lose.'

Paul nodded again. 'True, true. I mean, you make a valid point, but don't dismiss the leap of faith it's taken you to get to this point. I started with the council after twenty-five years in industry. But, you know, 2020 put paid to that. And to my pension plan. They kept me around just long enough to handle the firings, department by department. And then it was my turn.' He still looked deeply emotional about the whole experience. 'Wish I'd been brave like you.'

Jamie and Kath exchanged glances, thrown a little by an emotionally literate male in their mix. It didn't happen very often.

And, for all his receding hairline and tired, shiny suit, he suddenly looked all the kinder and more approachable for it.

'Was it the carpentry you'd have liked to explore, then?' Kath asked, clearly unable to watch a soul struggling without offering some support.

Paul nodded. 'That's the dream. No more forms in triplicate. No more BS from people who don't seem to grasp that the numbers never lie, even if they do.' He sighed, as though it really were time to let go of the fantasy. 'But when I retire, I promise you I'll be there with my lathe ...'

'Sounds like a plan,' Bonnie said sympathetically. 'And in the meantime, you're helping people like me. And I know that you're appreciated.'

'Well,' he breathed, looking positively choked up, 'isn't that a thoughtful thing to say.' He glanced around one more time and made for the door. 'Best bit of my week, dealing with my up-and-comers. Bittersweet, though. Good luck, Bonnie. I'll be in touch soon.'

As the door swung closed behind him, there was an audible sigh in the tiny kiosk.

'Bloody hell,' said Amy after a moment. 'If that isn't a testament to following your dreams, I don't know what is. All those years and then out on his arse. And scrabbling around at his age for any crappy job to refill his pension pot? Imagine if he has a heart attack and never gets to retire. All that time just waiting for his golden years ...'

Kath shook her head. 'You know, it's awful, but we see it all the time in A&E. Newly retired blokes, or those in the final stretches ... Makes you want to seize the day, doesn't it?'

Amy nodded. 'You know, Jamie – this interview I'm going for today? There's no way I'm going to get it. And it seems to me as though it might actually really suit you. It's got all sorts of prospects, apparently. They want to build a marketing team and help grow this new brand's market share. Like, it's a start-up that's gone viral or something.' She paused and looked uncomfortable. 'And I had to Google half the stuff in the job description, so it's not like I'd be going in at the top, you know?'

'I'm not pinching your interview slot, Amy,' Jamie said with feeling.

'There are no slots – it's one of those open calls. You know, like speed dating? Awful fucking cattle market, to be honest, but I suppose they get to see lots of candidates, and sometimes it's the only way people like me – the ones who are instantly forgettable on paper – can actually get a face to face. You know, hope that they "see something in you". Please come too?'

'Not the worst idea,' Kath chimed in. 'I mean, see what else is out there before you jump straight from Harrison's into something new . . .'

Jamie shrugged. 'You're forgetting the small homeless hurdle in this equation.'

'Come anyway,' Amy said. 'Even if it's just moral support for me? Or so you can see what I'm up against and be end-lessly sympathetic every time I miss out on yet another job. Help me "craft my message", or whatever it was you were saying. Please?'

'I'll be endlessly sympathetic anyway and I've got nothing to wear,' Jamie said, shrugging as though that absolved her of any requirement to join in this fruitless charade.

Amy face lit up. 'Well I can go in first, and then we can meet in the loos and swap clothes. Wouldn't it be a hoot if they hired us both?'

'You're both quite mad,' said Bonnie. 'But you have to admit, Jamie, it's a bit like breaking up with an abusive husband, only to move in with the first bloke to show you any attention . . .' Her face puckered slightly, as though she'd managed to touch a nerve with her own insightful observa-tion. 'Maybe you need to see how desirable you are in the job market in general? You said you want your career back, but you're just moving into another dead-end job.'

'Seriously,' Amy said with feeling, 'my CV is already unrecognisable since you worked your magic on it. And Kath's suit comes with a shot of espresso and inner confidence.' She grinned. 'By the time Bonnie has finished with me, they'd be fools not to hire me on the spot. So why can't you do the same for yourself?' She paused, clearly worried she was about to overstep the mark, 'I mean wouldn't you rather be in a dynamic office with lots of fit blokes and cappuccinos, than wiping bums in some gothic mansion.'

'They're not geriatric, Amy,' Jamie protested. 'They're just getting on a bit and their kids can't help out much. Plus, you know, there's the whole housing-included thing.'

'Okay, so just go along for interest's sake,' Bonnie said firmly. 'And if this speed-dating interview thing is half as demoralising as I suspect it might be – sorry Amy – then at least you can be pleased that you've dodged a bullet.'

Jamie nodded, struggling to align her ambitions as a single mother with the idea of a new brand to build and dusting off all her psychological and NLP know-how.

'I'll come for moral support,' she said with a sigh, wondering if she was opening a whole new can of worms. But also identifying in that moment the source of her ongoing inner conflict. It wasn't just a lack of opportunities to get back on track with her career, it was a lack of infrastructure in her life.

Nowhere to live, nobody to lean on and no resources to cover the shortfall.

Bo had to come first.

Always.

Chapter 22

Jamie hovered outside the ladies' loo in the main reception area, the vaulted ceilings and vast glazed façade of the building making her incredibly uncomfortable. Something about all the pointy corners and sharp edges perhaps? Or simply knowing that some poor soul was expected to keep all of this clean?

Or perhaps it was the equally stark fact that she was about to walk into the exact scenario that made her feel panicked, small and inarticulate every single time?

She still wasn't sure how Amy had talked her into this, but there was no denying that the information pack she'd been given on registration was impressive. Well thought out, nuanced and creative, and yet without even giving it too much thought, Jamie had spotted at least two missed opportunities to present this brand, this new company, in a glowing light. Perhaps that was the hidden test?

She fidgeted nervously, trying to avoid the glare of the highly polished women on reception, who clearly couldn't understand why anyone would turn up to an interview wearing jeans and a sloppy sweatshirt. At least her hair and make-up were faultless, though, thanks to Bonnie's efforts and the contents of Amy's handbag. She discreetly attempted the power pose she'd learned from a Ted Talk and earned herself a small snort of derision from the reception desk. Where was the solidarity, people, she wanted to holler, if only just to see if it would echo in this vast, glazed cathedral to materialism.

She glanced at her watch, mentally calculating how much time she could reasonably allocate to this boondoggle before she had to collect Bo. She could call it interview experience, she could say she was supporting a friend. She could even, quite reasonably, call it checking out her options before she committed to Henry and Ruth. But, call it what you will, it still felt like an entirely unnecessary, nerve-wracking waste of time.

She looked up at the sound of heels on the polished marble floor, to see Amy approaching at speed. Her neck was flushed and her eyes were filled with unshed tears. 'Well, I guess I fucked *that* up,' she said, by way of greeting, hustling Jamie into the ladies' and unbuttoning Kath's suit.

'Hey, hey, wait up – tell me what happened?' Jamie said, more concerned for how upset Amy was.

Amy shook her head. 'They were fine, perfectly nice and polite. They just made me feel stupid, that's all.'

'What did they say?' Jamie asked, hackles beginning to rise on Amy's behalf.

'They assumed it was a typo – that I only had two GCSEs,' Amy sniffed. 'And the problem is, Jamie, I can kind of see their point, you know? It seems a bit ridiculous, doesn't it? In this day and age, that anyone would leave school with chuff all to show for it.'

'But how are they to know what's going on in your life? School is just a part of that, and you can't view it in isolation. And it's not as though you were misleading them; it was an entry-level application.' Jamie hugged her tightly, almost as she would with Bo when the world just felt too much. 'Come on, let's get out of here. Fuck 'em, they don't deserve you.'

Amy shook her head. 'No way. This is a seriously good company, Jamie. They're, like, so switched on up there. They even have a professional coffee machine.' Which had clearly made an impression upon her. 'You have to go and see. Before you make any decisions – please?'

Amy slipped out of the slender sheath dress and held it out to Jamie, who hurriedly pulled off her sweatshirt so Amy wouldn't stand there shivering.

Zipped into the dress and pulling on the tailored jacket over the top, Jamie paused for a second, the fabric uncomfortably tight across her shoulders. 'We really didn't think this through,' she said.

'It'll be fine,' replied Amy. 'Just stand tall and don't hug anyone.' Her tears had dried, only to be replaced by some kind of mild hysteria.

Jamie shook her head. 'No, I mean shoes!' Amy and Kath clearly had similarly delicate, ladylike feet, but Jamie's size 8s had no chance of fitting into the neat black courts Amy was wearing.

Amy's giggles ratcheted up a notch. 'Just wear your flip-flops and look eccentric?'

Jamie shook her head, the contrast between her perfect blow-dry, the neat little suit – too neat some might say, seeing how tightly the fabric also pulled across her tummy – and her unmanicured toes in battered Birkenstocks, was hardly top-flight material.

As much as it didn't really matter, Jamie couldn't help feeling rather sad to be making a lousy first impression – old habits died hard.

Stepping out of the glass elevator, Jamie felt a swoop of nausea. Whether from the rapid ascent above the rooftops of Harnley, or because of the interview panels awaiting her, she couldn't really say. Amy's assessment of the applicant day was spot on – so many nervous souls clutching registration packs and being ferried from panel to panel by androgynous and efficient assistants with headsets and clipboards.

Two young men sporting a smattering of facial hair and tight, expensive suits were laughing together as they waited for the elevator. 'Yeah, can you believe it? Turning up here with two GCSEs and a pouty look, thinking her hot, sweet little arse was enough to get her a job that other people would kill for. People who're actually prepared to put in a day's work.'

Jamie stilled, her anger catching in her throat at their unthinking cruelty, knowing full well that it was Amy they were talking about. Knowing that they were unaware of their own innate privilege and the irony of their words; so accustomed to their very presence earning them due consideration?

She turned, about to give them a piece of her mind, as the doors of the elevator began to close, their last words hanging in the air as their descent began. 'I'd definitely tap that though, wouldn't you?'

Jamie blinked hard, shocked at the wave of fury that washed over her. It had been so long since she'd been in an office environment, she'd actually forgotten the casual, inherent sexism and harassment that just seemed to be an accepted part and parcel of any large organisation.

The #metoo movement still had a lot of work to do, so long as professional young men like that still clearly felt that words didn't count. Although based on their lascivious laughter, Jamie wouldn't necessarily bet the farm that those words wouldn't translate into actions with little encouragement.

She frowned, knowing that in a strange way, she'd been in a bubble these last few years, protected from this kind of bollocks. To the point that she'd almost bought into the myth that it was a thing of the past, the world had awoken to the problem and was being held to a higher standard.

She was clearly out of touch.

'Name?' asked one of the assistants curtly, stepping closer to Jamie. Far too close, if you wanted her opinion.

'Jamie Matson.'

The assistant glanced down at Jamie's flipflops with a sneer, before scanning the various pages on their clipboard, eyebrows lifting in surprise when she found what she was looking for.

'Right. Jamie Matson, you said? Okay then, you'll be over here to interview with the Executive Committee.' Another confused glance at the flipflops. 'For one of our *executive* roles.' They stressed the word, as much, it seemed, to confirm to themselves that they hadn't made some kind of mistake.

'And all of these?' Jamie asked, nodding towards the three distinct clusters of nervous-looking souls awaiting their own interrogations.

'Entry-level,' a dismissive nod towards the back of the office suite. 'Sales and administration over there. And, as I've said, you're over here. To see the *Executive* Committee.'

Settled in a chic but uncomfortable armchair, Jamie looked around, wondering when the buzz of a busy office had morphed from exciting to exhausting in her mind. Was it some time after becoming a parent, she wondered, or was it simply that the legacy of discomfort in a crowd had yet to recede?

She settled down to wait; the men around her seemingly used to the form, ostentatiously reading the *Financial Times*.

All of it was a power play, of course, but the waiting didn't help when you had a child to collect from school.

Eventually, 'Jamie Matson? Come this way.' A shrewd glance, another raised eyebrow and Jamie was ushered into a vast glass box masquerading as a boardroom. A rather ostentatious display of pastries and exotic fruits laid out, untouched, on the sideboard. 'Do help yourself,' the pin-thin woman in front of her said, with a wave of her hand.

'I'm fine, but thank you,' Jamie replied, wondering what kind of chutzpah would be required to load up one's plate in the face of this intimidating panel of faces appraising her. Her stomach rumbled at the sight of the custard danishes and for a half beat she contemplated doing just that – it wasn't as though they were going to offer her a job, after all – the flipflops had put the final nail in that particular coffin. And she really was famished.

'Your qualifications are very impressive,' boomed a vast, rugby player of a man from the far end of the table, as Jamie sat down. Danish-less.

'Thank you,' she replied simply.

'The rest of your application, however, is somewhat underwhelming, it has to be said. More support staff than executive level, but nevertheless your background in psychology's enough to get you into the boardroom. Colour us intrigued.'

Ugh. Colour me irked, thought Jamie. There was a horribly combative edge to every interaction she'd had in this building and it made her feel intensely uncomfortable.

If Amy had wanted someone to empathise with just how awful this cattle market approach to employment was, then Jamie was already on board. Feeling just a little less human, less of an individual than she had, even moments earlier.

A brief silence descended.

This was the part, as always, where Jamie had to spell out

all the particular hurdles at which she had fallen. Justifying her life. Taking time out to have a baby. Stepping off the graduate fast track to find a work/life balance and a regular pay cheque, only to find even her cautious approach stumble in the face of a global pandemic.

Both should surely be forgivable, and yet . . .

'It hasn't been a traditional career path, I grant you,' Jamie began, with absolutely no intention of apologising for her choices to this panel of anonymous faces. Couldn't they at the very least have introduced themselves? Or was that just another ploy to keep their applicants off balance? She opened her mouth to continue only to find that Rugby Man much preferred the sound of his own voice.

'You might be wondering,' Rugby Man said, glancing at his colleagues, 'why we've invited you to talk to us, when your application made no mention of an interest in a management position?'

Jamie nodded, intrigued despite herself, knowing full well that she had only ticked the boxes for a nine to five admin position. Wondering why they even bothered asking, if they had no intention of listening to her wishes.

But Rugby Man droned on, detailing their plans for this new brand, the overseas travel that would be an essential part of any management role, and adopting a strangely patronising tone when he explained their plans for product development.

Ill-considered, half-arsed plans, if you wanted Jamie's opinion, but apparently her response was not required.

And, as she listened to his colleague – sharp suit, sharper

cheekbones and hair blow-dried to perfection – reeling off the remuneration package and benefits she might enjoy as a successful candidate, Jamie felt utterly detached.

All these long months she had spent dreaming of a scenario like this: a job – no, a career – with money, security and opportunities for growth and advancement.

All this time, thinking that this was exactly what she needed, what she and Bo both needed, to get their lives back on track.

But she had somehow missed the most important point of all: if she took this opportunity, grabbed hold of this incredible, financial life raft, then she simply wouldn't be here.

Couldn't be here.

Not in the middle of the night when Bo couldn't breathe, or to help him after school when his life felt overwhelming.

Would he thank her, she wondered, from a beautiful, clean home, supervised by a succession of after-school clubs and babysitters? Would the elevation of their living standard be worth her absence?

All these long, long months, Jamie had been dreaming of getting her life back on track – getting away from minimum-wage working, but could she actually *manage* a career right now or was a 'job' actually more than enough? Had she spent hours and nights longing for something she couldn't actually accommodate into her reality?

Chapter 23

Why, Jamie wondered, as she gathered together her things, feeling Kath's suit jacket straining at the seams as she reached down for her bag, did nobody ever listen?

Even when she had explained that her family commitments meant that a job in this office, without travel, would be preferable, the whole panel had just looked at her blankly.

'You are completely overqualified for anything we have here,' Rugby Man had insisted, frowning. 'We're offering you something much, much better.' He spoke slowly, as if perhaps they had overestimated her intelligence.

'It's a problem just waiting to happen, if you're completely overqualified,' Cheekbones had chimed in. 'There would be no real loyalty on your part, would there, if you could just up and leave at any point when you inevitably got bored, or felt unfulfilled.'

Jamie was still quietly fuming. Wasn't that up to her to decide? If she was prepared to take a lower-level position, a lower income, to fit around her personal circumstances, then why did employers insist that was a problem?

She'd hit this hurdle time and time again, which had

ultimately led to the position at Harrison's; Nick Harrison not giving two hoots if she was overqualified or not, so long as she worked her socks off for minimum wage.

Jamie glanced around the room as she left – did none of these people have families, children, commitments outside their work?

Probably not, she conceded. Oh, to be thirty-something and utterly single-minded.

She shook her head, thinking of Bo, watching the minutes tick by.

Somehow both disappointed and relieved to be walking away.

Riding down in the glass elevator, Jamie felt the sweat grow cold now, clinging to her back, biting into the custard danish she had swiped on her way out of the boardroom. Every mouthful a small rebellion. The rooftops and treetops below her loomed ever closer, her hometown laid out below like a Lego city.

Bo would love seeing this, she thought distractedly as she chewed.

Everything came back to Bo.

Even if the nameless suits upstairs – and she still couldn't quite believe the absence of introductions – would never see her point of view, or understand her priorities.

All these companies she'd applied to over the years? They always talked a good game – mentions of job shares and flexible hours, keen to impress how modern and diverse their hiring practices were – but when it came to accessing any of these schemes, all too often the gatekeepers were young, male and clueless about the realities of juggling parenting and work. Theory never a patch on experience.

Which probably explained why so many smart, qualified and experienced women were being shunted out of the workforce. All that talent. All that skill. Eclipsed by presenteeism and the 'boys' club'.

Any misgivings at having walked away had evaporated by the time the lift hit the lobby. Talk about a glass ceiling, the entire office structure had been laid out with barely visible, glass boundaries.

Boxing their workforce in.

Although she couldn't deny that their pastries *were* excellent.

She glanced around, looking for Amy, feeling intensely uncomfortable in Kath's suit and longing for her well-worn jeans and sweatshirt. It didn't matter that they came from Primark – they were hers. Without pretence.

She didn't need a smart suit, Jamie realised, to have faith in her own abilities and skills. It was just a shell.

Part of the shell game of equality and exposition.

So perhaps this bizarre experience had been worth it after all, if only to remind her of her own capabilities and self-worth. And the fact that she wasn't a pliable twenty-three-year old anymore – she knew what she wanted.

And she hadn't known that this morning. Not definitively.

Too many memories of *The Big Trip* and living the dream

still crowding in, colouring her expectations and aspirations. But life had moved on; it was about time that Jamie's inner monologue did too.

All this time, she'd been fixated on rebuilding their finances, rebuilding the life they'd had before. Before 2020.

But at no point had she stopped to consider whether their needs remained the same. The whole experience of losing everything material and yet still considering themselves lucky for coming through with their tiny family unit relatively unscathed by grief and more permanent loss. Except, of course, their wonderful Anik. It had changed them.

Their priorities.

And their needs, so many of which she could see clearly now, looking back, had actually been wants.

She smiled when she thought of Father Bill and his gentle chastisement of those at the food bank who always wanted more: enough is as good as a feast.

She glanced around, looking for Amy, hoping she wasn't still red-eyed in the ladies', just as her phone vibrated in her bag. A string of texts from Amy, each incomprehensible on first sight.

U bn aages – hope thz a gd sign

I'll get Bo frm school 4 U

Dont want U 2 miss out

Msg B&me whn UR dun

Meet U @ Bonnies XXX

A row of emojis followed – crossed fingers, smiley faces and an optimistic thumbs-up.

Jamie stilled, speechless, as she realised what Amy had done. In the last decade, she could count the number of times anybody had thought of her like this on one hand. Proactively considering what she might need. What Bo might need.

Not waiting to be asked.

Just taking the initiative.

And now twice in one week.

Jamie tapped out her reply, including far too many emojis for a grown woman, but somehow without the correct vocabulary to express the depth of her gratitude. Such a small thing, perhaps, but the sensation of feeling supported and considered, part of something bigger than just herself and Bo, was overwhelming.

Proof, if indeed proof were needed, that she didn't actually need yoga classes in her lunch break, or first-class travel or any of the other perks these nameless Suits had been so insistent on lauding as incentives.

She needed enough money to live on, and she needed a community. Even these hardest of times made easier by a metaphorical village in which to raise her son and keep her sanity.

She couldn't quite see Cheekbones or Rugby Man rising to that particular challenge.

But a smile lit up her face at just the thought of Bonnie and Amy and Kath; she felt warm and comforted by the very idea of going home to the annexe at The Old School House and entrusting her livelihood to Ruth and Henry.

It wasn't a conventional decision, but it was absolutely the right one.

Chapter 24

'Hi Mum – Amy got me from school and we had Haribo!'

The route to Bo's heart was simple and predictable and his huge grin spoke volumes – he flourished in the company of adults. Comfortable to be himself – uninhibited and so often sounding older than his years.

'I thought she was you to begin with though, because she's wearing all your clothes.' He narrowed his eyes accusingly. 'I hope you didn't do dress-up without me?'

Jamie shook her head with a smile. 'I wouldn't dare. But we did swap clothes so I could look really smart for a job interview.'

'Another one?' Bo's face dropped. 'Why do you need to go for another one when Henry and Ruth said you could work there? And you said we could *live* there?' He kicked out at the ground in frustration. 'You *said*. And then I could go to Stoneleigh for secondary school.'

Jamie felt herself pulled under for a second, under the weight of responsibility, yes, but also under the desperate desire to do the right thing by her son. Her adorable, quirky, struggling son.

A decent school and a clean, dry apartment to live in were always going to trump any notion of career advance or fulfilment. She would find her fulfilment elsewhere.

Always supposing she herself was up to the task of looking after Ruth and Henry, because she was under no illusion it would all be cups of tea and bridge parties.

Caring had never really been on her radar. It was something she occasionally read about with an uncomfortable sympathy: parents of children with specific needs, or wives looking after their husbands in their declining years – rarely the other way around if the broadsheets were to be believed. And of course, those selfless souls in their pink tabards in the nursing home down the road.

A verb convoluted into a job description.

'Don't worry, Bo. In fact, I've already left a message with Ruth to see which day we could move in. I only went to the interview to double-check we weren't missing a trick.'

Either way, it seemed, she would be missing something.

But she wasn't a dewy-eyed ingénue; she was a mother first and foremost, and any ambitions beyond that would have to wait. She tried not to dwell on the fact that in less than a decade, she would have all the freedom in the world – even though the prospect wasn't quite as appealing as one might imagine.

Bo chattered on as they walked along the High Street, Amy giving him the kind of undivided attention that could only come from a shared love of all things Monet, Manet and

Marvel, or simply a fresh ear on his obsessive and particular monologue. Walking home, through the twilight of their town, Jamie realised how much she had missed the sense of community from being a part of this little strip of independent shops and fabulous people. And even though there were hardly any open doors now, so many hopes and dreams scattered and lost, Jamie realised that one way or another she was beginning to feel like a part of something again.

Almost as if she were coming out of hibernation.

Was it the gently unfurling leaves on the trees around her, or the lighter, brighter evenings?

Or was it simply allowing herself to accept her circumstances, and accept that she wasn't alone in experiencing them?

'I don't know about you, but I'm knackered,' Amy yawned. 'There's something exhausting about bigging yourself up, have you noticed? Like, trying to make yourself come across as this calm, capable person who they'd actually want to employ, while on the inside you just feel worthless and crap and like it's all a charade?'

Jamie hesitated, but only for a moment, because this girl beside her was barely an adult and if Bo ever talked that way – or even felt that way for a moment – well, she hoped somebody would reassure him. 'As long as you know it is actually all a charade for everyone involved. Truly. They're all putting on a show, too, Amy. Even the way they describe the job – it's like dating apps, or property particulars. You learn to read between the lines, but it's all experience. And, however any pompous idiot with a clipboard and modicum of power might imply, can we please be clear that you are not worthless or crap? Promise me.'

Amy frowned, tugging at the end of her plait and avoiding meeting Jamie's eye. She shrugged tiredly, defeatedly, and carried on walking, dragging her feet with each step.

Nineteen years old and she was already on her way to giving up, Jamie thought. Kath had mentioned Amy's struggle to recover from Long Covid in passing, as though it were a thing of the past, but from where Jamie was standing, Amy looked simply drained. Physically and emotionally.

So not, perhaps, quite past after all.

'Promise me,' Jamie insisted.

'You know,' Bo said quietly, leaning towards Amy in a rare show of physical affection, 'sometimes it's just quicker and easier to accept that she's right. Saves hours in the long run.'

Jamie blinked, unable to quash a yelp of surprised laughter. 'Bo!'

He grinned at Amy, now partners in crime. 'She'll look all shocked and surprised at my fabulous insight now, you just see.'

'Cheeky,' said Amy, a proper smile breaking through the funk.

Jamie shook her head. 'Well then, since I am obviously right, can I also remind you that there's an element of luck to all this, Amy. Being in the right place at the right time and all that.' She couldn't deny that serendipity had played a monumental role in her situation, although she preferred to think of it as karma at play. Karma, at least, gave her the comfort of agency and being proactive, rather than simply leaving things to the ineffable concept of fate.

'My gran says you make your own luck,' Amy said, suddenly serious.

It seemed to Jamie as though Amy's gran had a *bon mot* for any occasion and that Amy had them all on instant recall. She wondered what Amy's gran thought about her granddaughter feeling as though her future prospects were becoming increasingly futile.

'What does your gran do, Amy?' Jamie wondered aloud, thinking that perhaps she'd short-changed the woman without ever meeting her. Perhaps she was a counsellor, or a teacher who really knew her onions.

Amy shrugged again, the sullen look returning. 'Lurks around the bookies mainly. Can't understand why I don't just sign on and cut myself some slack, you know? Like everybody else in my street.'

'Sounds boring,' Bo piped up.

'I know, right?' Amy said, with feeling.

And Jamie couldn't help but smile that her unusual little boy, who struggled to bond with almost anyone, had succeeded in connecting with Amy where she herself had obviously failed.

'I mean, how are you going to pay for your paints and stuff if you don't get a job?' Bo continued earnestly.

'Paints and stuff' clearly being a far more pressing need for both of them than, say, rent or electricity. Jamie smiled, letting them chatter on until they reached the corner of their street. She ran a mental inventory of the larder, grateful in that moment to have not only supplies, but options.

Amy's phone sounded with an airhorn and she tapped at the screen, looking increasingly confused.

'You okay?' Jamie asked. The fact that Amy was silent for a moment worrying in itself.

'I don't understand,' Amy said, scrolling down the screen. 'I think – I think maybe they've offered me a job. From the interview.' Her voice had got higher and higher, as she blinked in excitement, even as her brow still furrowed. 'But it says here it's an intern— an internat—?' She held up the screen so that Jamie could read it for herself.

'An internship,' Jamie read aloud.

'I don't even know what that is.' Amy breathed out slowly, a smile lighting up her whole face, eyes dancing. 'But it's something, right?'

Jamie smiled too. 'It's definitely something – it's like work experience, or training. It's different everywhere you go, but it means they see something in you, Amy, and they want you to work with them for a while. Maybe they'll have a job for you at the end of it?'

'Do you think?' Amy said, breathlessly as she continued to read the lengthy email on the tiny screen. 'But—'

She thrust the phone towards Jamie again, her smile fading to nothing.

'This can't be right. It says they will "contribute towards my travel expenses". Nothing about proper money, like, wages and stuff.' She huffed furiously. 'They want me to work full time, just to get my bloody bus fare paid? Cheeky bastards! Surely nobody can afford to work for bus fare?'

Jamie shook her head. There would always be somebody, someone, without any overheads, who might leap at the chance, but it didn't feel helpful to say that to Amy right now. 'Maybe it would be good, for a month or so, though, Amy. You can see all the different departments at work and see if anything sparks an interest?'

'Watch other people work then, really? And I'll bet I'd lose my Job Seekers Allowance as well, wouldn't I? 'Cause I wouldn't actually, technically "be available for paid work" – so really, I'd be paying them to make their tea and do their photocopying!'

Amy's face tightened in on itself. 'This whole day's been a complete waste of make-up.' She shoved her phone angrily back into her pocket. 'Didn't I tell you – and they've confirmed it – potentially useful, but totally worthless. That's me.'

'You're not worthless to me,' Bo said quietly, having listened to the whole conversation without making a sound. 'You showed me how to draw hands. I've never been able to draw hands properly before.'

Amy forced a smile.

'Why don't you come back with us and have some tea,' Jamie said. 'Don't go home feeling upset. Stay, and I'll even make pudding. Come on – we'd love the company.'

Amy looked discomfited for a moment. 'Really? Come for tea with you guys?' She hesitated before pulling a silly face. 'I'd really like that actually. I can show Bo here how to draw ears if you want. Make myself useful to someone today. I can even help cook if you'd like.'

Amy's teenage moods were mercurial at best, but the prospect of a home-cooked meal rather than yet another kebab seemed to have eclipsed the ignominy of her supposed 'job offer'.

'It won't be anything fancy,' Jamie warned her as she rummaged in her bag for the house keys.

'And I can show you my sketch book!' Bo almost shouted in excitement. 'The big one with all my charcoal drawings in it.' He clutched his small sketchpad tightly, not one of his possessions so valuable to him as his artwork. His people. His collections of life around him, through which he apparently made sense of the world, and saw far beyond whatever people chose to show on the surface.

Jamie made to unlock the front door, feeling good about this slightly unusual playdate she'd somehow arranged for Bo, about helping Amy's day improve, when the door swung inwards, already unlocked.

Her heart ratcheted up in seconds, her hands cramping tightly around her keyring as she instinctively slid the large Yale key between her fingers. 'Amy, can you be an angel and keep an eye on Bo, stay out here for a moment, please?'

Amy nodded, stepping back and taking a firm hold of Bo's hand, even as he instinctively flinched away, reaching for his mum, the tension in the air almost tangible.

Jamie stood in the dark foyer of the building, the sensor on the hallway lights long since having given up the ghost.

She paused and listened intently. She knew she had locked this door when they left that morning.

She pushed against it gently and fear immediately took a backseat to an overwhelming sense of fury as she took in the sight of Kieran Jones, in her kitchen, swigging juice from the bottle. Juice from her fridge, for Bo's breakfasts. Her fridge in her flat. At least until the end of the month.

'I let myself in,' he drawled unnecessarily as he caught sight of her standing stock still in the doorway. He nodded towards the tape measure and pad on the kitchen counter, covered in scrawling numbers and diagrams.

'You may have keys and you may be the landlord, but you absolutely cannot just let yourself in to *my* home,' Jamie said, her hand clenching and unclenching reflexively on the door-knob. Fragments of memories from her time at the Citizens Advice Bureau and all those endless property programmes on TV coming back to her. 'You are legally obliged to give me twenty-four hours' notice and you know it.'

He looked smug. 'And who's to say I didn't? The disgruntled tenant on the verge of eviction, or me? Me – a reputable, *reliable* property owner?'

He drained the last of the juice and tossed the empty carton into the sink. 'Unless you've changed your mind? I'm still open to discussions about other ways you could cover the rent hike, Jamie.' He stepped towards her, his eyes skimming over her body and triggering an acute wave of nausea to hit her throat.

'Get. Out,' she said. 'I have no problem reporting you,

Kieran. And zero desire to stay living in this shithole any longer than I've already paid for.'

He paused, recalibrating, glancing out through the open door into the apparently empty corridor. 'Your choice. But we're here now, aren't we? You and me?' He stepped closer. 'And I feel like I've really got to know you this afternoon . . .'

He nodded towards the storage unit in the corner and Jamie saw that he had been rifling through all of her things. Her books shoved back, with their precious pages crumpled. Her best underwear spilling out from its drawer, wisps of silk – from a life she no longer led, but couldn't quite bring herself to say goodbye to – and even the contents of her wash bag spilled across the floor.

'Quite the dark horse, aren't you, Jamie? Under all that denim and rage. Hardly a feminist icon. Sad really.' Another step closer. 'So, who do you think they're going to believe? Me? Or the kind of desperate single mother who still flaunts herself in these?' He tugged a pair of black silk knickers from his pocket and casually caressed the fabric.

Jamie took a breath and tightened her hand into a fist, the key biting into the very bones of her fingers, preparing to step forward. To gouge his face if necessary. To almost welcome the opportunity to vent her rage . . .

'I'm going to go out on a limb and say that most people find video the most reliable witness these days, don't you think?' Amy said, stepping into the empty doorway, her voice cold and hard and her eyes glittering with fury. 'So, get your *kit* together, get your *shit* together and GET OUT!'

Kieran baulked, eyeing the iPhone she held aloft, weighing his options.

His hesitation gave Jamie long enough to tug her own phone from her pocket. Nine. Nine. 'Are you going or am I dialling?' she said, stepping beside Amy, blocking the corridor where Bo stood hidden in the shadows.

'Bitch,' he hissed in her face, right up close, his breath heavy with garlic and beer, as he strode from the room and out of the building. 'Whore,' she heard, echoing through the stairwell.

'Get your kit together, get your shit together and get out,' came Bo's quiet voice from the corridor, echoing, as he so often did, any word or phrase that truly resonated with him. 'Did you know Amy was bad-ass, Mum?'

'I did not,' Jamie choked, pulling both of them into a hug, squeezing tightly until they both protested. 'But I'm very glad she is.'

She took a calming breath, shocked at herself and the wave of fury that had overwhelmed common sense there for a moment, and looked around the flat, no longer any form of sanctuary so long as Kieran Jones held the keys. She mentally calculated the contents of each room: Bo's meds, his artwork and the photographs on her laptop were the only things of true value.

Both a blessing and a sadness depending on the circumstances really.

She glanced at her phone and made a decision.

Chapter 25

'I'm so sorry to just turn up like this . . .'

Jamie tugged at the weighty holdall, even as the minicab driver sat, deliberately oblivious, awaiting the very last of Jamie's cash.

Ruth shook her head with a smile. 'Like I said on the phone, Jamie, it's not a problem.' She instinctively reached out to shepherd Bo away from the fumes still chugging from the car's exhaust and into the fresh bite of the chill evening air. 'We'll get you settled in and then have something warm to eat, yes? Henry has become a bit of a midnight-muncher so he'll be over the moon to show off his skills with the toasted sandwich maker.'

Ruth smiled, and for a fleeting moment, Jamie saw that she wasn't the only one who was nervous about this new arrangement.

As the minicab pulled away with an impatient churn of the gravel drive under his tyres, there was an awkward hesitation – neither of them quite knowing the etiquette of starting a new job, impromptu, in the middle of the night, or indeed welcoming a new lodger-slash-employee in one's nightdress and slippers.

Ruth, it seemed, was made of sterner stuff than Jamie had reckoned because she was the first to rally. 'Right then, you two, here's your keys. Drop your stuff and catch your breath. No need to do anything tonight, is there? All the beds are already made up, so I'll just get the kettle on and see you in a few minutes for some sustenance?'

Everything was a question, but there was no expectation of an answer.

If she were honest, Jamie found it immensely comforting to have someone else take charge for a moment. For her not to be the only parent, the only adult, the only decision-maker at every single point of inflection in her life.

A fleeting sensation of feeling mothered herself almost choked her with the intensity of her longing. Just because she was a mother herself, a grown woman with responsibilities and commitments, didn't mean that she too didn't crave that comfort from time to time. Especially in moments like this. When the weight of responsibility, of making the right choice, weighed her down. Suffocated her, really, if she were honest.

Becoming a parent had been her choice and she wouldn't change it for the world. But had she really known how unendingly relentless it would be? How exhausting – not just physically when Bo was a baby, but emotionally, now? And always.

And, as always, the more pressure she piled on herself to

'get it right', the more the second-guessing and catastrophising added yet another layer of draining emotions.

'Go on, love, get yourself settled. There's no shame in asking for help, you know. In fact, some might say it's the bravest thing a person can do. Go on then, catch your breath,' Ruth said, pressing a set of keys into Jamie's hand and gently ushering her towards the side door.

Jamie simply nodded, only too aware as she turned to unlock the heavy stable door that it was in fact supposed to be her role to be caring for Ruth, and certainly not the other way around.

'Mum! Come see . . .'

Jamie blinked back into herself, breathing out slowly, leading from the front. Bo's unerring ability to read every nuance of her moods never really left space for the plastered-on smile that so many mums seemed to rely on. That child really outdid himself on the empathy front some days. It would just be really useful if it wasn't today.

'Look what Ruth did!' Bo called again, ranging from room to room in their quarters. There was a vase of bright orange tulips on the kitchen counter, together with a few basic supplies to get them started. Pasta and a jar of sauce, but also a fruit bowl stacked with oranges and bananas and bright, crisp apples.

Fresh fruit. Not something that they could always rely upon and, although she knew it frustrated the team at the food bank, rarely a component of their weekly parcel.

Tinned was fine.

Except it really wasn't, and the sight of the huge, fat oranges with their dimpled skin and the promise of sweet juice probably meant far more to her than Ruth could have realised.

Or perhaps not?

The more Jamie looked around at the thoughtful considerate touches in the studio, the more she saw how much effort Ruth had put into preparing their space.

A few framed posters in Bo's room – flourishes of impressionist art brightening his tiny bedroom. A stack of DVDs and novels on the shelves by the sofa, not to mention cosy throws and cushions that certainly hadn't been there when Jamie came for the interview.

And there was no way that Ruth had made this space so welcoming in the half-hour since Jamie's panicked phone call. And to think that all this thoughtful preparation had been going on, while Jamie hedged her bets and considered her options at that farcical interview.

A hot flush of shame warmed her chest.

She'd accepted the job here, hadn't she?

But would she have had any qualms about leaving Ruth and Henry high and dry, if the offer at that start-up had been doable. Acceptable.

A way back?

'Mu–um – come see!' Bo insisted again, running through and tugging at her hand. 'There's bubbles for the bath.'

Jamie followed him, his exuberance eclipsing any

worries she might have had about this abrupt turn of events. Apparently, a vast bottle of Matey was enough to capture his attention for the evening.

'And remember, you get your own bedroom too,' he grinned, almost as though he was excited on her behalf. 'That has to be better than the sofa bed every night?' He cuddled himself into her side and squeezed tightly. 'Thanks, Mum.'

'You don't have to thank me, Bo,' she said automatically.

But he pulled back and looked up at her, brow furrowed. 'Why not, though? I know the other job was fancier, Mum. A better job, probably. And Amy said you were amazing – like really professional. But I like it here. And I really want to go to school here. So, I know that at least *some* of this is for me, not for you.' He grinned again. 'Although you have to admit that having your own bedroom is waaaaaay better than being in the sitting room. Isn't it?'

The wobble to his voice, the imploring look – it was an easy white lie to tell.

'Of course,' she said, digging deep to find sufficient conviction to convince, pushing aside any nascent hopes of reclaiming her old status in life. 'A door! A bedroom door of my very own,' she teased him, 'not to mention lovely, lovely people to work for. These are not things to take lightly. Or indeed the offer of a toasted sandwich way past your bedtime . . .' She held out her hand for his. 'Shall we?'

It was clear that their untimely arrival had become a bit of an event at The Old School House. Henry's eyes were bright with excitement and Ruth's idea of a casual snack appeared to include several place settings and a variety of condiments, some of which were way past their useful, or possibly safe, life expectancy.

'I didn't know what you'd like,' Ruth said, fidgeting slightly, all of them so keen to make a first good impression.

'Come and take a look, Bo, and tell me if this takes your fancy.' Henry was, as promised, manning a large and fancy-looking panini machine. Presumably another gift from the absent son, but clearly this one deemed useful enough to unpack.

Henry nodded at Jamie with a conspiratorial smile, checking in, checking to see if she was okay.

Again.

Jamie had never quite imagined that her knight in shining armour might be a married octogenarian.

For there was no doubt in her mind, especially after the hideous showdown with Kieran earlier that evening, that Henry – and Ruth of course – had rescued her. And it took a conscious effort not to think about where she and Bo might have found themselves without them.

Her phone pinged in her pocket and Jamie couldn't help but smile when she saw the domino run of texts on her lock-screen. Kath. Amy. Bonnie. All of them logging in, checking she was there safely. Offering a bed 'just in case'.

She couldn't actually remember the last time anyone had done that.

The downside, perhaps, of being independent, capable,

decisive – on the surface at least – as she'd travelled the world and then juggled motherhood and a business of her own making.

Tapping out her grateful replies, she saw Ruth watching her with a smile.

'Nice to have good friends looking out for you,' she said with a nod of approval.

Jamie nodded too.

Because quietly, without fanfare, without worlds in common beyond their hope for something more, that's what this little group had become.

Friends.

Chapter 26

'I can't tell you how nice it is to have a bit of life in the place,' Ruth said the next morning, after Bo had been dropped at school following a wonderfully chaotic breakfast all together in the main house. Pancakes and blueberries and bacon. Enough to make Bo's eyes pop out on stalks. And for Jamie to feel a little uncomfortable to be the recipient, rather than the cook.

A welcome breakfast, Henry had insisted, whose thoughts were apparently never very far from his next meal.

And welcome it had been, as first-day nerves had bubbled up the moment Jamie had opened her eyes and looked around their annexe, wondering what exactly she had let herself in for. Kath's words of caution were never far away, yet mitigated by the simple relief of being away from Kieran Jones, away from the mould climbing the walls and one step closer to earning Bo a place at Stoneleigh.

The small act of filling in the change of address card at school that morning, registering their move into a new catchment area had felt like a huge victory. The pen being mightier than inevitable daggers drawn and the endless appeals with the LEA they'd been facing. With one flourish of her signature, she'd felt bold and optimistic about making her son's hopes a reality. Sure, she'd quietly crossed her fingers as she signed. But that was just common sense; nobody wanted to tempt fate when it came to something this important.

And even though she knew it was still a lottery, she allowed herself to savour the moment. Despite Andrew Davies's conviction that she still needed to do more, it still had to be a step in the right direction.

And now, as Ruth and Jamie made a leisurely tour of the house, noticing all the smaller details that she had missed on that first fleeting visit, Jamie smiled, feeling inexplicably settled and home already. The large brass bell for summoning the children in from break took pride of place in the hallway, and here and there were pitted wooden desks, complete with inkwells, now serving as side tables. History woven throughout the house.

Jamie did try to get Ruth to be specific, as promised, as they continued their tour room by room, to discuss exactly what her role here would entail and what would be expected of her.

At least technically that was what they were *supposed* to be doing, but four rooms and the sweeping staircase into said tour, notebook in hand, and Jamie was honestly none the wiser.

She knew about Helena, Ruth's best friend and bridge partner, and the trouble she was having with her hip.

She knew about the plans Ruth and Henry had for 'refreshing' the sitting room, just like that programme on the telly 'where everything looks like Cape Cod'.

And she knew that nobody ever answered the phone in this house, as it plaintively peeled out in the entrance hall. Ignored deliberately, it seemed.

'I'll just run down and grab that for you?' Jamie said, noticing that Henry was standing merely metres away, but seemingly oblivious to its summons.

Ruth shook her head, 'Oh no, we don't answer the land-line, Jamie. More trouble than it's worth.'

'But—' began Jamie, herself unable to ignore a ring-ing phone, a knock at the door, or even an unopened letter for long.

Ruth shook her head again. 'Just leave it, Jamie. It's nor-mally just people trying to sell us nonsense we don't need, or asking if we've been in an accident that wasn't our fault.' She paused. 'Of course, sometimes it's Theo, because that boy does know how to fuss, but we're trying to train him out of it.' She smiled and gave a dismissive wave of her hand as though there wasn't a multitude of subtext in just that casual mention of their son.

Returning to their tour, they headed along the landing upstairs, the large picture window looking out over the roof-tops below, over the leafy driveway that led to Miles Street, and the little house with the yellow door.

She now knew about Willow, the 'sweet but troubled girl' who had been just that bit quicker off the mark to secure the lease. Apparently in the hope that starting over without too much financial pressure might yet rebuild her shattered self-confidence.

Jamie could relate.

Briefly, shamefully, she'd felt an intense flicker of resentment towards this young woman, a woman she hadn't even met, for being the recipient of the Waverly Trust's largesse. For living in the little house with the yellow door, yet free to pursue whatever career she chose.

There was no reason, of course, to assume that Willow's needs were any less than her own, yet there was an incipient prickle of irritation that Jamie struggled to ignore. Was it the name, which spoke of a wistful childhood of privilege and sweeping meadows, or the fact that the girl was young and single, with no obvious commitments beyond the basics?

Was *Willow* really the most deserving candidate for such an overwhelmingly generous opportunity?

She checked herself, shocked and rather disgusted by her own train of thought. The very idea that she might be morphing into one of those judgemental, competitive – my cat's blacker than yours – type of people made her feel physically nauseated for a moment.

After all, hadn't Henry and Ruth been there to catch her, a total stranger, when she fell too?

'We always used to have a lodger, but it didn't seem safe during all that Covid whatnot and then, I suppose, we fell out of the habit.' Ruth straightened vases and photographs on the lengthy sideboard, making swathed curves in the fine layer of dust on the mahogany surface. 'Shame though, because it's always so helpful having another pair of hands around, another pair of eyes.'

She paused, having glanced out of the window to check that Henry was where she'd left him, quietly pottering in the garden with a wooden trug and a trowel, gathering weeds. 'I probably don't need to spell this out to you, Jamie, but a large part of your role here will be just that – keeping an eye out. Henry isn't as young as he thinks he is, and I do worry. He's not always that stable on his feet ...' Ruth gave Jamie a meaningful look.

Quite what she was trying to communicate eluded Jamie, outside the obvious – that Henry had the soul of a thirty-year-old in the body of a pensioner.

'Of course,' she replied, gratified to see the look of instant relief on Ruth's face.

'Between us, of course,' Ruth said, with feeling.

Jamie nodded. 'And so, around the house?'

Ruth waved a hand loosely, 'Just do what you can to keep the ship afloat, dear girl. But Henry – Henry is the priority. As much as I adore a fresh set of sheets, or a homemade lasagne, none of that really matters, does it, in the big picture?'

Jamie followed, as Ruth pointed out the airing cupboard, where sets of sheets were beautifully ironed and stacked inside their matching pillowcases. Some of them were ageing and neatly darned in places, but there was no denying that Henry and Ruth apparently liked the finer things in life.

The simple things. Or the memorably quirky.

But what they valued was clear: art and comfort – taking care of the soul, as well as the body.

'And this room?' Jamie asked, pushing open the door to what she assumed was the guest room at the far end of the corridor, only to step back in time. Posters of pop stars long forgotten and fading certificates of musical achievement were stuck all over the peeling Laura Ashley wallpaper. The small single bed an island, the walls a sea of memorabilia and photographs of happy, laughing teenagers, with bad hair, awful skin, and bright futures.

Or perhaps not.

Ruth shook her head and with a sad, soft smile, pulled the door closed. 'You don't need to worry about Gemma's room. We like to leave it be, and I'm happy to dust it myself.' She looked older for a second, tired and drained, simply by communicating her wishes. 'I'll tell you all about it one day, Jamie. But for now . . .'

The door clicked closed with a sense of finality and Ruth walked quietly and quickly away, slipping into her own bedroom. Closing the door behind her, their conversation apparently over.

Hours later, Jamie had begun to make some headway in the kitchen. Not least actually putting away some of the crockery stacked on every surface. She stood back and stretched her aching shoulders, quietly proud of the system she had instigated.

Everything low down. Everything within reach.

And the brand new and neglected dishwasher now quietly burbling away under the counter, removing the worst of the dust and the grime from those items that were routinely out of circulation.

She wondered how many other areas in the house presented the same problems.

Something that one didn't think twice about, while shoulders and knees still gave range of reach and movement. And yet, no doubt, utterly inconvenient and frustrating for Ruth and Henry.

Jamie made a mental note to work her way around the house – a small change here and there – anything to make the mundane a bit easier and less of an 'event'.

As ever, even with a job that required so little headspace, Jamie couldn't help but overcomplicate things. To look for the smart solutions and clever tweaks. She hadn't yet mastered the ability to dial down her brain, but she couldn't help wondering whether she might be happier if she did.

At least then, she might be able to quash the intrusive thoughts about Gemma and the room that time forgot. Was it possible that Ruth and Henry simply had two children, both living overseas, or was the darker, more tragic explanation more likely? Either way, it was almost impossible not to see the visible pain etched across Ruth's face at even the mention of her name. She sighed as she worked, unable to imagine the agony of losing a child, whatever the circumstances, her heart going out to Ruth and wondering how best to show her support. Before realising that Ruth had already made her wishes perfectly clear.

'Well, this is looking rather organised, Jamie. You certainly don't let the grass grow under your feet.' Henry had wandered through from the sitting room, his mug in hand, no doubt looking for biscuits and a refill. It was already a wonder to Jamie that his sparse, rangy frame continued to triumph over the constant snacking. Although obviously, his omnipresent cardigan might camouflage a multitude of sins.

'You might have to pace yourself though, Jamie. No brownie points for overachieving here, I promise you. This house is a needy mistress; she'll always take as much as you're prepared to give and then a little more ...' He leaned back against the stove, cradling his mug and seemed to take a moment to organise his thoughts. 'Just while Dotty's having her nap, I thought I'd come and see how you're settling in? If there's anything *you* might need?'

Jamie shook her head. 'All good. I'll go and get Bo in a couple of hours, but actually I've just spent the morning finding my feet, working out how I can best help out, you know?'

Henry nodded, before glancing back furtively over his shoulder towards the stairwell.

'Now about that, actually—' He leaned in closer. 'I want to be really clear about what we need from you, Jamie. I know the brief has probably been rather vague, but that's because we're walking on eggshells, you and I. And it's easier, really, to have you here as a housekeeper, or home help, or whatever one calls it these days, than to be frank about it and ruffle Dotty's feathers.'

'Dotty being . . . Ruth?' Jamie said quietly, trying to read Henry's intense insistence.

'Yes, yes, yes,' he dismissed her interruption, 'but the thing is, Jamie, she just won't accept that she needs any help. Not just with this ridiculous house, but sometimes life in general, you know. Shoe laces, or carrying things, *remembering* things . . .' He raised one eyebrow meaningfully. 'So, while the kitchen looks wonderful, and thank you for all your effort, I do need to be clear about your role here. The priority is Ruth. Always Ruth, do you understand?'

He reached out and squeezed her hand, surprising strength behind the papery skin and liver spots.

He nodded. 'Good then. We like to fill our world with generosity and kindness, Jamie. Help out where we can, you know. With our little Trust and so on. But I rather worry that the tide might be turning . . .'

Jamie nodded, wondering how on earth it would be possible to balance her twin briefs here, a gentle smile emerging as she thought of the intense affection and concern that both Ruth and Henry had invested in the other's well-being. All these years together and still their affection for each other was almost tangible.

It was the first time in a long time that she'd even considered what it might feel like to have a partner. To share the load. In life, not just in business.

'Why do you call her Dotty?' Jamie asked, realising that

she ought to check there wasn't something she was missing. Something more than the odd forgetful moment.

Henry's face broke into a smile that lit up his tired eyes. 'It was 1978. She had the most beautiful dress – tiny polka dots all over. And she wore it to pieces. All summer – and it was a hot one. So light, so soft – ethereal really, the way she turned to the sun.' He paused, embarrassed for a moment. 'The most beautiful woman I had ever met.'

Jamie swallowed hard. That was somehow not what she'd been expecting.

Chapter 27

'Dare I ask?' Bonnie grinned as she swooped into Jamie's small annexe the next day, immediately filling the room with colour and chaos. 'Are you wiping bums 24/7? Or is that just something to look forward to?'

She pulled Jamie into a rib-crushing hug before clasping her shoulders at arm's length and scrutinising her face properly.

'I'm fine,' Jamie laughed at the intensity with which Bonnie tried to read between the lines. 'All good so far, actually. Although I'm not entirely sure it will be smooth sailing all the way. Ruth thinks I'm here to look after Henry, and Henry's convinced he hired me to take care of Ruth.' She smiled. 'It's rather sweet actually.'

Bonnie shook her head. 'What could possibly go wrong?'

She looked around, taking in the light and airy space that Jamie and Bo now called home. 'This isn't too shabby, though, you know? I mean, seriously.' She nodded to herself as she noseyed around, picking up ornaments, books, generally ignoring any social mores or boundaries. Making Jamie twitch. 'Good call,' Bonnie murmured.

'Looks like it,' Jamie said. 'I mean, I think it's going to be quite satisfying, getting them sorted out and the house running smoothly.' She shrugged. 'I mean, I dare say the novelty might wear off – it's only been a day! And to be honest, I can't help but wonder how Bo is processing all this. It's a lot of change.' She paused, her brow furrowed for a moment. 'Although, you know, he barely touched his inhaler all night . . .'

Bonnie fixed her with a hard stare, 'Look, we both know that this is hardly your dream career path, but there's a lot to be said for taking a beat, just to consolidate, you know? Catch your breath, the pair of you? Literally and metaphorically, I guess. It's hardly as though you and Bo have had the easiest run of late. So, something constructive, where you get to literally get your house in order, might be exactly what you need. And just enjoy having a dry, safe space?'

Bonnie nodded again, as though she'd said what she came here to say. 'And now, I need *your* help. Well, technically Kath does, but she's on shift today.' She reached into her voluminous turquoise handbag and pulled out a battered iPad in a fuchsia ostrich-skin case. 'Her bloody husband has been at it again.'

Jamie tried to focus on the screen that opened up, but Bonnie was busy waving the iPad around indignantly.

'He's done this kind of thing before. And I'm never quite sure if it's a control thing, or just petty jealousy that Kath has a life and friends, while he's away on the rigs half the time, but she's really upset.' Bonnie shook her head furiously, curls flying. 'He's changed all her passwords on her socials – Facebook, email the lot. Locked her out and she can't get back in, not even to delete the comments he's posting. In her name. Arsehole!' Bonnie said again with feeling, apparently the designated moniker of disdain for Kath's idiot husband.

Jamie blinked. It just went to show, you really never knew what went on behind closed doors; she'd been all sympathetic to Kath only last week, thinking how hard it must be having Craig away on the rigs. That maybe there was an innocent explanation to Craig's ill-considered spending. Now she just wondered whether it wasn't a good thing for his personal safety that miles of icy North Sea separated him from the wrath of his wife and her friends.

'What do you need me to do?' Jamie asked. 'I'm not exactly tech savvy. I mean, I presume she's tried asking him? Or, you know, pet's names and things.'

Bonnie nodded, stabbing at the screen despite her ferocious manicure. 'And obviously, the girls follow their mum's accounts, so they're seeing all the crap he's writing. Honestly, that man has the brain of an amoeba sometimes.'

'How did he even do it, though?' Jamie frowned, trying to remember how complicated her own passwords were. A few exclamation marks and the odd capital letter were as far as she went in beefing up her online security, if memory served. Ripe for the hacking, in fact, by anyone who knew her.

'Well, they've been married for a decade, so he knows *all* her details doesn't he? Date of birth, dead pets, all that. It's terrifyingly easy, actually,' Bonnie replied, eyes narrowed. 'Arsehole!' she said once again, her indignation and fury on Kath's behalf both touching and terrifying.

'She can contact the sites though, yes, say that she's been hacked?' Jamie asked.

Bonnie shook her head. 'She's been trying to contact them half the night, but she's been on shift, hasn't she? And the longer he has access, the more filthy shit he's posting on her feed. God, he's a nasty piece of work when he's had a skinful.'

Jamie thought of Kath, of the long hours she worked and all the kindness and consideration she had shown Bo over the years. It still seemed a little surreal to her, aligning the calm, competent and endlessly kind nurse they had so often turned to in the middle of the night in A&E, with the vulnerable Kath, the 'real' Kath, juggling so many struggles and difficulties in her own life. How on earth did she manage to change gears, Jamie wondered, to be there for her patients in their life and death moments, even while her home life seemed to be anything but calm and supportive.

Thank God she had sweet, easy-going kids. And long may that last, because Jamie was half convinced that a few (entirely normal) teenage tribulations might yet tip poor Kath over the brink.

'Let's have a look at that iPad, see what we can do,' Jamie said, glancing at the clock on the wall and deciding that she couldn't think of a better way to spend her lunch break.

*

'Er, hi?' Jamie said, as she walked into the main kitchen an hour later, distracted and hungry, her mind entirely elsewhere.

Sitting at the head of the kitchen table, muddy boots leaving a trail of filth across the very tiled floor she'd spent ages scrubbing, was a large man. Not large as in fat, but somehow padded, like a lumberjack, his hairline receding, yet his face confusingly that of a healthy, ruddy teenager. His large hands were clasped around a doorstep sandwich that shed Branston pickle across what had been, momentarily at least, the immaculate table top.

'Hi, yourself,' he said, spraying crumbs. He swallowed his mouthful and took a swig from an enormous mug of tea. 'I'm Chris. The garden guy?' Everything about this guy was super-sized, it seemed. In fact, if it wasn't for the slightly cherubic look of cheerfulness, Jamie would probably have felt rather on edge being alone in his company.

She couldn't help but glance at the scene of destruction he had created, but said nothing. It was hardly her place to say, was it?

He had the grace to look sheepish. 'Sorry,' he said awkwardly, rubbing at the crumbs on the table with his sleeve and categorically making it worse. 'Not something I normally need to worry about in here.'

He had a point. Only yesterday, the carnage in this kitchen could hardly have been worsened by a few muddy footprints and a spackle of pickle.

Jamie waved a hand. 'Leave it, honestly.'

He frowned. 'Doesn't seem fair. Boots off tomorrow, I promise. And how about I cut some flowers to brighten up the place.' He leaned forward. 'Henry thinks they belong in the garden, though, no matter how much Ruth likes a nice arrangement, so brace yourself for having two masters.' He smiled and his obvious affection for the pair of them made it clear he had only the best of intentions in forewarning her.

'The sooner you realise that you can't please them both at the same time, the easier your job will become. Promise.' He stood up, dirty plate in hand and looked around, confused. 'So, are we using the blighted dishwasher of abandonment then?'

Jamie nodded. 'Seems mad not to.'

'Ah, but using it means accepting the premise, doesn't it? Another bribe from Theo, in lieu of, you know, actually getting on a plane and visiting his folks.' He shook his head. 'Not for me to say though. Obviously.'

'Obviously,' Jamie smiled. For all his imposing size, Chris seemed a likeable enough bloke. 'Have you always had a gardening business?'

His guffaw took her by surprise.

'Ah, now that's what I would call an overstatement. I mow Henry's lawns and help out with the heavy stuff. That's it.' He coloured briefly before rallying. 'I'm in home security actually. Well, to be more precise, I *was* in home security. Quite a nice little business for a while there, but then – well, it wasn't the best timing to be self-employed, was it? One of the many millions falling through the gaps.' He shook his head. 'Anyway, Henry's a sweetheart and he chucked a few hours my way when I was really stuck.'

Jamie nodded. It seemed to be a habit of Henry's.

'To tell you the truth, it's not really my thing. The gardening,' Chris said, staring down at his mud-encrusted fingernails. 'But beggars can't be choosers, can they?' The soft smile he gave her was filled with empathy. 'I just need to find something with a bit more focus,' he tapped his forehead, 'to keep the old grey matter busy and distracted.'

He stepped forward and shoved his plate into the dishwasher, the pickle still welded to its surface, but Jamie said nothing. It would take the work of a moment to rinse it once he'd gone and he suddenly looked so awkward and uncomfortable.

'Well, I'm guessing that was far more than you actually wanted or needed to know,' he said. 'I'm Chris, by the way, did I actually mention that?'

'You did,' Jamie replied, holding out her hand, 'and I'm Jamie. But I'm guessing you knew that already.'

He shook her hand carefully, as though it were made of bone china. 'Welcome to the refuge,' he said. 'It's a good place to land, Jamie. They're really decent people and, honestly, I'd do more for them if I could. Willow's a sweetheart too – you'll meet her, no doubt – and she helps out a lot, but I worry that she's a bit more fragile than she seems.'

He nodded, as though he'd said what he wanted to say, and then strode away out into the garden.

Henry and Ruth really did like to populate their world with lost souls, Jamie realised, still feeling small for that out-of-character moment of resentment she'd felt towards Willow earlier on.

They were all here because Henry and Ruth had reached out a hand, offered refuge in a way. And, of course, it seemed they all had their own baggage, their own backstory. But not least, it seemed as though they were all in need of a little kindness, a little space to catch their breath.

Bonnie had seen it, recognising this place instantly as the sanctuary it was.

Jamie, on the other hand, true to form, had been on the lookout this last twenty-four hours, on edge, still waiting for the catch.

Chapter 28

Housekeeper. Cleaner. Carer.

Whatever her label in this new household, Jamie felt the very least she could do was to throw herself into it with energy and enthusiasm, despite Henry's warnings to pace herself.

Indeed, Jamie took a certain pride in dissembling Ruth and Henry's bathroom that afternoon – on the basis that she would have a better shot at keeping everyone hale and hearty if she took a few days to rectify the neglected basics. But Kath's predicament was never far from her mind.

Even as she filtered down the nineteen bottles precariously balanced around the shower and bath, to the three that still actually contained shampoo, conditioner and shower gel, she felt a simmering rage at the injustice of Kath's situation.

Long hours, for rubbish pay, and yet still she was a phenomenal nurse and, to all appearances anyway, a caring hands-on mother.

It was truly difficult to see what Craig actually brought to the table. Nothing but trouble.

She lobbed a terrifyingly ancient loofah across into the

bin bag with satisfying precision. 'Yes!' she cheered, under her breath.

She herself had never even entertained the idea of playing happy families just to become a mother.

She liked to paddle her own canoe. A singular soul.

Lonely, sometimes, of course – but also safe.

Hadn't it always been that way? As she scrubbed at the stubborn limescale around the shower, white flakes fleckling around her, she tried to recall a time when she hadn't been braced for the worst in people, braced to be let down, her mother's cautionary tone still echoing in her subconscious even after all these years.

And the only times she had struck out – defiantly, deliberately – and been bold and fearless, taking a chance and trusting other people to be decent, hadn't she been burned herself?

Doubly galling.

For the greater burn had actually been the validation of her mother's prescient distrust of 'other people' – even though, in their family of two, always just Jamie and her mum, there could only ever be 'other people'.

Her mum may be long passed, but her voice in Jamie's head stubbornly remained and so Jamie found herself an adult now, a parent, yet without many of the social skills that everyone else she knew took for granted.

Their relationships, friendships and intuitive interactions so very, very different to her own.

Learning to trust was hard, when Jamie had never quite

mastered how to reach out *just a little*, without giving all of herself.

But how did a person even begin to master the necessary moderation? The two extremes of amplitude both carried a legacy of hurt and loneliness for Jamie, yet still the pendulum continued to swing.

She glanced at her watch, counting down until she could collect Bo from school.

It was strange being here, at work, yet also now apparently at home, but without him here.

Bo was somehow always around; he wasn't the kind of boy who was invited to sleepovers and parties. A double-edged sword really, because they both knew he would struggle to cope, yet he still wanted to be invited, included. Of course he did.

As Jamie rinsed down the bathroom, gratified by the satisfying sparkle, she wondered whether now – here, in this amazing house – they might be able to turn the tables, invite his friends back to the annexe and create the social life he simultaneously craved and feared.

The apple really didn't fall far from the tree, Jamie thought, as she gathered up her cleaning supplies and hefted the bin bag.

Small change; big difference – the fundamentals of her plan to get Ruth and Henry back on track, room by room – so why not apply it to her own life, and Bo's too?

*

Fidgeting in the crisp spring sunshine on the dot of 3.30, Jamie stayed away from the small cliques of mums at the school gates. Feeling both relieved and excluded, as always.

She liked to remind herself that she'd tried, of course she had – at first anyway.

When Bo was small.

When all the kids were loud and uncensored in their joy of movement and expression.

Before, overnight it seemed, confidence and flare became 'extra' and, by extension, apparently, embarrassing.

Weird.

It was easier to step back, step away.

She watched as Bo walked out of the school building, his school bag slung across his body, his uniform as immaculate as when he'd left that morning, and his shoulders weighed down by more than Key Stage 2 textbooks.

Small huddles of friends emerged too, bantering and shoving each other, footballs at the ready. Shirts untucked and trousers with muddy knees. Shouting, teasing, loudly abrasive.

Jamie breathed out slowly. There was no point in letting Bo see how much this divide upset her too. Even as she noticed some of his classmates looking every inch as uncom-fortable as Bo might, as they attempted to clumsily join in. They were prepared to try, at least, but at what cost?

She flinched as Robbie Clark bounced his football off somebody's head. Saw the tears well in the poor lad's eyes with the shock, before he could rally. 'Wank-er-er!'

he hollered in response, even as Jamie watched his small hands tremble.

All part of the 'game'.

Bo walked towards her, barely missing a beat, and then kept walking, as they fell into step. No hugs, no hi, no 'how was your day'.

They had their routine down pat.

Safer this way, even at ten, than Bo running the gauntlet of the High Street alone.

Three streets. Three streets to breathe out and recalibrate, turning the corner into Kingsley Way, she watched her boy come back.

'I'm starving,' he said, bumping his shoulder against hers. 'Lunch was shit.'

'Bo!' A startled laugh, quietly shocked, but also secretly pleased. Small transgressions, assertions of independence, surely long overdue.

'Utter shi-t,' he said again, with feeling. Plosives had always been Bo's friends. There was little he enjoyed more than muttering under his breath, over and over. She could only hope that 'shit' wasn't about to replace 'crap' as his latest echolalia of choice, or Andrew Davies was about to become her most frequent caller.

'It really *was*.' Wide-eyed innocence. 'And seriously, Mum, I can hear my stomach rumbling. I think I must be growing.' He puffed up his chest, his slender rib cage visible through the thin cotton of his shirt.

'I think so too,' Jamie agreed, knowing how much he longed

for a few extra pounds, a few extra inches, just a bit more heft. She felt in her pocket, closing her fingers around two pound coins and her own stomach grumbled in an echo of Bo's.

Five days until pay day. There was no point checking her wallet.

Two pounds couldn't feed them both and the fruit bowl awaiting them in the annexe had already taken a serious hit.

They walked steadily across town, the streets becoming quieter, flats becoming houses, now-familiar trees marking their route home. The church and the community centre up ahead signalling the midpoint of their journey, and indeed of their town.

'Do you have tons of homework or can we swing by the food bank on the way home. Maybe I can whip you up a chickpea extravaganza?' she smiled, trying to make light of their limited choices. Thinking of the few supplies they'd abandoned back at the flat, the ingredients for a batch of flapjacks carefully hoarded for days like these.

To her surprise, Bo smiled. 'Yeah, that'd be great. Do you think Amy will be there? She was going to lend me a book she has about Andy Warhol.'

'I think Amy is at work today, Bo. She decided to make a go of that internship, remember? But we can text her later and ask.'

They turned the corner towards the community centre, and as always, whatever time of day they chose to come, Jamie was shocked by the gentle queue of subdued people awaiting their parcel of food. So many people.

How had it come to this?

She hesitated for a moment, searching for a friendly face, before joining the queue as it snaked out of the building and along the pavement. For every small group deep in conversation, there would be another looking uncomfortable, displaced, embarrassed to be there. Or worse, sighing rudely, as though even waiting was beneath them.

'Ms Matson? Bo? I thought that was you.'

And to her shame, when the food bank had been nothing but a godsend to her, Jamie felt that same wash of humiliation. At being here, at being seen here. And by Bo's officious headmaster at that.

He was lifting several green plastic crates from the boot of his car, filled with donations from the school food drive.

She swallowed the nausea and felt Bo press tightly into her side. She would wager they were both thinking the same thing – please God, let there be no pupil volunteers helping him out.

But, to his credit, Mr Davies read the situation in a heartbeat, stepping away from his car and striding over to join them in the queue. 'Just me,' he said to Bo reassuringly.

Jamie nodded, the ability to make polite conversation completely deserting her. Eyes followed their every interaction, it seemed. Andrew Davies too smart, too groomed, skin too glowing with overfed good health to blend in among them.

'I'm glad I caught you actually.'

Jamie felt her heart sink. There was no doubt, of course,

that Bo was missing a huge amount of school, and while he wasn't falling behind academically, there was the looming 'yet' in every conversation they had. She only felt relief as he continued.

'I wanted to give you both an update about Stoneleigh – I've written to the headmistress, like we discussed, and your change of address can only help. She particularly appreciated your letter, Ms Matson. I don't know what you wrote, but it must have been eloquently persuasive,' he smiled.

A saccharine smile. His words were presumably well meaning, but why, oh why, did he always feel the need to stand so close to her, towering over her?

She wondered whether he was even aware of how that made people feel – eclipsed by his presence, the need to tip one's head back just to see his face. And how incredibly vulnerable that one simple act made her feel.

She instinctively lifted one hand to cover her exposed throat. Even knowing that he was supposedly 'one of the good guys' – not all men, and all that – she couldn't help the way her nervous system responded.

She felt patronised and threatened, struggling not to let those primaeval ripples of fear evolve, as they so often did, into anger and frustration.

'But I will say again,' he continued, 'that if you're looking for special consideration, then those assessments we discussed would probably be more useful than sending personal pleas independent of the system.'

Jamie forced herself to smile politely. 'Bo, why don't you

pop inside and say hello to Father Bill?' she said firmly. She needed Bo's headmaster on side, but she resented being put on the spot like this, in front of Bo. Undermined too, if she was honest.

She wanted what was best for her son, of course she did. She just wasn't convinced that Andrew Davies, for all the letters after his name, was actually better placed to say what that looked like.

'Anyone can see that Bo's a very talented young boy, Ms Matson.' Mr Davies watched Bo walk away. 'But it's hard to watch him struggle among his peers. Socially, I mean. I think a little understanding might go a long way to smoothing his path.'

Jamie bit her tongue, not convinced that schoolboys were known for their understanding, or empathy, but then perhaps he didn't mean other people.

Perhaps he meant Bo.

'I'm very aware that the system isn't a one-size-fits-all, but it's the system we have. And sometimes, in preparation for life in the real world, it's important that our students – and indeed their *parents* – realise this. That's why these assessments are so important, Ms Matson. Once we've established that Bo has special needs, then there's a system in place to address that.'

Jamie bristled instinctively. 'Words matter to Bo. You must see that. And what you call "Special Needs"—' She exhaled angrily. 'His *needs* are simple right now: a loving and supportive mother, a decent school and somewhere safe to live, with food on the table. And believe me when I say that none of that has always been a given. It just feels to me as though the school is more interested in ticking boxes than looking at him as an individual.'

She could hardly rail at this clueless, but apparently well-meaning, buffoon when he had no idea of their reality. She could hardly roar at him about how bloody amazing it was for Bo to have somewhere clean and safe to live now – without mould climbing the walls and making him ill. Or for herself – no longer having an abusive landlord letting himself into their home, offering sex in lieu of rent.

No longer being hungry.

She felt a groundswell of rage for what they had been through these last few years and, even as sanity prevailed, and pointed out that none of this was Andrew Davies's fault, he still happened to be in the firing line when Jamie hit breaking point.

'Look,' she said, stepping back to give herself breathing space and trying to calm herself. 'Look, I know – of course I do – that Bo runs to a different beat. I'm not stupid. But all this pressure to explain and measure and assess *why* he feels the way he feels – he's ten years old, Mr Davies. Who am I to tell him that anything he *feels* is wrong? Especially when he comes with so many gifts – you can't teach the intuition or the artistic flair that he carries with such grace. So can we please not talk about "Special Needs" as though he is in some way "less", when to me, he is in every way "more" than any child I have ever met.'

Jamie was breathless, the words seemingly taking priority over oxygen in that moment.

She frowned, her anger cooling to replaced by the omniscient guilt of parenting. 'So, at some point, he might have to jump through hoops and do all sorts of assessments that will, undoubtedly, be confusing and upsetting, and focus on all the ways he isn't "normal",' she made quote marks with her fingers, 'but I'm damned if we won't celebrate his uniqueness and build his self-confidence *first*. Let him make that choice himself, when he's old enough to make that choice. Himself. And to understand what that means.'

'Okay then, Ms Matson,' the headmaster couldn't hide his disappointment at her decision, 'just make sure that you fill in all those forms and get them in on time.'

He spoke with such deliberate precision, Jamie couldn't help but wonder whether he doubted her ability to keep up her end of the equation. As though declining the assessments for Bo made her somehow lesser, as a mother, as his advocate.

There was an awkward pause before he turned back to his car boot, stacked with tone-deaf donations from parents at school with clearly no real understanding of how the food bank operated. Luxury jars of jam and chutney – unwanted gifts and nonsense – outweighed actual groceries ten to one. What was wrong with porridge oats, or pasta? Or even some tinned fruit? And why did nobody ever think to donate razors, or shampoo, or even sanitary towels?

She sighed. 'Do you want some help carrying that lot?'

He paused, frowning. 'I know you and Bo have had – are

having – a difficult time, Ms Matson. And for all that we disagree about Bo's educational needs, I do like to think of my school as its own community, for all the good and bad, and you are both a very important part of that. So, if you ever need us, please do say.'

Hollow words left trailing as he walked away laden with boxes and Jamie stepped forward in the queue.

After all, it was one thing telling somebody they were a 'part of something', but if it didn't ring true, didn't *feel* true? Jamie glanced around her, offering a gentle smile to familiar faces. Wondering why being here felt so different.

Of all places.

Not something she could have predicted in a million years, but here, she felt understood. The daily hardships, struggles and trade-offs weren't hers alone.

Chapter 29

Jamie and Bo arrived back at The Old School House with his school bags and their week's groceries laden between them. But it was only as they crunched up the final straight of the gravel drive did it occur to Jamie that perhaps she shouldn't be so tactlessly obvious about her reliance on charity, when Ruth and Henry had gone out of their way to give her both an income, however modest, and a home. They weren't to know that she'd already allocated every penny she could spare towards paying down her creditors and wiping the slate clean, trying to ensure that their fresh start would be unencumbered by bad decisions and bad debt.

Somehow, even though she knew all too well that the charges on her credit card had been anything but fancy – just boring necessities, trying to get by – she still felt embarrassed by the yoke of debt, as though it were the domain of frivolity and overspending, rather than simply subsistence.

Voices echoed from the open kitchen windows, laughter and the clink of glassware, and it was actually the perfect accompaniment to this bright spring evening, the cusp of summer almost within reach now. The swathes of bright yellow forsythia in the shrubberies lining the driveway brightened the bare branches whose leaves were only now just feeling brave enough to fully unfurl.

'Let's pop this lot away first and then go and say hello,' Jamie said, ushering him quickly and quietly towards their own small domain.

In the short time they had been here, it was obvious to Jamie that Ruth and Henry liked their lives to be busy, the constant comings and goings meant there was rarely a lull in their day. She wondered how and when they found time to catch their breath or gather their thoughts, before realising that perhaps that very lack might be their prime motivation.

There had been so many ribbons of conversation with Ruth just left hanging, these last few days, so many moments when confusion would cloud her face for a fleeting moment before she 'clicked back in'.

And, yes, while it seemed as though keeping busy kept these moments at bay, there was always a sense that there was so much more unspoken. So much more taking up space in her mind, blurring her thoughts. Perhaps, deliberately, blurring her memories.

Bo tugged at her hand, pulling her focus. 'We don't have to go in, Mum, but Henry said he would let me refill the birdfeeders.'

Possibly the only ten-year-old boy in Harnley who would rather muck about with birdfeeders than with a football.

'And – and he said we could cut some of the flowers to bring into the annexe – just for us.' Bo's face was hopeful.

Anything for a splash of colour; he'd been known to iron out the Tunnock's teacake wrappers and use them in his artwork.

There was nothing about her son that was black and white.

Jamie simply nodded. Sometimes it was easier.

'Don't take too many though, Bo. Henry's very proud of his garden and the flowers last longer outside.'

'Ah yes, but Ruthie is forever telling me we should appreciate their beauty inside too!' Henry smiled as he strode towards them, a small sherry glass in one hand and a bag of bird feed in the other. 'Right then, young man. As promised. The sun is past the yardarm and it's time for you to shed this schoolboy nonsense you seem to insist upon by day and become my apprentice.'

Bo laughed, his face lighting up. School bag instantly jettisoned onto the gravel drive and his mother forgotten. Dancing up onto the tips of his toes, he was by Henry's side in a moment, barely drawing breath before he began peppering Henry with questions. All of which were taken very seriously and answered with absolute authority.

Whether Henry actually knew what he was talking about would remain to be seen, but Jamie had certainly never heard of a cranesbill woodpecker before. Or indeed been aware that garden blackbirds would eat small frogs if given the opportunity.

Henry smiled and gave a small flourish of a wave, knowing he'd been rumbled perhaps, as the two of them headed off across the lawn, before Jamie could even suggest that Bo get changed. At some point, a spare set of uniform would have to rise up the list of priorities, but until then, she could only hope that Bo's natural aversion to mud might overcome his more enthusiastic tendencies when it came to gathering flowers.

Stacking their groceries away, Jamie couldn't help but look forward to a time when she might choose her own, rather than playing Ready Steady Cook with this well-meaning but somewhat random assortment. Still, two years ago, she wouldn't have known where to start with a lentil or even a can of stewing meat. So, in a way, it was all a learning curve. A silver lining of sorts, should you be inclined to look really, *really* hard for it.

She'd left the stable door wide open, partly for the welcome sunshine and partly to keep one ear out for Bo. Yet still it made her jump when Ruth materialised in the doorway with a small exclamation.

'Oh Jamie, didn't I say? You really don't need to shop – we have the nice van from the supermarket deliver. Frees up so much time and saves one carrying the heavy stuff.' She smiled conspiratorially. 'Obviously I mean the laundry detergent and not the Croft Original.' She raised her own small glass of sherry, the matching pair of Henry's, in salute.

Wandering casually into the annexe, sweeping her eyes around the space that Bo and Jamie had yet to make their own, Ruth frowned. 'And do go ahead and put things up on the walls and whatnot. Make yourselves at home – I have no intention of being one of *those* landlords.'

Jamie nodded, appreciating the gesture, but uncomfortably perturbed by Ruth's casual encroachment of her space.

But then, Ruth made a valid point: not all landlords were created equal.

Jamie forced herself to breathe evenly, to quell the rising panic before it took hold. 'We don't really have much to hang up, to be honest,' she said, hoping her voice sounded normal. 'But I'll give Bo free rein and it will look like the Tate Modern in here within the week.'

Ruth looked delighted. 'He has such ... flair, your boy.'

The hesitation was miniscule, but Jamie loved that she had clearly tried to get the words right. Words, as she'd tried to explain to Bo's headmaster, sometimes being everything.

She nodded. 'He's so sure of himself and what he loves when he's at home, and hopefully here too. It's just so much harder at school, you know?'

Ruth nodded with feeling. 'Such a foul time for anyone who doesn't tick all the regular boxes. If only they knew what the future held – I mean, it's never the mundane and ordinary who go on to success, is it?'

She stepped forward and picked up the can of stewing meat with a concerned frown. 'Oh Jamie, love. This isn't proper food. Grab something from the chest freezer if you need it.' She wavered, glancing at the large chrome pedal bin and Jamie could see exactly the impulse that her manners forbade her from following.

Saving Ruth's blushes, she reached forward and took the can from her hand. 'Works fine in a steak and kidney pie though – quick mid-week supper.'

Ruth nodded, clearly unconvinced. 'If you say so. But

there's all sorts in that freezer, Jamie. Most of it will probably outlive me and Henry if you don't tuck in.' She shrugged. 'Something about the last few years has made both of us more inclined to cater for a rainy day, you know. Not *stockpiling*,' another shudder, 'so much as making sure we don't need to go out and about if we don't want to.'

So much unspoken.

Superfluous.

They understood each other perfectly on that front.

'Anyway—' Ruth breathed, 'I actually came over to say your friends popped round. I've left them in the kitchen with Willow. She's been rather helpful actually.' She plucked a grape from the remains of the bunch in Jamie's fruit bowl, perfectly at home. 'Just the boost that young Willow needed, I think.'

Jamie frowned. 'Friends?'

Ruth popped another grape into her mouth and turned to leave, clearly assuming Jamie would follow. 'Such a blow when things don't go to plan. Especially when you're young, and let's face it, not coming from the easiest situation in the first place. Be gentle with Willow, won't you? All that hard work to get a proper foothold on life, away from the system. All lost to that bloody exam algorithm fiasco, poor kid. But you have to give the girl credit – she may have lost her university place, but she still got her degree. Online. Can you believe it? How many young kids show that much determination?' Ruth shook her head. 'Not without cost though. I think not finding a job after all that effort was the final straw, to be honest.'

Ruth dropped her voice to the least subtle whisper as they approached the kitchen in the main house. 'Inevitable really – sweet girl has a few mental health issues to deal with now, too.' Ruth breathed out, deliberately rallying. 'But she'll get there. In time. And she knows we're all here for her.' She aimed for confidence, that much was clear, but there was a tremor of concern in Ruth's voice that was hard to ignore. 'Anyway,' she continued, 'for now, at least she knows enough to give your friend some free advice.'

Jamie followed her instinctively, trying to work out the gist of what Ruth was actually saying, a volley of instantly recognisable laughter from the open kitchen windows confirming her suspicions.

'Bonnie's here?'

'Yes, yes, yes, that's what I've been saying. Bonnie and the lovely nurse, Cat, is it?' She shook her head. 'And that husband of hers needs a bloody good shake, doesn't he?'

Much as the encounter at the food bank with Bo's headmaster had unsettled her, so too there was a bizarre sensation of worlds colliding as she stepped into Ruth's kitchen. Bonnie and Kath were both seated at the large island, incongruously sipping from the same delicate thimbles of sherry that were apparently the norm at The Old School House and looking delightedly overwhelmed by the whole set-up.

A slender wisp of a girl, her skin and hair both Scandinavian-fair, perched on one of the tall stools, her legs twisted around each other in a tight pretzel. Her long fingers looked fragile and uncertain as they shredded a few mint leaves over and over again on the worktop in front of her, none of them making it as far as the pan of new potatoes bubbling on the stove.

Willow, presumably.

Her widening, flinching gaze when Jamie entered the room made so much more sense in the light of Ruth's, possibly tactless, comments.

'Hi,' Jamie said softly with a smile, much as one might to a nervous dog, or pony. 'It's great to meet you at last, Willow. I've just had Henry and Ruth singing your praises for the last few days.'

A minute flash of colour to those porcelain cheeks.

'Likewise, actually,' Willow replied. 'And Ruth dragged me upstairs earlier to show off the en-suite. You're the miracle worker round here.' She turned and offered a nervous smile to Bonnie and Kath who were grinning like loons, taking it all in. 'Until Jamie arrived, the dishwasher was quite verboten, you know.'

Kath looked stricken.

'But *why*?' she breathed, glancing down with maximum appreciation at the expensive bit of German engineering purring happily through a wash cycle.

'Honestly, girls,' Ruth tutted. 'We all managed to live happy and fulfilling lives before dishwashers and Apple TV, you know.'

Bonnie shook her head. 'I refuse to believe it,' she said firmly. 'But I will say that you know your cocktail hour,

Mrs W. Never had a sherry before.' She pronounced it with a flourish, making it sound like her new, French darling.

'But we're here to talk about my *chéri*, remember, Bon. And his backstabbing ways.' Kath brought her back on track, the strain of the last few days making her friendly, open face look pinched and tired. 'Before I get summoned into HR for bringing the NHS into disrepute. Again.'

Ruth shook her head, 'It's a rotten business, all this.'

Bonnie turned the screen of her iPad so that Jamie could see Craig's latest exploits.

It was hard to fathom, with photos like that, how Kath was remaining quite so calm and composed.

'Do you have a plan?' Jamie asked her.

Kath nodded. 'I'm going to kill him,' she said, and for a moment, not one person in the room knew whether she was joking.

'Well,' laughed Ruth nervously, 'at least you'll know how to make it look like an accident.'

All eyes turned.

Ruth's face was a picture of innocence. 'What? If my husband – someone who allegedly loved me – pulled a stunt like that, and I was a nurse with access to the strong stuff, I'd certainly give it full consideration.

'Or,' she continued, glancing sideways at Willow, 'we could ask very nicely and get, er, *somebody* to do that hacking thing they do and solve the problem ourselves.'

Jamie frowned, unable to reconcile this fragile wraith of a girl with someone who might have the requisite skills.

Willow barely moved, yet the anxiety that tensed in her slender body was somehow visible.

'What?' she said tersely, in response to Jamie's questioning look. 'Just because I *can* do it, doesn't mean I enjoy it!' She sighed, looking around the room at their hopeful expressions. 'Oh for fuck's sake. Pass me my laptop.'

Compared to Bonnie's bright pink iPad, Willow's laptop was a behemoth of a thing, presumably with the wherewithal to run air-traffic control should she so choose. She hunkered down, shoulders hunched tightly, fingers flying across the backlit keyboard that rotated through the colour spectrum distractingly as she worked.

But Willow wasn't distracted. Her focus was absolute.

She hit return and let out an exhalation of fury. 'SelfishWhore2022 – isn't he a keeper?' She slammed the laptop closed, looking utterly drained. 'I don't know much about men, Kath, but to use a password like that?'

Kath blinked slowly, watching as Willow scribbled her new passwords down on the back of an empty envelope for her – a row of characters that were unintelligible and, there-fore hopefully, Craig-proof.

Bonnie opened her mouth to speak and then closed it again.

There was nothing any one of them could say to make Kath feel better at this point.

'Look, just phone me if you're worried,' Willow said, scribbling her mobile number down too. 'He shouldn't be allowed to get away with this. I mean, I don't even know you, and I'm furious on your behalf.' She paused. 'So, you know, if you need retribution . . .'

Ruth nodded her approval. 'You girls have to stick together, you know. Everything seems so much harder when you try and deal with it on your own,' she said with feeling, sipping innocently from her glass of sherry. 'It's a good thing to let friends in, let them support you a little.'

And was it Jamie's imagination, or was that comment aimed just a little in her direction too, a passing glance from Ruth seemingly seeing far more that Jamie had imagined she'd shared.

Chapter 30

The next morning, Jamie swept the yellow duster across the polished walnut table in the entrance hall, taking a distinct pleasure in watching the clean swathes mark their passage through the dust. The price one paid for living in an old house filled with character, she presumed, grateful that their own annexe was mint-fresh. Glancing up at the pockmarked oak rafters above her head, it was clear that keeping this lofty hall dust-free was going to be her personal nemesis, her very own Forth Bridge, and yet still she took a very real pride in bringing order and cleanliness to Ruth and Henry's somewhat chaotic existence.

The trick, she thought to herself, as the smell of beeswax filled her nostrils and the tabletop submitted to her ministrations, would be walking the line between keeping their fabulously welcoming boho spirit alive, while also keeping everything shipshape and spotless. Making sure that the welcoming world they'd created wasn't lost in a bid for efficiency, the feeling of sanctuary more important than the gloss on their walnut burr.

As always, her thoughts travelled to Bo – wondering how his day was going.

Last night was the first night since they'd been here that they'd been up in the wee small hours, shower running for steam, and inhaler in hand. It was hard not to feel guilty, as though she'd somehow dropped the ball for a moment, relaxing perhaps rather too much in the safety and security of life here at The Old School House, away from the damp and the chill. But this time, there had been no obvious trigger for the attack, nothing she could put her finger on.

Until they'd arrived at school and Bo's worst fears had apparently been confirmed – Robbie Clarke inexplicably, yet apparently deliberately, chosen as his partner for the Big School Art Project.

Only time would tell whether Mrs Taylor's firm belief in boys working through their issues by having a shared goal would end in tears.

Bo's tears, if Jamie were allowed to put money on it.

Well-meaning people were so often blissfully unaware of the grenades they tossed into her son's life, into her life. Bracing herself to deal with the consequences would only get her so far. Practicalities would have to prevail – she made a mental note to pick up Bo's monthly prescriptions later that day.

She polished even harder, as she thought of all the things she'd like to say to Mrs Taylor when the shit inevitably hit the fan, and then her pulse shot up a gear. She clasped at the table in surprise, as the phone rang out just inches from where she was leaning over the table. Peeling crossly, it seemed to her, in full anticipation of being ignored. The handset vibrated in its cradle; nothing so helpful as caller ID on this decidedly vintage Bakelite model. Nothing wrong with its lungs though, as the ringing somehow seemed louder and more insistent with each successive demand for attention.

She glanced around; she knew the rules.

And yet . . .

Spotting Ruth and Henry in deep conversation in the garden, apparently debating some crucial planting scheme whose importance eluded her, Jamie fought the inner conflict. But . . .

But what if all these calls, and all the stress blanching the colour from Henry's face, could somehow be appeased with the simple act of answering the increasingly frequent phone calls? Simply having a conversation.

Was she tackling their issues because she couldn't handle her own, she wondered briefly, barely registering the movement before her hand was lifting the receiver from its cradle. A moment of blissful silence and then, 'Hello,' Jamie said tentatively, 'The Old School House, Jamie speaking.'

'Who is this?' The voice at the other end was clipped and unfriendly, with a faint transatlantic drawl, but also perhaps, taken by surprise that someone had actually picked up the call.

'Theo?' Jamie ventured a guess. 'It's *Jamie* here.'

'So you said. And yet I'm none the wiser. Although you obviously know me.'

Jamie blinked hard, surprised not only by his terse, irritated response but also that she had somehow, rather arrogantly, broken Ruth's cardinal rule: answering the phone only invited trouble. And Jamie felt a prescient tremor of discomfort that she had done exactly that.

She took a breath and injected a smile into her voice, pushing aside her own personal feelings towards this man at the end of the phone, on the other side of the Atlantic. A man she had never met, and yet who had a lot to answer for, in her opinion.

'Only by reputation,' Jamie replied, surprising herself with this unusual temerity. So much easier, as always, to champion other people's needs than her own. 'And I'm Jamie Matson. I'm here to support Ruth and Henry with—'

'You're the new carer?' Theo interrupted. 'Or house-keeper, or whatever they're calling you.' He paused. 'And I presume Mum's given her usual orders not to answer the phone and yet here we are.'

An awkward silence descended. Damned either way really.

'What can I help you with today, Theo?' Jamie replied, determined not to let this disembodied voice ruffle her feathers. 'Your mum and dad are both out in the garden, enjoying the sunshine, but I can fetch them for you if you'd like?'

A beat and then, 'No, that's not necessary. But they're well?'

And there, in a nutshell, lay the main reason that Ruth avoided these calls, because what could she honestly say? That Ruth's memory lapses were becoming more and more noticeable, as Jamie got to know her and how incredibly adept she was at covering them up. And Henry? Well, Henry was somewhat harder to read, and Jamie was still struggling to get the measure of him.

Probably best not to share that particular concern just yet.

'Well, they seem to be doing okay and they're certainly busy. It must be reassuring to know they have such a wonderful circle of friends close by?'

'So they can all get sozzled on sherry and moan about their wayward offspring together? Oh yes, it sounds like a hoot,' Theo said drily. 'But now what about you, Jamie? My mother seems determined to keep me in the dark about the goings on at the house, and yet she sings your praises from the rooftops.'

'Well,' said Jamie, a little taken aback that Ruth had even mentioned her in the rare and fleeting conversations she had with her son. 'There's not much to tell, to be honest, but Ruth and Henry are wonderful to work for and I hope that my being here, helping out, is making life easier for them. And it's such a fabulous place for us to call home, if only for a short while.'

'Us?' Theo's tone changed abruptly.

'Well, yes. Me and my son, Bo. He's ten.' Jamie paused, wondering if she'd somehow put her foot in it. Clearly Ruth hadn't seen fit to even mention Bo's existence and Jamie was at a loss to know why.

It was all very well stepping in, with the best of intentions, wanting to help open the channels of communication between her employers and their son, but Jamie was increasingly aware that she was walking through a minefield of historical half-truths and tactful evasions. Clomping into a delicate relationship with zero idea of the ground rules.

Every family had them.

Every relationship too.

The things one didn't mention, the soft triggers and hard deflections.

How incredibly arrogant of her to believe that simply because Ruth had trusted her to rearrange a few cupboards, she might also welcome Jamie's input into her family politics.

Theo's voice was tight when he replied, any pretence at welcome erased. 'Well don't go getting too comfortable. As you so rightly say, it's only temporary. And my parents aren't the soft target they appear, you know.'

'I'm sorry, did you say *target*?' Jamie stilled, her brow furrowing in confusion.

'You know exactly what I said, and, in all likelihood, what I meant. So please don't confuse my physical absence for a lack of oversight. Do we understand each other, Jamie?'

Jamie nodded instinctively, realising that this truncated conversation alone had given her a far greater insight into why Ruth and Henry might choose to keep their loving son at arm's length. Best of intentions, perhaps, but his sharp suspicious tone spoke volumes.

'It know it must be hard, being so far away, and delegating their care to me, someone you've never met. But please know, Theo, that I have nothing but respect for your parents and their wishes. I really am just another pair of hands in the house to give them, and hopefully you, some peace of mind.'

There was a long pause, crackling across the Atlantic, and then Theo exhaled heavily. 'Well, I guess only time will tell whether you're as good as your word, Jamie,' he said, and then hung up leaving Jamie standing in the hallway, the phone in her hand and feeling somewhat shaken.

Was it his innate distrust, the insinuation in his every word that her intentions were anything but honourable, that had so unsettled her, she wondered. Any feeling of pride or accomplishment at having taken control of the endless unanswered calls impasse long gone.

'Who were you talking to?' Ruth's sharp voice from the doorway made her jump.

For one brief moment, Jamie actually considered lying.

Flat out lying to her kind, trusting and welcoming new boss.

Simply because she herself hadn't truly understood the situation and had felt the need to interfere. To meddle. Because she could now see all too clearly that was what she'd been doing from the moment her hand reached out for the ringing phone.

'It was Theo calling,' she said, 'wanting to see how you were.'

'Was he indeed?' Ruth said with a wry smile. 'And I'm sure it had nothing to do with wanting to find out everything about you and whether in fact you're going to fleece us for our life's savings and flog off the family silver?'

'No, he – I mean, he was checking that . . .' her words petered out as she reran the conversation in her head. 'It must be hard for him,' she said in the end, wanting to give this man the benefit of the doubt, if only because Ruth and Henry so clearly adored him. Even putting aside their discomfort at his arm's length interference in their lives.

'It is,' Ruth said. 'But then you have to remember, Jamie, that he's a grown man and he chose to absent himself – not just from our lives here, but from the whole bloody continent.' She shook her head. 'It's not just Theo, darling girl. There's a whole generation of adult children who aren't prepared to look after their ageing parents; rightly or wrongly, they just don't want to do it themselves. But, dear lord, do they bitterly resent the closeness and the access of those that do.'

She gave Jamie's arm a gentle squeeze. 'At my age, Jamie, life is in the little moments, the everyday experiences and small surprises like the ones we share together, here. It's not about the big trips, or the visits, or the high days and holidays. And Theo knows that. Deep down. He knows he's only seeing half the picture.'

'Well, maybe it will reassure him when we meet?' Jamie said. 'And he can see that Bo and I aren't part of some elaborate confidence trick?'

'Maybe,' Ruth nodded. 'But don't hold your breath, Jamie. Theo actually finds comfort in playing out the worst-case scenario. He has no time for following his feelings or trusting his instincts, the way Henry and I like to live. He prefers to believe in statistics that never lie, apparently.' She shook her head again. 'That boy and his numbers.'

Jamie nodded, trying to imagine what that would be like. To be so afraid of feeling, that a cascade of impenetrable numbers was preferable.

And then she thought of Bo and his sketchbook, and how overwhelming life could be for him at times; the security he found in the sweep of his pencil, the insights of his creative mind playing out safely on the page.

'He only worries because he loves you,' Jamie said after a moment. 'And for what it's worth, Ruth, I'm sorry I didn't take your wishes into account when I answered the phone.'

'Look, Jamie,' Ruth said, leaning back against the cast-iron radiator in the hall and easing off her gardening gloves, 'over the years Henry and I have found that dealing with Theo is a bit like dealing with the press. You have to stay on message and limit the detail. He's just too far away to bother with the day-to-day mundanities, and for all his bluster, we both know his fragilities. Logic might dictate that having you here would give him peace of mind, but that's just not how his brain works. And so we speak, at a prearranged time, on the Zooms so he can see our faces, rather than feed his insecurities every time he picks up the phone.' She shrugged. 'It may seem callous, but it's for the best. Okay?'

Jamie nodded. For all her concerns about Ruth these last few days, there was no doubt that when it came to Theo at least, she clearly knew her own mind.

Chapter 31

'Oh no, Jamie, you don't have to worry about sorting out anything in there. Or cleaning. Organised chaos is my system of choice.' Henry slipped past her, surprisingly fleet of foot and pulled his study door closed abruptly later that day. Yet not quite fast enough to eclipse the anarchy of his alleged system.

Jamie breathed out slowly, reminding herself that this was not *her* study, or *her* home. She could return to the sanctuary of the annexe at any time, to the soothing order of her shelves and cupboards and the relative calm of life with Bo, who thankfully was equally evangelical about having everything in its place.

But of course, it was so much easier for her and Bo to streamline their lives when they carried so little, their baggage purely emotional.

For Ruth and Henry, these four walls contained decades of memorabilia, some of which would presumably mean nothing to a casual observer like herself, yet surely carried a wealth of hidden emotion.

Not to be organised, streamlined or denigrated by her objective assessment of worth at least.

Presumably also the reason that Gemma's bedroom door had been locked shortly after her arrival.

Or so she assumed.

She couldn't deny that taking charge of The Old School House and re-establishing some semblance of order had been incredibly rewarding this past week – room by room, working her way through the house and priding herself on finding clever ways to make everything just a bit easier for Ruth and Henry. Just a bit more accessible, without ever invoking the dreaded notion of *accessibility* which, it turned out, was guaranteed to provoke their immediate ire.

It was the objectivity, of course, which made the transformations so much easier.

Presumably that same objectivity that made Henry wary of letting her into his domain.

'It must be time for elevenses, anyway,' Henry said, with a nod towards the kitchen.

'Why not,' Jamie said, stepping back and noticing his body relax, relief obvious on his face. 'How do you feel about hot cross buns?'

Willow was curled up in the kitchen window seat with a magazine when they walked in and, once again, Jamie felt that irrational twinge of annoyance in her presence. Her wafty ethereal presence somehow pressed Jamie's buttons. Whatever Willow's history – and clearly there were so many more layers to the story than Ruth had alluded to – Jamie still felt a knee-jerk resentment that it was Willow, and not her and Bo, who now lived in that little house with the yellow door.

Childish, possibly. Mean-spirited, perhaps.

It was not something she would ever admit to, to anyone.

And it made no rational sense to be territorial about this space – for God's sake, Willow's arrival predated her own – yet still Jamie felt disconcertingly irked that an easy conversation with Henry over hot cross buns would now – inevitably – evolve into a morning tea party.

Everything at the house was seemingly an excuse for a gathering – morning coffee, afternoon tea, bridge games, long lunches, cocktails at six and suppers that lingered into the night, conversation and laughter wafting through the annexe's open windows.

Never an empty room.

It was no easy adjustment from the small world that she and Bo had inhabited these last few years. And in many ways, if she were honest with herself at least, their cocoon had been so much simpler at times. Without the draining need to be interesting or entertaining, she had felt some of her old sense of self return. Without the pull of invitations, necessitating juggling of childcare, wardrobe and work, she'd been able to fully breathe. To relax, rather than startle at an unexpected phone call.

But she couldn't deny there were days, weeks possibly, when she'd felt lonely.

Alone.

Waiting for Bo to come home from school just to hear the

sound of his voice and revel in his excitement and joie de vivre. She breathed out slowly and managed a friendly smile as she filled the kettle, reminding herself of Willow's kindness to Kath and the curiously emotional cost it seemed to have taken Willow to do it. 'Fancy a cuppa with us, Willow? We're having buns too.'

Willow glanced up from her magazine. 'Buns? Yes, please.' Quietly reading, her slender arms wrapped snugly around herself and the sun catching on her blonde hair, it was hard to reconcile the gentle ease of this young woman with the tightly wound, tech genius who had given Kath such peace of mind last night.

'What do think about layering some *Euonymus* in the herbaceous borders along the south side, Henry?' Willow asked, turning the magazine she was reading so that they could all see the coloured array of shrubbery. 'If you timed it right, you could have colour all year. See—' her whole face glowed with enthusiasm, 'this one is a beautiful rhus. You could use it in flower arrangements and whatnot too. And if you had more dahlias and alyssum in the borders too, then you would have three tiers of planting.' She caught her breath. 'Never a dull moment.'

'Sounds wonderful,' Henry said simply. 'When can you start?'

Willow laughed. 'Oh Henry, you are funny.' She unfurled, quite literally, long limbs and floating linen. 'Shall I get toasting?'

Jamie nodded, passing her the chopping board of sliced

buns and then hesitating. 'Are Ruth and Chris about as well?' Acceptance being the first step and all that.

Henry nodded. 'I'd pop another few in if I were you. And, Willow, I'm not joking – let's jump in the Volvo and hit the garden centre. I'd be over the moon if you took on those bloody borders for me. Chris has been fighting a losing battle with them for months and he's this close to bringing in a rotavator. So, no time to lose really.'

Willow looked aghast. 'He can't do that – there's decades of planting in those borders!' She grabbed the notebook and pen that Jamie had placed beside the phone and began scribbling a list in earnest, almost visibly jolted by the thought of Chris desecrating the wide swathes of planting that circumnavigated the walled garden.

Henry looked terribly pleased with himself and gave Jamie a knowing wink, despite the fact that Jamie had somehow missed exactly what they were supposedly in cahoots about.

Was he trying to fix Willow up with Chris? Somehow, she couldn't quite see the slightly chubby, chatty grafter being the perfect match for this ballerina-like girl. Even if they did apparently both share an interest in Henry's greenery.

Speak of the devil and Chris came lumbering into the kitchen, reversing quickly to remove his filthy boots when he spotted Jamie. 'Sorry,' he mumbled.

'Dear God, it's cold out there and it's supposed to be spring,' he moaned, warming his hands on the massive teapot and leaving muddy fingerprints on the canary yellow china.

He rubbed at them with his sleeve and only succeeded in spreading the muddy marks around further.

Henry shook his head. 'Well you've got the wrong clothes on, haven't you. It's hardly T-shirt and shorts weather, is it?' He eyed up Chris's broad shoulders. 'And I'll wager my coats won't do the trick, will they?'

Chris ladled three sugars into his cup of tea and demolished a hot cross bun in two bites.

'Did you not want jam on that?' Willow asked, bemused, as she sipped at her tea delicately.

Jamie turned away to hide her grin; Henry was way off base on this one. She refilled the kettle, accepting that they were getting nothing done for the next half-hour. Acceptance made it easier to breathe through the constant comings and goings. She'd tried telling herself they were finite bubbles throughout her new working day, but all too often they merged together, as various lost souls came and went from this kitchen. Seeking out Ruth and Henry's compassion, welcome and wisdom.

She glanced at the clock, allowing the conversation to billow around her – she would tackle the dining room next, she decided, as a little something to look forward to.

She hadn't entirely realised that she'd spoken aloud until Chris chortled beside her. 'Each to his own, eh?'

Henry frowned. 'You can't tackle the dresser in the dining room though, Jamie, until I've had someone out to mend it. Some of the shelves are a bit iffy – that's why we stack the best china on the table.'

'And also why you can't actually eat at the table,' Jamie said gently. 'Do you want me to phone around for some quotes?'

'Or maybe Chris could take a look?' Henry said. 'He might welcome the warmth today? What do you think – you're a details man, aren't you, Chris?'

Chris nodded agreeably. 'Better with a tape measure than a lawn mower, if I'm honest, Mr W.' He downed his tea, nabbed another bun and wombled off into the dining room.

'There we are – problem solved,' said Henry happily. 'He's quite the dark horse, our Chris. Got caught up in the whole self-employed debacle, but he used to run his own security firm. Alarms and the like.' Henry frowned. 'Never got the impression he enjoyed it much though.'

Willow shook her head, unexpectedly irritated. 'Well, it's not as though gardening is exactly his calling either, is it?' she muttered quietly.

Henry turned back to the platter of buns and took an age selecting one, offering Jamie another of his quiet gentle smiles that she had yet to fully understand.

'I'll need to pop to the shops,' Chris announced, striding back into the kitchen with a new-found purpose, scrolling his tape measure closed with a practised flick. 'You need new brackets for sure. And some staining and wood glue.'

'Brilliant,' said Henry, reaching into his trouser pocket and tossing him the keys to the Volvo workhorse on the drive. 'Can you swing by the garden centre and help Willow with some heavy lifting too. She's after some shrubbery.'

As the two of them left a few minutes later, somewhat

railroaded into their expedition, Henry sat back and poured himself another cup of tea.

'For all your matchmaking,' Jamie said, stacking the dishwasher, 'they're not a good fit, you know.'

Henry looked at her with wide, innocent eyes. 'And what makes you say that?'

Jamie shook her head. 'They just don't seem like a couple.'

'Oh ...' Henry put down his cup and stood up. 'Well, you're right there. But then, who said I was trying to match them with each other?'

He left the room, murmuring his thanks for the elevenses and disappearing into his study before Jamie could quiz him further.

Chapter 32

Jamie fidgeted at the school gates, her mind running on to the list of tasks she had hoped to achieve. Time at The Old School House ran to its own surreal clock, where nobody seemed to work to any goals or deadlines – just happy to keep on keeping on.

Or perhaps that was just Ruth and Henry?

Perhaps the sherry and corduroy quotient had been misleading, and she'd inadvertently wandered into a hippy-dippy commune set-up?

'Hi.' Bo strode towards her across the playground, his tired face puckered in frustration. Jamie barely had time to change gear before Bo was on his way, expecting her to fall into step beside him.

Yet another bad day, apparently.

'Can I—' she began.

'Just leave it,' he said tersely, cutting her off. To anyone who knew him, it was obvious that he was barely holding the tears at bay, and the last thing she knew he would want was to lose that fragile thread in sight of the school gate.

Jamie simply picked up her pace.

'Ms Matson? Ms Matson!' She could hear the headmaster's voice calling after her, as they left the school grounds, but when she glanced at Bo, he gave a tight, definitive shake of the head.

No doubt there would be a phone call later.

Feigning deafness, they turned the corner and Jamie found that her own pulse was racing, ratcheted up as her imagination attempted to fill in all the blanks.

'Bo – do I need to go back and talk to Mr Davies?'

Bo blinked and the angry young man beside her morphed into the small boy he once was – still was – in so many ways. His face collapsed as the tears began to flow and his words were jerky and incomprehensible among the sobs. She could do nothing but fold him into her arms and wait for the storm to pass, praying that none of his schoolmates would choose this route home.

'I . . .' He hiccupped through another volley of sobs. 'Mrs Taylor was trying to help but . . .'

Jamie shepherded him along the road and onto the overgrown footpath that looped back towards their new home. A longer walk this way, for sure, but quieter and a timely opportunity for Bo to catch his breath.

The quiet cocoon of 'home' no longer quite so quiet.

Fronds of green leaves hung over the path, and within only a few yards, it was almost impossible to believe they were still in the heart of town. This little network of footpaths crisscrossing behind the scenes, behind the houses, out of sight and out of mind. Thankfully.

Bo kicked at the tufts of dying daffodils with an unusual ferocity. Whereas normally he would be sketching them, today he seemed bent on destruction.

But until he chose to share – which, these days, was no longer a given – Jamie felt helpless. Distraction her only means.

'So, it turns out that Ruth really likes catalogues. I was tidying up today and you'll never guess what I found?'

She paused, waiting to see if she'd piqued his interest.

Another kick at the dying narcissi, yellowing into mustard corpses.

'Anyway, right now, waiting for us at home is the new IKEA book, a Lakeland storage guide and a bumper stationery catalogue. I thought we could have hot chocolate and marshmallows and dig in for a bit.'

Bringing out the heavy artillery – rationed for days of intense stress and maximum friction. And, if she were honest, it wasn't just Bo who benefitted from this particular routine. There was something infinitely soothing about flicking through the pages, stepping out of reality and into an ordered world of co-ordination and design.

A little like the interiors magazines that Bo admired so much.

Only for real life.

Or a version of it, at least.

Bo looked up, eyes red and sore. 'The *very* new IKEA one?'

Jamie simply nodded and squeezed his hand gently. Kept on walking.

'We did a project about nutrition today. Sort of. In art class, really, so we had to draw our weekly shop.' A deep breath, catching slightly, and Jamie instinctively felt in her pocket for his spare inhaler. 'And I couldn't remember, not really, what we used to choose. You know, before.'

Jamie nodded, understanding dawning.

'So,' Bo continued, 'I just drew what we had this week and then Robbie Clarke started shouting his mouth off about me living like a refugee – and his drawing was rubbish, but it was all avocadoes and steak and that quin-lola stuff.'

'Could you just—'

Bo rounded on her. 'Do *not* just say ignore him! You have no idea what it's like. What *they're* like!' His fists were curled tightly, knuckles white; her gentle little boy pushed into fury. 'And then Mr Davies decided to help by saying not everyone could afford the same and they should be considerate – so when he left, they all started calling me Oliver Twist. For someone who works with kids, he's bloody clueless too.'

'Bo!'

Bo had the grace to look apologetic. 'Adults have no idea, though, Mum. Not really. By lunchtime there was a meme on the Snapchat with my face on it – you know, the "Please sir, I want some more" picture? So that's everywhere now.'

Jamie felt winded. He was absolutely right, of course. Being a teenager, or even this ghastly cohort of 'preteen', was a whole different ballpark once the internet got involved.

Bo kicked angrily at another cluster of dying flowers, and Jamie was kind of relieved to see that at least he avoided the living ones.

'That's not even the worst part,' he seethed. 'Mrs

Grant – the know-it-all art teacher? She only went and drew on *my drawing*!' He yelled the last two words angrily. 'To show me how to do better. She actually *drew* on my picture, Mum. Like, with a pen and everything!'

The tears were back now, racking through his slight body and Jamie couldn't help but think that he was right – for people who worked with kids every day, they were, in fact, bloody clueless.

There was no doubting that her son's artistic gift was somewhat precocious and likewise Jamie knew that some-times that fact alone irked those who considered themselves to be talented. Art teachers in particular, it seemed, based on their last parents' evening. But to deface his work?

Had they *met* Bo? Did they have any understanding of how he took ownership of each and every creation so completely and utterly?

And as for throwing him into the spotlight about his choice of food to represent?

She stopped suddenly, half tempted to go back and give them a piece of her mind.

'It's not worth it,' Bo said astutely, trudging onwards with-out her. 'If anything, it'll only make things worse.'

'Well,' Jamie breathed, her brain scrambling to find some silver lining, 'at least, you're heading home to steak pie and lashings of mashed potato – Robbie Clark can keep his manky quinoa salad, I reckon, don't you?' She gave him a smile, a conspiratorial us-against-the-world, two-fingers-up moment of solidarity.

He nodded, thought for a moment and then grinned. 'And at least I'll be actually doing art when I'm a grown-up, Mum, won't I? Not trying to teach it to a roomful of kids who just don't care?' He paused, frowned. 'But somehow that makes it worse actually – because I do care; she just didn't care about me.'

Crunching tiredly up the driveway half an hour later, Jamie and Bo had fallen into easy conversation, trying to guess what his classmates might be when they were grown-ups, and ditto what some of his teachers had been like when they were ten.

Distraction, as so often, the cure for many ills.

It had been highly illuminating and, as always, Jamie had no doubt that her son's imagination would carry him far, thinking outside the box, in whatever his chosen profession. Once he was allowed free rein, and distinction became something to be celebrated rather than crushed.

Henry was standing beside the Volvo and waved in greeting, his eyes narrowing as he seemed to read the reality of Bo's day in a heartbeat. 'Just the lad I've been waiting for. Jamie, could you spare him for half an hour? I'm sorting out the shed and I've found half a ton of paints. Thought I might spruce up the old girl and bring a bit of colour to proceedings.'

Bo turned to his mum, clearly torn between his beloved catalogues and the thought of what a 'ton of paint' might look like.

Jamie nodded. 'Uniform off first. And we can have hot chocolate and catalogues at bedtime. How does that sound?'

But Bo was gone, shot into the annexe, tugging off his jumper as he ran.

'Bad day?' Henry asked.

'Sounds like it,' Jamie replied. 'And I've yet to work out whether it's the staff or the kids who are making things hardest for him.'

'He's a sweet boy, Jamie. And I know he finds it harder than most, but he's a credit to you. He'll find life so much easier once he finds his tribe.' He nodded, almost to himself really. 'He just has to get through this bit, find the joy where he can and in whatever form that takes. Even if it's painting the shed with a geriatric old sod like me.' He smiled. 'Now, where do you stand on him getting covered head to toe, because I thought some paint-slinging might be quite cathartic?'

Jamie blinked hard. Shocked, but also pleasantly surprised that Henry seemed to recognise her son's needs so astutely. She'd been bracing herself, for a while now, for the next stage of Bo's life, knowing that she would need to be on call, yet willing to be ignored, after school each day. Indispensable, still, yet equally superfluous to whatever teenage boys found to fill their time.

Ruth appeared in the front doorway, out of breath and waving two vast plastic ponchos. 'Found them! I knew they were here somewhere.' She thrust one of the ponchos into Jamie's hands, the faded Niagara Falls logo now evident on the front. 'That should do the trick.'

She leaned into Jamie's side, dropping her voice. 'Sometimes it's just easier to go along with Henry's plans, once he gets an idea in his head. Leave him to it and hope for the best.' She briefly clasped Jamie's hand, smiling. 'And, to be fair, some of them are very good ideas. Very good indeed.'

Chapter 33

'He still misses teaching sometimes, I think,' Ruth said, as she and Jamie enjoyed a quiet moment on the terrace, nursing a cup of tea. Henry and Bo were now tinkering in the greenhouse, their voices contented murmurs against the evening birdsong. Supper could wait.

Ruth watched them intently, running the single pearl up and down its fine gold chain around her neck. 'I think he misses Theo too.'

Jamie nodded, waiting in the half-light. There was so much about their family that she didn't know, couldn't interpret from the many, many photos around the house. It seemed they were willing to open up their home, but their history remained a closed book to her. Perhaps rightly so . . .

And yet, Jamie couldn't help but feel she might understand their needs a little more if only she knew what motivated some of their somewhat unpredictable decisions and choices.

For all their bohemian charm and welcome, there was a rod of steel stubbornness in both Ruth and Henry that Jamie had yet to find a way to overcome. Bo had come the closest, 'pottering' about after school every day with Henry in the garden. Fixing whatever needed attention, or simply embarking on eccentric projects with no perceivable goal in mind, other than whiling away an hour or two.

It seemed to be exactly what Bo needed – decompression.

Often, they would work in silence, side by side, heads bowed low over whatever scheme they had cooked up that day. Bo's pleas for 'just a bit longer' always winning the day. Henry's patience knowing no bounds, even on the days that Bo was frustrated or angry.

She hadn't fully appreciated, until now, that Henry might be getting just as much out of the arrangement.

Volleys of laughter from the greenhouse echoed around the walled garden and, in that moment, Jamie felt as though their own small oasis was a step out of time with the rest of the world.

The pearl stilled.

Whatever lay outside the vast redbrick walls that so bothered Ruth and Henry, the future that so intimidated Jamie herself – it all felt somehow 'other' on a night like tonight.

They were here, they were safe, and nobody was going to bed hungry.

To ask for anything more, to reach for anything more, felt like avarice of the most insidious kind. And yet still, the insistent voice in Jamie's head that wanted more for herself, for her son, refused to be quieted.

She wanted to give him a life that was his, rather than dependent on the kindness and goodwill of others.

She wanted him to have what she herself so longed for – independence.

'It's never long enough, you know, Jamie.' Ruth's soft voice broke into her thoughts. 'Having them as your own, having them in your life every day. Even the days that seemed to go on forever, when you wished for bedtime, longed for a moment to yourself. Begrudged even, that constant call on your energy, your body, your time . . .' She slid the pearl back and forth in a steady rhythm. 'And then they're gone. And you long for just one more of those days – or even an hour . . .'

She swallowed hard and turned to Jamie, eyes bright and filled with unshed tears.

'We never talk about Gemma, you know. But everything we do is in her memory.' She waved a hand back towards the house behind them. 'It was all I could do to have her photos around, for years afterwards.'

Jamie reached out her hand, offering comfort, but Ruth shook her head.

'Don't be too nice to me, Jamie. It's more than I deserve.' She stood up and walked inside, Jamie hesitating before following her into the sitting room. 'All the things we do now, with our little trust, and trying to help out – you know, find the people who need a bit of a boost back on track more than most? It's all too little too late for my own family.

'Theo's in the States and he tells me he's happy there. Can't face coming home, though. And Gemma . . .' She picked up the framed photograph from the centre of the mantelpiece,

Theo's dark skin in direct contrast to the pale lucidity of his sister's. 'It didn't seem to matter what we did for Gemma, we couldn't overwrite her history.'

She replaced the photograph reverently. 'So, we do what we can to keep going. And we try to do it without regrets – I certainly don't regret adopting either of them, Jamie. Being their mother was the greatest gift of my life. But losing Gemma? Knowing how much pain she must have been in to make an irrevocable decision like that?

'I'm not sure any of us will ever get over that, Jamie, and it was on my watch. I wasn't there to reassure her, or to change her mind when it mattered most. I was her parent, but I didn't see how much she was struggling. And she didn't tell me. Didn't trust me enough.' She finally stepped closer and took Jamie's outstretched hand, acknowledging her sympathy with a gentle nod.

'And so, we do what we can in her memory because her twenty short years on this planet left their mark, whether she would have believed that or not. I'm not sure the twisted logic in her mind would ever have allowed her to know how much she was adored. Our gorgeous girl, lost to us, but somehow still here, Jamie, influencing every choice we make and everything we do.'

'And Theo?' Jamie ventured, seeing the reality behind life at The Old School House more clearly for the first time, just a small glimpse into Ruth and Henry's motivation for gathering lost souls around them and setting them back on their feet. Understanding their need to reach out, to people like her, to Willow, to Chris – and who knew how many others over the years. A band-aid for their own grief? Or perhaps just two thoroughly decent and loving people, finding comfort in diverting the possibility of such a tragic outcome for anyone else.

'Does Theo understand that you're still hurting?' Jamie asked tentatively, her heart breaking for this wonderful woman, and the loss she had endured. How could losing a child not shatter your whole life, along with your heart? Jamie felt a deeper respect for the welcoming chaos of Ruth's kitchen; respite and renewal and simple acceptance on tap. No small achievement in the face of such tragedy.

Ruth nodded. 'Theo's still hurting too, though, Jamie. All these years later, it's still fundamentally changed who we are to each other. And this place . . .' she shrugged. 'He doesn't want to be here with the memories, so he can't understand why we don't want to leave. Why we can't bear to leave them behind, but would rather make sure our experiences don't go to waste, if that makes sense.' She sighed. 'When it comes to Theo these days, sometimes it's just easier to avoid the conversation.'

Jamie hesitated, wondering in that moment why it was always so much easier to give advice to other people than to take it oneself. Confrontation wasn't always bad if you were standing up for your rights and your beliefs – intellectually, she knew that. But instinctively she still veered away, every time, even to her own detriment.

But again, who was she to judge?

'Maybe I can help?' she offered softly. 'I'll field your phone calls, if you field mine?'

'You're a sweet girl, Jamie, but there's no harm in letting the answerphone do the heavy lifting.'

Jamie disagreed; there was no doubt that ignoring the ringing phone brought stress into the house, so why not simply deal with whomever was trying so insistently to get their attention?

And then she realised the hypocrisy of what she was thinking – Ruth's loss certainly made her own struggles pale by comparison and yet the denial and avoidance they both employed to get through each day bore striking parallels.

It was hardly as though Jamie had stood up to fight for what was owed to her – from Nick Harrison, or from Kieran Jones. She'd been licking her wounds here instead, rather than rallying to reclaim her lost wages, her lost deposit. It was galling to realise how much she'd given away just to avoid further confrontation.

Even so, either way, evasion and procrastination had been so much easier than facing the uncomfortable truths; hypocrisy at its finest.

And so, Jamie said nothing more, even as she wrapped her arms around her diminutive boss, whose soft, clean hair was scented with fresh tomatoes and basil from the salad she'd been preparing. Who folded into her embrace with a tremulous sigh and, it seemed, a sense of relief at having shared her burden.

'I'm here to help,' Jamie murmured, her gaze caught on

the image of Ruth and Henry, two small children wrapped around them like monkeys, their faces mirrors of laughter and belonging. Understanding just a little bit more why she was here.

Chapter 34

'Mum! Mu-um!' Bo's voice was high-pitched and tremulous, calling from the garden, a hiccup of panic summoning Jamie instantly back out to the terrace.

Bo held out his hand in front of him, a look of stunned amazement on his face, even as the shockingly bright red blood dripped down his wrist. Jamie swallowed the instant wave of nausea that hit at the sight of it, at the amount of it, releasing her instinctive grip on the inhaler in her pocket.

Not one of those emergencies.

'I'm so sorry, Jamie,' Henry said, hobbling across the lawn to catch up with Bo. 'It just slipped. A complete accident, but I think he might need stitches.'

Jamie breathed out slowly, soothing her son and lifting his hand above his heart on autopilot. 'Oh Bobo – let's have a look then.'

The puncture wound was deep. Neat and clean but still rather prolific and the heavy iron smell filled Jamie's nostrils and made her stomach roil.

Bo, on the other hand, seemed fascinated, leaning in to

get a closer look. A novelty perhaps to be heading for A&E with his lungs full of air and all of his senses?

Ruth came out onto the terrace with a ten-pound note and the car keys for the Volvo. 'Some blighter has spent all my parking change, but there's usually a few coins in the glovebox.' She passed Jamie the keys and Bo the tenner. 'Get yourself a hot cup of tea while you wait, darling boy. You okay to drive him in, Jamie – I think I'd better take care of this one here.'

Henry was pale, sweaty from his dash across the lawn and clearly guilt-stricken. 'A complete accident,' he kept saying, eyes fixed on Bo's oozing hand.

'I was stabbing a hole with an awl and I missed,' Bo explained, looking sheepish for a moment. 'I was supposed to wait . . .'

Henry shook his head. 'Not your fault.'

Well, it sounded a little bit like Bo's fault, from where Jamie was standing. And maybe, just maybe, a little bit Henry's fault too for giving the boy an awl, for God's sake, to muck about with in the first place. More backgammon, she decided, less weaponry.

Driving down the High Street, one eye on the speedometer, Jamie pressed her foot down hard on the accelerator.

While Bo had been chattering away happily beside her, she hadn't actually been too worried.

Boys would be boys.

Or so everyone had told her – although she'd yet to

experience the penknife injuries, bruises from fencing with branches or black eyes from scuffles on the rugby pitch with Bo.

But now he was quiet, a faint but recognisable drag with each breath hitching in his chest. Two puffs on the inhaler, Jamie holding her own breath as she drove, as always vesting so much hope in that small blue canister.

The shock setting in now, enough to catch his breathing in that familiar cycle.

'Bo? We're nearly there, sweetheart. And I think this is definitely one of those times we can drive right to the door, don't you? Like in the movies?' Her running commentary of events was normally reserved for the jump seat in the back of an ambulance, rather than negotiating her way round a one-way system in Friday traffic.

'I'm okay,' Bo said quietly. 'No need for drama. I was just thinking about Henry.'

Jamie took the roundabout rather too quickly, scaring herself, both of them leaning into the curve. 'Henry?'

Bo nodded, a whistling exhalation, 'I think he's lonely, Mum. I mean, it's nice that he wants to spend time with me, but I think he misses his boy.' He paused. 'Did you know they have a son who lives in America? Their daughter died,' he said, quite matter-of-factly, 'so I think it's worse that he's so far away. Don't you? Like they're both gone?'

Her son. Never missing a trick.

They pulled into the car park at the hospital and Jamie wondered once more at how deeply her boy seemed to feel everything. Not just physically, but emotionally he was a sponge, taking on everyone's feelings.

'I think that right now, we should concentrate on you, young man, and we can work out what to do about Henry later, okay?' The temptation to dash across the car park as the cloth wrapped around Bo's hand darkened was hard to ignore, but Jamie made sure they walked slowly, steadily.

Pushing open the door, she came face to face with Kath, her exhausted expression lighting up at the sight of a friendly face. Her hair was tousled and there was no doubt that this had not been an easy shift so far.

'Here he is,' Kath announced to the doctor beside her, 'my favourite patient.' She knelt down beside Bo. 'Just you go and grab yourself a seat, young man, and we'll get you set up in a mo, okay?'

She shook her head with a reassuring smile as she stood. 'Honestly, Jamie. This does not qualify as a Friday night out. We've talked about this.' She turned to the doctor, his hair buzzed into an army cut that could only serve to highlight his cheekbones and intense grey eyes. 'Luke? This is my friend Jamie and her lad over there is Bo – looks like suture kit and a nebuliser. Can I crack on, while there's a lull?' She gestured around the half-empty waiting room.

Never normally one to endorse the notion of nepotism, Jamie's moral standing took a blow every time they came to A&E – she would never turn down a little queue-jumping when it came to Bo's health. Even as she guiltily acknowledged that every parent in the room probably felt the same way.

Luke nodded. 'He'd triage on top anyway,' he said to Jamie kindly, reading the conflict on her face. 'And I'll pop by in a minute and give him a once-over. But to be honest,' he smiled at Jamie, 'you really don't want my embroidery skills.'

Kath snorted as he walked away. 'To be fair, he does have enormous hands.' She gave Jamie a nudge, 'And he's never normally so smiley with the patients. I'll give him your number, if you like.'

Jamie shook her head. 'Please don't. It took me years to get over my *Grey's Anatomy* addiction; I don't think having someone like Luke on my radar could ever end well.'

They ushered Bo into his favourite cubicle, and yes, Jamie thought to herself, it *was* weird for any ten-year-old to have a favourite cubicle in A&E, but there you go. That was their life and sometimes it was just easier to accept it, rather than question it and tie yourself in knots.

Not too bright, or too busy, or too near the large air vents in the ceiling. With the trolley tucked against a solid wall, rather than an insubstantial curtain.

Like mother, like son.

Although Jamie's habits tended more towards restaurant tables and cinema seats than NHS trolleys.

Bo nodded, comforted, even as his face took on that waxy sheen of pallor that Jamie knew all too well. 'I've got this, Jamie. Take a seat?' Kath was calmness and efficiency personified, settling Bo, dealing with his breathing even as she prepared the suture kit for his hand. The saline rinse, the steri-strips and gauze.

Jamie took her usual seat, feeling equal parts relief to have handed over his care, and impotence at being unable to help. His needs eclipsed her skills and, not for the first time, Jamie wondered if she should have medical training just to be his mum. Not for the career that Kath had chosen, driven by altruism and compassion, but just to get through the week.

'We're good,' said Kath calmly, as much to reassure Jamie as Bo. 'And I'm sorry to say, Bo, that you probably won't even have a cracking scar to show for your troubles.'

Kath glanced over her shoulder at Jamie, as she secured the sterile gauze over her incredibly neat handiwork. 'Will you pass on my thanks to Willow, by the way. All calm on the North Sea front since she worked her magic. I owe her a bottle once I've got a few beans to spare. Although who knows when that will be – Tanya's taken my request for a pay review "under advisement" whatever the hell that means.'

Jamie shook her head. 'Then save your beans, Kath. I'll pass on your thanks and maybe just swing by when you get a moment. She's a funny gherkin, but she seems quite sweet. A bit lost maybe, but very kind.'

Kath nodded. 'If I can prize Bonnie away from her philanthropic schedule, I'll bring her along too.'

Jamie frowned. 'Surely she's charging for *some* haircuts?'

Kath nodded. 'Mostly. And doing well, I gather. Well enough not to need the food bank for a bit, so she's started volunteering there instead.' She shook her head. 'You can imagine Father Bill is over the freaking moon about the whole thing. She's another one of his success stories right there – another lamb set back on the path to righteous what-ever . . .' She waved a hand dismissively. 'I'm kind of proud and jealous at the same time, which is never a good look. But at least I still have you and Amy for company in the queue of shame, while Bonnie's photo's gone straight up on the pinboard in Bill's office. Another soul saved.'

Jamie nodded, somehow not surprised by Bonnie's decision. Deciding it was not the best time to mention the bounty in Ruth's freezer – that she and Bo might soon be opting out too.

Either way, Jamie was a long way from walking into Tesco with her own shopping basket and free choice.

Decadence indeed.

For now, she was just grateful for the hot cup of plasticky tea from the vending machine and the fact that Bo was already looking so much better.

'How're we doing in here?' Luke stepped through the cur-tains and checked Bo's chart, glancing at the readings of the Pulsox on the monitor. He sat down gently on the end of Bo's bed, looking serious. 'Now then, since you've caught your breath, young man, I think it's time we talked about this owl. Not every day we get an owl attack in A&E.' He raised one eyebrow, looking very serious. 'Could you describe this owl to me? So I can circulate an e-fit to the necessary authorities?'

Bo laughed, the sound muffled and hollow inside his mask, and shook his head.

Jamie caught Kath's eye and they both smothered a smile,

unsure whether Luke's shenanigans were for Bo's benefit or for Jamie's.

Luke drew a few quick circles on the back of Bo's notes and held out the clipboard to Bo. 'Is *this* the owl we're looking for?'

Bo shook his head and took the pen, and with scarcely a flourish, he sketched a swooping barn owl, light as its feathers, the mottled tawny and cream somehow clear despite being sharpie on white.

Luke blinked in surprise. 'Bloody hell,' he said, turning to look at Jamie fully for the first time. 'Your kid is some kind of genius, right?'

Jamie nodded. 'He likes art, what can I say? He doesn't get it from me.' She paused. 'You do know it *wasn't* an owl, right? They were doing woodwork or something . . .'

Luke nodded. 'I know, I know. But where's the fun in that?' he said, turning his full attention back to Bo.

As Luke gently and kindly gave Bo a full check-up, murmuring to Kath as they worked, Jamie sat back and watched. For a brief moment she'd felt that all-too-familiar panic, scrambling logistics in her head for the days ahead. And then she realised – there was no scramble required.

No missed shifts.

No stressful stand-offs and negotiations.

And not just because it was Friday.

But because now her job – the job that deep down she was still embarrassed to resent just very slightly, being so very different from anything her hopes and ambitions would have decreed 'acceptable' just a very short time ago, also offered her so much more than an airy annexe and a living wage.

It offered security for both of them; a safety net on the days Bo couldn't go to school. No judgement, no questioning of her priorities or commitment required.

A different kind of job satisfaction, perhaps.

Chapter 35

Jamie returned home with Bo in the early hours to find the lights blazing in the main house and Bonnie perched at the kitchen counter, reassuring Henry. The open-door policy at The Old School House now apparently extending to Jamie's friends indefinitely.

'You're back!' Henry exhaled with relief, his face pale and his hands shaky. 'I'm so, so sorry.'

'You have absolutely nothing to apologise for,' Jamie said sincerely. Bo had guiltily updated her as they sat in the hospital for hours, that he'd totally ignored Henry's warnings and set to, by himself, eager to make their project his own. Quite what that project entailed, however, remained a closely guarded secret.

'Hey, Bo. How're you feeling? I come bearing gifts.' Bonnie reached into her handbag and pulled out another jar of Father Bill's vegan hot chocolate. 'Kath texted me and said you'd been in the wars, so everyone at the—' Bonnie caught herself just in time. 'Everyone sends their love.'

'Thank you,' mouthed Jamie across the kitchen, wondering

when she might get over this ridiculous awkwardness about having needed, possibly still needing, a bit of help.

It was disingenuous at best, she thought crossly, to still carry all this mortification around with her every day, even as she gratefully accepted the kind of support she'd always shied away from. Something to consider when she'd had some more sleep, maybe?

'Ruth went to bed, I'm afraid,' Henry said. 'But she sends her love too. She's awfully cross with me for meddling, and for letting you get hurt.'

Bo frowned, scuffing his trainers against the floor. 'Shall I go and tell her it wasn't your fault?'

'Better in the morning?' Jamie suggested.

'Well, I've had three cups of coffee and some waffles, so I'm officially on the night shift now,' Bonnie laughed, patting the seat beside her. 'Come and tell me what's new, Bo. Henry seems to think you're the perfect apprentice. Gory holes and blood loss excepting.'

Bo's face lit up at the compliment. 'And the doctor at the hospital said I was a genius. Good day for being Bo.' He shrugged. 'Although I think he was just trying to get Mum to notice him, to be honest. He had nice eyes, all speckly like an egg.'

Bonnie lifted her head and stared hard at Jamie, a smile lifting the corners of her mouth. 'Is that right? All speckly, eh?'

'And bluey grey, like an egg,' Bo continued, oblivious to the mirth his comments had provoked.

'Maybe you could do one of your portraits of the doctor,

then, so your mum doesn't forget what he looked like?' Bonnie said, ever ready to stir the pot.

'The only thing I'm interested in remembering right now is the location of my pillow and my duvet,' Jamie cut in. 'Bonnie? Could you walk Bo round to the annexe and I'll be there in just a sec?'

She turned to Henry, still sitting, his hands still shaking. 'How about I make you some hot sweet tea and walk you up the stairs? I think one trip to A&E is enough for one night, don't you?' She flicked the kettle on to boil, poor Henry suddenly looking exhausted. 'You didn't need to wait up, Henry. Bo is fine. Really. And he's an old hand at the hospital run.'

Henry nodded. 'I'd forgotten, Jamie, that you need to have eyes in the back of your head when they're that age.'

Jamie nodded. 'He's easier now, if you can believe it. Into everything when he was about five. My favourite dress ended up as the star turn in one of his collages, and he made a fabulous mosaic with vitamin pills when he was eight. He's not so much a danger to himself as a magpie, really.'

'He's a good boy, though, Jamie. You can be proud of him.'

'I am,' she smiled. 'Every single day.'

'He seems happy here—' Henry began and then stopped. 'I mean, apart from tonight, he seems more comfortable in his skin, you know?'

'I think so too,' said Jamie, spooning sugar into a mug. 'I think letting off steam with you, being creative − without judgement − is doing him the world of good. And Henry? I really don't see it as meddling, whatever Ruth may have said in the heat of the moment. Bo needed somewhere like this, just to be himself and I'm really grateful to be here.'

It was the first time she'd voiced that particular sentiment aloud, and it wasn't out of politeness. Tonight, more than ever, had brought home what exactly she needed in her life right now. Dreaming and wishing aside.

With Henry in bed, just walking down the stairs in the main house felt like something from a novel. The gentle creaks of the building made it feel like a living entity, part of the family. Ruth's beloved ostrich stood sentinel by the front door, an umbrella propped against it legs, an emergency support that had the happy by-product of making the ostrich look as though it were on its daily commute.

For all its foibles, not to mention the constant chaos, The Old School House could be a surprisingly peaceful place for Jamie to be. Peaceful in every sense of the word.

Even tonight, as she'd hustled to get Bo to the hospital, taking Henry's Volvo rather than the Uber/ambulance continuum she was used to, Jamie had been aware that things were just a little easier.

Not a lot. Not a lottery win.

But a little bit easier.

Enough to allow her to catch her breath, anyway, as she navigated through the ebb and flow of worries that came with parenting alone. With parenting a child like Bo.

And wasn't that exactly what she'd longed for?

She had friends for the first time in years who had a

modicum of understanding of her life, her priorities and what exactly was keeping her awake at 3am.

And the ephemeral feeling she'd been struggling to name suddenly became clear, as she flicked the light switches in the kitchen, shutting down the house for the night.

She was no longer lonely.

For all the times she'd been surrounded by people these last few years, yet felt utterly invisible and misunderstood.

For all the times she'd reached out to old friends, only to find that the bonds they shared were friable at best.

For all the times she had longed, with all her being, to rebuild her life exactly as it was before . . .

But it had never somehow occurred to her that she herself was changed, that Bo was changed. They were forever different for having lived through their own private and personal apocalypse.

So, really, if she stopped to think about it with clear eyes, wasn't it obvious that their needs might actually have changed too?

Jamie pulled the back door closed and heard the Yale click into place.

Bo saw it.

Henry saw it.

Both of them with some second sight that intrigued her.

The ability to see what somebody needed – beyond what they *wanted* – was a special gift indeed, and Jamie felt incredibly lucky to have landed here at The Old School House. Not least so that Bo had finally found a like-minded soul to talk with, to see the world through similar eyes.

The lights were still on at the end of the drive, Willow doubtless burning the midnight oil looking for jobs to apply to, still attempting to build a career that held no interest for her beyond paying the bills.

The shafts of moonlight through the trees lit up the rows of newly bought plants, just waiting to be nestled into the loamy, dark soil. Willow's true passion was never going to be on a computer screen, when it was obvious that her real joy came from muddy fingernails, seed catalogues and planting schemes.

Just as Chris loathed the filth and the delayed gratification of gardening, it was exactly those things that lit Willow up from inside, making her eyes dance and her conversation illuminated.

Jamie smiled to herself, thinking back to Henry's comment a few days ago.

She hadn't been that far off the mark in assuming he was matchmaking; but she saw now that it was a different kind of match that he'd had in mind.

She thought of Chris walking back into the kitchen, numbers and measurements filling his head, flicking that tape measure closed with contented finesse.

Henry, again, looking beyond the obvious.

She couldn't help but wonder what he saw when he looked at her. Or was it simply the naked longing for a home in which to feel safe, in which to raise her son, that had caught his attention.

Or did he see something more in her?

Jamie pushed open the door to the annexe to find Bo and Bonnie fast asleep on the sofa, re-runs of *Friends* burbling quietly in the background.

It was no small thing for her son to trust implicitly.

And Jamie couldn't help but wonder whether, by gradually loosening the reins on her own insecurities, by letting people into her tightly curated world, she was finally, *finally*, leading by example for her son as well.

Chapter 36

It was the rain lashing against the huge windowpanes that woke Jamie the next morning, as she stretched and luxuriated in her cosy double bed for a moment, before the events of the night before crowded into her mind and propelled her from her duvet.

Fear and worry were never far from her mind, even here, cocooned away from threatening landlords, abusive bosses and the chill damp of their old flat. Some days it felt as though Jamie had simply transported her anxieties about Bo to a new location, rather than actually resolving anything. Even if that clearly wasn't the case and her boy was flourishing in this new environment. So much so that, just occasionally of late, she'd found herself relaxing for a brief moment or two, dropping the hyper-vigilance that had become so ingrained.

She let out a breath of relief, finding Bo fast asleep, curled up on the sofa with the TV remote still clasped tightly in his hand, cheeks pink and eyelashes fluttering gently with his dreams.

It was Bo's face, more than any other, that made Jamie long for the skill that came so naturally to her son: his unerring ability to capture the very essence of a person with just a few pencil strokes.

His sketch pad lay open on the coffee table in front of him, rarely out of his reach, and Jamie knelt down on the polished wooden floor, unable to resist the urge to flick through his recent sketches. It was like taking a sneaky peek inside Bo's mind; his moods and his thoughts always reflected in his art.

Just by glancing at one of Bo's portraits, you could see how he felt about the person. How he saw them in the world – warts and all. It could, at times, be a very humbling experience.

She quietly settled back on her heels and turned the pages one by one.

Bonnie – her hair springing out in tight curls, her burnished skin glowing, even in black and white. The light in her eyes sparkling with tender affection.

Willow – hunched crossly over her laptop in the kitchen, a swirling pit of coffee steaming angrily beside her. And then Willow again, on her knees, planting the new shrubs, her whole posture changed – a study in quiet contentment.

And Amy – with her lopsided smile, as she made one of her perceptive quips that were always just a touch too close to the bone.

Jamie flicked on through the sketchbook: Henry, Ruth, even Kath, had been immortalised on these pages. Their tiredness, their kindness, their open affection for her son were all captured in the lines and shading of his work.

She glanced at her sleeping child. Knowing that, for all

the challenges his unique little brain threw into his life, his perspective was a talent not to be ignored. And, as much as she shied away from focusing on his differences, there was no doubt that the empathy and kindness he showed to those he loved was also a rare gift in a young boy.

Rarity.

Perspective.

Gifted.

Better labels surely than the ones that were all too often applied to her gorgeous son?

She turned the page and caught her breath. For the image there was so life-like in its energy, she was taken aback.

Robbie Clarke – his face contorted in rage and judgement. Lip curled, nostrils flared. Hatred in every pore.

Was this the image that confronted Bo every day at school?

No wonder he was struggling, becoming more and more withdrawn about his day, finding respite in the creative non-sense with Henry every evening.

The temptation to tear the sketch from its bindings and march into Andrew Davies's school office on Monday was overwhelming, but Jamie stilled her hand as she looked more closely at the picture.

For what she had first seen as rage might equally be fear.

What she had taken to be judgement might yet be isolation.

How did Bo do this? How did he see beyond the obvious in a way that eluded Jamie so completely?

She closed the sketch book quietly, confused by the

emotions that assailed her and determined to find out more about Robbie Clarke's home life before she leapt to judgement. Was it possible that the rift between Bo and this boy had more to do with what they had in common than what separated them? Was that in itself enough to frighten Robbie into this harassment of her son?

Jamie glanced over at the window as a volley of rain was blown against the glass and could only hope that Bonnie had made it home before the worst of the downpour began. The hurriedly scribbled note on the coffee table that she was heading to the food bank to pack parcels before opening the kiosk reinforced Bo's opinion that Bonnie was indeed one of the good ones.

Even though, had anyone asked Jamie, she would have been forced to pause, to carefully phrase her suspicions that Bonnie was driven by more than altruism. She seemed driven by an energy that Jamie couldn't quite name, yet still somehow identified with. The very notion of stopping, staying still and actually being in the moment with her thoughts, was enough to drive Jamie to action every single day.

Jamie knew deep down, of course, what it was that her own mind was trying to avoid.

She couldn't help but wonder if Bonnie did too.

Summoned to Saturday brunch in the kitchen with Ruth and Henry, Jamie was astonished to see the feast that was laid out: scotch pancakes and bacon, a vast sticky bottle of maple syrup, not to mention freshly squeezed orange juice.

Bo's eyes widened in appreciation.

It was a far cry from their usual Saturday morning queuing for provisions.

'Come on, come on, tuck in,' Henry urged, incongruous in his wife's floral apron, waving a spatula as another batch of pancakes cooked on the stove. Flour everywhere.

'If a man can't appease his guilt with a decent brunch, then all is lost, am I right?' Henry said with a hopeful smile.

Bo laughed, glancing down at the sterile dressing on his hand. 'So you mean, I can skip PE *and* get pancakes?'

Jamie just shook her head. 'I thought we agreed last night, Henry? No guilt required.'

Ruth put down her teacup with a gentle clatter. 'We've all tried telling him, Jamie . . .'

Chris emerged from the dining room, his hair sprouting in eight different directions and his clothes covered in wood shavings. 'Didn't you get the memo? Henry reserves the right to overthink everything.' He adjusted the weighty toolbelt that circled his hips and grinned. 'And we love him for it, because it saves us the bother.'

He clapped a calloused hand on Henry's shoulder. 'Come and have a look before it's too late to make any changes.'

They both left the room, Chris whistling a jaunty refrain, and Bo turned to Jamie with ill-concealed impatience. 'Can I start?' His morning hunger still that of a ravenous child.

'Of course you can,' said Ruth with an indulgent smile, pouring him a large glass of orange juice and filling a plate for him.

'Are you just being polite,' Ruth dropped her voice so that Bo couldn't hear, deeply engrossed as he was in arranging his pancakes into a perfect stack, 'or are you really not cross about last night?' She held out a hand to stop Jamie interrupting. 'I mean, I wouldn't blame you if you were – I would just hate to see you leave us so soon.'

Jamie caught hold of Ruth's hand, shocked for a second by how cold it was. 'Leave you? Of course not. And, Ruth, honestly? Accidents happen, especially with ten-year-old boys. I think it's the constant curiosity.' She poured herself a cup of coffee, at ease in this kitchen in a way that would have shocked her only a month ago.

'Bo loves spending time with Henry – it's wonderful for him to let off steam after a whole day of swallowing his every thought and impulse at school. And knowing that Henry seems to understand where Bo's coming from, in a way that I struggle with sometimes . . .'

Jamie smiled reassuringly. 'It's been pretty amazing for him, Ruth. Honestly.'

And then she thought of the sketchbook again. The angry contorted faces of school and the contentment and ease of Henry in the greenhouse wearing his battered straw hat.

She had to trust in Bo's opinion.

Ruth nodded, grateful it seemed for the reassurance. 'Well, for what it's worth, you and Bo being here has given Henry a whole new lease of life. And it's so tricky, isn't it? I mean, for anyone on the spectrum to find a like-minded soul who understands. Although, I do confess I envy Bo's generation sometimes. So much less stigma, I think. So much more support.' She sipped her tea again. Calmer. Reassured.

But Jamie felt the words jar against her reality. 'I'm sorry, Ruth. I think you may have misread things a bit. Bo's a whizz with a paintbrush, I'll grant you. And he takes a creative view of the world, but—'

Ruth's face coloured immediately. 'I'm so sorry, Jamie. I certainly didn't mean to overstep. Obviously, with Henry, we've known for years and for some reason I just ... Well, there's no excuse is there, for jumping to conclusions. Bo is a wonderful, creative little boy and that's all there is to it.' Ruth's flustered apology may have been heartfelt, but Jamie could tell that she was still unconvinced.

And to think that Henry, with his gentle humour and incredible empathy, might yet be considered autistic.

Call it denial, call it confusion – but none of it sat right with Jamie.

Because, as always, every scrap of information Jamie had ever scrutinised online over the years flashed through her mind, every book, every movie; a constant portrayal of uncontrolled impulses and difficulty reading emotions, lack of eye-contact and words.

None of these applied to Henry.

Or to Bo.

In fact, every time the ephemeral 'spectrum' had been mentioned by well-meaning teachers – and Jamie steadfastly chose not to think about why it might be mentioned *quite* so very often – she could only think that these descriptors couldn't be further from the creative boy she knew and loved.

Whose empathy was, if anything, almost detrimental in its sincerity.

Ruth fidgeted uncomfortably, clearly on eggshells but equally, it seemed, wanting to say something.

'I don't know if you've noticed, Jamie, but Henry has this innate ability to cut through the chatter and see the heart of a problem. He just sees life differently. Although he wasn't diagnosed until he was in his forties actually, when we were talking to various professionals about Gemma.' She gave a strangled laugh. 'It didn't seem to matter how many times we said that Gemma was adopted, they would still go on and on about genetic predispositions. Anyway,' she puffed out her cheeks as she exhaled, 'long story short, we found out that his mind processes information in a different way. As did Gemma's, actually. All a bit of a farce at the time, but there we go.'

She paused and slowly refilled her teacup. 'All I'm saying is, that in the end, it made life easier for Henry to *know*. Less pressure to conform and less guilt when he couldn't, if that makes any sense?' She shrugged. 'Anyway, that's my Henry.'

Jamie nodded, echoes of past conversations reverberating in her mind, even as she watched Bo deliberately separate the pancakes and the bacon and the blueberries into sections on his plate, brow furrowing in concentration, orange juice abandoned. Pulp, no doubt.

She turned to soothe her thoughts into a coherent response

to Ruth and caught sight of Willow in the garden. The rain streaming off her coat and her hair plastered to her forehead, seemingly chattering away to the plants as she nestled them into their new home. As happy as Jamie had ever seen her.

And who was to say what counted as 'normal' when it came to following one's bliss.

She thought of that hideous expression that one man's meat was another man's poison, and realised that Henry's distinct perspective somehow gave him that insight without being told.

She turned and gave Ruth a smile, no harm done, as she quietly wondered what Henry saw when he looked at her and Bo. And whether, no matter how often she chose to steadfastly focus on Bo's incredible creativity, she might actually be doing her wonderfully unique son a disservice by burying her head in the proverbial sand.

By hiding behind her desire for him to choose for himself.

When, maybe, how Bo saw the world wasn't a choice he was making at all.

Chapter 37

'Are you sure it's okay? I can work around him—' Old insecurities were never far from the surface, no matter how reassuring Ruth and Henry's words.

Another day off school for Bo, another day of worrying and juggling for Jamie.

And of course, the guilt.

The guilt, that somehow among all the chaos and, indeed, all the blessings of her new position, there was still a part of her mind that longed for more. That shouted louder than her gratitude, craving intellectual engagement and prospects.

Prospects.

A word only used by Jane Austen and university marketing departments, and yet so accurately summing up the absence that Jamie still felt in her current situation.

A word that Amy could surely identify with, having taken up residence on Bonnie's sofa at Sunday lunchtime and apparently having yet to leave, the internship at the start-up already abandoned. Loutish demands and total lack of personal space or respect had been the final blow. It was one thing to work for nothing; it was another to feel unsafe while you were doing it.

Jamie pulled out her phone to text her; if Amy felt in need of moral support and could relocate to Jamie's sofa instead, then at least she could keep Bo company. Keep an eye on the poor wheezy lad so Jamie could get on with her day.

And what a glamorous day Jamie herself had in store: collecting prescriptions, driving Henry to the chiropodist (he'd been unable to drive himself home last time after what could only be described as some fairly heavy-duty 'filing' – urgh), and of course making sure that she pulled her weight.

With a job description so vague as to be indefinable, it was actually only Jamie's sense of duty and reluctance to take advantage that kept her working so hard. Neither of her employers seemed bothered either way.

And since the only measure of the days of the week was Bo's school timetable, Jamie was finding it increasingly hard to find an anchor in the passing of time.

With Amy settled on the sofa with Bo, a vast bag of popcorn from Ruth's larder and more coloured pencils than seemed strictly necessary, Jamie had left the two of them looking significantly happier.

She'd tried to overcome her reservations about Amy setting up an Instagram account on Bo's ancient iPad, only to be fobbed off with a speeding scroll of artists and art appreciation accounts, Amy whizzing them past her eyes on her own feed before Jamie could fully focus, even as Bo bounced

Penny Parkes

with anticipation at the treasure awaiting his attention. Still, at least *they* had a fun morning in store.

Henry grumbled like a toddler in the passenger seat of the Volvo as they navigated their way through traffic, and Jamie made a rather ridiculous detour to avoid driving past Harrison's and indeed *The Big Trip* shopfront. Bonnie had gently confided that there were plans mooted for it to become a nail bar and the very thought of it had been like a kick to the stomach. All these months later, and she still felt a sense of ownership for her and Anik's little unit on the High Street and the catalogue of happy moments and achievements that had taken place there. Ripping out their dreams to replace them with Perspex screens and nail baths was a step beyond what she could contemplate. Truly the end of an era.

'Are you taking The Knowledge, Jamie? Why on earth are you tackling every back street in the postcode. Please say you're not moonlighting as a cab driver?' Henry flinched disproportionately as Jamie gentled rolled over another speed bump, not himself at all this morning.

'Are you okay?' Jamie asked, pulling into the chiropodist's car park and switching off the engine. She could run all her errands during his appointment, so they had a few minutes in hand. 'You seem a bit out of sorts.'

Henry shook his head. 'I'm fine.'

'Convincing,' Jamie said sarcastically, forgetting herself for a moment and earning herself a hard stare.

'Sorry,' she mumbled, 'but I am allowed to be worried about you.'

306

He shook his head. 'Do I seem that decrepit, Jamie? Is that why suddenly everyone thinks they know what's best for me? Is that it?'

Jamie flinched at this sudden and abrupt outburst, so far from his usual mild manner as to be disconcerting.

He looked shamefaced for a moment, before reaching into his jacket pocket and pulling out a folded envelope.

'Sorry. Shouldn't be taking it out on you.' He handed her the envelope. 'Our dear son is on a mission again.'

Jamie reached into the envelope to find a slender glossy brochure and an accompanying note.

'Retirement living for the discerning,' she read aloud. 'Bloody hell, Henry – that's a slogan designed to attract some high-quality twats.' She coloured instantly, once again overstepping the mark.

For that was the problem with this bizarrely informal working and living situation – where were the boundaries, the hierarchy, the professional respect? They were all replaced by a pseudo sense of friendship or family.

'My thoughts exactly,' said Henry drily. 'Theo says he's worried about us, but it doesn't seem to occur to the lad to get on a plane and come and see for himself that we're absolutely fine. That we have you. That Willow and Chris are coming and going all the time. We're hardly going to find ourselves stuck on the floor in need of rescue.' He reached out for the envelope and shoved it into the door pocket of the Volvo crossly. Out of sight, out of mind. 'And his letter says it all – when does the divide kick in, eh Jamie? From falling over, to the risk of "having a fall"?' He made air quotes around the words with his fingers, which were trembling with his indignation.

'Why don't we arrange to have another Zoom call with him later, make it more of a daily thing perhaps, just to reassure him?' Jamie suggested.

Henry shook his head. 'Let's not start that. It's bad enough that he phones constantly, always worrying, always putting a dampener on the day.'

Jamie frowned. 'But I imagine the fact you never answer the phone is hardly reassuring.'

'I wouldn't mind so much if he just phoned for a chat. You know, to tell us his news and find out what we're up to. But instead, it always feels so intrusive, like he's checking up on us.' Henry sighed. 'And I do so miss the little tyke.'

'Maybe we should just invite him over. Properly? With an invitation or something,' Jamie suggested, half wondering if these two were just stuck in a stalemate of stubborn misunderstandings.

Henry shook his head tightly, his face visibly taut at the very suggestion. 'This is not my first rodeo, Jamie. I'll have you know that I did invite him, actually.' He paused, exhaling tiredly. 'I gather Dotty has told you all about our dear, sweet Gemma?' He looked every inch his age for a second. 'Not much of an innings, poor girl. But it would have been her fortieth birthday next week. I don't know where the years have gone, to be honest. But I do know that Ruth wanted us all to be together, as a family – it's a milestone birthday whether she's here with us or not. But our Theo already has other plans, it seems. Some stock-market fandango he "can't possibly miss". And I get to be the one to break it to his mother.' He shook his head tiredly. 'Never one to embrace an emotion he can possibly avoid, my son. Too busy worshipping the almighty dollar.'

He glanced at his watch and pushed open the car door, barely catching himself from sprawling on the tarmac, as his foot caught in the dangling seatbelt. He righted himself before Jamie could even dash around the car to help him. 'We'll just gloss over that, shall we? Could happen to anyone! See you in half an hour!'

And with a slam, the door was closed, and Henry was marching into the chiropody clinic, failing to disguise that he'd given himself a bit of a shock.

Jamie shook her head, leaning across the empty passenger seat and retrieving the envelope. She wasn't spying, Jamie told herself – hadn't Henry actually given her the contents to look at? But as she flicked through the pages of luxurious yet sterile accommodations, she couldn't help but wonder how well Theo actually knew his parents at all.

The very notion of them stripped away from The Old School House would be like surrendering a part of their very identity. And she could hardly imagine them making the most of the gym suite or the bowling alley, or even the in-house beauty therapist.

She frowned as she saw two items circled boldly in red Sharpie: Dementia care. Parkinson's Support Group.

She swallowed hard, always fearing there might be so much more to Ruth and Henry's situation than met the eye.

She tried to recalibrate, utterly thrown, some of Henry's more eccentric 'quirks' suddenly cast in a whole new light. That thing he did with his head, and his habit of ramming his hands into his trouser pockets, especially when he was stressed. Even that funny stiffened slow motion she'd seen on occasion.

And she had dared to presume that it was Theo, a thousand miles away, who was out of the loop.

Dad – we need to talk.

Tx

That was how he'd signed off his note on the accompanying compliments slip, bearing the logo of his New York office. A million miles removed from his parents' reality. But, it seemed, with one firm eye on the future.

Returning to the house later that morning, Jamie was still distracted by those red circles on the brochure. She couldn't help but wonder yet again whether regular communication might subvert some of Theo's obvious concerns about his parents.

But again, with the lack of boundaries, she wasn't quite sure where her responsibilities lay. She could potentially, as their carer, update their son and put his mind at ease.

But as their housekeeper, though, it would be a hard no.

Jamie's brow furrowed in thought as she eyed the phone in the hallway, calling out her hellos.

She found Ruth in the kitchen with Bo rolling out shortbread biscuits. 'We got snackish,' Bo explained with a grin, tugging a morsel of uncooked dough free and eating it happily.

'And Amy was having a moan about her finances, so I put her to work decorating the en-suite,' Ruth said casually to her husband. 'You made such a wonderful job of streamlining our clutter, Jamie, I'm afraid it rather highlighted how shabby the paintwork has been getting in there.'

Henry just nodded. 'Well, there's still plenty of paint in the shed.'

Bo pulled off another chunk of dough. 'And even though I'm good with a paintbrush too, I wasn't allowed to help because I'm supposed to be *resting*.' He sounded thoroughly annoyed.

'Well, that is true,' Jamie said, 'and the paint fumes aren't really going to help your chest . . .'

'I always buy the ones without VOC,' Henry interrupted. 'Can't stand the smell myself otherwise, so he could go up and have a look if he wants to.'

'Can I?'

Jamie noticed with surprise that it was Ruth he turned to for approval.

'Hang on a minute,' Ruth turned and pulled a second tray of golden shortbread from the oven. 'Why don't we all go and have a look and take Amy a snack while we're at it? You pour some juice and grab a tray.'

And to Jamie's further bemusement, Bo didn't hesitate. He

seemed to know exactly where everything was and quickly laid out a beautiful tray of glasses, juice and side plates, just waiting for the shortbread to cool enough to be lifted from the metal sheet.

'Amy's been up there for hours,' Bo said. 'She didn't like her new job, Mum, so she wants to find another one.'

Jamie nodded. She'd already received chapter and verse on the disgraceful behaviour towards the interns at the start-up. All six had walked out en masse, but Jamie was under no illusion that six more willing candidates would be easy to find in the current market. Their evasive promises all too convincing, and certainly not the only culprits to take advantage of the young people desperate to get their foot on the corporate ladder either. The very thought made her impotently furious and oddly protective.

'Well, then, let's hope your shortbread cheers her up,' Ruth said with a smile. 'Although, actually, she really did seem bizarrely chuffed about the painting and deco-rating idea.'

Walking into the bright and sunny en-suite a few minutes later, it was immediately clear to Jamie that Amy's enthusiasm may well have stemmed from a slight, possibly deliberate, misunderstanding of her brief.

Her mural was outlined in sweeping brushstrokes across the largest wall. Mirroring the vast oak tree outside the window, Amy had truly brought the outside in. Small details were already picked out – an owl, a squirrel and what looked like a tiny elf were dotted among the foliage.

'It's the Magic Faraway Tree,' breathed Bo in awe beside her.

'Goodness,' managed Ruth in shock. The mural clearly nothing like the clean sweep of Elephant's Breath emulsion she'd had in mind for the job.

Henry said nothing, but his smile spoke volumes.

Amy bit her lip nervously. 'Do you like it? I mean, I can't believe this morning I was so lost about finding a job and here I am now, doing the one thing I'm actually good at. The one thing I never really realised could be a *job*, you know? Like, I thought it was just my hobby . . .'

Ruth glanced awkwardly at her husband, and then stepped forward into the tiny room, leaving the others packed into the doorway watching. She reached out to touch the small section that Amy had begun to fill in with detail, almost as though to convince her own eyes of the trompe l'oeil. The leaves seemed so dense, so lifelike, it really was hard to concede that they lay flat, in two dimensions, on Ruth's bathroom wall.

'It's actually rather incredible, Amy,' she said quietly. 'And taking a shower will never be the same again.'

You had to admire her tact. For it was obvious to all of them, except Amy, that this was absolutely not what Ruth had asked Amy to do, but the growing wonderment in her eyes reassured Jamie that this was not going to end in tears.

'Do you think you could add in a parrot?' Ruth said eventually.

'And a baby Groot?' Bo suggested. 'Or maybe I could do that?'

He turned longingly, again to Ruth, rather than his mum. 'Can I? Can I help too?'

Her simple nod made his face light up and Jamie made a mental note to remind her son the seemingly obvious fact that Amy had been rather late to learn: do a job you love and you'll never work a day in your life.

And if only she could work out where her own passions lay these days, perhaps in time, she herself could follow suit.

Chapter 38

It had been a long time since Jamie had found herself in the role of hostess, the gaggle of women evicted from Ruth's kitchen as they prepared for their own guests. Ruth and Henry's regular bridge gathering merely an excuse for sherry and gossip, so far as Jamie could tell.

Over in the annexe, setting out glasses on the island, she watched Bonnie and Amy bickering with each other, as Kath patiently listened to one of Bo's long-winded recounts of some particular detail of his day.

Her own small kitchen was filled with laughter and conversation and, even though she was exhausted, there was something uplifting and energising about having company.

Counter-intuitively perhaps.

And not her normal approach by a long step.

Yet somehow Bonnie wasn't the kind of friend who took no for an answer and when she'd turned up at the end of the day, Kath in tow, along with bags of Doritos and salsa, it would have been churlish to turn them away.

Jamie set down the tray of drinks on the coffee table between them all, finding space among the bags of snacks that Bonnie had neatly torn open to act as plates. 'What?' she'd said in response to Bo's shocked look of surprise. 'It saves on washing up.'

Snuggling in beside her son, Jamie couldn't help but smile as she listened to Bonnie giving Amy her two-pence worth.

'Look, from where I'm standing your heart was never in that internship anyway. Put aside for a moment the fact that they were arseholes taking advantage of desperate people and focus on what you learned. Do you actually see yourself putting on a suit and going in to an office every day? Sitting at a computer and shuffling from meeting to meeting – half of which are power trips for the boss and could just as easily have been a bloody email?'

Kath snorted with laughter. 'Ain't that the truth. They could save millions in the NHS budget just by cutting all the unnecessary showboating.'

Jamie leaned forward and crammed a Dorito into her mouth, watching Amy's expression closely. 'You know,' she said, swallowing hard and remembering why she never normally ate such pointy snacks, 'I have never seen you looking so happy as you were this afternoon. And I get that you need a regular income, so maybe being a full-time artist is something to aim for, but why not have a stab at being a decorator for a bit? I might be wrong, but so many people seem to be doing up their houses round here.' She took a long drink to soothe her throat. 'I think maybe lots of them have just got sick of the sight of their own four walls these last few years.'

Kath nodded. 'It's true. I work all hours God sends, but I'm still sick to the back teeth of my magnolia blah.'

Amy shook her head. 'But that's not the kind of painter I am,' she protested, shuddering at the very mention of magnolia.

Bonnie huffed. 'Listen, sweetheart. Let's be blunt. Your art is your passion but you've got to pay the rent, am I right? So maybe you earn enough painting walls three days a week, so you can splurge on your canvases on the other two?' She shrugged. 'It's your call, honey, but you might have to make your own opportunities if you don't want to go back to school. Or else accept that your future will involve a lot of answering phones or taking coffee orders. Wouldn't it be better to do something art-adjacent?'

Bonnie waggled her finger in the air as she spoke and Jamie decided that it would take a tougher soul than her to disagree. Amy it seemed, though, was made of sterner stuff than her freckles might suggest.

'Bo suggested I should skip regular school and just apply to art college instead.' She jutted her jaw as though to challenge anyone who might suggest this was a pipe dream. 'They won't care about my GCSEs once they see my portfolio.'

Jamie caught Kath's eye and they shared a moment of understanding. What it was to be young and invincible, before the knowledge acquired by being the parent rather than the child eclipsed all those romantic notions. And while she applauded Bo for thinking about what would be ideal for Amy, she couldn't help but wish that he hadn't got her hopes up.

'Maybe there's a foundation course you could find,' she began hesitantly. 'But finding an income stream that's flexible might be a good idea either way. Use your talents to your advantage.'

Kath nodded. 'It's expensive being a student these days. God knows what I'll do if either of mine get into higher education.' She paused, 'Although the way their school reports are looking, it's probably not something I need to lose any sleep over.'

Bonnie laughed. 'Well, ladies, I am living proof, if it helps, that you can be a successful business owner without following the sheep blindly. Even if it does mean a few hard choices.'

'Bonnie, my love,' Kath said firmly, affection in her every syllable, 'you have been a business owner for less than a month. And while I have no doubt that you will always find a way to land on your feet, I think you might have a way to go before we're calling on you to be a role model.'

'Oi,' said Bonnie indignantly, laughing. 'Cheeky!'

'I think you're a good role model,' Bo chirped up from the depths of the sofa cushions, Dorito dust all down his front. 'You got your job sorted and now you go back and help Father Bill.' He reached for another handful of crisps. 'I bet he likes that.'

'I know he does,' Kath said, smiling at Bo. 'In fact, I had to listen to chapter and verse on what an inspiring soul she is, our Bonnie, when I was down there earlier. He gets so excited about his past successes, like we're all some part of a giant catch-and-release scheme. And he remembers everyone, you know. He must have reeled off a dozen stories of families he's helped, who in turn, are helping, or donating or volunteering now. Kind of like a proud grandpa, bless him. But still, it gives one hope, doesn't it?'

'Everything changes, everything stays the same,' Bonnie said profoundly, nodding. 'He's furious with me though too.' She shook her head, watching Jamie carefully as she spoke. 'I've been given an opportunity to expand the kiosk, but he thinks I should take it steady – not overreach.'

Jamie frowned. 'But sometimes you have to take a risk to grow, don't you? I mean, there's hardly room for you in that kiosk, let alone another stylist.'

Bonnie nodded again. 'You're absolutely right. But, to be honest, there's another reason I'm hesitating.' She reached into her handbag and pulled out a printed page of property particulars. 'This is the unit that's become available, you see.' She bit her lip. 'I have zero desire to step on toes.'

Jamie blinked hard, utterly blindsided.

She didn't need to read the particulars to know the exact dimensions of the space, the location of every electrical outlet or indeed the very breakdown of the monthly overheads.

Standing empty for months, as lease after lease had fallen through, had somehow enforced the notion that, in Jamie's mind at least, Number 42, High Street had forever remained hers: *The Big Trip*.

Empty now, stripped bare, but still carrying the remnants of her dreams. 'Wow,' she said after a long pause.

'Do you just hate the idea?' Bonnie leaned forward,

conflict etched across her face. 'I know what that place meant to you. *Means* to you.'

Jamie shook her head, rallying. 'Of course I don't hate it, Bonnie. I just – you took me by surprise is all.' She tried to envisage the layout without her own failed legacy crowding out the space. 'It's so much lighter and brighter than where you are now, isn't it? And you know, I think it's a brilliant idea actually, Bonnie. You could really grow into the place.'

It was Bonnie's turn to look surprised. 'But . . . So you're saying I'm not stepping on toes, opening old wounds? You mean, you don't actually *mind*?' she asked.

'Why should I mind? You mad muppet.' Jamie was emotional in her conviction. 'Aren't we all here to support each other's successes as well as our hiccups?'

'Well now, don't I feel stupid for keeping it a secret from you guys?' Bonnie said, leaning forward to give Jamie a hug. 'Thank you,' she whispered into Jamie ear. 'I've been really worried about telling you.'

Jamie smiled. 'No need,' she replied. Even though in her head, she wanted nothing more than to be back with Anik, planning and dreaming about their new business, filled with hope and potential.

Just as Bonnie was now.

She missed Anik so much – her best friend. Her only friend for so long. And so pointlessly lost to them for the want of masks on the Tube, or indeed the willingness to wear them.

And now here she was, still rubbish at friendship. But trying her very best.

No matter how Jamie longed to be part of a group – like on the sitcoms on the television – she had somehow never perfected the social skills required. Or indeed been prepared, if she were brutally honest, to allocate the sheer number of hours involved in maintaining such intense bonds.

Or perhaps to invest that much of her limited energy.

It frightened her in a way, the draining of her own energy for the benefit of anyone other than Bo. Because who knew when she might be expected to rise to the challenge of an all-nighter in A&E?

Her own life, on hold, on call.

A large part of her mental load already and constantly engaged in just keeping everyone she loved upright and breathing.

And, let's face it, even without the looming spectre of the nebuliser, parenting Bo was hardly a picnic on any given day, with or without a group of mates to help traverse the ever-changing landscape.

Yet somehow, it was the powerhouse that was Bonnie that had beaten down Jamie's last reservations about letting people into her life. That, and a certain degree of desperation.

The least she could do was support her now, in return. No matter how much it hurt.

Although Jamie couldn't deny that her life was richer for having these amazing women in her orbit.

These outspoken, savvy, clever women – who were, some-how, just as adrift in their lives as she was in her own.

All of them, it seemed, without the perspective to step back and evaluate their own choices, their own situations. Their own careers.

She herself had only to listen to Amy, to watch her innate instinct with colour and style to know – really *know* – that she could excel in home design, if only Amy herself could see it.

And as for Kath, all of her innate caring skills seemed to be sapped away by the endless bureaucracy of the NHS; the trauma of the last few years in the hospital etched into her face and her psyche. She was worth so much more than the pittance they paid her, while expecting her heart and soul on every graveyard shift.

Maybe Kath hadn't actually been joking when she'd told Jamie that she would bite her hand off for a gig like this? Caring for Ruth and Henry. Caring full stop.

'Do you think we should have invited Willow to join us?' Jamie said suddenly. 'I feel bad because she's always home alone, I think.'

Bonnie shook her head. 'I saw her heading out actually. Henry got her tickets to some lecture at the RHS. You know, the plant people?'

'It's mad, isn't it? She's so incredibly skilled with computers and totally saved my bacon, by the way, but she doesn't give a shit. And I know that even the IT jobs are hard to come by at the moment, but all she really wants to do is muck about in the garden.' Kath frowned, bemused.

'Landscape design, not mucking about,' said Bo. 'That's what she wants to do. And she knows loads of stuff about it too.'

Jamie turned to him. 'Is that what you've been up to after school with Henry?'

Bo shook his head. 'Henry's teaching me to make stuff. But Willow comes and chats to us sometimes. She's trying to persuade Henry to make a plan for the garden, and Henry's trying to persuade her that it's her calling and she should apply for a job with the plant people.' He wrinkled his nose. 'Although that's definitely *not* why he got her those tickets. Not at all.'

'Subtle,' smirked Bonnie with a smile and innocent look when Bo stared at her.

'He's quite the puppet master, I'll grant you,' Kath said. 'But when you look at that amazing cabinet that Chris is making in their dining room, you have to admit he's not always wrong, either.'

'It's like that fish meme,' Amy said, nodding. 'You know – if you judge a fish by its ability to fly, it'll live its whole life thinking it's stupid.'

'Einstein,' Kath said, nodding.

'He didn't say that, though,' Bo interrupted, ever the stickler. 'But I still think it's true. If you judged my school report on just my football skills I'd be screwed.'

Jamie blinked, even as the others laughed, utterly taken aback. It was the closest she'd ever heard Bo come to making a joke. For sure, he had always been happier in the company of adults, more comfortable with their conversations than he was with the mercurial threads of his peers, but jokes?

Dare she hope that he had finally, finally, relaxed into himself? Accepted his somewhat atypical take on the world and possibly even dared to embrace it?

She paused, taking in the brightness of his gaze, his cheeks a little pinker now after a day's rest and fresh air, sketching and scrolling through Instagram with Amy all morning, pottering with Henry all afternoon.

Or perhaps it was Henry she had to thank, their two perspectives so alike. A kinship that had given her son his confidence and his humour back.

A similarity of thinking that Ruth had astutely recognised before she herself had been ready to acknowledge it.

And, not for the first time, she wondered whether her own unique perspective might yet have some value.

The apple didn't fall far from the tree after all.

Chapter 39

'Out of interest, Henry, why do you never give *me* career advice, the way you do to everyone else around here?' Jamie blurted, as she reapplied Henry's dressing to his big toe the next morning. The chiropodist had been nothing but thorough, that was for sure.

The question had been tormenting her mind all night after her conversation with the girls.

'I don't do that—' Henry protested, trying not to look as though the very sight of his missing toenail might tip him over the edge. 'I just encourage people to follow their gut and their natural skills, rather than tying themselves up with logic all the time.'

Jamie frowned. 'But I tie myself up with logic ALL the time, though.'

'Well, yes, but that's mainly because you're always putting Bo's needs first. Running just-in-case scenarios and making sure you're prepared for every eventuality. You're a mother, Jamie, first and foremost. So right now, it's probably better to embrace those priorities, rather than wear yourself out fighting against something you can't change.'

Jamie stilled, lengths of micropore tape dotted on her fingers. She felt oddly let down that Henry's 'vision' for her seemingly began and ended with being Bo's mum. Not that she didn't revel in the role, but she had to believe that her skillset extended beyond parenting. Besides, being a mum could hardly count as a *career* choice, no matter that it was increasingly a full-time job . . .

'Is that why you offered me this job, Henry? Am I basically here to parent you and Ruth as well?' she said, quietly winded as the thought occurred to her for the first time.

He shook his head. 'Your tiny sandwiches and your pep talks may be a triumph, Jamie, as indeed is your perfect "dippy egg", but you are categorically not here to parent me. Or Ruth. You're here because you are a kind, caring soul who needed a little respite from the world. And we needed a little help. But if there's one thing this house is good at, apart from leaking in inconceivable places, it's offering sanctuary.

'An oasis for a while, for you and for Bo. Besides, you *know* what's going to make you happy, Jamie. You just aren't quite ready to admit it yet.'

Jamie wrapped the last of the gauze around his toe, ignoring the childish urge to wrap it just a fraction too tightly. She stuck down the end with tape and sat back on her heels.

'And what might that be?'

Henry smiled. 'You tell me—'

'God, you're frustrating!' Jamie sighed.

'Starting to feel a bit more sympathy for Ruth now, aren't you? Forty years she's put up with me.' Henry made as though to tip his imaginary cap, but his affectionate smile was genuine, even in the face of her annoyance.

Jamie gathered the tape, ointment and scissors together and clambered to her feet. 'Then she probably deserves a medal by now.' She hesitated. 'I'm not being ungrateful, Henry, because of course you were right – Bo and I absolutely needed to step off the treadmill of struggling to exist for a little while.' She paused, acknowledging the truth of her statement. 'You can't really think about the future when it's taking all your energy just to get through the day, can you?'

Henry shook his head. 'And you know that to be true. It's not a failing on your part, Jamie. You were just stuck in survival mode there for a while.'

'But I'm not any more,' Jamie replied, realising it was actually true. It was no longer a pipe dream, just to be able to dream. Wanting more didn't make her ungrateful; maybe it meant that she was healing. 'Cup of tea?'

They walked through to the kitchen and, as she filled the kettle, Jamie realised how that one simple shift out of survival mode had somehow changed everything.

She wasn't constantly thinking ahead about how to keep Bo fed, or keep the heating on – making choices between necessities, compromising constantly, even with Bo's health. She hadn't worried about Bo being cold even once since they'd moved here, and the sound of his laughter was no longer a distant memory.

The fact that she'd struggled to do up her jeans only that

morning was a big deal too. Something to be celebrated rather than feared.

Their time at The Old School House was a feast after years of famine – culinarily, socially, emotionally. Henry and Ruth had given them that.

'The thing is,' Jamie said quietly, taking advantage of this rare quiet moment alone, 'I know, Henry. About the Parkinson's.'

'Ah,' he said simply. 'I wondered.'

'And it's just Ruth and Theo who know?' Jamie checked, not wanting to blunder into a situation that required tact and sensitivity.

Henry nodded. 'We're all doing a fantastic turn on the denial front, right now. It's all feeling a bit deja-vu to be honest. Watching another slow decline. But at least I've had my four score years and ten – or very nearly. There's nothing very fair about this, but I'd still rather it was me, not Dotty. She's got her own troubles, of course, no point trying to hide it. '

'I wish you'd said,' Jamie said quietly, gently. 'I want to help and I'm here to take care of you – both of you.'

Henry held up his hand, cutting her off. 'Not strictly true, dear girl. I always said from the outset, didn't I, that you were here for Ruthie. My little Dot. I need to know that someone's going to be there for her – not just to help with the house, but really *there* for her, when this gets ugly. And, forgive me, for judging on appearances, but it seemed to me that you needed to let someone into your life too. At least when we first met.'

He smiled again, looking rather pleased with himself. 'It's a funny old thing, thinking about your own legacy. The mark you leave on the planet and the things that happened differently, just because you were there. And I meant what I said earlier – I am very proud of you. Watching you take a few chances, stepping outside your comfort zone. It's all too easy to retreat when life batters you over and over again.

'Now, that – wouldn't that be quite the legacy? Seeing you and Bo flourish again.'

Jamie sighed, the tumult of emotions in this one short conversation leaving her reeling off kilter. As though the camber of the road was wrong as she took each bend, her body and mind each taking their own path, only to rejoin again as though nothing had happened.

'I've never given my legacy a moment's thought,' she said, wondering if that were entirely true.

Her mobile trilled in her pocket and shattered their shared moment of reflection, Jamie's heart rate shooting up instinctively, until she could see that it wasn't Bo's school calling.

'Hello?' she said cautiously.

'Hi, I'm calling about Amy? She's given me your name as a reference. Apparently, she did some decorating for you and your family?' The woman's voice was pure cut glass. Abrupt. Disinterest laced with suspicion.

'That's right,' Jamie said. 'She did a wonderful job with our bathroom. In fact, I couldn't recommend her highly enough.'

Henry pulled a face across the kitchen, clearly intrigued.

Jamie shook her head and lifted one finger to her lips. She knew what he was like; he'd be gesticulating to her to put the call on speakerphone any second.

'She has a fantastic eye for colour. So if you need any design input—' Jamie began.

'Oh, I hardly think that's necessary. Did she leave a huge mess, was her work up to scratch, was she punctual – these are the things I need to know.'

'She was tidy, professional and prompt,' Jamie replied, wondering how on earth Amy had found this arsey gem of a client barely hours after she'd so roundly pooh-poohed the very concept. 'And she does beautiful murals too, trompe l'oeil and the like. She's a real find, actually. Although, to be honest, I hadn't realised she was taking on new clients. Normally she's very particular and has quite the waiting list . . .'

There was a long pause at the end of the phone and Jamie panicked for a second that she had overplayed her hand. But she knew clients like this, women like this – they were only really interested in what they couldn't have.

'Well, I appreciate the heads up.' The woman's voice softened, and she ended the call abruptly. Jamie would bet her entire day's wages that she was on the phone to Amy within seconds.

'You see,' Henry said quietly, stirring an illicit second sugar into his tea while she was distracted, 'you know exactly what you're good at.'

*

His words echoed in Jamie's head all afternoon as she worked with Chris to reassemble the dining room. She'd taken Henry's words to be a compliment, yet perhaps he'd been implying that she was a master of manipulation. And that didn't sit quite so comfortably.

'I hear your mate Amy's gone into the decorating lark?' Chris said, pencil wedged firmly behind his ear as he slid the final shelf into the newly renovated dresser. 'Do you think she'd put in a word with some of her clients for me? Stands to reason if you've got the decorators in, then you might need a carpenter too, right?'

The shelf slid into place with gilded perfection, its surface smooth and glossy and Chris gave a small exhalation of satisfaction.

'Are you taking the leap too?' Jamie asked. 'No more home security for you?'

Chris shook his head. 'Life's too short, isn't it? The last few years have rather hammered that home. But I won't lie, Jamie. The whole idea of starting over is kind of overwhelming.'

She nodded, the first few years at *The Big Trip* still fresh in her mind like yesterday. 'If you ever want to talk about it, I've been there,' she said. 'Although since the business I was involved in went under, maybe I'm not the best person to hand out advice.'

Chris laughed. 'Or maybe you're the very best person to highlight potential pitfalls? You know, like, don't run a luxury travel business in a global pandemic?' He slung his arm around her shoulder and gave her an avuncular squeeze.

'Mate, you're still standing and so's your wee lad. That's all that matters, isn't it?' He paused. 'But I think I'm kidding myself if I think that being properly self-employed will be anything like running my security franchise. I didn't realise at the time how much support HQ were actually giving us.'

'It's scary,' Jamie agreed. 'But then think of Amy, with nothing to lose and everything to gain. I feel a bit guilty, actually, that Bo might have lit the touch paper there – given her a nudge to pursuing her artistic dreams rather than going back to school and getting her exams. Painting walls to pay for her canvases and all that.'

Chris shook his head. 'I think it might have more to do with you girls – I mean you've all got each other's backs, haven't you? I saw the way you rallied when Kath's husband did a number on her.' He looked wistful for a moment. 'Easier to leap when there's someone there to catch you, isn't it?'

Jamie paused, the stack of china in her hands suddenly weighing her down. Was that what Amy had been lacking all along? Was her own choice to parent Bo alone setting him on the same path?

For as long as Jamie could remember, she had never really felt like enough.

But she had to hope that she was enough for her son at least – one dedicated, adoring parent who would always, always put him first.

Ahead of friendships, ahead of ambition.

'And anyway, the world's gone a bit mad, hasn't it? I

keep waiting for the Roaring Twenties to fully kick off and then we'll have another art-deco revolution.' He patted his toolbelt reassuringly. 'And I'll be right there, ready and waiting.'

Jamie couldn't help but grin. This hefty bloke, so intimidating at a distance, but such a gentle sweetheart up close. 'I always reckon you have to make your own opportunities in life. No point waiting for someone to hand things to you, or the perfect serendipitous moment. Although I'll never dismiss the hand of fate in whether you find success. It's more about being proactive, isn't it?'

She ran her hand over the beautiful joinery that Chris had worked with such apparent ease. It was obvious he was a natural.

'You know, this is going to sound crazy, but what if you and Amy worked on a room together – took your Roaring Twenties, take-back-our-social-lives idea and really went to town. We could ask my friend Daniel to photograph it, try and persuade some influencers to write about it – he's a whizz with a camera. It could be your calling card until you can get a bigger portfolio together?'

Chris's face lit up. 'Bloody genius idea. Do you think Amy would go for it?'

'I don't think it's Amy you need to convince.' Jamie walked over and pushed at the double doors. Creaking and stiff from lack of use, they groaned into submission, swinging open to reveal the school's long-neglected assembly room – a small stage of shiny varnished wood, glowing orange in the sunlight, and the lectern still proudly claiming its spot in the centre, covered in dust.

Henry and Ruth's plan to convert this into a party room or playroom for the family had been long-since abandoned.

The parquet floor was still intact, and the floor-length windows made the room the perfect blank canvas for anything Chris and Amy might cook up. A showcase for their talents.

'What do you think?' she said with a quiet smile.

For in that moment, Jamie saw what Henry had obliquely alluded to. She wasn't just Bo's parent, she was his *advocate* and had been his entire life. She could see beyond what he wanted, focusing her energy on his needs and his aspirations. The Big Picture.

And it was no small talent, to speak for others.

To be an advocate for people other than her son sounded like the most perfect way to make a difference. And since getting things done was her unappreciated superpower – although it might not look good on a CV, ineffable and arrogant at best – it also gave her a unique opportunity: the chance to change lives.

Chapter 40

But the project for Chris and Amy was the furthest thing from Jamie's mind the next morning – one look at Ruth and Henry's pale faces and their lacklustre start to the day, standing around in their dressing gowns at eleven o'clock in the morning rather than neatly dressed at the crack of dawn, told its own story.

The calendar clicked over to a date none of them could ignore or avoid.

Jamie stepped in and filled the cafetiere, placing a few slices of toast into the fancy Dualit machine – doubtless another present from Theo – who really should have been there, today of all days, rather than sending white goods and gadgets as his proxy.

She hesitated, unsure for a moment whether it was tactless to broach the subject unprompted, before deciding that faint heart rarely won the day. 'Would you like me to bake a birthday cake. For Gemma. Well, for you obviously, but . . .'

Jamie faltered under their twin, hollow gazes. 'Sorry, bad idea,' she murmured in retreat.

Ruth shook her head. 'Actually, darling girl, I think it's

a wonderful idea. But I think it's something I'd like to do myself, if you don't mind.' She turned to Henry with a soft smile. 'How does carrot and walnut sound to you, my love?'

Henry swallowed hard and nodded. 'Well it was her favourite. That and those awful chocolate lime sweets. But even they've disappeared these days.' He paused. 'Would you ladies mind if I took a short stroll to clear my head? Leave you both cooking up a storm, and then we can have tea and cake later?'

'Maybe you should—?' Jamie began, eyeing the tremble in his hand before he shoved it deeply into his pocket. Out of sight and out of mind.

'I am perfectly fine to go by myself, but I will take my mobile with me if it makes you feel better.' He strode over towards the back door with purpose.

'I was just going to suggest that you got dressed first,' Jamie called after him, watching his reaction to her gentle kindness.

Well, at least she'd somehow managed to elicit a small, affectionate smile on this hardest of days, Jamie thought, before turning her attention to Ruth. Who seemed to be intent on emptying out every single item in the larder, in the search for the baking powder she was already clasping in her other hand.

Nobody said that today was going to be easy.

'Why don't we ask the girls over for lunch?' Ruth said, as she laid out her ingredients in serried ranks, before rearranging them again in a way that apparently made more sense. 'Your girls, I mean, not mine. There's only so much tea and sympathy, and husbands with dodgy prostates, that a person can stomach from my little lot.' She paused. 'Plus, if I'm honest, they all knew Gemma, you see – back in the day – and while that *should* make it easier, somehow all that shared grief just makes it suffocating.'

Jamie nodded; it was understandable that distraction might make the day flow more smoothly.

'I'll send out a group message,' Jamie said, 'and see if people can juggle their work and whatnot.'

Ruth shook her head. 'Good lord, now doesn't that just go to show how out of touch I am. Who can come to lunch midweek at a moment's notice? Let's make it supper, then, Jamie. A cosy kitchen supper. With lots of wine and gossip and laughter.' She looked utterly bereft for a moment. 'Exactly what Gemma would have chosen herself, as it happens. Couldn't stand big parties or "fuss". And heaven help you if you attempted a surprise. Do you know, when she was eight . . .'

And Jamie sat back and listened; the best way she could think of to support Ruth today would be to offer a willing ear to her reminiscences. Reminiscences, Jamie now realised, that Ruth treated as something of a guilty pleasure.

And that was something that Jamie was determined to change. If Ruth and Henry, and, in all likelihood, Theo, still felt unable to talk about Gemma all these years later, without each word being loaded with guilt and blame and intense emotion – well, it was hardly likely that they were ever going to resolve their ever-growing rift.

'So, what were Gemma's favourite foods?' Jamie asked after a while, watching Ruth's face light up with enthusiasm, as she shared stories of barbecues and picnics and pot-luck suppers. Each dish carrying with it a special memory or moment. And then they began to design an incredibly eclectic menu for their kitchen supper.

Together.

Hours later, Kath, Bonnie and Amy, Willow and Chris milled around the kitchen, glasses in hand, bickering over the soundtrack they should choose from Amy's Spotify. Bo couldn't stop laughing at the silly titles of nineties music as they skipped through the decade, looking for something that Gemma might have danced to.

'It was all about that girl with the lacy gloves, you know, the one who was always getting her kit off,' Henry volunteered from the head of the table, well into his third glass of wine and dealing with the day in his own particular way.

Ruth, on the other hand, had been busy overseeing Jamie's culinary efforts.

The kitchen table was laden with treats, not so much courses, per se, as a veritable walk-through-time buffet: devilled eggs alongside vol au vents and focaccias, and a vat of macaroni cheese with a bubbling golden topping that made Jamie's mouth water in anticipation. A vast black cherry cheesecake sat waiting in the fridge and then, of course, there was Ruth's cake.

The centrepiece of the proceedings.

It teetered on a cake stand for all to see, a Leaning Tower of Pisa in claggy carrot form. 'Oh Dotty, my love, it couldn't matter less, you know,' Henry attempted to reassure her, as the cake gave one last shudder, before its failing structural integrity admitted defeat.

'It's hard to stay up without eggs,' Kath sympathised, when Ruth gasped in disappointment.

'I don't know what I was thinking!' she exclaimed. 'I had it all organised so beautifully, didn't I, Jamie? Tell them! I was like Delia bloody Smith with all my ingredients weighed out in tiny bowls.' She paused and frowned, 'I just don't know how I managed to forget the eggs . . .'

As Kath and Amy rallied, portioning the collapsed birthday cake into bowls for later, on the basis that it would still be 'undoubtedly delicious', Henry caught Jamie's eye. 'Happens every time she gets stressed or worried you see, Jamie. It's like she struggles to process two thoughts at the same time any-more – and that from the Queen of Multitasking our entire married life. The next few days might be a bit interesting, I'm afraid, after such a big anniversary. There's bound to be fallout from this, but I wouldn't begrudge her a moment, would you?'

They both looked over to watch Ruth among friends, laughing and joking with each other, gently teasing her about her cake, and also the mad array of dishes on the table awaiting them.

Bo had finally settled on a 'Best of the Nineties' mix, after Ruth had confided that Gemma's teenage years had been one long battle for the stereo between her and her brother.

There was a small awkward pause at the mention of Theo's name; in this ridiculous evening of loving affection, there was no doubt that his choice to absent himself from Gemma's fortieth had cut deep for both Ruth and Henry.

'Now look,' Henry said, stumbling to his feet, and raising his glass, waving at Bo to pause the music.

Jamie made a mental note to pour him some water the moment he sat down and then sat back to listen to his toast.

'It's a bittersweet occasion, as you know. But both Ruth and I couldn't be more grateful that you've given up your evening to help us mark this particular date. A date that should have been a celebration. A big one. And so, rather than dwelling on all the reasons that's not the case, I wanted to celebrate the wonderful, remarkable young woman that Ruth and I were fortunate enough to call our daughter.'

He turned to Bo and Willow and nodded. Bo scampered across and hit the lights, just as Willow clicked a small device in her hand and the whole back wall of the kitchen lit up with a projected image, a new soundtrack slowly growing in volume with each successive slide.

A small girl nervously looking up at Ruth and Henry, awkwardly posed to capture the moment for posterity as they clasped their adoption paperwork.

Then seemingly that same day, in that same dress, laughing as a small wiry terrier clambered onto her lap on the lawn just outside.

With each passing image her tense, nervous smile morphing into the real thing.

And then suddenly a stunning Ruth in a bikini, half buried in sand, her nose pink with the sun, as the same small girl, wearing a spotty swimsuit this time, gleefully emptied yet another bucket of sand over her legs.

Gemma and Ruth – together, it seemed, always.

Gemma, now with bunches in satin ribbons, grinning at the camera, with gaps in her teeth and jelly smudged down the front of her party dress. The birthday cake bore the legend '5 today'.

Stevie Wonder's dulcet tones echoed around the room, and Jamie couldn't help but agree – image after image of Gemma segueing on the wall, throughout her childhood here at The Old School House – she was indeed lovely, and wonderful. The chords of the song caught in her heart and Jamie found herself with tears flowing freely down her face.

She wasn't alone.

As mud pies and trips to the zoo became discos and giggling groups of girls, and Theo's awkward teenage presence loomed into the periphery of the pictures, the music built to a crescendo only to morph into Jamie's own personal musical nemesis.

That song from *Mamma Mia* that every parent felt like a visceral punch, as time slipped through their own fingers, faster than anyone could ever predict.

'Sorry,' whispered Willow as she saw the reaction in the room.

'No, no. Don't you dare apologise,' sobbed Ruth. 'It's absolutely perfect,' she managed, tears streaming freely. Decades of grief given voice, it seemed.

Jamie wiped her eyes and tried to focus on the photos as they scrolled by, Ruth so young and so vital as she embraced her beautiful daughter. Henry – with actual hair – popping open champagne to celebrate a moment that only two people at the table could remember, but in which every one of them felt invested.

Then suddenly, teenage Gemma in the Madonna years that Henry had joked about, weighted down with bangles and scowling unconvincingly – suddenly far too cool for school.

Bookworm Gemma, earnestly curled up on the window seat in the sitting room, golden evening light highlighting the auburn streaks in her hair as she was engrossed in Virginia Woolf. A teetering pile of A-level texts at her feet and a packet of Minstrels torn open bedside her.

The girl becoming a woman. The gappy grin, replaced by an uncertain smile. So many moments of Ruth and Henry hugging her, loving her, supporting her as she wobbled through adolescence.

And then the final photo taking them all by surprise – a crackly video, a last glimpse into the life of their adored daughter, as she swung back and forth on the tyre swing under the oak tree in the garden. Ripped jeans, flowing hair and the sound of her laughter.

'Oh my God,' gulped Kath quietly into Jamie's shoulder.

And yet any doubts about the wisdom of Henry's surprise were erased with one glance at Ruth's face, enchanted, or possibly transported, by the sound of her daughter's carefree laughter, overwriting the soundtrack of loss, and giving Ruth one more moment of joy to be savoured and revisited on days like these.

Bo hesitated by the light switch, trying to read the emotions of the adults in the room. 'Mum?'

Ruth glanced over at the sound of his voice. 'They're happy tears, Bo darling, don't worry.'

His relief was almost palpable. 'Can I still give you your present then?' he asked tentatively.

Jamie stilled, wondering what other schemes her boy had been plotting without her. 'It's fine,' Henry leaned in to reassure her. 'It's more than fine actually, it's just wonderful.'

And so, Bo shyly stepped forward and presented Ruth with a frame, only Ruth being able to see the image within.

She pressed her hand to her heart and let out a small whimper. 'Oh Bo. You angel. Thank you. Thank you so much.' She pulled him into a tearful hug, and Jamie held her breath. She needn't have worried, as Bo tentatively put his arms around Ruth in response, hugging her back.

Unprompted.

'I thought,' he ventured, 'you might want to hang it above Gemma's reading nook. It seems like she was really happy there.'

Ruth nodded, words beyond her, as she turned the frame to allow the others to see the exquisite charcoal drawing of Gemma reading, her profile lit by the sunshine of the garden beyond, and her expression in wonderfully calm repose. Happy, contented, thoroughly absorbed in the moment. Her skin glowing with health and vitality and her eyes dancing with enjoyment.

A moment in time captured to perfection and a true work of art.

The art of friendship, as only Bo knew how.

Chapter 41

Jamie filled her plate with the slightly mad concoction of flavours and sat back down, watching Bo dissect his vol au vent into its component parts and pick at each section in turn. She was amazed by how well he was coping with the chaos – because this 'birthday' supper had become chaotic in the extreme; nobody staying seated for long, hugs and laughter, swiftly followed by tears and more memories.

Henry's video had seemingly loosened the stopper on Ruth's recollections. And her funny little stories peppered their conversation with no logical flow – just shared as they popped into her mind.

'Willow, you are so wonderful for helping Henry put that together,' Jamie said, as Willow sat down beside her, nabbing Kath's empty seat while she went back for thirds. 'It's amazing how a picture can truly speak a thousand words, isn't it?'

Amy nodded in agreement, holding up her phone. 'We should really capture this moment for posterity too. Everyone here together.'

Bonnie held out her hand for the phone, looking tired, her tangerine dungerees almost luminous in the lamplight and her hair pulled back tightly. 'I'll take it. I'm strictly behind the lens tonight.'

Jamie herself had somehow smudged cheese sauce on her smartest T-shirt, her own hair caught up in a tousled approximation of a bun with a purple glitter party hat lopsided on her head. 'I'm not sure we're too worried about appearances tonight, Bon.'

Amy grinned. 'All the best photos are the candids anyway – leave it with me.'

Bonnie rolled her eyes, but with good humour. After all, hadn't they just seen the power of a simple photograph to bring back a moment, a memory. A feeling.

Kath wandered back towards them, her plate filled with more food and licking her fingers gleefully. 'Dear God, that macaroni cheese must be laced with crack cocaine or something. I can't get enough of it. And yes, can I second the motion – and I'm kicking myself for not thinking of it, actually. Those photos have done more for Ruth's memory than hours of conversations ever would.'

They glanced over to see Ruth regaling Bo with stories of a go-cart that Theo and Gemma had built together and just how many times they'd ended up in pieces.

Bo, meanwhile, was telling Ruth all about his new favourite Instagram feed and it didn't seem to matter that neither one was properly listening to the other.

Amy grinned at Jamie apologetically across the table. 'I think I've rather created a monster by getting Bo online, I'm so sorry.'

Jamie shook her head. 'He really loves it though, doesn't he? I thought to begin with it was all the other artists that he liked, but there's a really strong community on there for kids like Bo, isn't there?'

Batlike hearing as always, Bo turned to reply, 'It's true. It turns out *loads* of people think like me, Mum, did you know? I mean, they're not all artistic geniuses, to be fair – some of them can actually do all that stupid maths and stuff. But it's nice to hear about their lives – and it turns out that everybody's got their own Robbie Clarke, you know.'

Amy nodded. 'It's true. I mean even Superman had Lex Luthor.'

Bo rolled his eyes, 'Meanwhile, in *this* century, Iron Man has Thanos . . .'

'Cheeky,' Amy laughed, clearly taking no offence as the two of them engaged in some kind of nerd-off that Jamie struggled to follow. Maybe it was odd that her ten-year-old's new best friend was a decade his senior, but the joy that Amy brought to his life was not to be belittled. Their conversations leapt around with no logical train of thought, except to them, of course.

And Bo seemed to have words to describe more of his emotions and experiences these days.

Words, Jamie realised, that she herself had always shied away from – were they triggering, or labelling? She wasn't sure.

But the first time she'd heard Bo use the phrase 'neuro-divergent' with such casual ease had knocked her sideways.

Hearing him babble on this evening was a revelation.

Never before had she been so convinced that rushing him into a pigeon-hole would have been a mistake; letting him develop, find his tribe, and find his voice with no boundaries, just unquestioning support, had to be the right path.

If only that path could end up at Stoneleigh.

She wondered if her latest heartfelt letter to the headmistress would be enough. And at what point her campaign might constitute harassment rather than commitment. Enclosing a small portfolio of Bo's best work had been the carrot she hoped they couldn't resist.

Who wouldn't want a talent like Bo in the mix?

Or indeed this sweet, funny – and yes, quirky – boy in their community?

She glanced around the table at the unlikely group of friends that had somehow, without her even noticing, become her world.

Henry, revelling in his role as wise village elder, and Ruth mothering all of them.

Sitting back and sipping her drink slowly, she could only be grateful that fate and circumstance had thrown them all together.

Guided them into friendships, relationships and indeed pushed them to seek out opportunities more suited to their natural talents and proclivities than any spurious notion of success.

Because, surely, even the very definition of 'success' was just a question of perception?

Here, in Ruth's kitchen, feeling safe, supported – and yes, loved – had to fulfil that notion by any other measure.

So many of their new experiences only possible at all because they had come together, rather than soldiering on.

Alone.

As the food was devoured and their high spirits calmed into quiet contemplation, Bonnie leaned against Jamie's shoulder, heavy with exhaustion after a long day on her feet. Together they watched the slide show still playing silently against the back wall of the kitchen.

'Would you just look at how happy Gemma seems in so many of these,' Bonnie said quietly, reverently. 'It really does go to show that a person can properly hide how they're truly feeling, doesn't it?'

She paused for a moment and then plucked a breadstick from one of the glasses on the side. 'Do you think that made it worse for Ruth and Henry? Knowing she'd been suffering in plain sight, and they'd had no idea how bad it was?'

'Honestly?' Jamie replied, watching Ruth's face across the table, illuminated by the flickering images and still entranced by the video even on its fifth revolution. 'I don't think there can be anything worse than losing a child, so it's all relative then, isn't it? And who's to say how much more horrific it would be, to suspect it was avoidable?'

Bonnie sighed. 'I've been thinking about this a lot actually. Father Bill reckons that lots of the people at the food bank are drowning. But trying to hide it, you know? And I don't just mean paying the bills, but like, genuinely struggling to keep themselves, like, their mental health afloat when there's no hope of anything different on the horizon.' She snapped the breadstick in half with ill-concealed frustration. 'And it's not like the government are going to step up and offer a lifeline, is it?'

'No,' Jamie agreed. 'But I guess it's not all that surprising after the last few years.'

She herself could bear testament that a little hope went a very long way – the lifeline here at The Old School House had been transformative for her and for Bo. She may have left those hideous months of stress behind but they were still fresh in her memory.

'Doesn't it still feel like life is hard for too many people on too many levels right now, though?' Jamie said quietly. 'And to be honest, I think it's something we should all be talking about more.'

She glanced around the room, wondering how many of her friends in this room could truly claim to be coping right now. To be completely happy and content with their lot.

Bonnie nodded. 'If only we could get past the pride and the stigma, eh?'

Jamie sighed. 'If only.'

Chapter 42

Jamie woke up early the next morning, the dawn chorus bold and throaty, as the light crept around the edges of the wooden shutters in her bedroom. She stretched to ease the taut muscles in her neck and gave a quiet groan as they protested loudly. Stepping out of bed, she curled her toes against the chill of the flagstone floor and wrapped herself in her vast, fluffy dressing gown. Oh yes, she thought with a smile, she was all about the glamour, as she shoved her feet into Bo's Power Ranger slippers and padded quietly out into the sitting room. Kath lay gently snoring on the sofa under heaps of blankets and pillows.

She'd claimed she was too tired to go home, but it was a near certainty that she was simply trying to avoid yet another row with Craig while he was home on leave.

Friend that she was, Jamie would allow the myth of 'giving him space to enjoy the kids' company' for another day or so, before a few quiet words might be required. Jamie eyed up the kettle, before deeming it too loud and plucking one of Bo's apple juice cartons from the fridge instead. Easing open the stable door to the garden, she felt her spirits lift at the sight of the streaks of pink across sky and the amber sunlight breaking through to warm the treetops.

She walked round the corner to her favourite bench for morning coffee, huddling tighter in her robe, only to find Ruth had beaten her to it.

'Couldn't sleep?' Jamie asked, sitting down beside her.

'Something like that,' Ruth replied.

They sat in comfortable silence, until Jamie managed to break the moment with an unintentional slurp as she reached the bottom of the tiny carton. 'Sorry,' she said, but Ruth only smiled distractedly.

'I know a lot of people turn to the church after a loss,' Ruth said quietly, 'but for me? My God is the light behind the clouds. Look, Jamie. Look at that blush of pink and the layers of promise and hope – it's like a renaissance master-piece, that sky.'

Jamie breathed out slowly, relief coursing through her body, Henry's words of caution last night clearly amounting to nothing. In this instance, anyway. Although it did make perfect sense that each incremental decline in Ruth's faculties seemed to have been precipitated by a stress-filled event.

'It's so beautiful at this time of the morning, isn't it? As though the whole day could lead anywhere,' Jamie said, wondering where this particular day might yet lead.

Ruth nodded. 'Dawn and stars – the changing of the tide. Like autumn and spring. You can keep your summer and winter – I like the promise of something.' Her voice cracked a little. 'Like the moment when Theo comes home, before he speaks, or weighs in with an opinion, or his disappointment.

'Just that first moment – when he's just my boy, at home, with me. However rare that might be.'

Jamie put her arm around Ruth's shoulders and they leaned their heads together, steepled in understanding and empathy. Mothers of sons.

'It's so very easy to let the grief become the longest shadow, you know, Jamie. The way our Theo has. He just plasters on that veneer of success and won't even entertain the memories. It's like they've been overwritten by the loss for him. To him, this is just the house where she died. But for me, it's where she *lived*, Jamie. And I still can't believe he didn't join us yesterday.

'The years we had with Gemma were the best times in my entire life and I wouldn't trade them for anything.' Ruth gave a small nervous laugh. 'Even if it would be nice to remember where I left my glasses, or what Helena's boring husband is called, or even if I really did unplug the electric blanket when I got up this morning. I just don't have space in my brain for everything, so I think it just chooses to prioritise.'

Jamie nodded. It was certainly a nicer way to think about Ruth's scattergun memory – as a proactive choice to focus on happier times . . .

'Bo still asleep?' Ruth asked after a moment.

'We've got an hour or so yet until he surfaces,' Jamie said simply, glancing at her watch. She gave a gentle laugh, her son's early bird tendencies still a mystery to her. 'And if you'd told me a few years ago that I'd be up to watch the sunrise just to give myself a few moments' headspace, I'd have laughed you out of the room.'

'Well, if we're honest with ourselves, it's always our children who shape our world, isn't it? I mean, we try to believe it's the other way around, of course we do, just to give us some illusion of control,' Ruth said. 'But one can't deny that it's their experiences that become our present, and that shape our understanding of the future.'

Jamie blinked, unused to Ruth being quite so philosophical.

'I suppose so,' she said slowly. 'I mean, I'd prefer to think that Bo and I have worked together to find our path, though. Rather than either one of us calling all the shots.'

Ruth looked at her sideways and Jamie found herself shrugging.

'Okay, so maybe we do adapt around what works for Bo, more than we do for me. But that's just parenting, right?'

'Not for everyone,' Ruth said bluntly.

'But Bo isn't everyone,' Jamie protested. 'I mean, I know I'm not great at acknowledging it, but we all know that he has particular foibles, particular needs and routines. Sometimes it's just easier to be adaptable, you know, to accept that all plans are made to be changed and that it's no big drama. Sticking doggedly to a plan that isn't working, now *that's* the very definition of insanity.'

Ruth nodded. 'You make a valid point. But maybe not everyone in Bo's life can be expected to drop everything and change direction the way you do?'

Jamie nodded. It was an uncomfortable truth she rarely felt equipped to address.

'But when it comes to school and that pushy headmaster – well, for what it's worth, I think you've done the right thing there,' Ruth said quietly, 'waiting until he feels involved in the process, rather than having the process imposed upon him. It's been a brave move too. And a bold one. But I, for one, am incredibly proud of you.'

'Thank you,' Jamie replied simply. 'I can't deny though, I've been drowning in maternal guilt on this one. Principles and prevaricating can only take you so far. But I'm trying to follow my gut, you know? I can't just turn off the worry. Although it's been a gamble, for sure, but he's been happy and safe while we got our ducks in a row.' She paused. 'I just wanted him to feel heard. To feel seen, rather than judged. If that makes any sense.'

Ruth nodded. 'Life's a gamble in general, though, isn't it? But I'm a big believer in raising the stakes when it matters – and if you can't take a chance on those you love, then really what's the point of it all?'

In her lifetime, Jamie hadn't crossed paths with many people like Ruth, and she couldn't help but wish they'd met sooner. Or occasionally just daring to imagine her own mother being so open and willing to adapt to the world around her, like Ruth. Rather than tightly curating their own little world of 'safety' and fearful dissatisfaction.

'I probably don't say it enough, you know,' Jamie said, 'but I love being here. And I know Bo does too. There's something in the air here, isn't there – and obviously it comes from you and Henry, not the bricks and mortar – like, somehow it's a safe space to explore possibilities. To be a builder, not a cynic. And I've no idea how you've managed it, but I'm so grateful to be a part of it.'

Ruth smiled and patted her hand, her eyes beginning to glaze, as they so often did as she wearied. 'Well that's nice. And we love having you here, but don't throw in your lot with us entirely, Jamie, we're far too old, and liable to disappoint.'

Jamie nodded, indeed feeling oddly disappointed by Ruth's reaction. 'Don't worry. I'm nothing if not adaptable these days—'

'And, if I were to be so bold, so that someone at least, might learn from my mistakes?' Ruth interrupted her, glancing up at the window to Gemma's empty bedroom instinctively. 'Part of parenting is about leading by example.' She took a deep breath. 'Whether it's how to process grief, or talk about feelings, or . . .' She took Jamie's hand and gave it a gentle squeeze. 'Or maybe just allowing yourself to embrace your own talents, rather than apologise for them? Actually *show* Bo that it's okay to be exceptional? Show him it's okay to be vulnerable, or different. Rather than just talking about it.'

Ruth looked at her sideways. 'I mean, for some people, that might be a good place to start?'

'For some people?' Jamie queried, with an affectionate smile, even as Ruth's well-intentioned words cut deep.

Ruth shrugged. 'We all have to dance to our own beat,

my darling girl. Life's just more fun when we're all dancing together,' she said enigmatically, tipping her face back
to catch the first warm rays of sunshine, looking utterly
exhausted.

'Sorry to interrupt, ladies.' Henry hovered at a distance,
plucking at the buttons of his cardigan in obvious discomfort. 'Ruth, my love, I've got Theo online. A video call.' He
frowned apologetically. 'He says he wants to talk to us both
together.'

Jamie felt Ruth physically deflate beside her.

Standing up, she held out her hand to guide Ruth to her
feet. 'I'm here if you need me. And we'll have a nice coffee
together afterwards?'

She watched them walk back towards the house,
hand in hand.

Everyone's family was its own particular enigma, of
course, but the Ruth that she knew was so outgoing and
loving. It pained Jamie to see her shrink at the very prospect
of yet another challenging conversation with her son, all of
them at cross-purposes. Their agendas not so much overlap-
ping, as clashing, yet all with the best of intentions.

Support was really the only thing Jamie could offer.

Chapter 43

By the time Bo had woken up and navigated his carefully choreographed morning routine, Kath had given up on getting near the bathroom and dashed out the door, one of Bo's snack bars in her mouth and tugging on her uniform clumsily in her haste to be on time for work. To Jamie, after her early start and late night, it felt like lunchtime already.

Waiting for Ruth and Henry to finish their video call, hearing raised voices through the open windows, Jamie could only hope that they would find the common ground that so clearly eluded them.

She didn't mean to eavesdrop. She didn't want to intrude on their privacy, but sound did travel and it was hard to ignore the occasional outbursts. Theo, as always, like a broken record – not really listening to his parents and their wishes, trying to impose his solutions upon them with little regard for the wonderful and fulfilling life they had built here.

His world was all about the logic, the logistics and the finances.

The figures in his spreadsheets dictating the facts.

He obviously worked hard and he was clearly gifted when

it came to playing the financial markets, but yet his ethos jarred with Jamie. For her, money had always been the currency to fund the life you wanted. The means, not the ends.

But then, hadn't Theo already made his views about Jamie and her role here perfectly clear? Her very presence was an unknown vector – just a complication born from his parents' ongoing guilt about Gemma. A do-over.

But even as the 'hired help', Jamie could have told him that his high-handed approach would get him nowhere in his quest to ship Ruth and Henry across the Atlantic to make his own life easier and salve his conscience.

More raised voices and then the slamming of doors.

Gentle, loving Ruth driven to anger. So out of character as to be confusing.

Jamie stilled for a moment, the rude thought intruding into her mind that perhaps parents were *always* different people away from their beloved offspring?

Was it perhaps possible that her own fearful, controlling mother had been the life and soul of the party when Jamie had not been around?

Was she, herself, more relaxed and less braced for drama when Bo was safely occupied elsewhere?

It was a galling thought, but one that she had no time to entertain or explore right now.

Right now, her priority was to keep Ruth and Henry company, while keeping them safe. And if that meant stepping in to soothe their familial situation then so be it.

*

359

Henry sat alone at the kitchen table, the iPad still propped up in front of him and paperwork strewn across the scrubbed oak expanse.

'Don't worry. He's logged off. And Dotty's gone for a little fresh air,' he said tiredly, shuffling the various folders and printouts into heaps, even as they slithered disobediently in his failing grasp.

'Henry, let me?' Jamie said, stepping forward to help. The beatific smiles of the elderly couple adorning the front cover of one of the folders gave her pause. Were they back to looking at retirement communities again?

She frowned instinctively, even as she read the words 'Equity Release' – not knowing *exactly* what that meant, but aware enough to realise that Henry hadn't been twiddling his thumbs all this time. While Theo had been posting him pamphlets, he and Ruth had been making plans of their own. She gathered together page after page of neatly written calculations and extrapolations.

She glanced up and saw Henry watching her expression. 'Nobody wants to feel like an obligation, do they?' he said quietly. 'And at the end of the day, Theo has made it perfectly clear that he has no desire to live at The Old School House ever again, so Dotty and I may as well make the most of the time we have left and maybe even make a difference.' He glanced at the pages of calculations. 'It's the price of freedom, really.'

He walked away, out into the garden in search of his wife, leaving Jamie to try and work out what their apparent plans for the future meant for her own.

In just a few short moments, the firm sense of security she had so enjoyed since landing here at The Old School House was completely undermined. Not wilfully, maliciously or thoughtlessly, but by a caring couple who had no wish to be infantalised in their dotage, or indeed to visit every moment of their inevitable demise upon their only child.

Chapter 44

Hours later and Ruth had barely spoken a word all day. And now, as the afternoon faded, she simply sat at the kitchen table, her hands wrapped tightly around a mug of tea that was now so cold and congealed that there was something floating on the surface. But she wouldn't let go.

Any attempt to relieve her of the mug and her hands would tighten, even as her glazed eyes looked right through whomever was trying.

Jamie had failed.

Henry had failed.

And even Chris's usual chirpy-chappy-chippie routine, which was normally guaranteed to raise a smile, had fallen flat.

A small part of Jamie had wanted to join her; to simply sit down and log out of the chaotic turmoil that had been roiling in her mind since that morning.

So many unanswered questions.

And that fluid, ineffable feeling of security from being here at The Old School House? Well, it seemed as though that too had simply left the building.

'Look,' Jamie said in the end, Henry and Chris having long left them to it, whiling away their afternoon in the assembly room, making plans and measuring things. 'I know Theo's call didn't exactly go to plan this morning . . .'

Ruth turned to her, blinking slowly, as though emerging from a trance. 'Gemma?' she said.

Jamie nodded. 'Maybe it *is* all about Gemma? And this place too, probably? From what you've told me, it seems like he's been bottling up so many emotions for years that it's bound to be an emotional conversation to talk about the future.'

Ruth patted her hand distractedly. 'You're a good girl,' she said with a tired smile. 'Trying to defend your brother.'

Jamie stilled, the air knocked from her lungs. 'Ruth?'

'Let's not waste the day while he has another one of his moods,' Ruth said, standing up abruptly and brushing something from her lap, as though brushing away whatever torment had been filling her mind all day. Jamie reached out a hand to steady her, but Ruth gave her a querulous look. 'I'm fine, Gem. Don't look so worried, love. Some baking therapy is exactly what we need, you and I.'

And with that she marched over to the larder and began pulling out ingredients in disjointed, jerky movements, like a marionette.

'Henry!' Jamie called, unable to quash the wave of panic that overcame her. 'Henry, can I borrow you for a minute?' She forced herself to breathe in deeply, oddly overcome with emotion at the sight of her beloved boss, her new friend, so entrenched in false memories and wily, convincing confusion.

Henry stood in the doorway for a second as realisation dawned. 'Can you – do you mind just playing along for a short while? It passes. But not always quickly.' His tone was apologetic, but Jamie's concern was mirrored in his eyes.

'Are you ready for this, Jamie?' he whispered, steadying himself at every mention of his daughter's name.

Jamie shook her head. 'I don't think any of us will ever be ready, Henry. But we'll be here.'

Her phone buzzed in her pocket and she reached down, her eyes never leaving Ruth as she bustled around the kitchen, whistling to herself. Happy, it seemed, locked in the past for a few fleeting moments, or possibly hours? Back in a time when she and Gemma would bake their worries away.

Kath's voice memo wobbled into the room, her habit of dictating on the run now all too familiar. 'Love, if I pick Bo up from school, can I crash at yours again tonight? And yes, I am attempting to bribe you!' Her gentle laugh betrayed a world of anxiety and not for the first time Jamie felt an urge to gather everyone she loved under one roof – this roof, in particular, it seemed – to protect them from the world at large.

Or at least errant and arrogant husbands.

'Sounds perfect,' she replied and hit send.

'Now then, what are we making today?' Jamie said, walking over to Ruth's side, drawing the line at calling her Mum in whatever delusion this was, but nevertheless the swell of love and affection she felt as she tied Ruth's unravelling apron spoke of a bond between them that Jamie had longed for all of her life.

She swallowed hard, only wishing she'd known this feeling sooner – love, yes, but also respect and a genuine longing to spend time in her company – before the twilight years were able to steal away with the very essence that made Ruth, Ruth.

Jamie heard Henry sigh, both of them knowing that after the stress of the last twenty-four hours, this was hardly unexpected, but still . . .

'And then, well, I said, "You're not the boss of me, Robbie Clarke!" and I ate the whole cupcake in one big mouthful,' Bo reported proudly, the smears of vanilla frosting still spackling his cheeks as testament to the tale.

His wonderfully oblivious cheer had been exactly what they'd all needed, truth be told, although Kath had clocked the situation with Ruth in an instant.

'Sundowners,' she'd said with a nod. 'It's so hard, I know,' she'd repeated as Ruth insisted on calling Jamie, Gemma, and acting as though Theo were simply out with his friends, working off a teenage strop. 'Change of scene sometimes helps? Do you want me to get her showered and ready for bed? We could have a TV supper in PJs and break the routine a little?'

Jamie turned to Henry, all too aware suddenly that this was where her responsibilities presumably kicked in. Henry, however, was miles away, watching his wife hum to herself as she licked the spoon, flicking cake batter up the wall as she did so, and not giving a fig.

He walked over to her and rested his hands on her waist, kissing the tip of her nose. 'You're making quite the mess of things, my love,' he said.

And to Jamie and Kath, it wasn't entirely clear in that moment whether he was referring to the cake-smeared walls or the plans they'd made to grow happily and contentedly old together.

'God, is it weird that I see them together – warts and all – and I still find myself wanting that?' Kath said quietly.

Jamie shook her head. 'Not weird. Just goes to show that everyone's different. I mean, I look at them together and wish they were my parents. How sad is that? Me – a grown woman, a parent herself? Just wanting to feel mothered occasionally, while you see the love story.'

Kath pulled Jamie into her arms for a hug. 'We all deserve to feel mothered occasionally, you daft bat. Even when we're all grown up. I think it's more the unconditional love and support we crave, if I'm honest. But that's what mums are for, isn't it?'

Jamie sighed. 'You tell me. Mine didn't do that kind of emotion. Think more hedgehog than fluffy bunny.'

Kath kissed the top of her head and gave her a squeeze. 'Ah, but even hedgehogs have soft centres, Jamie. Maybe you just never got to see hers.'

'Ruth doesn't mind showing her vulnerable side, though,

does she?' Jamie said, watching Henry cuddle his wife, even as she laughed and tried to pop cake batter on his nose. To anyone watching, the epitome of happiness, a love story spanning the decades. But in this case, quite literally, with Ruth's mind somewhere back in the nineties, while Henry tried to make the best of it here in real time.

'Maybe not with you,' Kath said gently, 'and maybe she's mellowed with age. But I'll wager you'd get a different answer if you talked to Theo. Probably even if you'd known—'

'Gem? Gemma, love? Come and help me with these cupcake cases will you, darling girl?'

Bo frowned, staring at his mum for reassurance, his eyes widening as it seemingly occurred to him that there might be a ghost in the room. 'Can she see . . . ?' he began.

Jamie shook her head and crouched down in front of him. 'Ruth's a little confused right now, love. She thinks I'm Gemma. She's been very stressed and her memories have got a bit muddled up, that's all.'

Bo frowned. 'I could lend her one of my notebooks, if you think that would help. Maybe to write things down so she doesn't feel confused, because that must feel horrible to think that your daughter is still—'

'I am not confused,' Ruth's cross voice cut through their whispered conversation. She glared at Bo as though trying to place him, whispers of the present making him seem familiar and yet his name and the reason for his presence apparently eluded her.

'Shower time!' Kath said perkily. 'Come on then, Ruth,

and show me this new bathroom painting. I've been longing to see it.' And with no nonsense, just a firm hand, she shepherded Ruth from the room, leaving a scene of devastation behind her – not just cake batter, but Henry, with a smudge on his nose, looking utterly lost.

His wife still present in their marriage, but somehow absent too from the life they had built together. At least for the next few hours.

A small taste of what the future held for him, for their relationship and for everyone in their orbit.

'Let me,' said Jamie, stepping forward to salvage the mess that Ruth had created in such a short time. The cake batter filled with a hearty quantity of pistachios, still jacketed in their shells and, as it turned out, cornflour instead of self-raising.

'I'm not sure even you can work your magic on this little lot, Jamie,' Henry said sadly, picking a pistachio from the counter, peeling away the shell and popping it in his mouth, deep in thought.

Although, from the distracted expression on his face, it was obvious to everyone in the room that it wasn't the nut-filled batter that was preying on his mind.

Chapter 45

'You look well.' Daniel hovered uncertainly on the doorstep of The Old School House the next morning. It was a far cry from their usual haunts – the break room at Harrison's or the pigeon poop-spackled bench on Harnley High Street – and Jamie hadn't realised how much she'd missed his reassuring presence until he was standing right in front of her.

Text friendships were all well and good, but there was nothing like a—

'Oof,' she exhaled, as Daniel scooped her into one of his bear hugs, his beard rough against her forehead, yet comforting by its very familiarity. 'It's so great to see you . . .'

'You too,' Daniel said. 'I hadn't realised that our barmy conversations about life, love and the universe were what made that job actually bearable.'

'Is Harrison being utterly foul?' Jamie asked sympathetically, having half wondered whether he would take his bad mood out on her colleagues. Ex-colleagues, she should say.

'Probably no more than usual,' he replied with a shrug, 'it's just harder to process when there's nobody left who's willing to mock him behind his back.'

Jamie smiled, so pleased that he'd responded to her call for help with such alacrity. Food and photography. That was what made Daniel tick and it was wonderful to see his face light up as he looked around her new home.

'My friend, this is so much better for you than stacking shelves for a petty tyrant,' he said with feeling. 'I'll bet Bo adores this place, doesn't he? It must be like living in an adventure playground for him.'

Jamie nodded, loving his enthusiasm. 'You'll barely recognise him, Daniel. He's in his element. So much happier, at home anyway.' She rolled her eyes, 'School is another story, *obviously.*'

Daniel nodded, no explanation necessary.

'Come on then, make me a cup of tea and tell me what you're plotting now.' He hefted the camera bag more firmly onto his shoulder and glanced around with a huge grin on his face. 'Suits you, you know, this place.'

'Old and draughty?' Jamie replied.

'Was thinking more stylish and eccentric, but maybe you're more on the money.'

'That's it – no chocolate biscuits for you then,' Jamie said sternly, but unable to disguise her smile, loving the way they fell back so easily into their comforting repartee. He was a unique soul, that was for sure, but maybe the fact he'd been through so much in his own life was what made him the thoughtful, caring friend she valued so much.

Daniel was good company. Easy company. And that was not to be taken for granted.

She filled the teapot and hunted around for sugar. Three spoonfuls. No matter what anyone said about the future of his teeth.

'So,' she said, settling down at the island beside him. 'We have a plan to make-over a room here, as a showpiece for some amazing talent, actually. But I thought it might be nice to have a "before" photograph too, you know, so people can truly appreciate the magic they've wrought. And Henry's really excited – that's one of the owners – because they've always wanted to do up this room but never had the time, you know how it is?

'Anyway,' she carried on, caught up in her own enthusiasm for the plan, 'the idea is to turn the old school assembly room into a kind of art-deco orangery – Chris is an amazing carpenter, Amy is doing the paintwork and colour scheme, and then Willow is going to furnish the room with some wonderful plants and flowers. Beyond that, nobody really knows, but that's the plan anyway ... They're all starting over and launching new careers, hopefully, so I was thinking a picture's worth a thousand words, right?'

He nodded, leaning forward, intrigued. 'So they're not actually in business yet?'

Jamie shook her head. 'It's a new venture for all of them.'

'Brave,' he said, 'in the current climate, I mean.'

Jamie nodded. 'They *are* brave, though, aren't they? Starting over is always scary. But I'd rather be scared than filled with regret.'

'Well, that was said with feeling,' Daniel said, frowning. 'Are you okay?'

'I'm fine. I mean, it'll be fine. Right?'

'Er – yes?' Daniel watched her carefully. 'I can listen and take photos at the same time, you know.'

'I know. I was just thinking that starting over always seemed to be such a leap – reserved for dreamers and risk-takers. And now, it's just something we all have to accept as a part of life. Almost everyone has to make a course correction at some point, but still none of us feel brave or certain about doing it.'

'Again though, better to change direction than be stuck on a collision course,' Daniel said, opening his camera bag and arranging his various lenses methodically on the kitchen counter. 'And you definitely dodged a bullet at Harrison's.'

He clicked a wide-angle lens onto the camera body of his beloved SLR. A vintage find on eBay, but nonetheless beautiful and highly effective. Particularly in such talented hands.

'And here's me asking for favours on your only day off.'

'Hardly,' Daniel replied with a cheeky smile. 'I mean, if you're all about spreading the word of new ventures, new talent on the scene, then maybe we could credit my photographs too?'

'Perfect,' Jamie said. 'Come and see the space, and then you can tell me all about your new photography business.'

'Steady on,' Daniel said, shaking his head with resigned amusement at Jamie's tireless enthusiasm, her absolute belief in his talents. 'You haven't seen the photos yet, and I'm not sure an obsession with *Location, Location, Location* actually qualifies me to be a property photographer, you know? It's a far cry from sweeping views and wildflower meadows.'

'Maybe,' Jamie conceded. 'But the housing market is insanely buoyant around here. Or so I'm told.' She shuddered at just the memory of Kieran Jones and his conviction that better times, better tenants, were on the cards. 'So there has to be space for someone with a bit of artistic vision when they're doing fancy brochures and websites, right? In fact, if you can do video tours, I reckon you're really on to something. I still can't believe people were buying houses during the lockdowns on the strength of just a FaceTime tour?'

'Madness,' Daniel agreed. 'But when needs must ... I mean, I emigrated to a whole new country on the strength of liking the BBC World Service. So, you know, maybe I'm not the best person to ask about sane decision-making.'

'No plans for heading back into chef-ing then? No yearning for a hot, sweaty kitchen?'

He shook his head. 'I think it's better to accept my particular course correction for what it is, but I can't pretend I wouldn't rather talk about houses and property all day, than Harrison's linguine and panna cotta.' He paused. 'There's a new show on Channel 4 I've become rather obsessed with, actually, they—'

He broke off as Jamie pushed open the double doors and stepped into the light-flooded room, dust motes hanging in the air and only serving to accentuate the other-worldly sense of time held still.

'Wow,' he breathed. 'This is insane.' He turned full circle, focusing on every tiny detail. 'You know, if it was me, I'd want to keep it as it is. Preserve the history of the school.'

Jamie shook her head. 'There's no shortage of reminders throughout the house, and having all this dead space unused is what's crazy.'

She squinted and tilted her head, trying to envision the design that Chris and Amy had been bickering about ever since they'd floated the suggestion. Henry was surprisingly laid-back about how it turned out, so long as he no longer had to look at the orange pinewood stage and lectern.

The only hold-up in proceedings, in fact, was waiting for him to find a good moment to broach the subject with Ruth.

Ruth, who had been particularly tetchy since Theo's latest 'thoughtful present' had been delivered first thing – did he really think a shower seat was something that a person might like to receive unprompted? As olive branches went, it was ill-considered at best.

The telephone pealed loudly in the hallway, echoing around the whole house.

'Isn't somebody going to answer that?' Daniel frowned, perplexed by Jamie's lack of response.

She shook her head. 'Not normally. You get used to it after a while.'

The phone cut out as the answerphone cut in, only to start ringing again almost instantly.

Jamie checked her mobile out of habit, checking that nobody at school was trying to reach her. What Ruth and

Henry chose to do wasn't really her business, no matter how uncomfortable it made her feel; they had laid down the law on this too many times already.

The phone, Gemma's bedroom and the study.

Three parts of the house that had nothing to do with her role here. Apparently.

'So,' Daniel said, once the phone had finally accepted defeat, 'what kind of look are you aiming for with this? Sort of lost and atmospheric? Did the owners want some shots as a memento as well?'

'Why would I need a memento for something I can see every day just by opening a door?' Ruth's voice was curt as her gaze flickered back and forth between Jamie and Daniel. She looked hurt and rather angry as she took in the scene.

'I expected better of you, Jamie, than to let those grasping estate agents into my home when I have expressly told them, time and time again, that this house is *not* for sale.' Ruth's hand gripped tightly on the doorjamb, her face blanched of colour.

'No, no, no,' Jamie was quick to reassure her, 'Daniel's just a friend of mine, taking some photos. He's not an estate agent.'

'Not yet,' Daniel murmured under his breath, earning himself a bewildered look from Jamie that he'd thought that might be helpful in the circumstances.

'Sorry,' he mouthed, turning away, to let Jamie handle the situation.

'Ruth,' Jamie repeated herself, 'Daniel isn't here to sell the house – he's just here to take photos.'

Ruth scowled at him suspiciously. 'Did you check his ID? They can be sneaky, you know – all smiles and compliments while they're selling your home out from under you.'

Jamie blinked hard. She had no way of knowing whether this was some paranoid episode or a further insight into the squirrelly finances and correspondence that Henry and Ruth had previously gone to great pains to keep private. She'd been meaning to look up what the realities of an equity release scheme entailed, but life just kept getting in the way.

'You know you can always talk to me – in confidence – if there's something that's worrying you,' Jamie said gently.

Ruth shook her head, folding her lips inwards as though to physically prevent herself from speaking.

'Why *are* you taking photographs then?' Ruth said abruptly, changing gear and then listening intently as Jamie explained the whole saga.

'And I'm so sorry to take you by surprise,' Jamie finished. 'Henry was going to talk to you himself . . .'

Ruth sighed, nodding, as she formulated her reply, 'Daniel, was it? And a friend you can trust, Jamie? Take your photos then, but I'd like some copies too please, if I may?'

Ruth made to leave, then paused once more in the doorway. 'It's a wonderful idea, all of this, Jamie. So cheering to see you all supporting each other. It's always what I hope for actually, bringing people together, making our own community among all the chaos, you know?'

She looked around the room again, giving Jamie the odd

impression that she was taking it all in, as though for the last time.

'We won't change anything without your approval, Ruth. You have my word,' Jamie said earnestly.

Ruth shook her head. 'I dare say it doesn't matter anyway,' she said sadly, as she left the room.

Daniel still held his camera in his hands, waiting for the go-ahead.

'You know,' he said very quietly, holding his camera up to his eye and then hesitating, 'I'm not sure your boss is okay.'

Jamie stared at Ruth's departing figure, smaller and more frail than she had been only a week before. The video call with Theo had certainly taken its toll.

'I'm not sure either,' she murmured. 'But I'm working on it.'

Chapter 46

Jamie lay back on the picnic rug later that day, the early evening sun illuminating a small oasis in the middle of the lawn. Picnic tea had been Bo's favourite thing since he was small and, as she'd rummaged in Ruth's freezer at lunchtime, unearthing sausage rolls and vegan quiches, the idea had quickly taken shape.

Totally worth the effort to see Bo's tired face light up with teary excitement as he'd walked down the drive with Jamie to see the spread she had laid out.

Jamie's smile, too, had grown wider when she saw that the tartan rug and Tupperware she'd assembled had since been supplemented with tumbling heaps of cushions, a huge bowl of strawberries and a tray of drinks, ice still clinking and popping as it warmed up in the sunshine.

Willow sat back on her haunches by the flower borders, now a riot of colour and depth. Her hands covered in mud, along with a wide streak of dirt along one cheek, she was almost unrecognisable from the taut, wan girl that Jamie had first met. 'I think Ruth may have got a little overexcited,' Willow laughed. 'She'll be out in a minute, once she's got the flapjacks out of the oven. I hope you're hungry, Bo?'

Bo dumped his school bag on the ground, looked up at his mum and grinned, eyes sparkling. 'Can I see if Henry wants to join in too?' But he was already halfway across the lawn, heading to the greenhouse, where the cricket on 5 Live could be heard burbling away behind the glass, a sure indicator that Henry was at work nearby.

'I've barely been gone half an hour,' Jamie exclaimed, taken aback at how her rather scruffy spontaneous picnic now resembled something from an E. M. Forster novel. All they needed now was a tray of fine china tea cups and—

She laughed, one hand pressed tightly to her chest to quell the emotion. Ruth really had thought of everything.

She emerged from the kitchen doorway balancing a vast tray bearing an entire tea set and a tiered stand of flapjacks and tiny sandwiches. 'Tea, darling?' she said, almost giddy with glee.

Jamie dashed over and relieved her of the weight before the entire ensemble could come crashing to the ground. 'This looks amazing!'

'And Amy will be here in a minute with some Babycham, or whatever the like is these days – we're celebrating again.'

'Make way for your very own, highly in demand, painter and decorator extraordinaire!' Amy skidded to a halt on the driveway, her bike wheels spraying gravel into an almost impressive arc. A Spar bag swung from the handlebars, the bottle of Appletiser poking through the fine plastic, no doubt a fizzy grenade by this point.

'Wow! That's fantastic, Ames. I'm so thrilled for you,' Jamie said, as she accepted the swamping hug with good grace.

'Well, I owe you one. Whatever you said to that Mrs Kendal sure put a rocket up her bum. She went from snarky and suspicious to fawning and appreciative in a heartbeat. Wouldn't let me leave until she'd paid a deposit to secure my services.' She gave a filthy laugh. 'It's a good job I actually intend to go back and do the work, you know?'

'Amy!' Ruth looked shocked, even as Jamie and Amy exchanged a smile.

'Mum! Mum! Bonnie's on the radio!' Bo called as he and Henry hustled across the lawn with his ancient Roberts radio crackling.

'It's true – I was just adjusting the dial and there she was – on Radio Harnley clear as day,' Henry added.

'And we'll be back with more from our local entrepreneur Bonnie Fuller after these messages from our sponsors ...' 'Grant in the Afternoon' was well known in these parts for cherry-picking the sponsors he wanted for his show and they all couldn't help a chuckle as there was a parade of local car dealerships, sunbeds and tapas bars.

'Well, now – how did she manage that?' Ruth asked. 'She's only been open five minutes. Oh, she's a clever girl that one. See Amy, how some smart thinking about her clients, about her business, has really made a difference. Although maybe at some point she'll actually listen to some advice and change the name of her salon too.'

Henry looked up, catching the fleeting smile on Jamie's

face, knowing full well that it had been her urging that had given Bonnie the nous to approach Radio Harnley in the first place. Even if Jamie herself might confess some small surprise that she'd been successful so quickly in securing a spot.

'It's not a salon, it's a kiosk,' said Bo, through a mouthful of flapjack.

'Shhh!' they all said, as Ruth quietly poured out the tea for everyone and they sat around on the rug, listening intently to the radio as Bonnie came back on the air.

Her dulcet tones echoed across the local airwaves, as she chatted confidently with 'Grant in the Afternoon'. 'The thing is, Grant, I'm convinced you don't need to spend a fortune to look good or to build your confidence. And everybody knows that feeling, right, when you step out of the hairdressers, with an amazing blow-dry, feeling like you could take on the world? Well, why wait to have that feeling every eight weeks, when the right style could give you that boost every day? Heaven knows, it's hard enough finding our feet in the world these days without doing it with a lousy haircut.'

Her conviction was rather beguiling actually, and Jamie felt a warm swell of pride for her friend's achievement, not to mention her eloquence in framing her ideas and her views on air. No small achievement.

'And,' continued Bonnie, 'while so many people are picking themselves up and starting again, I'd like to help. So, to any listeners out there – if you bring along proof that you have a job interview, I will cut your hair for just a small donation to the local food bank in lieu of payment.

'Life shouldn't be a competition, don't you think, Grant, when it can be so much more satisfying as a collaboration, a team effort.'

'But it's just you right now? You are your business, am I right, Bonnie?'

'I'm the one wielding the scissors, yes, Grant. But there's so much more to a business than just the face-to-face work with your clients. And I think it's really important to acknowledge that we each have our individual skills, don't we? As I was reminded recently by some incredibly astute young friends: we can't judge a fish by its ability to fly.'

'That's us!' Bo said excitedly to Amy, his chest puffed out proudly. 'We told her that!'

'Shhh! I missed that bit now,' Ruth said, talking over yet more of whatever Bonnie was saying.

'I'm not ashamed to tell you that there have been some really challenging times over the last few years, Grant. Some pretty awful experiences in the workplace convinced me that life was too short to be bullied every day. Especially somewhere we're all entitled to feel safe. And yes, throw in a pretty brutal case of Covid, and some changes had to be made.

'And try as I might, I needed a little help to get back on my feet. And that's okay, you know. To need help, and to have the courage to ask for it is one of the hardest things. Without the food bank at St Mark's, without the entrepreneur scheme from Harnley Council, and without the advice and cheerleading from some very special friends, I wouldn't be here talking to you today.'

'As a successful business owner?' Grant finished for her.

'At all,' Bonnie said bluntly, quietly. 'Actually.'

There was a collective intake of breath across the picnic rug. Hard swallows of mini meringues, and iced apple juice. Shocked glances traded as they all fell silent to listen.

'It's really important to realise that however bad things seem, there is always someone there to help. Probably someone who has already walked a mile in your shoes, and they know the way,' Bonnie said. 'Just a conversation on your darkest day can change your life, can save your life actually.

'So, when you come for a haircut, come for a chat. Come for a laugh – I have some cracking jokes up my sleeve. But more importantly, to anyone listening, come and say "hi" so you don't feel like you have to manage life on your own. Come, even if you're shiny and bald and the last thing you need is a haircut,' she joked to finish, her voice choked with emotion.

'Well, what an incredibly brave and impressive story,' Grant said, the wind clearly taken out of his sails by her revelation.

'Not really,' Bonnie said. 'It just really irks me that there's an awful lot of talk about how people with mental health issues struggle to find their place in the world. Am I right?' She sighed deeply across the airwaves, 'It's just that nobody *ever* seems to mention how people who struggle to find their place in the world often end up with mental health issues.

'So, let's talk about that! To anyone listening, maybe check in with the person next to you in the queue at the food bank, or at the job centre, the post office, or even at the checkout in the supermarket . . . Let them know that nobody has to do everything on their own. Am I right?'

There was an awkward pause and then Grant brought the interview back on track. 'Our guest for today, the inspirational Bonnie Fuller, and you can find her new hairdressing salon—'

'Kiosk,' Bonnie interrupted, her voice still husky with emotion, echoed across the lawn by Bo, Amy and Henry listening.

'Indeed,' said Grant. 'You can find *Crap But Cheap* – which sounds anything but crap – on Harnley High Street now.'

'Where Dave's Churros used to be—' Bonnie couldn't help interrupting again.

'And now for these words from our sponsors . . .'

'Slip into oblivion with a Sleeptight mattress,' crooned the velvet tones of the voiceover artist.

Henry gave a shocked snort of discomforted laughter at the incredibly unfortunate timing of that tagline, but Jamie was still too stunned to react.

She couldn't reconcile the Bonnie she knew – bold, loud and bright in every sense of the word – with what she had just heard. The Bonnie that was so cheerful and determinedly full of optimism, the first to offer a hand of friendship.

But of course, she'd had no way of knowing that this very exuberance was the legacy of surviving such dark times. Or worse – the thought hit Jamie hard – that perhaps everything she knew about Bonnie might yet be an elaborate facade concealing how she really felt.

And as much as she loathed talking about feelings, or even acknowledging them in any way – could she honestly call herself Bonnie's friend if she didn't even ask the question?

Chapter 47

'That poor girl.' Ruth's hand hovered over her mouth, the colour drained from her cheeks.

'No wonder she goes back to St Mark's to volunteer every evening,' Amy said thoughtfully. 'Even when she's exhausted.'

'It's more than giving back and saying thank you, isn't it?' Jamie ventured, the jigsaw pieces of the puzzle that was Bonnie Fuller dropping into place in her mind. 'Maybe she just doesn't want to be alone?'

Henry nodded sagely, glancing lovingly at Ruth, their bond almost tangible across the chaotic picnic rug. 'Haven't we all been there, though, when it's easier to work longer and longer hours than confront the reality of your situation? Focus on your career while your life is quietly falling apart?'

There was a moment of quiet as his words resonated with everyone there.

'Like when I stay up late drawing, even though I'm tired, because going to sleep is scary sometimes?' Bo said quietly, looking up to his mother for confirmation.

Jamie nodded. 'I think Bonnie needs a big hug and some of this flapjack, don't you? She's been very brave today, sharing her story on the radio, trying to help other people.'

'Being brave is exhausting,' Ruth said with feeling, watching Bo carefully. 'And it always makes me hungry, don't you find? Even making a phone call I don't want to make, or sometimes just having to be somewhere I don't want to be.' She nudged the plate of flapjacks towards Bo, accompanied by a knowing look. 'Bo?'

He flushed, rumbled. 'Maybe I will have just one more flapjack then ...'

Ruth nodded, understanding, seeing exactly how exhausting and demoralising Bo's day at school had been, even without this bombshell about one of his favourite people. A bombshell that must surely have shaken her too. Her quiet fragility these last few days noticeable to all of them; moments of lucidity and clarity, like now, to be savoured rather than taken for granted.

'I'm glad Bonnie's still around and she didn't move away,' Bo said, through a mouthful of oats. 'She brought all of us together, didn't she really?'

Ruth caught Jamie's eye in sympathy, as Bo's misunderstanding of the situation became clear, both of them wondering whether it was strictly necessary to burden him with the reality of just how very far removed Bonnie had obviously longed to be from this life. Here. In Harnley. Before she'd known them.

*

Kath's car pulled up on the drive twenty minutes later, Bonnie crammed into the passenger seat, even her exuberant hair squashed into submission in the tiny Fiat.

They were bickering even as they both emerged from the car, half affectionately, half cross with each other.

'All I'm saying is that I'm here for you. And you don't have to put a brave face on for my benefit.' Kath looked frustrated as her words were falling on apparently deaf ears.

'You've got enough on your plate with your job and your kids and your useless husband,' Bonnie countered. 'You don't need to worry about me – the pills work and I'm fine. *Now*.'

'Well then, next time you're not fine?' Kath said, holding her ground.

Bonnie nodded.

'Can I second the motion?' Jamie said, walking over and reaching out a hand to Bonnie. 'Any time. Honestly.'

Bonnie rolled her eyes and sighed. Holding up one hand to halt any further outpourings. 'Guys, I am *fine*. Honestly. It's one of the reasons I wanted to speak out, because if you'd told me a year ago that I'd be here, with friends, with a business, with prospects even – well, I wouldn't have believed you, that's all.' She gave an embarrassed shrug. 'A lot can change in a year, and I thought that was a strong message to send, you know?'

Jamie nodded, her own life transformed in a matter of weeks by good company and a safe place to call home.

That alone, in fact, giving her more by way of comfort than she could possibly imagine.

'It's a solid message to start the conversation with,' she agreed. 'But still, everyone knows that life comes with ups and downs – mainly when you're least expecting them – so can we at least lay down a marker, that you don't need to suffer in silence?'

Bonnie threw her arms out wide, her tangerine kaftan top wafting in the breeze. 'Have you ever known me to be silent, Jamie? Have you?'

Jamie smiled and shook her head. 'But that doesn't mean you're saying everything that needs to be said, now Bon, does it?' She gave her a knowing look.

'Exactly what I was saying,' Kath joined in. 'And no, we're not ganging up on you. There's this strange concept where friends care about each other and look out for each other.' She paused and dropped her voice. 'The way you have for me, time and time again.'

And as Jamie poured more tea and handed out more food, the same thought echoed around in her head over and over again.

There would always be hurdles on the path to happiness, even putting aside pandemics and recessions. But the biggest hurdle she could see was in trying to manage any of it alone.

And hadn't they all been guilty of thinking that it was easier to try it, though.

Not wanting to be a burden, or to elicit pity.

Stepping back from life at the very time it would have been healthier to step forward.

Putting on a mask, a brave face, just to get through the day and losing oneself in the process.

She looked at Willow, at Amy. Could hear Chris whistling happily as he turned wood in Henry's shed, promising to join them when he'd finished his set of beautifully smooth cherry table legs.

Every single one of them had been lost without some gentle guidance.

She looked up and saw Henry watching her, almost as though he could read her mind. He nodded, just once, apparently happy with what he saw.

Bo began fidgeting beside her. 'Can I go and help Chris in the workshop?'

'Or you could play French cricket with me?' Amy said, leaping to her feet. 'In fact, we could all play together and work off those flapjacks.'

Henry heaved himself up out of his folding chair, trembling slightly with the effort. 'Bo, there's a tennis racquet and some balls just by the backdoor. Be a good lad and grab them for me?'

Bo shook his head. 'You can't play cricket with a tennis racquet.'

'You can play cricket with a floorboard if you have to,' Henry corrected him, 'but this is French cricket. Less running, more whacking – you'll like it.'

As Bo ran off, still a little confused, to gather supplies, Jamie noticed Kath make a beeline for Henry, their intense conversation a static point among the sudden activity on the lawn, as picnic supplies and rugs were hastily gathered together to clear the way for games.

'Everything okay?' Jamie called.

Henry waved dismissively. 'Everything absolutely fine. Now then, I'll just limber up my bowling arm ...'

Kath frowned but said nothing more, moving back to field along the edge of the lawn as Bonnie tucked her voluminous skirt in her knickers and kicked off her shoes.

They were all in the mood to let off some steam, it appeared.

'I'll be your runner, okay, Bo?' Amy said, taking charge. 'So, your job is to thwack that ball, and let me do the sprinting about like a nutter, okay?'

Bo grinned – this was his idea of how sport should be.

'Mum! Mum!' he said. 'You be on our team, okay?'

Jamie nodded, oddly touched that not only did he still want her around, but that he had no problem expressing that. And around other people too! Definitely something to savour while it lasted.

'On it,' she said with a smile, as they all milled around, their chilled and disorganised approach making their impromptu game all the more fun. In fact, very quickly, there were no teams at all – everyone mucking in to field and support whomever was wielding the knackered old tennis racquet.

'Goal!' cheered Ruth at one point, as Bonnie thwacked the ball with such force that it penetrated the canopy of branches overhead, cleaving a perfect circle through the foliage and they all laughed.

'Allez, allez, allez!' shouted Henry from the sidelines, clapping and hollering.

Bo's cheeks were pink and his eyes sparkled with mischief, as he chased Amy down the lawn to claim the ball when it came back down from orbit. 'Mine!' he cried happily, tumbling over his own feet in his haste to be victorious. His exuberant dance of jubilation soon had Amy and Bonnie joining in, their moves jerky and uncoordinated but none the less hysterical.

It didn't escape Jamie's notice for one moment that Bo's inhaler sat firmly in her pocket. Superfluous to requirements. His laughter and cheekiness ramping up with each successive round, as he realised he had a captive audience in Amy, Bonnie and Willow.

Her little boy – happy, confident and at one with himself.

Amy delighted that her celebratory picnic was back on track.

And Bonnie – who presumably welcomed such silliness after the heightened emotions of her day – whose face lit up with every joke, every hug, every dodgy dance routine.

She looked up and caught Jamie watching her and smiled.

Indeed, there was something about this summer evening that was magical on so many levels; not just the walled garden and the shouts of laughter, but the warm smell of grass and the riot of colour in Willow's newly planted borders. It was like a tiny oasis away from the world, away from her worries and challenges, pressing pause on thinking about the future and enjoying the moment.

Together.

Every single person here had been to hell and back, and yet they were still standing. With whatever life had thrown at them, they had called on their reserves and rallied. Coming back from rock bottom.

Jamie's eye wandered to the beautiful fat vase that stood tall on her window sill, at Ruth's particular insistence, outlined by the sweeping curve of the clematis.

Jade and charcoal and grey woven together throughout the mottled ceramic, but then each fragment joined together with seams of liquid silver, catching the light and holding the vase whole.

Kintsugi.

And she realised, in that moment, what Ruth and the Japanese ceramicist had clearly known all along – something that had been broken could end up being more precious. The fault lines becoming a thing of beauty and part of life's story. In embracing those flaws, imperfections and misfortunes, one could even create a stronger, more beautiful piece of art.

A stronger, more beautiful life.

As the silver seams caught the evening sun, Jamie realised what a privilege it would be to guide that process, to silver the joins, and lay new foundations upon which to build a better future.

It was hardly a job description that she recognised, but it was the first prospect that had lit a fire within her, energising her just at the very thought.

Advocate. Restorer. Optimist.

Not bad labels to aspire to.

Chapter 48

'Can I come too?' Bo said, stirring at the merest mention of an outing to see Father Bill. Almost as though he'd actually been missing their weekly trips to the food bank.

What had her world come to, when her son was excited by the prospect of a trip to the food bank after school, she wondered the next day. Sure, their tummies were full, and their lives were busy, but was it possible that Bo, like Jamie, rather missed feeling a part of something bigger on occasion?

Ruth had been up early, driven by some unknown force to streamline their lives. And now the hall was filled with boxes – some for the food bank, some for the charity shop and some filled with assorted paraphernalia that Jamie would be quietly replacing around the house once Ruth had settled down for her nap.

'Are you okay to do all this, Jamie?' Henry asked apologetically, lowering his voice and one eye on Ruth. 'She seemed so agitated about the whole thing. It was easier just to go along with it, to be honest. But now we've created more work for you.'

'I want to help too, though,' insisted Bo. 'It'll be so much nicer to donate than to collect, won't it, Mum?' he added with a grin, managing to surprise her, as always. Less about the hot chocolate then, more about community spirit, that he almost certainly hadn't learned from her.

'I'm happy to help, Henry. And don't worry about it – my friend Daniel's going to meet us there and help unload. I'm far more worried about you two.'

Jamie watched him carefully tuck his trembling hand in his trouser pocket, all innocence. 'I'm fine, Jamie. Just relieved not to be the one lugging all these boxes around.' He gave her a twinkly smile. '*The Antiques Roadshow* and a sherry with my wife sounds infinitely nicer, don't you think?'

'Bonnie!' Bo darted away from Jamie's side before they could even open the boot at the food bank. He'd taken the news that Bonnie had even considered 'leaving' rather hard, until the determined tilt of his chin told Jamie that a decision had been made, and now he seemed intent on making Bonnie feel indispensable wherever possible.

It was not a bad plan, to be honest.

Jamie took one of the lighter boxes, filled with spices and condiments, all box-fresh and unopened, and walked over to where Bo was thrusting his sketchbook up higher so that Bonnie could see her new portrait. She blinked, frowning as she leaned forward herself, just to look a little closer.

Not, in fact, a portrait of Bonnie in Bo's usual style; face turned a third away, in semi-profile. But a drawing of them all, together, playing French cricket – arms outstretched, laughter creasing their faces, and the atmosphere rising from the page as though the moment captured were alive.

'I know, right?' Bonnie said, shaking her head, eyes never leaving the page. Each fresh glance revealing another detail, another expression captured with just the sweep of a pencil.

Bo gave an awkward smile. He was getting better at people talking about his work, although quiet appreciation was still his comfort zone. And even that was progress. Only a few months ago, nobody had been allowed to even see his work.

'I feel honoured, Bo, I really do,' Bonnie said, somehow knowing exactly what to say. 'Thank you for sharing this with me. And for making me look so good in the picture too.'

Bo shook his head. 'This is for you, to keep. So you can always look at it and remember how much fun we had together. Just in case you ever feel like moving away again.'

Bonnie frowned, her face scrunched up in confusion. 'Moving a—?'

'In case you feel like *leaving*,' Jamie interrupted apologetically. 'Like you were talking about on the radio?'

Understanding dawned on Bonnie's face, and she clapped her hand to her chest. 'Well,' she breathed out, visibly moved, 'isn't that a thing.' She leaned down, her voice a little wobbly. 'The perfect thing, in fact, to remind me of how life can change in such a short time. You are very thoughtful, Bo.'

He looked, Jamie thought, properly pleased. He was often called clever, or talented, or a host of less flattering monikers. But thoughtful seemed to have touched a chord with him. 'I did think about you a lot,' he replied nodding. 'Thank you for noticing.'

Her gorgeous boy, literal as ever. And, Jamie glanced at the unusual sketch once more, expanding his horizons in every way. His sketch book, as always, a barometer of how he felt about life at any given moment.

'Crikey, Bo. I won't need my camera much longer at this rate,' Daniel said, walking over to join them, laden down with bags of provisions from Ruth to donate. He leaned in and squinted. 'Your perspective is incredible, you know that?'

Bo nodded, pleased. 'That's because I'm listening more than I'm talking,' he replied earnestly, the synonym utterly escaping him.

And Jamie had to concede that, either way, he made a valid point.

Bonnie's exit curtailed by their arrival, she quickly mucked in to help them empty the last of the boxes from the car on this, their final pitstop. 'Come and see what Father Bill's been up to while you're here. He's all on a high because some of his "graduates" popped in to say hello, so now he's cooking up a "scheme",' Bonnie grinned, balancing her omnipresent turquoise bag on top of the final box so she could carry it in.

Jamie could easily imagine that it was a curious dichotomy for him, celebrating those moving on and no longer in need of the food bank, but with a revolving carousel of new faces arriving all the time. It hadn't even occurred to her that she might now qualify as a 'graduate' – one of the food bank alumni – albeit mainly thanks to Ruth's well-stocked freezer and endless goodwill, rather than any change in her financial circumstances. But still, it was a progress of sorts.

'Jamie! Bo!' His weathered face lit up as predicted. 'I cannot thank you enough for all these donations, but you do know you can just pop in to say hi?'

Jamie gave him a slightly goofy smile by way of greeting. 'I can't take the credit, I'm afraid. My new boss asked me to be the middle-man.'

Daniel plonked down the heaviest box with a groan. 'Not sure what that makes me then. Hi, I'm Daniel.' And as always, his wonderfully old-fashioned manners came to the fore, as he shook Father Bill's hand with genuine pleasure at the introduction. 'Jamie has told me so much about what you do here. It's a wonderful thing.'

Father Bill beamed. 'Isn't it though? I mean, if you put aside the fact that it's a tragedy this food bank is even required, then I really feel we're making the best of a bad situation. In fact,' he glanced down at his watch, 'come see, come see. Before rush hour hits.'

He guided them away from the drop-off zone and into the main hall and Jamie instantly felt a surge of conflicting emotions. Gratitude, of course, not just for the lifeline, but also the unlikely friendships she'd made here; but also a shiver of prescience at how very close they were, her and Bo, to being back here once again. For nothing had really changed with her new job, only perhaps a postponement of the inevitable if Theo had his way. Her fate was still in the hands of others and Jamie longed to reclaim that measure of security and independence that she had so valued; the ability to paddle her own canoe and even take the odd spontaneous detour, without her entire financial life being derailed.

'What do you think?' Father Bill spread his hands wide, his face a transparent combination of pride and anticipation. 'Just like I said – we're making it happen.'

Eight small café-style tables were clustered together at one end of the hall, chairs around them and a small play corner set up nearby, filled with books and toys and colouring-in sets. Three women were sitting there, sipping coffee and allowing their small ones free rein, bags of food at their feet. A moment's respite in their day and a wonderfully benign, welcoming atmosphere surrounding them.

'Obviously it's not fancy and to be honest, the coffee isn't exactly great, but we're trying to create a safe space. You know, just to catch one's breath?' He dropped his voice. 'And following Bonnie's suggestion, we have posters in the ladies' loo. Just saying that if you order a particular drink at the counter, it means you're in trouble, you know – in danger, at home – and we can quietly intervene. All very discreet.' He gave Bonnie an appreciative nod. 'It's the kind of thing I wouldn't have thought to do, to be honest.'

Jamie smiled at Bonnie, trying to gauge her reaction at Bill's praise. She was beginning to think of Bonnie as some kind of onion: the more layers they peeled off, the more layers appeared underneath. Did this insight, perhaps, go some way to explaining Bonnie's abject lack of interest in dating of any stripe?

Meanwhile Father Bill was still talking, Daniel and Bo following him around the hall like the proverbial sheep. She suspected Bo was more influenced by the prospect of the promised hot chocolate but Daniel was wide-eyed. Emotional too. Perhaps all of this a far cry from what his family had experienced at home in Syria when times were bad?

Everything was relative, after all. Even the notion of hard times.

'I've been really trying to set up a small creche here, just for a some occasional respite, you know? But you wouldn't believe the bureaucratic hoops involved with DBS checks for all volunteers and whatnot.' Father Bill looked utterly disillusioned for a moment, until he rallied. 'So for now, at least, we just have this drop-in set-up,' he waved a hand towards the women and children clustered around the tables, 'so nobody ever needs to be completely alone, if they need company.'

He nodded firmly, as though convincing himself that his work was fulfilling a need, even though it was only an approximation of what he'd hoped for.

'Every little helps,' Bonnie said supportively. 'And I think you're on the right track about having a willing ear and some companionship on offer. We're all happier knowing we're not the only one in the same situation – I mean, look at me and Jamie, and Kath and Amy. Aren't we so much better off for having each other? A shoulder to cry on? An ear to bend?'

Father Bill nodded, his forehead creasing in thought. 'You

know, I wonder if maybe having a counsellor here might be more useful than a creche?'

Jamie had zoned out for a moment, fascinated by the tableau of young children at the tables, only half an ear on what Bill was saying. Until she heard Bo's voice pipe up, clear and distinct and throwing her for six.

'Well, my mum could do that, can't you, Mum? She's a qualified counsellor, you know. I've seen her certificates. In a frame and with gold letters and everything . . .'

And Jamie felt four pairs of eyes turn towards her as though in slow motion.

Chapter 49

Jamie gave a nervous yelp of laughter. 'I can promise you that I am not what you're looking for.'

'Why not?' interrupted Bonnie briskly, with a dismissive wave of her hand. 'If you have all the credentials – why *not* you?'

Jamie looked around – Daniel and Father Bill merely looked intrigued, Bo actually looked rather proud. Bonnie was the only one who had taken the idea and run with it.

'You do though, Mum, don't you? When I was looking for stuff for my collage, I found all those certificates.' He paused. 'They looked very smart actually.'

Jamie smiled. They were indeed very smart – and every one of them a labour of love. Not just the hard work and studying, the hours of practical assessment and the money – God, to think about the money she had drip-fed into her own education over the years . . .

But they had been a part of a bigger plan. Not just a job that gave her the chance to explore the world and her dreams while paying the bills, but the long shifts at the Citizens Advice Bureau giving her the warm glow of reaching out, giving back.

She gave a small shake of her head at the middle-classed audacity of her younger self. Or had it been arrogance – that she could appease her social conscience while still giving her son the kind of comfortable life she felt he deserved.

Naivety, she decided with a sigh, was probably a far more accurate descriptor.

Still, those days were long gone.

'And you said, Mum, you said you wanted to explore your options. The other day . . . You said.'

'Oh Bo, do you always have to remember *everything*?' Bonnie asked, flashing a sympathetic look at Jamie.

Bo shrugged. 'I don't seem to have a choice. Sorry.' He looked worried for a moment. 'I do *know* it's annoying some-times. Well, not to me obviously . . .'

Jamie's momentary frustration dissipated instantly in the very presence of Bo's earnest concern.

'I can absolutely promise you that there are more qualified people out there who would be all too willing to help, Bo,' Jamie said gently, turning to Father Bill. 'I'm hardly equipped to offer advice when my own life is in such total disarray, am I?' She gave him an apologetic smile. 'It would be like the blind leading the blind. It's one of the reasons I stopped volunteering at the Citizen's Advice – the sheer hypocrisy. I am not the role model you want for this.'

Father Bill folded his arms across his tautly rounded belly and looked down at Jamie, brow still furrowed. 'We are not looking for a role model, Jamie. And whyever would you denigrate your own worth so flippantly? The people who come here would surely welcome a knowledgeable ear, some life experience and advice, perhaps, but more importantly, don't you think, a little empathy?'

Bo leaned in towards his mum's side, his whisper anything but subtle, 'That's kind of like sympathy but better,' he said, smiling up at Bonnie as he repeated her own words not quite verbatim. 'Like when you wear their shoes and agree that life is tricky.' He frowned, confused for a moment as he considered his own words. 'Well, I suppose it would be if you had different-sized feet?'

Jamie looked up and caught Bonnie's eye, trying not to laugh at Bo's earnest expression and eagerness to help.

Daniel stared down at the floor, the corners of his mouth twitching. 'One size does not fit all, young Bo. That's why life is a different journey for everybody.'

Father Bill just sighed, an almost avuncular air around him as always. 'Quite. But had it actually occurred to you, Jamie, that perhaps you are actually *more* qualified now than you were before. You've lived the experience. First hand. You know more than some well-meaning but utterly clueless middle-class woman wanting to help.'

Jamie looked up, unable to conceal the shocked flash of hurt on her face.

But Father Bill held up a hand to allay her response. 'And very genuinely making a difference, for the most part. But you cannot deny that there are always a few whose main motivation is virtue-signalling their good deeds, rather making a useful contribution.'

Jamie's angry riposte fell away from her lips unspoken. She couldn't deny that he knew whereof he spoke. And there had been all too many bored, privileged, underqualified but overly confident people applying to support the less fortunate. Just as long as it could fit around their lunches or tennis matches . . .

'Experience is better than theory,' Daniel said, nodding. 'So, actually, Father, if there are any other displaced persons, people, who might like to talk, then I too am here to help.' He shifted awkwardly. 'I don't have any answers for them though, I'm still finding my path, but maybe sometimes it's just nice to talk to someone who really knows, you know?'

Jamie smiled at him, touched that he'd barely been in the door five minutes and already he was confirming her view of him as a thoroughly decent soul.

Bonnie exhaled with a puff. 'You see the difference, Jamie, this imposter syndrome – I've been reading up and that's definitely what it's called – it's a properly female affliction in the main.'

Jamie nodded. It was undeniable. All too often, men tended to apply for jobs that were beyond them, adept at talking themselves up, whereas women were far more likely to err on the side of caution, and consequently missed out time and time again. 'And where have you been doing this reading?'

They all knew the answer

Instagram and TikTok now apparently the fount of all knowledge, science and pop-psychology.

Bonnie would be graduating with honours any day, based on her screen-time stats and hunger for titbits of insight.

'But just because it's on the internet, doesn't mean it *isn't* true,' Bonnie protested.

Jamie smiled. 'Point taken.'

'Well, if I can't persuade you that "counselling" is the best way to put your talents to good purpose, how about *listening*?' Father Bill offered, with a smile that suggested their conversation had ended up exactly where he'd intended.

Jamie frowned. Some days, it felt like all she ever did was listen, yet still she felt a quickening of intrigue as he reached into his jacket pocket and pulled out a folded piece of A4.

'I wondered, you see, when one of our "graduates" sent this my way, whether it might not be the perfect solution . . .'

He held out the printed email message to Jamie, and her pulse skipped immediately as she saw the sender's address. Stoneleigh School. Who were apparently asking around for recommendations for a 'School Listener', preferring, it seemed, that such a sensitive role be filled by someone who was known to the school or its governors.

'I only mention it,' Father Bill said, looking distinctly pleased with himself by this point, 'because there's some indication in their by-laws that children of staff be given priority when it comes to places at the school. Nepotism, favouritism, call it what you will. They like to build the school as an extended family it seems, so even the janitor's kid gets a better shot at being offered a place there.'

Jamie blinked, and reread the email for the third time. She

was totally qualified for the role – in fact, this was one of the rare occasions when she couldn't imagine it being a problem that she was *over*qualified at that.

The remuneration was a pittance, but for a few hours' work a week that she could doubtless fit around her commitments to Ruth and Henry?

The upside would be immeasurable.

And maybe another step towards building the kind of portfolio career she now understood was the only way forward, if she wanted to keep her life in balance.

Perhaps even beginning to rebuild confidence in her own abilities – if only she knew how.

Sometimes the best advice was indeed the hardest to hear.

'Tell me what I need to do,' she said, clutching the printout as though it were a winning lottery ticket.

Chapter 50

The next morning, Jamie awoke with a sense of clarity that had been somewhat elusive of late. She could hear Bo humming to himself in the kitchen, his morning routine in the annexe well established by now, and woe betide his mother should she interrupt his carefully choreographed breakfast. She lay back in the warmth of her duvet and scrolled through her phone to find that Daniel had emailed her the best of the photographs from the photo shoot: stunning images of the assembly room filling her small screen, atmospheric, haunting. Undoubtedly, it would be a beautiful showcase for the skills of everyone who had contributed their time, talent and energy.

But there was one image that haunted her more than the others, and not for the sweeping history of the room, the intricate skill of Amy's mural or indeed the delicate beauty of the sunlight through the antique glass. It was the small, pale face in the doorway that held her attention.

Ruth.

Her hands clasping the doorframe and her face alight with worry and uncertainty.

Her genteel confusion was becoming more pronounced by the day and Henry's apparent denial of that fact alone gave her pause. It would be all too easy to dismiss a few quirks as eccentricity, but Jamie knew better. Not just by some gut instinct, or by the late-night research she'd been doing to prepare herself for that very eventuality, but by Kath's professional take on the situation.

The very last thing Jamie wanted to do was add uncertainty to Ruth's world. Not when it was becoming increasingly obvious that change was no longer her friend. Routine. Security. Familiar faces. These were the bread and butter of Ruth's carefully curated world.

Ingratitude sat heavy in her stomach as she zoomed in on the image, Ruth's expression so starkly reminiscent of a lost child. How could she possibly squeeze her commitment to them, even if the role at Stoneleigh was part time?

She sighed heavily and tugged the duvet closer, cocooning herself from her moral dilemma, that fleeting bubble of clarity already burst.

Somehow, in such a short space of time, she had come to feel like one of the family, and her commitment to Ruth and Henry extended way beyond a pay packet and a place to call home.

It was hardly as though she were abandoning Ruth and Henry, though. The position at Stoneleigh was just one small chess move, an attempt to secure her son's future, as it became increasingly obvious that her tenure at The Old School House was anything but secure.

Certainly, if Theo had anything to do with it.

She sighed, unable to ignore the judgemental voice inside her head.

Ungrateful. Irresponsible.

How could she step back when everything about Ruth's recent behaviour suggested that stepping forward, stepping *up*, was the best course of action? In accepting this role at The Old School House, she'd promised to be here and there was simply no way to reframe applying for a second job as a sign of that commitment.

'Argh.' She pressed her face into the pillowy softness and growled her frustration. God knows, if she spoke to any of her friends the way she spoke to herself, she'd be Billy-no-mates in no time. Her inner monologue so hypercritical and disapproving, it was a wonder she could muster the energy to get out of bed some days, let alone take on the daily plate spinning that was her everyday reality.

Running the conversation over and over in her head, role-playing the best way to basically say that she had big plans for letting everybody down – and on a long shot at that – she tackled the morning's cleaning with a suppressed vigour. The bathroom took the brunt of her frustration and the mirrors had never gleamed with such a shine, even as they reflected Jamie's conflicted, exhausted face back at her.

And she was tired. So very tired.

Not just of tying herself in knots trying to be all things to all people, but from the ingrained habit of checking on Bo throughout the night. Even as he slept soundly, his breathing so much more even and measured in his toasty bedroom here in the annexe, the terrifying sounds of dragging suffocation no longer a nightly event. But still, every time she rolled over, into that shallow phase of sleep, her subconscious would whisper to her. Had she heard something, missed something? How would she feel if she went back to sleep without checking, and Bo had been struggling for breath as she'd selfishly slumbered on?

Could she live with the guilt?

She frowned, driving the hoover across the hallway floor, frustrated with herself. Her daily, and nightly, efforts to be the parent her own mother had failed to be were wearing her down. Eroding her sense of self. But really, who was she competing with, except a ghost? And, of course, knowing what it felt like to be the child whose mother never, ever, made her a priority, except as a part of their own agenda.

She just didn't seem able to find a sense of proportion.

For that she needed perspective; for that, she needed her new friends and their blunt, unbiased appraisal.

Perspective.

Another sweep along the hallway rug.

She thought of the voice in her head. Gladys. And yes, she had named the caustic old biddy who was so willing and ready to put her down.

Only silenced, it seemed, by a sense of impartiality – of objectivity – that she herself could not provide.

Could it be true, then, that the same held sway when it

came to the big life choices and ambitions? In the same way that Henry could guide Willow and Chris towards their natural aspirations, without all the background noise that clouded their own judgement?

She frowned, an idea nibbling at the edges of her mind, elusive and fragile. Evaporating into fronds of nothingness and frustration as she reached for it. Jamie sighed, feeling as though an opportunity for something special had just been lost to the powering sound of the hoover and her own awkward determination to make the best of every situation. To be the best that she could be.

Irritation vied with concern in her head, as she wielded the hoover with more force than accuracy, back and forth, over and over across the large hallway.

'Jamie? Jamie, love? Are you okay?' Henry's voice loudly interrupted her machinations. 'Only, we quite like the pattern on that rug and it's probably clean by now.'

He leaned forward and switched off the hoover at the wall, nodding towards the kitchen. 'How about we have some elevenses and a little chat, before you're down to the weft.'

'Sorry, I was miles away,' Jamie apologised, startled from her thoughts, embarrassed to be caught navel-gazing on the job.

He guided her into the kitchen and they both stopped in surprise to find Ruth at the table, her enormous Filofax, well worn and well stuffed, open in front of her, and a sense of palpable anticipation in the air.

'I've had a thought—' Ruth began eagerly. 'I was thinking

that we might invite some people over,' she said, a pen in her hand and a list of names already begun on a notepad beside her. 'If we're going to all the trouble of making over that room, it seems a shame not to show it off.'

'As in – properly *invite* people, rather than just assume they'll show up?' Henry asked, perplexed. The open-door policy at The Old School House made their social life more of an organic entity and it was clear from Ruth's ill-concealed excitement that something more organised was actually rather a big deal.

'Exactly,' Ruth said enthusiastically, adding a few more names to the guest list, before pausing and crossing one of them off again with a frown. 'Too handsy.' She ran her pen down the list, deep in thought, then crossed another name off. 'Dead, of course. How dull. I'd quite forgotten.'

And then she hummed to herself as she flicked through the pages, caught up in decades of memories, it seemed.

'You know so many people,' Jamie began, mentally tallying her own social circle on the fingers of two hands.

Henry shrugged, 'Well, over the years, there have been many souls come and go from here. Many Willows. Many Chrises. Many—'

'Oh,' Jamie couldn't help the small, disappointed sigh that escaped her. Here she was, thinking herself something special. A part of the family, and meanwhile she was just one of many. The latest in a long line, in fact.

Ruth tapped her Filofax, 'And this may just look like a big old address book of names and nonsense, Jamie. But to us, it's been a lifeline.' She smiled, her eyes bright and engaged, the skin crinkling into well-worn laughter lines. Somehow, it seemed that Ruth had found plenty of joy in her life, alongside the tragedy – the legacy of both etched into the very being of her face.

'There's no hiding that life here hasn't always been easy, Jamie. But Henry and I made a choice, years ago ...' She tapped the Filofax again. 'Reaching out and sharing our privilege was the only way we could find to keep going. Offering a safe haven, a willing ear, a safe bed. None of these are big things—'

'But to so many of our friends over the years, they've been life-changing,' Henry finished for her.

'And for us, as well,' Ruth said, nodding. 'It cuts both ways, you see, Jamie. Helping. Sharing.' She closed the book and ran her pencil down the list of names. 'So many lives entwined.'

'It's one of those tough life lessons, I'm afraid, that there's nothing like grief to show you who your friends are – the people who cross the street or look the other way because your pain makes *them* feel uncomfortable?' He shrugged. 'Sometimes it's best to just let them go.'

Ruth nodded. 'And actually, you'll find that empathy hides in the most unexpected of places – that's part of how all this began.' She waved a hand around, nearly knocking a vase of tulips flying. 'It was so much easier to be around other people who were struggling, for whatever reason, and all of us being comfortable together, finding our feet, without the need to plaster on a smile. Offering a little respite and a helping hand, you know? Because the world does insist on turning, even when it feels as though it shouldn't.'

Jamie nodded. Everything they were saying made sense. Their path through the grief so generous that it brought a lump to her throat, and yet . . .

Yet, seeing that list of names written down in black and white brought home a reality that she somehow hadn't been prepared for.

To Ruth and Henry, her role was transient. All that soul-searching – only to find that, of course, she was replaceable. A temporary player in the story of their lives, even if – to her and Bo – they had felt like so much more. Like family.

Henry frowned, 'You all right, Jamie? You don't seem yourself today at all?'

'I'm fine,' Jamie managed.

Ruth and Henry exchanged a worried glance. 'Out with it,' Ruth said firmly.

Jamie shook her head, 'You don't need chapter and verse of all my worries. You've got enough to be dealing with and I'm just here to help out, not add to the burden.' She gave an awkward smile.

An uncomfortable truth that didn't improve with being spoken aloud.

'I have to disagree with you there, Jamie,' Henry said firmly. Crossly even, it seemed. 'In the time that you and Bo have lived here, it's been like a breath of fresh air. For both of us. You must know that you and Bo have brought more laughter and joy into our lives than we've seen in a long, long time. Goodness knows, your crazy friends alone have brought this place back to life. And it hasn't escaped either of our notice that you have a very similar outlook on life. Be honest – you've spent more time helping them find their path forward than you have thinking about your own. And as you've seen, Ruth and I are huge advocates of the paying-it-forward way of life. So, let's be clear on one thing? To us you have never been "just the help", okay?'

Jamie nodded, moved by his words and by the kindness in his eyes.

'Your efforts don't go unnoticed, Jamie. And Ruth and I think the world of you.' He glanced at the Filofax and Ruth's neat list of names and realisation dawned.

'Oh Jamie,' he said fondly, patting her arm, his hand trembling. 'Don't ask me how or why. There is no rhyme or reason to life, I've found. But sometimes people cross your path and join you for the journey. You and Bo – you're not passing through, even when you inevitably get the kind of job and future you both deserve.'

He smiled and cracked open the cake tin, offering her one of the last two flapjacks, in a solemn and meaningful gesture. 'No burden on your part, dear girl. Just know that we're here for you, Dotty and I. It's no small thing that you've achieved, raising a gorgeous boy like Bo by yourself. Where's the harm in having a little back-up, eh?'

'Family by any other name,' added Ruth, taking Jamie's hand in her own, her skin soft and pliable with age, entwined with the red raw of Jamie's. 'Although I do wish you'd wear those bloody Marigolds I gave you . . .'

Jamie laughed and pulled her into a hug. Feeling relieved, feeling mothered. And, oddly, feeling as though she had their blessing whether she chose to stay, to go, or some random hybrid in between.

They would make it work.

Because together didn't always mean sacrifice, she realised.

Sometimes, together meant sharing the load. A concept so alien and yet so enticing to her, that she felt a small give in the weight she carried on her slim shoulders. Every day. Without question.

Her phone buzzed in her pocket and she reached for it apologetically.

'Go ahead, go ahead,' Henry gestured, knowing that she was always on call for Bo.

Her face drained of colour as she clocked the school's number on her screen, getting to her feet instinctively even before she'd said hello.

Chapter 51

'He's fine. Jamie, He's fine.' Kath sat back on her heels, and tucked the blanket more tightly around Bo on the sofa in the annexe.

'I think it really was a panic attack, like they said. But it's still sensible to get you checked out, hey Bo? Stress can do funny things to our bodies. Especially when we're not expecting it.'

Bo nodded, pale and waxen, looking utterly exhausted after his stressful day. He tucked his earphones into his ears and closed his eyes.

iPad on. Subject closed.

Kath stood up and stretched, before guiding Jamie away from him and over to the kitchen counter. 'I can't quite believe they even tried to pull that, Jamie. I'm so sorry.'

Jamie nodded. She would save her anger and indignation for Andrew Davies when she saw him. 'I keep telling myself that school were just being proactive, taking the initiative. But, to me, it just feels like they were taking advantage of Bo, of his good nature.

'I mean anyone could have told them he might need

additional support – emotional support – for *any* kind of assessment. But they didn't even ask, and I don't believe it was their call to make. Can you believe, Bo told me that the headmaster said I was obviously incredibly busy, and that if Bo could manage to just quietly do the tests at school, it would be one less thing for me to worry about. Talk about manipulative.'

Her voice was tight with anger and frustration. Even though all the way home with Bo she'd been talking herself down.

The lioness could wait.

Kath looked gratifyingly shocked, which rather helped.

But not a lot. This whole farce just played into all of Jamie's long-held fears about being out of control.

Of her own life, of Bo's.

Of decisions being made for her, by people whose agendas weren't the same as her own.

Caution mistaken for apathy by people who hadn't a clue.

More labels, more stigma.

'I'm so over explaining that it's a conscious decision to wait. And why should I have to? All I ever wanted was to raise my son with the agency I never had as a child, and I'm still not convinced of the harm in that,' Jamie said tightly, trying not to cry.

Kath frowned. 'Nobody ever really understands, though, do they? Unless they've been there.'

They glanced over at the sofa where Bo was now curled up, apparently fast asleep, his arms wrapped around his pillow and his lashes long and dark against the pallor of his cheeks and Jamie felt herself soften a little. He was nothing if not resilient, her boy. It was just a shame that he had to be.

'Bless,' said Kath. 'I think he's worn himself out.'

'And he *really is* okay?' Jamie checked again, desperate to scoop Bo into her arms, but loathe to wake him when he looked so peaceful.

'He's really okay,' Kath replied, checking her watch and gathering her things, heading home for a welcome shower after a long, long shift.

'Thank you for coming,' Jamie said.

Kath pulled her into an awkward hug. 'Come here, you. You're just like your son – it's like hugging an angry cat! And you know you can always count on us. Me and Bonnie and Amy. We've got you. I mean, who'd have thought, that first day in the queue at the food bank, with Bonnie wielding her scissors like Zorro and Amy all buttoned up and embarrassed, that we'd be here now . . . Friends. Proper friends.'

Jamie swallowed hard. 'Who'd have thought.'

And who'd have thought that she'd be delighted by the company of an elderly man on a Friday night, Jamie wondered later that evening, as they sat side by side in the armchairs watching Bo doze on the sofa listening to music, his baby face already lengthening into a suggestion of the young man he would become. A man, Jamie hoped, who would be open-minded, loving and kind, above all else.

The heating cranked up and colour slowly returning to

his face. Ruth was doing Pilates next door with her friend Helena and for an hour or so, Henry and Jamie could relax, reassured.

Even so, there was an aching tiredness in Jamie's bones that she couldn't ignore.

Not from the frenetic cleaning and clearing at The Old School House, but from the weight of the decisions that fell only to her in the next few days.

She didn't want to burden Bo with any indecision – she wanted to lead from the front, with calm reassurance. Although the message from school had been crystal clear – they felt her hesitation was doing Bo a disservice and a formal assessment was in his best interests.

They were also, however, the same people who had triggered a massive panic attack by springing the assessment on him without warning.

So, ultimately, one really had to ask if they knew whereof they spoke.

'Mum?' Bo's sleepy voice from the sofa made them both jump. 'I'm sorry, I really thought I could do it today. I really thought I was ready.'

'It's okay,' she reassured him, glancing at Henry. 'You can take all the time you need.'

Bo shook his head crossly. 'You can't, you know. All the tests are against the clock.' He sighed grumpily. 'I just thought if I got them done then everyone might stop going on about it.'

Jamie nodded. 'I can see that.' She didn't like to mention

that if the assessments led to some formal diagnosis, they were likely to be talking about this more, rather than less.

A lot more.

'Well, when you feel ready again, why don't we go together? Maybe not to school, but to the psychologist Kath recommended. Apparently she's lovely.'

Bo nodded, deep in thought. 'The lady who came to school today had hairs up her nose. Have you ever tried to concentrate when there's someone looking right at you with hairs up their nose?'

Henry and Jamie smiled at his earnest intent. 'I don't think I could concentrate at all. Especially if there were bogeys!'

Bo nodded seriously. 'Or spinach in their teeth?'

'Or one long hair on their chin?' Henry added.

Bo hesitated for a moment. 'So you're not cross?'

'I am absolutely, categorically, one hundred per cent NOT cross with you,' Jamie said.

'But look out your headmaster,' Henry said, giving Bo a supportive smile. 'That was an amateur move, if you don't mind my saying. And I say that as a retired teacher. You never anger the Mama Bear, Bo.'

Bo burst out laughing. 'Even I know *that*,' he said, sticking his headphones back in and turning away.

'What's holding you back?' Henry said quietly. 'Because if it's the stigma—'

'No,' Jamie cut in. 'It's not that. If Bo is on the spectrum, then that's a part of who is, of what makes him unique. I'm not embarrassed or ashamed about that. Who would be?'

'You'd be surprised—' Henry murmured darkly. 'Times are different now, Jamie.'

She nodded. 'I can imagine. But really, for me, for us, it all comes down to Bo being whoever *he* wants to be, without labels. He's not a baby and he certainly knows his own mind. And he worries, you know, that all his talent, his artistic flair, would suddenly become a "symptom" rather than a gift. Just forever overshadowed by a diagnosis. And, look, I don't know if he's right, but as long as he's worried, then it's my job to be patient and to reassure. Not to pressure him.'

Henry nodded. 'It's hard to be objective when it comes to your kids. I'd say it's almost impossible and yet that's what's expected of us, isn't it?'

'Do you mind me asking, Henry, what would have been different in your life – if you'd known sooner, I mean. If you'd understood why you thought differently to all of your friends,' Jamie asked him.

Henry exhaled slowly. 'Where to begin? Well, I suppose, I wish I'd known that it's okay to be self-sufficient and happy with your own company. Making friends is hard and it's okay to walk your own path. Of course it is. But there's a lot to be said for *knowing*, intellectually I mean, that you are not, and never will be, completely alone in how you see the world. To take it for the blessing that it is, rather than the challenge.'

'I like being on my own, but with people around me,' Bo said, tugging his headphones free. '*My* people, though. Not just anyone.'

Jamie caught Henry's eye and smiled. They were always

slow to pick up on Bo's strategic use of headphones – not, in fact, always channelling music or content – just sometimes soothing 'the loud'. She wondered if he'd heard every word.

'And Henry's right,' Bo added. 'I like walking my own path. Even if people like my portraits more than they like me. Even if, sometimes, what I see on paper makes them uncomfortable.' He waved his iPad at Jamie. 'But I already know I'm not alone, Mum. And I don't want to be scared of who I am, because I actually quite like who I am.'

'Okay then,' said Jamie, taken aback. 'So, Bobo, what would you like to do?'

Bo frowned in thought. 'I do think I'm nearly ready to do this now. Properly though, this time. Not like a surprise, because you *know* how I feel about surprises. And only if you come with me, so you can tell them all about me the way *you* see me, Mum. Not the way the teachers at school took a snapshot and thought that was me all the time.' He paused. 'I'm a very different person when I'm at school.'

Henry nodded too. 'Quite right. Save the best of you for those you love. And get your mum to advocate for you, so you can learn from the best. She's quite something, you know, Bo. You're a very lucky boy.'

But Bo just rolled his eyes, his brow furrowing for a moment as a thought seemed to occur to him. 'I just think it might be nice to find out for sure. Not just think it really loudly and tiptoe around how my brain works a bit differently sometimes.

'I mean, like Willow said,' he continued, 'sometimes it's

424

the hardware, and not just the software, when the processor doesn't run properly? And then people might accept that it is what it is, like just how my head – my hardware – works.' He nodded, as though agreeing with his own decision. 'Maybe then, I could even have my own Instagram account, couldn't I, Mum? About how I think about things? Or my drawings?'

'Well, it seems to me, Bo, that you know exactly how you want to do this,' Jamie said, nodding. 'So that's what we'll do. And I'm so proud of you for thinking it all through.'

One half of her incredibly proud at the young man he was becoming and the steps he was beginning to take without her.

One half already pining for the days when his tiny hand would curl into hers as they skipped through the puddles, his gaze instinctively tracking her every movement and his smiles saved only for her.

Unfazed, Bo turned back to his iPad, done with the discussion. 'You should see this reel on Instagram, Mum,' he said. 'It's all about people like me – you know, who can really see people when we're drawing them, but absolutely cannot understand them in real life. It's good.' He stuck his headphones in his ears again and tuned out, eyes glued to the screen, the light dancing across his face.

'I have a love–hate relationship with his bloody iPad,' Jamie said to Henry. 'On the one hand, I want him to be here, in the moment, and experiencing the world first-hand. But on the other, I know how stressful he finds that – and these kids, these accounts on there ... He seems to really relate, you know? I feel like it's helping.'

Henry nodded. 'I do know. And it's a blessing and a curse. All this talk of "followers" instead of friends, and "likes" instead of laughs. The whole thing is a nonsense, of course – except *then* you see Bo with that iPad of his ...'

'And then it makes sense, right?' Jamie nodded. 'Bringing people together who have the same experiences, even if they're hundreds of miles apart?'

Henry nodded. 'He's finding his tribe there, Jamie. His identity. So, screw screen time and let the kid find his voice, I say,' he laughed. 'And I don't think you need to worry too much, you know – there's no flies on that one, are there? Besides he's a lucky boy to have someone like you advocating for him.

'It's a rare talent to speak for someone else, to see beyond what they think they know, Jamie. And it's rather gratifying to see you recognising that in yourself. Even better to see you using it to help others.' He smiled softly. 'I have to confess, I've taken such pleasure in seeing you rediscover your strengths these last few months. Maybe even finding your path forward?'

He looked so hopeful that Jamie forced herself to consider his words before automatically, instinctively, shying away from the compliment.

Chapter 52

Jamie rinsed the shampoo from her hair. Eight o'clock on a Friday and she was ready for bed. The stresses of the afternoon had taken their toll and all she could think of was snuggling in under her duvet. And maybe, just maybe, if she was feeling brave enough, tackling the six-page application for the role at Stoneleigh.

Covering all bases.

Next door she could hear Bo bumbling around his bedroom – his marathon power nap having seemingly reset his day. She frowned, trying to place the song – it certainly wasn't one of his usual, albeit eclectic, playlists.

Stepping out of the shower, she towelled herself dry, already running conversations in her mind for the following week. Role-playing, leaving no eventuality uncovered. If only she could control both sides of the conversation with Andrew Davies it would make life an awful lot easier . . . She half wondered whether her diminutive stature just screamed out to men that she was in need of their advice? Or perhaps it was the fact that she was deliberately flouting convention in raising a son alone, right from the get-go, as a conscious choice, despite all the mutterings across the years about how 'a lad needs his dad'?

Watch out for the Mama Bear, she thought determinedly, with a smile at Henry's assessment of their situation.

She ran a brush through her hair, and then paused. 'Mama Cass,' she said, a wide smile of recognition breaking across her face as she finally placed the song that had touched her subconscious.

Poking her head around the door, she saw Bo dancing in his own inimitable style – he'd clearly developed a taste for some of the seventies' classics Henry insisted on playing at full whack throughout the house.

'What?' Bo said, self-consciously, stopping when he spotted her.

'Play that one again?' Jamie asked.

Bo grinned. 'It's my favourite too. Words to live by, Mum. Words to live by.' And then he cranked up the volume. 'Make your own kind of music—' he sang happily, flinging out his arms as he twirled around, as though he hadn't a care in the world.

Jamie felt the tears run down her face before she even knew she was crying.

Watching him dance to the words, believing in the message that singing his own special song was the goal. Even if, indeed, nobody else sang along.

She pressed her hand to her chest; seeing him so happy, so in his element, was one of life's rare joys. And, as he sang along, she could only think about Henry's other parting comment.

True, he had been talking about Bo.

About the way Bo's mind worked.

But, it seemed to her, that this particular truth might be universal.

'. . . there's a lot to be said for knowing . . . that you are not, and never will be, completely alone in how you see the world.'

She could hear Henry's kindness echoing in those words and she refused to believe that she was the only one these days who was struggling to get her life back on track, who was standing at a crossroads – probably in rush hour, in the driving rain, knowing her luck – wondering which way now.

Which way now.

Those three words thrummed through her head, even as she tightened the belt on her towelling robe, and joined in Bo's gleeful dance.

Which way now.

She took Bo's hands and he spun her around. Doing her own thing might yet, like the song said, be the hardest thing to do. But in her heart, Jamie knew it was the *right* thing to do.

Ideas like this were like golden moments of promise – inspiration from the most unlikely places – and yet she was convinced that this was one of those life-changing moments she would forever look back on.

Dancing with her son. Making their own kind of music.

She smiled to herself – and yes, the idea, the concept, was still slippery and elusive at best, but she couldn't get past one simple truth: all the progress she had made, the friendships she had built, had only been possible because they had come together. Vulnerable, trusting and prepared to accept a slightly different definition of success. And an objective perspective.

To accept that there was no such thing as the perfect choice.

The very notion that she was now capable of making this intellectual leap seemed so bold, so out of character and yet . . . Jamie found herself utterly captivated by the very idea of guiding and supporting women like her, *people* like her, who had lost their way.

Those who fell through the cracks of the system, employed yes, yet unfulfilled.

Way off track.

Believing the voice of doubt in their own heads.

Living like imposters in their own lives.

She laughed at Bo's outrageous dance moves, showing off now, just to make her smile. Could she really find the strength, she wondered, to be so audacious as to bet on herself and her abilities.

To have a little faith that she knew whereof she spoke.

That living the journey was a blessing, not a hindrance as she'd always thought.

Jamie allowed herself to imagine advocating, supporting and lifting people out of the rut she herself had been stuck in for so long.

Could there be a more satisfying way to spend your days?

School listener was one thing, but it was only really one small step in the right direction.

The song came to an end and Bo flopped back on his bed, out of puff but laughing. 'Love you, Mum,' he said.

'Love you too, my gorgeous boy,' she replied.

She glanced at the clock by his bed. 'How do you feel about some company for tea this evening?' she asked.

The chaotic state of the sitting room no hurdle to this instinctive drive to share with her friends. To tell them about the life-changing notion that had arrived in her head thanks to Henry and Bo's questionable taste in music and a ballsy singer from decades ago, who knew exactly how to get the best out of life.

She tapped out an invitation on their WhatsApp group. Not for one moment did it occur to her to tidy up before the girls arrived. Not for one second had she quailed about what to wear and whether she would have time to make her tiny annexe welcoming.

All she had to do was be there and open the door.

With friends like these – true friends, she was beginning to realise – she was enough. Without bells and whistles and fancy eyeliner.

And nothing had really changed, except her perspective.

After all this time, after all these years, Jamie smiled as she pulled on her pyjamas and a huge comfy jumper.

She was enough.

Chapter 53

'I don't care what your ulterior motive is, Matson – this risotto is amazing,' Bonnie said appreciatively, ladling another spoonful from the pan on the kitchen counter.

Bowl food was Jamie's speciality – cheap, filling and no-frills.

And she was heartened to see that everyone had taken her at her word – wearing PJs by any other name – Bonnie surprising them all, turning up with her bounteous hair in a silk wrap and her face entirely devoid of make-up. Almost unrecognisable.

The uncertainty on her face eclipsed by laughter when she arrived to find Jamie and Bo quite literally in fluffy slippers and dressing gowns.

Jamie grinned. 'No motive, just in need of sensible input and objectivity.'

Kath snorted into her drink, 'Oh my love, did you invite the wrong people then …' She glanced over at her two girls, snuggled up on the sofa, trying to educate Bo about the joys of TikTok and teasing each other. He watched the conversation flow back and forth between them like a well-choreographed routine, bemused, as always, by siblings and their easy chat.

'He's looking so much better,' she commented to Jamie. 'It forever surprises me how quickly kids bounce back.'

Jamie nodded. 'And long may that be the case. Speaking of – where's Amy? She said she was coming with big news?'

'Your guess is as good as mine.' Kath replied. 'That girl runs to her own timetable, you know? She was up 'til like three o'clock the other morning, working on that mural in the assembly room. You've certainly got everyone fired up about that, by the way. I even saw Willow laughing in the garden with Chris when I arrived.' She smiled. 'Nothing like a group project, is there?'

'Funny you should mention that—' Jamie said.

'Here we go,' joked Bonnie. 'No such thing as a free lunch.'

'It's supper time, Bonnie,' Bo said, wandering over for a drink.

'Not in LA.' Bonnie stuck her tongue out.

'It's always five o'clock somewhere,' Kath agreed, downing the remains of her drink and refilling her glass.

'Bad day?' Jamie asked quietly, while Bonnie took Bo back to the sofa and pulled up the world clock on the iPad, effectively blowing his tiny mind and ensuring that Jamie would be peppered with questions about time zones for the rest of the week.

'Aren't they all, these days?' Kath said tiredly. 'How it's possible to love and loathe my job with such equal passion escapes me, but there it is.'

'And you still found time for us when I called in a flap? I'm so sorry,' Jamie apologised, her words cut off by Kath's waving hand.

'Never apologise for asking for help, okay? Promise me,' she said firmly.

'I'll try,' said Jamie, knowing full well that old habits died hard. She sat back against the kitchen worktop, legs swinging, watching the chaos of her evening unfold.

So many decisions ahead and, for once in her life, she didn't feel that detached, angry need to handle everything alone.

In the company of these women, she felt more connected, more alive and more supported than she ever had in her whole life.

For want of a week's groceries, she had discovered a true wealth of sustenance.

She shook her head, irked by her own whimsy and oddly tearful. She couldn't help but think that Father Bill would be so proud of them.

'Now, do I need to grab Amy for some food if she's still painting?' she said, pulling herself together.

'I'm here! I'm here!' Amy called out, pushing open the back door, her clothes splattered in paint and a huge grin on her face. 'We can start the party now – I have news!'

And, in the work of a moment, they were gathered together, poring over the letter that Amy proudly laid out on the worktop.

Jamie had to squint to read the detail and then her face broke out into a huge smile.

Art Foundation.

Not just a starting point, but a huge leap in the right direction for Amy to follow her ambitions.

'Well, I followed your advice and took a risk,' Amy said to her shyly. 'It's a part-time course for mature students and they didn't give a single feck about my GCSEs – they loved my portfolio though. So I'm in!'

'Amy!' Bo squealed, bouncing over to her, clasping her hands as he leapt about. Increasingly comfortable with a little physical contact, it seemed. 'You did it. You did it!'

'I am so very proud of you,' Kath said.

'Woman of the hour!' Jamie said. 'Any excuse to celebrate—' She rummaged in the cupboard and pulled out her emergency packet of Jaffa Cakes, even knowing full well that Bonnie would be off on her cakes versus biscuits spiel before she could even—

'You know they're not actually cakes, right?' Bonnie said, coming over to pull Amy into an enormous hug. 'Well done, that girl. Score one for determination, right? The fabulousness is, of course, a given.'

Amy smiled, embarrassed to be the centre of attention suddenly. 'Well, technically, I think I should be celebrating all of you – apparently it was your references and letters of support that made them even look at my portfolio properly.'

'Not many art students arrive with a following,' Kath beamed.

'Create your own opportunities, yeah?' Bonnie said with feeling.

'Takes a village,' Jamie said, filling a glass for Amy and whipping the plate of Jaffa Cakes out of reach from Bonnie's rapturous advances.

'Have you lot been at the fortune cookies again?' Amy grinned, carefully selecting one and nibbling at the edges with delicate concentration.

Bonnie leaned across and popped a whole one into her mouth, '*This* is how you eat a Jaffa Cake, Amy, for fuck's sake,' she said, spraying crumbs everywhere.

'Either way,' Jamie said, stepping into the breach before the two of them could start bickering, 'we're celebrating Amy tonight. And a victory of bold determination over—'

'—common sense and reasonable advice?' Amy cut in with a laugh. 'Come on, let's be honest. You all thought I should resit my GCSEs and start over.' She glanced over towards the sofas, where Kath's two teenagers were now entertaining Bo with – one could only presume based on the laughter – wildly inappropriate YouTube videos. 'I kind of owe Bo the biggest thank you, actually. He was the one who told me to stay true to myself, to ignore every rule, except my own.'

She held up a hand as though to fend off any recourse. 'And obviously I'm grateful for all your advice and support, but without Bo I wouldn't have had the courage to say screw it – my whole portfolio ended up being sketches from my graphic novel in the end, except a few photos and montages.' She settled back against the worktop with a new-found calmness and confidence. 'And it was *absolutely* what they said they weren't looking for, but they loved it.'

She shrugged, still rather emotional about the news. 'So I guess it goes to show—'

'That Bo is wiser and more insightful than all of us?' Bonnie queried.

'That we have to trust our gut,' Amy corrected her, shaking her head.

'My gut is telling me that I've had wa-aay too much risotto,' Kath said, nodding seriously.

'Or possibly, wa-aay too many glasses of wine?' Jamie teased her affectionately, handing her a Jaffa Cake and a large glass of water, insisting she drain it.

Chapter 54

Several hours later, after Bonnie had made herself at home by dragging Jamie's duvet through into the sitting room and Jamie had managed to swallow her instinctive flinch, they were settled around the room, draped across the furniture like students rather than an odd-job selection of grown women and children.

Jamie watched Kath smooth Lucy's hair back from her forehead as she dozed beside her, schlumpfed into her mother's side where sleep had overtaken her despite all her protests. So grown up, with her GCSEs looming, and yet still so innocent to the realities of adult life awaiting her.

Kath looked up and smiled at Jamie. 'It doesn't get any easier, you know. There's a lot more biting your tongue and letting them find their own path. It's so much harder than I imagined, watching them make their own mistakes. Any dreams and ambitions I might carry for them are completely secondary. Who knows what jobs they'll end up in.'

Jamie blinked, unable to imagine two years down the line, let alone five. And what that might look like for Bo.

Oddly, though, ambitions had never really featured on her

wish list for him. She'd always been too focused on security, safety and fulfilment.

For Bo, and, yes, for herself too.

Jamie sighed deeply. 'It's like the whole landscape of work has shifted while we were looking the other way. I'm suddenly looking at building a portfolio career, or working up a side hustle.'

Kath nodded, glancing to see whether her eldest could hear her from her perch at the kitchen counter, iPad still burbling away.

'The whole working world is a different place, J – the girls ask me about uni courses and job prospects, and I genuinely don't know what to say.' She lowered her voice still further. 'It just doesn't seem like excellent parenting to suggest that fate, or luck, play as big a role in success as they actually do.'

'And timing,' Jamie agreed. God knows her own life had been a succession of missteps out of sync with the zeitgeist.

'But even if you're lucky enough to get a decent gig,' Bonnie said, 'there's still this illusion about *job satisfaction*.' She said the last two words as though they were distasteful to her. ''Cos I don't believe that one career can ever meet all your needs. For all your life. We're all changing too, aren't we?'

Kath frowned. 'Yeah, but not everyone thinks like you, Bon. Some people need that status—'

'And the money,' Amy chimed in.

'Is enjoying your job a stretch too far then?' Jamie interrupted.

'Oh the luxury!' Kath breathed with a certain wistfulness

that spoke volumes. 'Can you even *imagine* ticking all of those boxes anymore. Didn't we used to see that as right, not a fantasy?'

'I've said it before, and I'll say it again: you make your own luck and your own opportunities these days, am I right? I mean, look at me – who was going to invest in my future, except me?' Bonnie said. 'I'm hardly what you'd call a good prospect.'

'You've got the right idea, Bon, and Henry too actually. He's a huge fan of stepping back and changing lanes,' Jamie agreed. 'I think he's bought into Bo's motto that all plans are made to be changed.' She smiled. 'I mean, look at Willow and Chris, even you, Amy. With just a nudge in a new direction – in the right direction, some might say . . .'

'You should absolutely take some credit for that too, you know,' Bonnie said firmly.

'It's true,' Kath said. 'You and Henry have a knack for seeing the blindingly obvious solution that all of us have missed,' she grinned, flicking a kernel of popcorn at Jamie. 'You two could make it official, call it Darwin's Job Club.' She seemed delighted at her own wit, and raised a glass in salute.

Bonnie just gave a snort of laughter, 'Survival of the fittest? Well, that's me screwed then, isn't it?' She cheerfully jiggled her upper arms in exposition.

'I meant adapt-or-die, you total muppet,' Kath said crossly, reaching out to top up her glass again.

'Cheerful,' Bonnie countered.

Kath merely stuck her tongue out as she attempted to pour a glass of wine with the lid still firmly screwed on.

Even with the constant, sibling-level bickering that Bonnie brought to every gathering, Jamie couldn't deny her gratitude for their unusual friendship. And she tried to avoid thinking about where she might be now, if she hadn't swallowed her pride and gone to the food bank, or indeed continued to scuttle in and out under cover of darkness.

It wasn't even a case of misery loving company, so much as understanding, truly empathising, with each other's experiences.

There was no awkwardness or one-upmanship.

No casual dismissal of their circumstances as a 'tricky phase'.

'Joking aside,' Jamie said slowly, 'if there was a group set up, a kind of community *hub*, specifically to help people change track, or get back on track – I mean, someone you could talk to and get decent advice from, or maybe be paired up with a mentor, I haven't quite worked out the details yet – but do you think people would actually use it?'

'Well, but like there's loads out there already, aren't there?' Amy said doubtfully, with a shrug.

'Yeah, but some of them seem a bit snooty and intense, to be honest. That or tone-deaf and patronising,' Kath said. 'Because, I have to tell you, there's been plenty of days lately when I've gone looking.'

Jamie nodded. 'And they seem to be far more interested in people who are actually *out* of work, eligible for benefits, that kind of thing.'

'Even that amazing group who offer the clothes and the interview practice for women – they're not interested in people like us,' Bonnie added. 'If you're managing – but not really – you just fall through the cracks in the system.'

'I think maybe there's thousands of people feeling lost right now – sort of invisible,' Jamie said, doodling on the sketch pad in front of her.

Kath nodded intently. 'Too bloody true. But you only have to look around this room to see that working out where your talents truly lie is actually the way forward.'

'Well, you're the psychologist, Jamie,' Amy teased. 'I'm still not convinced you can't just read people's minds and tell them their true vocation. It has to be quicker than all the soul-searching and desperation.'

Jamie flicked popcorn at her and shook her head with a smile. Sure, she knew how people's minds worked in *theory*, but that didn't mean she could read them! She was amazed at how often people were confused by this simple distinction.

Bonnie ploughed in, frowning. 'It's like that woman who designed the non-fogging mask thing for her disabled son, right? I mean, she was working at a petrol station to make ends meet – or not, obviously – but she clearly had the most instinctive skill for, what do they call it now . . . ?'

'Functional design,' Kath supplied. 'It's a whole growth market. You can study it at university.'

Jamie suddenly felt a little emotional, 'Seriously? I mean, like that's an actual degree course. I mean, like, Bo could actually—'

'He'd be a natural,' Kath confirmed with a nod.

There was a tug of relief somewhere inside her that Jamie had never really acknowledged before. Perhaps just knowing that there might yet be a place in the working world for someone who routinely refused to think *inside* the box. Or perhaps, just having her suspicions confirmed that the world was evolving, growing and adapting, even if it was taking her generation a bit longer to catch up, to jump on board.

'What are you actually thinking, Jamie?' Amy said, shooting Bonnie a look as though daring her to interrupt yet again.

Jamie wrinkled her nose, weighing up just how vulnerable she was willing to feel by sharing her idea before she'd fully thought it through.

'Okay, so hear me out? It's a bit all over the place, but I've had this idea . . .' She hesitated. 'So I've been thinking about retraining. I mean, I can't kid myself that working here is forever, and, in all honesty, I don't want it to be. So, I was thinking about social work, or teaching, basically trying to find somewhere I can make a meaningful contribution while still paying the bills . . .'

'Pipe dream,' muttered Bonnie under her breath, earning herself a look from all of them. 'Sorry,' she mumbled.

'Anywa-ay—' Jamie carried on, trying not to smile at Bonnie's chastened attentiveness. 'I can't stop thinking about what everyone said at the food bank the other day. There's all this support set up for the kids, all the support set up for the elderly, and then there's the women, well, the *people* in the middle – squeezed and pulled from every side and still expected to keep the finances on track.

'And I just can't get it out of my head – that they're, well, let's be honest, *we're* the ones keeping the ship afloat.'

'So what happens when we're drowning too?'

They all fell silent for a moment, Jamie's words touching each and every one of them in different ways.

'I just think that, so long as I can pay my way in the world – for me and for Bo – then really, isn't life too short to be just mindlessly working to live, when I could actually be making a difference too? Helping people get back on track? Bringing people together so that nobody has to do this alone.'

'I used to live to work,' Kath said, nodding, reaching that maudlin stage of tipsy that was half a glass away from streaked mascara. 'I don't anymore. I've lost sight of why I became a nurse at all actually.'

'I used to be an accountant,' Bonnie said quietly, seemingly to herself, yet shocking them all into silence. 'A very bad, very bored accountant.'

'What?' Kath exclaimed, blinking hard to recalibrate.

'I had this whole life plan, with pension contributions and everything,' Bonnie carried on, staring off into the distance. 'And it was literally sucking the life out of me – I was stressed and scared – most days actually. Arseholes in suits who took pleasure in intimidating people. Soul-destroying meetings that could have been emails. You know the form . . . And all it took was a global pandemic to wake me up.'

She turned to look at Jamie. 'All I'm saying is, I think you might be onto something. Adapting, you know. Evolving and stuff.'

Kath nodded. 'Second that. But with a touch more eloquence.' She rolled her eyes at Bonnie.

Jamie's smile quietly grew, buoying her confidence in this slightly madcap scheme. Setting up some kind of mentoring hub from scratch would hardly be a safe bet of a career plan, after all. 'But, we're agreed though, that's the way forward? Bringing people together? Taking a different view? A fresh perspective?' She frowned. 'If only I didn't loathe networking with such an absolute passion.'

Bonnie laughed and raised her glass. 'Then call it something else then, girl. You're the one running the show this time, remember.'

Chapter 55

One had to wonder, Jamie thought the next morning, why she ever sent Bo to school at all. Watching him now, in his element with Henry, he was like a different child – relaxed, chatty and totally engrossed in building what appeared to be a volcano in the kitchen sink. The sharp contrast to the wan, monosyllabic child that came home at 3.30 every day was enough to make Jamie question all the hoops she'd been jumping through, trying to squeeze him into a school system that really had no place – literally or metaphorically, it seemed – for a child like Bo.

Would home schooling be the end of the world, she wondered, before flashbacks of 2020 stopped her in her tracks. For all the stress of those blasted worksheets, Jamie had to acknowledge that it had been so much easier, for the two of them anyway, not to run the gamut of public life every day. Even if her maths skills clearly weren't up to par.

Jamie rubbed her neck, cricked and painful after a night on the sofa. The magnanimous gesture to surrender her bed to Bonnie and Kath last night not seeming quite so clever in the cold light of day. She tried not to think about the detritus of the night before that was still strewn on every surface in the annexe.

Bad move.

She made a mental note never again to listen to Bonnie and her willingness to procrastinate. Equal parts inspirational and surprising, the evening with Bonnie had been an eye-opener on so many levels and a timely reminder not to judge a book by its cover.

Yet Jamie suspected there were still more layers to Bonnie's story waiting to be uncovered. It felt like a privilege, some-how, to have been allowed a peek behind the scenes, behind the glowing smile and eccentric outfits. And now, Jamie couldn't help but wonder how many of them ever really wore their hearts on their sleeves the way Bo did – open and frank for all to see, for all to judge.

And where did one draw the line, she wondered. Between honest vulnerability and protecting oneself with a carefully curated facade, from a world that could be cruel at times.

All too often, in fact.

Bo cheered as the bicarb hit the vinegar and the 'volcano' erupted, spewing acidic-smelling froth high above the sink, as Henry attempted to capture it all on his iPhone. 'Kra-ka-tooooooooooo-aaaah!' hollered Bo with delight, his face lit up with satisfaction at a job well done.

Jamie glanced over her shoulder, some sixth sense alerting her to the hovering presence of Ruth, pausing in her now-habitual pottering around the kitchen, putting things into the larder, taking them out again. Rearranging until the small tins and pots made some sort of sense to her. Ruth nodded, satisfied in her own sweet way to have accomplished this most mundane, but apparently meaningful, of tasks.

And rather than raining on the boys' parade, she was watching with a reflective smile.

'Shall we go for take two?' Henry said to Bo, peering into the pot of bicarbonate of sofa. 'I reckon we've just about got enough.'

'But we've done it already. That was my homework,' Bo said, instantly losing interest now the 'explosion' had receded to a sad bubbling mess.

'Ah, but did you add the red food colouring, Theo?' Ruth said, stepping forward. 'Then you can pretend that it's proper lava.'

There was a sudden awkward stillness in the kitchen, a damp pall descending in a moment, with one misspoken word. Despite the increasing frequency of these slip-ups, they were still like a knife to the heart.

'I'm Bo,' Bo said, frowning. 'Not Theo.'

'Of course you are,' said Henry, watching his wife's face twist in confusion, but torn as to who first to reassure.

'Let's go next door and see how the others are getting on,' Jamie said, stepping forward and taking Ruth's arm. 'I don't know about you, Ruth, but I'm really excited to see the finished result.'

Henry offered her a grateful smile, but the tension in his face didn't leave, even as he turned back to Bo, now measuring out yet more bicarb in his quest for volcanic supremacy.

Leaving Bo in Henry's capable hands and trying to ignore any squirming misgivings about just how often Ruth was getting muddled these days, Jamie made her way through to the assembly room, pushing open the double doors, smiling with delight at the transformation underway. Amy, Chris and Willow all beavering away on their project.

Even Ruth looked impressed. 'They've been working so hard,' she murmured, switching back into the moment, all confusion forgotten. For the time being at least.

How it was possible for Ruth to switch back to astute and insightful lucidity in the blink of an eye eluded Jamie. But then, what did she really know about dementia? And what right did she really have to call herself Ruth's carer, when all she could really do was care.

In the literal, loving sense of the word.

'Isn't it glorious to see it all coming back to life?' Ruth said in wonderment.

It was hard to believe that the soft sage walls and muted weathered boarding hadn't always been there. Orange pine and institutional yellow replaced by soothing tones of Cape Cod – a hint of Fitzgerald in the decadent planters of glossy foliage that Willow was busy arranging around the outline of Amy's trompe l'oeil: an archway looking out to sea.

The whole atmosphere in the room was amazing, whether from the chatty camaraderie of the people creating in there, or simply the new lease of life and a touch of art deco enough on their own to raise the spirits.

'It really is fabulous,' Jamie breathed. She could already envisage the photo spread that Daniel had promised to put together. No payment required, just the promise of a homecooked meal. Just a meal, no matter how much the very thought made her feel off balance with the possibilities. Possibilities she would never have considered for a moment as they'd stacked shelves for hours side by side.

Pushing aside thoughts of Daniel, the Daniel who could effortlessly capture a moment through the lens of his battered Olympus camera, Jamie wandered around the room, Ruth at her side.

It was hugely gratifying to see everyone so invested in this showcase. Amy was singing away to herself as she daubed layers of paint onto her mural, her sweeping and inelegant strokes with the large brush belying the masterpiece she was creating. Chris, too. Happy in his element with sawdust in his hair and a ready smile.

Even Willow, usually wan and a little reserved, had flushed pink cheeks and a dancing gleam in her eyes as she filled antique copper planters from Henry's shed with dark glossy foliage.

Each of them following their passions. Following their natural talent.

And yet, Jamie would wager every one of the six pounds and twenty-seven pence in her pocket that not one of them would have considered this a career move: an avenue to gainful employment, away from GCSEs, or cyber training, or even the dizzying world of home security.

'All these years shut away . . .' Ruth said. 'It really does feel like we're giving this space a new lease of life, doesn't it? Not so much an assembly room filled with noisy young lads, but a proper oasis of calm.' She breathed out slowly. 'It's got such a welcoming atmosphere in here now, hasn't it? Lighter, you know? Like it wanted to be an orangery all along?'

Jamie shook her head and smiled. 'So you're saying it's fulfilling its destiny, finally?'

'Don't tease. You of all people should get what I'm trying to say,' Ruth scowled with good humour. 'Change isn't always a bad thing – it can be the key to a whole new story.'

'Speaking of . . .' Jamie said quietly, nodding her head towards where the French doors opened out into the sunshine. 'That's new.'

Ruth followed her gaze, serenely content at the sight of Willow and Chris now close together, deep in conversation, their hands fleetingly touching occasionally, their eyes never leaving one another.

'Isn't it lovely?' Ruth said. 'They're so delightfully awkward with one another too. And I mean, you never would have thought – he's hardly what one imagines for her. And yet . . .'

And yet, indeed, Jamie thought. For somehow the two of them together just seemed to make a strange kind of sense once you'd seen it. As though they were destined to fit their jagged lives together to become whole.

And, as much as Jamie had always loathed the very notion of needing another person to feel complete, she could see that, in this particular case, with all the inherent baggage, it was no bad thing.

'Where's Bo?' Ruth asked after a moment, deliberately turning away so as not to intrude on the romance flourishing over the trellises Chris was patiently building to Willow's exacting specifications.

'He's with Henry,' Jamie gently reminded her.

'Oh,' said Ruth frowning. 'No school today?'

'Not today,' Jamie said, unable to quash the small sad sigh that escaped her. Brilliant, articulate, wonderful Ruth, being slowly eroded day by day. Death by a thousand paper cuts. And her own son thousands of miles away. Missing everything.

Chapter 56

Jamie kept one eye on the vast shepherd's pie bubbling in the oven that evening – economies of scale her new best friend on the catering front – as Bo sketched quietly at the kitchen table in the main house, and she read over her application for Stoneleigh one more time. Ruth's words from earlier in the week echoed in her mind – don't throw in your lot with us – and yet still they weren't enough to quell the guilt.

Glancing at her watch, knowing the deadline was looming, somehow only fuelled her indecision. Not least the additional distraction of her nascent idea diverting her from the job in hand. She turned away from the duplicitous application form on the screen and began to lay the table, working around Bo, deep in concentration and totally oblivious to everything around him. Even the briefest outlines of his sketch already captured the defiant tilt of Amy's head as she painted next door and Jamie paused to watch his pencil fly instinctively over the paper.

'Well now, this all sounds very impressive.' Henry's voice sliced into her reverie, making her jump, her heart pounding against her ribs as she looked up to see him standing at the kitchen counter, glasses on the end of his nose, reading her laptop screen intently.

'It's not—' she began.

'Yes, yes, I can see that,' Henry said, with a wave of his hand that was either designed to allay her worries, or shut her up so he could finish reading. When he'd finished, he paused for a moment, his gaze straying to Bo at the table and nodding slowly to himself.

'Part-time?' he clarified.

Jamie nodded.

And then Henry leaned forward and typed on the keyboard before hitting return with a palpable sense of accomplishment.

Jamie's eyes widened in shock. 'What did you—?'

'I added myself as your reference. It seems like too good an opportunity to pass up, especially if it would help your cause with . . .' Henry nodded towards Bo.

Jamie breathed out slowly, relieved on so many levels. 'So you really don't mind, because it really would only be a few hours a week?' She sank back against the worktop, hand on her chest as she steadied her breathing. She laughed nervously. 'You know, for a moment there, Henry, I thought you actually pressed send.'

'Ah.' Henry looked awkward. 'Was I not supposed to?'

But before Jamie could respond, with a polite montage of suitable expletives, everyone began streaming into the kitchen, drawn by the clink of cutlery and the delicious aroma of a working supper.

Chris and Willow finished laying the table, no doubt making sure they were sitting together, and Amy gently teased Bo about whether her nose really was so very cute and freckled. Ruth wandered in to join them, smiling happily at having her kitchen so alive with young people and vivacious conversation. Never happier than when her house was full.

Henry lowered his voice and leaned in. 'Dear girl, we both know that it's only a matter of time before we need a little more, er, specialist help here for my Dotty. But that doesn't mean we won't need you here too. And this other position, with the children, might be just the antidote to our decline, might it not? Let's just keep talking, but please, don't mention it to Dotty until you've got the job for sure, okay?' Henry said, slipping away to ply everyone with sherry and avoiding Jamie's eye.

Plates cleared, bellies full and everyone exhausted after a long day, Jamie glanced at the kitchen clock and wondered how indecently soon she could call it a night and head back to the annexe, not least to proofread – belatedly of course – the application that Henry had submitted.

As Amy began pulling pints of ice-cream from the freezer to demonstrate her sundae skills for dessert, Jamie sat back, accepting defeat.

'Knock, knock?' Kath poked her head around the stable door and exhaustedly deflated into a chair at the table beside Jamie, dragging her handbag onto her laptop and rummaging inside.

'Absolute *fecking* arsehole,' she hissed under her breath for Jamie's ears only. 'Or should I say arseholes – plural?' She tugged a crumpled yet official-looking letter from her bag and attempted to smooth out the page with jerky, erratic sweeps of her hand.

Jamie saw Henry look up, watching their every move like a bird of prey, his hearing so much better than he ever chose to let on.

'What's your dearest husband done now?' Jamie asked, pouring out a large measure of sherry and pressing it into Kath's trembling hands.

Kath sipped the sickly aperitif offering a wobbly smile in thanks, as her body slowly unclenched and she gradually stopped shaking. 'Nothing new, Jamie. And isn't that the sodding problem.

'Letting the girls down when he said he'd be home.

'He isn't.

'Promising to repay all that money he took from the joint account last month before this month's rent is due.

'He hasn't.'

She reeled off these misdemeanours in a curiously flat monotone, as though she were simply worn down and fatigued by the continual litany of disappointments that comprised her husband, and very possibly her marriage too. She drained the delicate glass and held it out towards Jamie for a refill.

'And this time around, to add insult to injury, it seems he's taken out a credit card in my name – one of those transfer-the-balance-interest-free jobs.' She shook her head. 'Daft sod didn't even think to check what happens after the hook of the first six months, so now there's a metric feck-tonne of interest accrued. All in my name. On my credit rating.'

More sherry. More of the vibrating tension ebbing away.

'So you see – arsehole!' She sighed. 'I'm just trying to work out if I want to report him for fraud or just divorce his sorry arse.' Kath gave a yelp of nervous laughter. 'Well, either way, at least I won't be short of legal grounds.

'Bless. He really has thought of everything.'

Jamie reached out and squeezed her hand. 'I'm so sorry, Kath. You don't deserve this.'

'He doesn't deserve *you*,' Ruth chimed in from across the table, with absolute clarity and resolve, taking them all by surprise. 'Sounds like a rotten apple to me.' She gave a genteel shudder of distaste and then went back to arranging the bowlful of sugar packets into concentric circles. 'Unless the sex is great of course,' she added distractedly, 'but even then . . . Surely you girls can organise your orgasms without all this drama, by now, can't you?'

Henry guffawed with laughter, reaching across the table and patting her hand with absolute adoration imbued in every crease and wrinkle of his face, his eyes filled with love for his wife of so many decades, increasingly eccentric in her decline yet all the more endearing for it. At least for now. Until the final straight – a notion which none of them could even bear to give headspace to just yet.

'Orgasms aside,' Henry said drily, standing up and reaching for the emergency bottle of Scotch that stood sentinel on the sideboard these days, 'it's probably time for you to get some legal advice, Kath. Find out your liabilities and obligations.'

'Even if you chose to stay in the marriage, there's surely some way to separate your financial obligations?' Chris added.

And suddenly the conversation encompassed the entire table, apart from Amy and Bo, who had slipped away to work on the mural in the orangery, sundaes in hand, pulling Ruth along with them for her critical eye.

Kath shook her head. 'I've already asked. Marriage is a binding contract, you see, binding both of our assets and liabilities together.' She sighed. 'And that's just the business side of things. I look at you and Ruth, Henry, and I know – I mean, for certain, without a shadow of a doubt – that I don't have it in me to take care of him "in sickness and in health, 'til death do us part". If anything, I'm more likely to enact the death clause with my own hand if I have to stay.' She leaned forward and shoved the letter she'd extracted earlier across the table. 'And here unfolds the second act of today's Shakesperean tragedy—'

Henry picked up the letter and held it out at arm's length, blinking, trying to focus on the miniscule font without his reading glasses. 'I'm going to need longer arms.' He passed the letter to Jamie in defeat.

Jamie frowned as she saw the NHS logo in the top-right corner and Tanya's scrawling signature across the page, skim reading the block of legalese in the body of the letter.

'Tanya the Tyrant been at it again?' Jamie asked, skim reading the consequences of Kath's bold request to be remunerated for the hours she *actually* worked, rather than the pipe dream that was stipulated on her contract.

Kath growled, her anger pent up for politeness' sake, but simmering close to the surface.

'In basic terms, she's rejected my application to go up a pay grade, despite all my experience, and not to mention the very fact that I'm already doing the bloody job. With that one letter, she's basically told me, and my staff by the way, that she has no value for the work we do. We're *just* nurses. We're just background noise and in no way worthy of a living wage.'

Jamie reached out and squeezed her hand. The very idea that Kath – not to mention the other nurses – had been pushed way past breaking point with little or no support was heartbreaking; the very fact that nobody seemed to have noticed even more so. The best and the brightest of their medics still soldiering on, shell-shocked in a way, at what they had lived through. Even as placards and nonsense had rallied their immeasurable contribution. Already forgotten. The hypocrisy left a bitter taste in Jamie's mouth and glancing up, she saw her own expression mirrored on Henry's face.

'She even made it sound as though that were my fault for choosing to have children and making life more expensive for myself,' Kath carried on, exhaling sharply. 'And when I challenged her about it, she had the gall to say that at least I had a husband to cover my bills! Like it was 1972!'

Henry poured out several measures of Scotch and edged

them across the table. 'So where does that leave you, Kath? If you'll forgive me leaving the emotional support to Jamie and the girls. Could you actually *afford* to leave Craig, even if you wanted to? God knows there's enough people stuck in bad marriages because there simply isn't enough money to go around, but it never seems like a good enough reason to stay, does it?'

'Until you are the one who's stuck, and you don't have a choice.'

Henry and Jamie exchanged a loaded look across the kitchen table. A world of understanding passing in a moment.

'And what if there was another option, but it meant shelving your principles about private healthcare?' Jamie asked quietly.

Kath just downed her Scotch in one burning gulp. 'I don't think I can honestly afford my principles anymore, do you? I mean, I love the NHS – I've given the better part of my life, two whole decades, in her service. But if I can't support my family because my contribution is valued so little, then I don't really have a choice, do I? But the thought of those la-di-dah private hospitals just leaves me cold, you know, packed with people jumping over waiting lists, assured of their own superiority. Not my idea of nursing.'

'Nor mine,' said Henry. 'And yet I find myself in need, Kath. Ruth and I need to make some big decisions and, rightly or wrongly, we don't want to move into one of those care homes for couples. Sterile waiting rooms for God, that they are. Even if some of them do have wine lists and bridge clubs.'

'I can quite understand that,' Kath said, nodding. 'I think people are more hesitant now anyway, after everything that's happened, don't you?'

Henry nodded too. 'Quite. And so I find myself looking around for a private nurse to take care of Ruth's medical needs as things go, well, let's be blunt, downhill for her. Accommodation included, of course. I know all too well how brutal the rental market is around here . . .'

'Are you suggesting . . . ?' Kath began, eyes wide.

'Please say yes,' Jamie said. 'If there's one thing I've learned these last few months, it's that sometimes it really is okay to step back and take stock. And there honestly isn't a better place I can think of for you to do that.'

The queer serendipity of Kath's shoddy treatment wasn't lost on Jamie or Henry. Was it possible that the solution to all their worries and concerns had been right under their noses; one final misstep from Craig, and apparently Tanya the Tyrant, reframing such an offer into a lifeline rather than a demotion?

Kath's face twisted in embarrassment. 'Oh Henry, you are so sweet to think of me, but I have to think long term. Once you're out of the NHS loop, it's so hard to go back. And – please don't think me ungrateful or rude – but if I give up my flat and move in here, me and the girls . . . Well, what happens when you and Ruth really do need that extra care? When this house is just too much for you to manage?'

Henry nodded. 'Now that is a perfectly valid concern.

And one without an answer, I'm afraid. With the best will in the world, I can't promise not to drop dead any day now. But I just wanted you to know that there's an offer there, a possibility to save some money, regroup, start over – whatever you need, without the debt collectors banging on the door, or staying stuck in a loveless marriage through necessity.' He nodded again.

'It's something we like to do, Ruth and I – Jamie's probably already told you. We like to offer a little respite in the world; not to everyone, but to those who touch our lives, our hearts, our story. We couldn't be there for our daughter, Gemma, when she needed us, and so this is our way of making amends, paying our own good fortune forwards. The life Gemma could have lived has left a gaping hole in our world, so it helps us in trying to fill that void too.'

'And having you youngsters around keeps us young too, doesn't it, Henry?' Ruth said, appearing in the doorway, having apparently heard the entire conversation, her eavesdropping more of a problem than anyone liked to admit. 'You're always welcome here, Kath.'

'Thank you,' Kath said, more moved perhaps by Ruth's sincerity than all the logic and consideration of Henry's well-thought-out proposals. 'And I'd need to talk to the girls too. They're of an age where they deserve a say, I think.'

'I think you're right,' Henry said, nodding. 'Why not bring them along for a kitchen supper one evening? Let them gauge the lay of the land?'

'It's a lot of change all at once,' Kath said quietly, her brow furrowed in thought. Beside her on the kitchen table, her phone skittered from side to side, the screen lit up with an incoming call, and a picture of Kath and Bonnie, laughing uproariously, cheeks pressed together, hands entwined and eyes alight. The very image of happiness and ease. Bonnie's call went to voicemail, but Jamie didn't miss the fleeting flush of colour to Kath's cheeks and the tell-tale smile that danced in her eyes even as it did so.

Friendship took many forms, after all, and as they grew older and finally, *finally*, more sure of themselves, it felt long overdue for all of them to take a few leaps of faith. Each in their own way, into authenticity. For Jamie, thoughts of a relationship would always fall behind her role as a mother, and her desire to reclaim her agency in life. But for Kath, for Bonnie . . .

'And you know,' Jamie said, taken by surprise, but glancing away innocently, trying not to smile, 'if you *were* to meet someone new, I'm sure that Ruth and Henry wouldn't mind them being a part of the living arrangements here – in time. Especially if it was somebody they came to know and love.'

Kath looked up and held Jamie's gaze, understanding passing between them, and Kath wordlessly thanking her for the unquestioning and unconditional support. 'Or perhaps have already met?' she ventured shyly.

Henry watched them back and forth like the tennis at Wimbledon. 'Either way, the more the merrier,' he said, wonderfully, blissfully clueless. 'You girls are so lucky to have found each other aren't you. All of you – well, and

Chris – there for each other through thick and thin.' He paused. 'I can't imagine how anyone manages without that, can you?'

Chapter 57

'I kind of regret mentioning the accountancy thing now,' Bonnie grumbled a few days later, as she looked over the grant forms that Jamie had downloaded, and massaged her feet after a long day on her feet at the kiosk.

Yet Bonnie grumbled with good grace. The idea of making their little group something more official had obviously struck a chord with her too. So much so, in fact, that she'd volunteered her time to help with Jamie's exploratory plan. Market research of a sort.

As had Kath. As had Amy, on the promise of pizza afterwards.

A toe in the water.

Just to check.

Just to make sure that Jamie hadn't fallen foul of some slightly smug yet warped view of the world, in which everyone aspired to the same kind of team spirit and camaraderie that currently fuelled this little group of unlikely friends.

Making opportunities, pooling their time, resources and skills, and perhaps more importantly, bringing a fresh perspective and experience to the process of finding a career path that managed to be both fulfilling and financially rewarding.

In other words, the Holy Grail of all job searches, and not to be undertaken lightly, or indeed alone.

'I still can't believe you've got us all schlepping over to the community hall on a pissy wet evening for a pilot event,' Bonnie said, shaking her head but unable to disguise the proud gleam in her eyes. 'I mean, you don't waste any time, do you?'

'It has kind of got away from me,' Jamie confessed. 'But Henry and Ruth were really excited about the idea when I told them, and Father Bill said he could lean on some of his "alumni" for sponsorship or something, if the idea took off.' She shrugged. 'Although I have a horrible feeling it might just be us and a stack of flyers.'

Bonnie nodded. 'Well, at least you'll get a feel for whether there's any interest before I spend hours on these bloody grant applications for you.'

Harsh but true, and yet there was something about this whole idea that just felt right, serendipitous almost, and Jamie felt a compunction to at least explore the possibilities before she put them from her mind. Just another layer to the port-folio career she was apparently building.

For all Jamie's background in psychology, though, she had to confess that the buzz she still felt when she could read, even interpret, other people's needs when they themselves could hear only white noise, was somewhat addictive. If only she could apply the same logic to her own position so easily.

She gathered up all her papers and took a deep breath, 'Right then, I told Father Bill I'd be there from 6pm, so I'd better make a move.'

Bonnie shoved her tired feet back into her sparkly trainers. 'Lead on Macduff,' she said, hesitating as Jamie pulled open the door. 'And thank you for not making a big thing out of me and Kath. She told me you saw our photo and put the pieces together.'

Jamie smiled. 'I know nothing until you tell me what you're ready to share.' She couldn't resist pulling Bonnie into a hug. 'But if I were to know something, then I cannot possibly think of two lovelier people to know something about.'

Bonnie laughed and shook her head. 'Good to know.'

With Bo tucked up in bed and Henry and Ruth bingeing a boxset of *Downton Abbey* on the sofa in the annexe, Jamie was able to focus on the job in hand.

Even if she hadn't quite foreseen how nervous she would be; for all her cautions to the others about this being a pilot event and not to get their hopes up if nobody showed, it seemed that her own subconscious hadn't received the memo.

'Right then,' she breathed out slowly, standing outside the community hall. Hoping against hope that her fellow food bankers would show up, wondering whether she'd misjudged the correlation after all. But so many of the people she'd seen here, met here, had all fallen into the same groove.

Getting by.

Stuck in survival mode with any hope of job satisfaction way down the list.

Careers abandoned in favour of jobs and so very often, a special kind of loneliness borne of shame and disappointment.

Survivors, one and all.

Without the time or the ability to step back and consider whether they deserved more for the next few decades of their working life.

Father Bill greeted them as they walked into the hall, the queue to pick up food parcels as depressingly long as ever. He held a clipboard in his hand bearing the sign-up sheet that Jamie had hurriedly printed off a few days earlier.

Her face dropped.

Not one single name.

Not one person had thought it worth their time to have their say, to offer an opinion or share their situation, despite the carefully drafted leaflet she'd put together. The leaflet she'd felt would truly resonate with people in similar circumstances to her own. The leaflet that used their own little group as a case study and detailed all of her own training in psychology.

But no – apparently none of that was enough.

Thank God she'd discovered that before she embarrassed herself touting her cause around town looking for sponsorship. Jamie swallowed hard and glanced at the queue for the food bank again, feeling off kilter and confused.

'I'm so sorry we've wasted your time, Father,' she said sadly.

Father Bill looked confused. 'What do you mean?'

She nodded at the empty sign-up sheet, trying not to think about Kath and Amy coming here early, setting up a trestle table, taking time out of their busy lives to spread the word that it was okay to still have personal ambition, even when times were hard.

A smile creased his face, eyes twinkling beneath bushy, white eyebrows. 'Jamie, love, this is the third sheet I've had to print off.' He strode across the lobby and pushed open the door to a secondary function room. 'I've had to relocate your display – you're in demand.'

Bonnie clutched Jamie's arm excitedly at the sight of all the expectant faces turning towards the door, the small table already besieged, and her photocopied leaflets clutched in every pair of hands. Kath and Amy looked similarly over-whelmed by the response.

Jamie turned to Father Bill. 'How did you . . . ?' she began.

'You only have to read the room, Jamie. You've given everyone here a little bit of hope, just by suggesting they're allowed to want more, to ask for more than zero hours con-tracts and minimum wage. Being grateful to have a job at all can only carry you so far, especially when you're working all hours and still queueing here every week for your groceries. You've given them back their pride, Jamie. Just by making them feel seen and supported. And reminding them that they are not alone.'

A gentle round of applause began in those closest to them, those who had heard Father Bill's incredibly generous words, and then spread like a wave throughout the room.

Bonnie gave Jamie a nudge. 'I think you're going to have to give some kind of welcome speech.'

Jamie nodded, mute for a moment, as she clambered onto a chair and looked out at the sea of hopeful faces in front of her, all ages, all races all hanging on her every word. 'Let me tell you a story, about a group of women with nothing in common, but who met here every week, just like you, dependent on the kindness of strangers, even as their own drive, ambition and skills gradually waned. A group of women who needed compassion, understanding and some practical support to rebuild their confidence and get their lives back on track . . .'

Ten minutes later, Jamie clambered down, feeling wobbly with relief. The story she'd told hadn't ended with a happily ever after, but more realistically, with the promise and potential of better things to come.

And, perhaps more importantly, having shared the notion that they each had something to contribute. A big picture. A team effort. Call it what you will, but she noticed that the people in the room were now looking at each other with open curiosity, rather than staring at their feet, or pretending to read her leaflet over and over again to avoid conversation.

Bonnie pulled her into a hug, crushing the air from her lungs, 'Bloody well done, J. Very nicely put and rather cheering to hear what an inspiration I've been to you and the girls.' She grinned. 'I did tell you I was fabulous when we met, didn't I?'

Kath and Amy had squeezed through the crowd to reach them, both looking utterly exhausted yet equally buoyed by the response.

'Can you believe this?' Amy said.

'I think you might be on to something,' Kath agreed. 'All these people, falling through the cracks.' She waved a handful of the sign-up sheets. 'And you would not believe the talent and skillset in this room. Just sidelined into survival mode. And I've been asking around, Jamie – every single person on this sheet has been denied access to any job-seeking schemes locally because technically they're already employed. There's no interest in advancement. It's just a numbers game.'

Jamie nodded. She knew the feeling. And the bone-crushing disappointment at the job centre when she'd been chided time and time again for wanting a position commen-surate with her qualifications and experience. Hence stacking shelves for Nick Harrison, because according to her case worker, 'beggars can't be choosers.'

Looking at the people in this room tonight, that notion was almost breath-taking in its short-sightedness.

'Mum?' Bo's small voice shocked her from her thoughts, as she wondered how on earth they were going to get around to speaking to everyone individually tonight. And whether they'd be disappointed to be asked back for another evening when she could offer them her undivided attention.

'Bo?' Jamie did a small double-take to see Henry, Ruth and Bo standing in the doorway behind her.

'He wanted to bring you this, love,' Ruth said

apologetically. 'And to be honest, we all felt like we were missing out on seeing your clever plans come to fruition.'

Jamie crouched down, aware of just how much Bo hated crowds and yet he'd come anyway. 'I made you a sign for your booth,' Bo said shyly, turning a large piece of craft board to face her.

Jamie gasped. The image so compelling, so incredibly perceptive as to steal her breath away. 'Oh Bo! I can't even – that's just so beautiful.'

A wooden signpost framed the image, its pointed fingers all reaching in different directions. And on the other was her own face, lightly, in profile, looking away into the distance, hope and a kind of wistful determination in her expression. His swirling font outlined the words *Which Way Now*, with a smaller tagline forming her own shoulder ... *Looking to the Future*.

It was a work of art.

'I cannot thank you enough for this,' she breathed, kissing the top of his head as he surrendered to a hug. 'Bo, this is just so perfect. It says everything and more.'

'And it really looks like you, doesn't it, Mum?' he said proudly. 'You know, when you get that look on your face ...'

Jamie heard Ruth chuckle and stood up again, the sign clasped tightly in her hands, instantly one of her most precious possessions.

'He's got you there, Jamie. That's the wistful face you have on when you're doing the washing up or stripping the beds. The face that says you were born to do more than look after old farts like me and Henry,' Ruth said with a wry smile. 'I know you won't be with us forever, but I do like to think that staying with us for a bit, working with us for a bit, might even have helped you see the wood for the trees.'

'Ah lay off, Dotty, don't go taking credit for Jamie's fabulous plan,' Henry smiled, looking immensely proud of himself. 'Although I hope you'll have room for an elderly yet insightful volunteer?'

Jamie smiled. 'Of course. I would absolutely love that.'

Distracted for a moment, she saw Father Bill chatting intently to some very polished-looking souls in the hallway beyond. Could these be the mythical graduates he'd spoken of? The lucky few who had broken out of the cycle of need and who might yet be prepared to donate their time and support to a little group like this? They certainly looked as though life was just a bit easier these days, if only from their very demeanour, and the smooth confidence with which they spoke.

Loathe to interrupt, nerves prickling at her throat, Jamie turned, one hand still on Bo's shoulder, the beautiful sign in the other. 'If I could just have your attention for a moment, ladies and gentlemen? To say that we're rather overwhelmed by the turnout this evening would be an understatement, so might I make the following suggestion? Let's just pull up a chair. Tell us what *you* need from a group like this. Tell us your experiences and where they've been lacking. If we're going to build a group run by the people, for the people, then let's make sure it's fit for purpose from the very beginning.'

There was a general scuffling of chairs and feet and then a deep, yet tremulous voice from the back of the room. 'I think you may already have met the main objective. Until tonight, I genuinely thought I was the only person coming here who felt this way. And then I would feel guilty for wanting more.'

Jamie leaned over to try and catch a glimpse of the speaker, only to have everyone in the room in front of her try to do the same.

'I spent a lot of time telling myself I was grateful to have lived through the worst of the pandemic, when so many of my friends did not. And then I was just grateful to have an income, however modest, when the company I'd spent twenty years working for went bust. And yes, of course I want more security than working three jobs just to pay my rent. But how do you look to the future when you're spending all hours of the day just getting through the day.'

The murmur of assent in the room was building to a palpable energy.

Guilt. Gratitude. Longing. Ambition.

Loneliness.

'I think,' the man said, 'I just needed a bit of a boost, to feel seen – to reassure myself that wanting more, wanting my old life, my career back, was okay.'

Jamie nodded, touched by his honesty and by the wave of solidarity that rippled through the crowd. She glanced down at Bo's sign, his hand small and warm in her own. Looking to the future was a gift that they could all experience now. Together.

Chapter 58

There was a certain energy that came alive in a room filled with hope and possibilities.

It was an energy that Jamie had sorely missed, and as she looked around at the end of the evening, there was a subtle shift in those that were heading home, their minds now buzzing with options and opportunities. Maybe not feeling quite so alone, for once, or indeed adrift.

It was a very good feeling to know that, at least in part, she had been instrumental in that shift.

Father Bill wandered over to join her. 'You know, Jamie, I had my doubts about this. But to see so many people here tonight – faces I'm so familiar with – losing that down-trodden look I see every day, actually talking to each other properly . . . Well, that was rather special actually. And to hear you talking about stepping back and assessing one's natural talents and ambitions was very cheering.

'Sometimes I think people need to hear that it's okay to ask for more from their lives, just as long as they're prepared to take the rough with the smooth. And I'm perfectly aware that this food bank is just sticking a band-aid on a bigger problem, so actually it's heartening to see just a chink of light on the horizon for some of these folks.'

He gave her shoulder a squeeze and made his way back into the departing group, checking in with his more vulnerable souls with gentle and easy conversation. There was something of the sheepdog about Father Bill, softly persuading people onto the right path, that Jamie realised she could learn from.

Especially with the kind of people who pushed back instinctively the moment you made the smallest suggestion.

Ruth and Henry looked tired, hovering in the corner with Bo, and Jamie felt torn for a moment: she so badly wanted to see her son home and tuck him into bed, as indeed she had left him, but she also needed to see this through.

Bonnie's laughter echoed from behind her, and Jamie turned to see that Kath and Amy had completely disassembled the table and display in the work of moments, and that Bonnie was ushering the stragglers out of the door. 'You don't have to go home, but you can't stay here,' she chuckled, leaning into Jamie as she passed. 'I've always wanted to say that, but I'd be such a shit barmaid I thought I'd never have the chance.'

'It's true,' Kath said. 'She'd be fixing everyone's problems and denying them another whisky.'

'Or drinking all the stock more likely,' Amy countered.

'Look, you can mock all you like, but being a hairdresser is only 80 per cent hair, you know. It's 20 per cent therapy at the very least.'

'Oh, before I forget, I made you a list,' Kath said, handing

Jamie a piece of paper covered in handwritten website addresses. 'Local businesses who might offer discounts on interview clothes, or even donate. And also adult education options in the county, which to be honest, I'd already compiled for myself after one particularly hairy night shift.'

'We can get Willow to build all these resources into her website design too,' Amy said, nodding. 'Make it a one-stop click for anyone trying to get back on track in the county, you know. I mean, aside from all the government spaff for the unemployed and unemployable. You're targeting a slightly different person, aren't you?'

Jamie nodded. 'Although it does still feel a bit self-indulgent, doesn't it? I mean, a decade ago, it was a given that you might want to find work that was rewarding and filled with potential. I'm just not sure when we switched to being grateful for any scraps thrown our way.'

'I'm going to go out on a limb and say, sometime around 2022, when everybody realised that the world was never going to actually go back to how it was before?' Kath ventured, quietly insinuating her hand into Bonnie's and leaning her head on her shoulder.

Bonnie nodded. 'But, if I'm honest, it had the opposite effect on me. I just thought "fuck it, life's too short" and traded in my calculator for some fancy scissors. Gave up worrying what people think and followed my heart.' She smiled down at Kath, resting her cheek on the top of her head. 'Course, I've been basically broke ever since, but one hell of a lot happier.'

'I guess it cuts both ways,' Jamie mused, still unsure where she herself got off as any form of authority and weighed down by her newly diagnosed imposter syndrome. Still, watching the two of them building something special together, stepping outside their usual boundaries, filled her with hope that something new and unexpected was in store for each and every one of them.

'Argh,' Bonnie grimaced at her pun. 'Seriously, though, if my experiences are anything to go by, then a little mental health support in the mix wouldn't go astray either. It's hard making the leap from despondent to determined when your brain chemistry is in a tailspin. And I would know . . .' She hesitated for a moment, as though she were about to elaborate, before doing what she always did and pivoting to the practical.

'Now, take that yawning child home and Kath and I will finish up here. Go on, scoot.' Bonnie wasn't taking no for an answer, it seemed. 'And then ask Willow to crack on with that bloody website. I'll trade it for a haircut, tell her. She can't go round looking like she's just stepped out of *Game of Thrones* all her life.'

'Although maybe don't phrase it quite like that, if you're asking for a favour,' Kath added.

Jamie shook her head, indebted to each of these women in a way she couldn't yet express. But there was no doubt that it was the story of their friendship and support that had actually inspired the people here tonight, far more than any talk of retraining and mentoring.

The notion of knowing that somebody out there saw you, heard you, and was ready, willing and able to support you was an enticing concept. Even if they could hardly call themselves successful from a career perspective.

Although, she thought, with one last glance around the room, Bo's beautiful artwork tightly in her hand, she supposed that rather depended on your parameters.

Jamie gathered her stuff together, still buoyed beyond measure by the groundswell of support she'd felt throughout the evening, feeling a bit daft, if she were honest, about how incredibly nervous she'd felt earlier.

'Hi – Jamie, is it?'

She turned to see a woman striding towards her with purpose. Everything about her screamed authority, from the neat length of her skirt to the sensible heel of her shoe. And Jamie instinctively felt herself shrink.

Instead, she plastered on a smile and nodded. Perhaps this woman was one of Father Bill's guests. The ones he'd been so very keen to make a good impression upon.

'We haven't actually met, but I'm Hannah, and that really was a very impressive presentation. It's rare to see such a rapt audience, in my experience.' She laughed, somewhat self-deprecatingly, it seemed. 'I wish my Year 11s were so engaged.'

And then the penny dropped.

Hannah. As in Hannah Wilmslow. Headmistress of Stoneleigh School and arbiter of Bo's educational fate.

Hannah could not have missed the way Jamie's face lost all colour as she made the connection, but nevertheless the genuine affability in her general demeanour remained.

'Your son is wonderful, by the way. And his artwork is incredible,' Hannah said with a smile, glancing down at the poster in Jamie's hands.

'Thank you,' Jamie said, finally managing to breathe. 'I think so too, but then I'm rather biased.'

Hannah laughed. 'Quite right too.' She hesitated for a moment, looking around, almost as though to check who might be listening. 'Look, Jamie, if I'm not mistaken, I received an application from you this week. To join our team as our School Listener?' She held up a hand as though to pre-empt any interruption. 'And of course there is no doubt that you are more than qualified. I just have to ask – well, I suppose I need you to tell me – honestly – how much of your motivation to apply for the job is about helping our kids, and how much was about making sure Bo gets offered a place at Stoneleigh?

'And of course, I completely understand that he is your number one priority and rightly so . . .' She frowned, uncomfortable now. 'It's just you seem to have found yourself a rather wonderful vocation here.'

Jamie paused. Instinctively seeking out Bo, a flicker of doubt in her eye, ill-concealed. 'Bo isn't my *only* motivation,' she said, relying as always on her own instinctive honesty, 'but he is a large part of it. Although, God knows, I would have loved to have had a willing ear when I was at school. It can make all the difference sometimes, can't it? Just feeling seen and supported.' She smiled, trying to respect Hannah's frank enquiry. 'To be honest, that's part of the reason we thought about starting this group – that simple shift can be life-changing, even as parents, as adults.'

Jamie hesitated, knowing deep down that she'd blown it. That she should have obfuscated and fudged her answer, implied that she longed for nothing more in life than the role at Stoneleigh. She frowned, surprising herself to discover just how much the idea actually appealed, even while convinced that those kids deserved more than being her side hustle. 'I can't help thinking that if half the people here tonight had known, early doors, that changing lanes, changing careers, following their passions was even an option . . .' Jamie felt her words peter out.

'You know,' Hannah said, 'I sometimes wish that some-body had told me that it was okay to have ambitions beyond my children. I can't deny that I went into teaching, at least in part, because I could work around my family.' She leaned in, dropping her voice. 'And I still spend half my time feeling as though I have to choose between being a good feminist and being a good mother.'

Jamie blinked, taken aback by the wave of empathy that passed between them.

'I think I could be a really excellent school listener,' Jamie said, 'but I can't deny that my priority right now is Bo. Even this,' she lifted the poster that Bo had so carefully crafted in support of the evening, 'is just a part of shaping his future.'

Hannah nodded. 'If only we could advocate for ourselves as well as we do for our kids, eh?'

It was like a password of understanding. For how often in the last few weeks had Jamie mulled over that very word. Advocate.

A verb. A noun. And for her, it transpired, an ambition.

'Somehow it never feels quite so pressing when it's for ourselves, rather than our kids, though, does it? Even though, obviously, our lives and fortunes are inevitably theirs as well.' Jamie shook her head. 'Madness really.'

'Madness,' Hannah echoed. 'Although I try to tell my students that they'll have different jobs at different stages in their lives, and no doubt seeking out different rewards too. There's no such thing as a job for life anymore.'

Jamie couldn't help the smile that lit up her face. 'Right?' She glanced at the poster, with its many signposts. 'It's taken me until, well, very recently, if I'm completely honest, to realise that there's no point looking back at the career I used to have. It's just futile. Not only have my needs evolved, but my skills have too. I'm just not sure why I've been resisting that idea for so long.'

Hannah nodded. 'Okay then,' she said, reaching out to shake Jamie's hand. 'It's been wonderful to meet you, Jamie,' she said before slowly walking away.

Chapter 59

After a night spent tossing and turning, her mind insisting on replaying every moment of the previous evening, Jamie was exhausted. Rather than focusing on the resounding success of their little pilot event and all the amazing feedback they'd had, all she could think was that, when it came to Stoneleigh, she'd blown it. When it came to her own family's future, she'd misstepped.

So busy reaching out, driven to make sure that nobody ever felt the way she herself had done the last few years; alone and all out of options, resigned to a future of second choices and making do.

So busy looking outwards, that she'd dropped the ball for her own son.

And yet she couldn't deny that Hannah Wilmslow had a valid point. Those kids deserved better than being *her* second choice.

She yawned as she put together Bo's packed lunch, unable to even muster a smile at how this small practice alone had changed of late. No more free lunches at school, which Bo had loathed with a passion for singling him out, yet again, among his peers. Instead, he had breadsticks and dip. Fresh fruit. A fancy cereal bar, for crying out loud. They were surely dabbling in middle-class waters by this point?

A morning of errands for Ruth awaited her and she jotted down Bo's peak flow readings with quiet relief, already back to the point where Jamie felt safe having him out of sight. Even his outing last night had left him buoyed and excitable.

'Bo?' she called. 'Ten-minute warning, okay?'

To her surprise, Bo appeared, fully dressed and ready to go. 'Can we walk past the costume shop on the way, Mum, please? I've had an idea about Ruth's party and I wanted to check something.'

'Something costume-y by any chance?' Jamie smiled. Bo's enthusiasm for life always so infectious.

He nodded. 'If we're going to have an art-deco room for the party, then I thought maybe we could all dress up too? Like in *The Great Gatsby* or something?' He held up his iPad and Jamie could see that he'd done his homework – tab after tab open on the small screen – a glittering array of 1920s glamour.

'The Roaring Twenties?' Jamie smiled, watching the excitement and enthusiasm for his plan fairly illuminate her son's face.

'Raaaaaah!' he added. 'Doesn't that sound perfect?'

'It does,' Jamie agreed, roaring back at him and making him howl with laughter.

'Mu-um! That's not how grown-ups behave!'

Jamie shrugged. Maybe so, she thought, but by God that had felt good.

Suddenly the possiblity of bumping into Andrew Davies on the school run didn't feel quite so daunting. So long as she remembered to roar.

Metaphorically, of course, she thought with a smile.

'Jamie? Jamie?' She glanced up from trying to decipher Ruth's chaotically scribbled list of errands. Bo safely delivered at school, she was striding down the High Street, in her own little world of judgement and self-doubt. Her mind still insisting on replaying and re-engineering every word she'd said aloud in the last twenty-four hours.

She smiled to see Father Bill ambling towards her, his tank top straining over his tummy and his face glowing with an inner peace that Jamie could only dream about. Was it his faith, she wondered, that illuminated him from within, or simply his rigorously healthy lifestyle and endless good deeds?

'Morning, Father,' she said, his very presence vanquishing her despondent mood.

'Well, aren't you my favourite person today!' he said with a beaming smile. 'Your talk last night has everyone a-buzz. I tell you, if you were in need of convincing, then pop in and eavesdrop on the queue at the food bank this morning.'

He shook his head. 'Sometimes you really have to live a problem to see a solution, don't you? I mean, I've been running this food bank for twenty years, watching our numbers grow and grow. And somehow, the thought never occurred to me – whereas *you*? You were right there in the trenches and saw the need.' He looked abashed, almost apologetic. 'I was just so busy trying to keep everyone afloat, it somehow didn't occur to me to organise a lifeboat to safety.'

'I think we're going to need a bigger boat, though, Father, don't you? Based on last night.'

He smiled. 'Dare to dream, eh? Can you even imagine the difference it would make to this community though, for people to feel validated and supported again? Rather than just "handled", you know?'

Jamie nodded. 'I do indeed. Being stuck in survival mode is no fun. Paying the bills and getting by, but not really getting anything out of it – I mean, we can both agree that surviving is *not* the same as living, is it?'

'It is absolutely not,' Father Bill agreed. 'And you're not the only one who thinks so. Look, I know you're busy, but do you have five minutes?'

Stepping into Harnley Library, Jamie felt momentarily winded by just how much she'd missed the atmosphere, the smell of books and the feeling of stepping out of time. Small groups were clustered together, seeking out a little respite from life, whether through fiction, the internet, or indeed the coffee morning that seemed to be a source of somewhat riotous laughter and teasing.

'So, they did away with the quiet rules, then?' Jamie checked, their conviviality infectious. Certainly, when she and Bo had so often sought refuge in here over the years – the only place in Harnley to offer warmth and distraction without a price tag attached – there had been a draconian law of silence that somehow always resulted in more noise and giggling than was strictly necessary for a woman of her age.

She turned to Father Bill. 'What did you want to show me?'

He nodded over towards the coffee morning, which, Jamie now realised, was in fact a meeting of sorts. Informal, easy and yet being led by one of the incredibly polished women she had spotted in the hallway on their pilot evening. So refined and at ease, with her mane of glossy, grey-streaked hair and tailored navy dress, that she stood out like a llama in a field of sheep. 'Isn't she—?'

'Inspiring and wonderful?' Father Bill finished for her. 'Why, yes, since you mention it. She's also called Indira Norton and she's rather keen to talk to you. So, if you have the time, I would love to introduce you?'

And with that he strode away across the atrium towards Indira, and the group to whom she was apparently outlining the basics of putting together a CV from scratch. Their attempts at selling their own qualities in appropriate language seemingly the source of their hilarity.

'My culinary motivations outweigh my travel ambitions?' one seriously stocky man suggested.

Indira shook her head. 'Is that your way of saying you'd rather have a decent canteen than international clients?'

'He'd rather have a pork pie than a job full-stop,' his mate said, earning himself a friendly punch on the arm.

'Settle down, you two,' Indira said sternly, and to Jamie's immense surprise, they did. Two huge blokes, one with tattoos all down one arm, avidly taking in every word delivered by the petite woman in their midst, who clearly knew her stuff.

She glanced up, spotting Father Bill and Jamie and a smile lit up her face. 'Okay you guys, time for the next draft. Outline your career ambitions in two sentences, okay, and I'll be back in a mo.' She turned to her visitors.

'Hi,' she said, 'I'm Indira Norton. And you must be Jamie? You're so kind to drop by – I didn't want to interrupt the other night. You were marvellous, by the way.'

'Hi,' Jamie said, rather in awe of this woman's presence and energy, wondering whether she herself had ever looked so wonderfully put together and self-confident in her whole, entire life.

Indira leaned back on one of the book displays. 'Look, may I cut to the chase? I imagine you're as busy as I am. But I'm beyond impressed at everything you're planning and the concept for The Hub that you've outlined.

'I'm a huge fan of bringing people together to bolster their confidence and their opportunities. There's really nothing like a fresh take and a new perspective is there?

'Especially when you've been stuck in a rut for a while. Look, long story short, Jamie, I'd love to offer my support. If that's something you'd like?'

'Well, that's really kind of you to say and support is always welcome,' Jamie said with a smile, unable to resist a questioning glance at Father Bill, hoping for clarification.

Indira glanced over at Father Bill too, then, obviously realising that he hadn't quite given Jamie the full picture. 'So, the thing is, I run a recruitment company in Reading, but we're expanding and I've been allocated a fund by the board to invest as I see fit. It's a private company, but we like to think we're a little bit special, unique in some ways. All of our board members are women, for one thing, and we've all stepped off the career ladder at various points in our lives. Not always voluntarily. And projects like this one,' she nodded back towards the group behind her, 'are something we feel really strongly about. So, when we heard about this plan of yours . . .'

'If you don't mind me asking, how *did* you hear about us?' Jamie interrupted, totally thrown off guard by Indira's credentials, and then caught herself. 'It's just, we're new, we're small and we're decidedly local. Hardly making waves in the world of recruitment just yet!'

Indira grinned, her face lighting up and her skin glowing. 'Well, you've caught me there because you're quite right, of course. It's just that *we've* been actively looking, actively listening. Trying to see if our research is an accurate reflection of the post-Covid job market.

'Lots of people unemployed, for sure, but also many, many people *under*-employed.' She ticked off her salient points on beautifully manicured fingers. 'Frustrated and stuck in low-paying jobs, for which they are – in the main – massively overqualified. Clogging up the system, in a way, by filling entry-level jobs that other, often younger, people are desperate to fill.' And then threw up her hands, dropping the corporate spiel for a moment. 'Look, Jamie, the whole natural order of things is out of whack.'

Jamie shared a quiet smile with Father Bill – it was so rewarding to hear their own thoughts and opinions endorsed by this inveterate professional. Not that they needed validation, she corrected herself, but it was rather nice to know they weren't wildly off base with their plans and dreams for The Hub.

'So, we wondered whether some seed money, a small investment from us, might help you to explore what this project could achieve locally with the right backing. You know, like an extended pilot programme? And then we could help out too, if you needed input or advice for your members?'

Jamie fell silent, wondering if this woman was too good to be true. But then, either way, where was the harm in thinking about it?

Father Bill leaned into Jamie's side. 'And she's not just blowing smoke this one, I can promise you. Even Mr Google will verify she's a force to be reckoned with.'

Indira laughed, her face creasing into genuine amusement, smoothing down her skirt as she stood up and righted the wobbling book display. 'Well, quite. Look, I'm aware that I've kind of ambushed you, Jamie, and that was not my intention at all, but I just got rather caught up in the whole idea the other night, swept up by all the possibilities, and I've been pestering Father Bill to put us in touch.

'So here, let me leave my card with you, Jamie, and we can chat one day next week when you've had a chance to do your due diligence with Google et al.' She smiled warmly at

Father Bill. 'And, Jamie? If you happen to look on the company website for my bio, you'll find that a few years ago I was exactly where you and your friends are now. Frustrated, and struggling to make ends meet, wondering how on earth to get back on the moving treadmill once I'd fallen off quite so definitively.'

'Indira—' Jamie began and then paused, trying to formulate a response that didn't include a string of shocked yet grateful expletives. 'What did you do? To get back on?'

Indira tilted her head, the curtain of sleek hair falling to cover one cheek. 'Honestly? It really was no one thing, just a series of small steps – not least believing that I was able to – that seemed to make the difference. And finding a mentor, somebody willing to talk and to listen. Just as you've all realised, everything is so much easier, feels less impossible, when we step out of isolation.'

She smiled again. 'I only wish there had been a group like this at the food bank a few years back. It would have saved me a lot of heartache.'

Jamie tried and failed to hide her surprise. It just didn't seem possible.

'We must let you get back to it,' Father Bill cut in, watching the group in the corner dissolve into mayhem in her absence. 'But tell me, before you go – are the little ones well?'

'Hardly little anymore, I'm afraid, Father,' Indira laughed. 'Sanji is at university already, if you can believe it? But he sends his very best wishes and says that your hot chocolates are still the best he's had in years.'

'I do so love it when our food bankers have some good memories of their time with us,' Father Bill said, visibly moved. 'Makes me feel that everything we've been doing is worthwhile, you know. Not just when we see people safe and fed, finding life just a bit easier, but just occasionally it's nice to see someone truly flying. Gives us all hope that there's better times ahead.'

'There's always better times ahead, Father. You know that,' Indira said, leaning forward and kissing his cheek, making him blush. 'Imagine if we all join together? All these grassroots movements across the country?' She gave Jamie's arm a gentle squeeze. 'We're the ones driving change, you know that, don't you?'

'Because we've been there,' Jamie murmured. 'So we know.'

'Advise from a position of weakness, support from a position of strength – that's always been my company's approach. No more waiting for life to get easier, but taking the reins and making it happen. Let's make ourselves accountable and then make a difference.'

Jamie nodded, quietly lost for words, watching Indira draw Father Bill over towards her group, both of them volunteering their time and their experience in the hope of making that difference, however small.

Accountability.

The word remained, resonating with Jamie on so many levels, as she left the library and walked down the High Street to do Ruth's errands, the list flapping in her hand as the breeze blew the hair back from her face, seemingly taking with it every preconceived notion she'd been carrying of what success might look like.

All these formidable women, hiding in plain sight.

Hannah Wilmslow. Indira Norton. And, of course, Ruth.

Not shouting loudly, but whispering in the storm; quietly and considerately changing people's lives. Inspirational in every sense.

One day, she thought hopefully. They may not have the job titles or the influence – yet – but *one* day, she dared to dream that people might yet say the same about them. About Bonnie, and Kath, and even herself.

Never underestimate the women, she thought with a smile, buoyed beyond measure.

She walked past the empty shell of *The Big Trip*, and for the first time, she didn't feel the rush of hot salty tears at this visceral reminder of her own failed venture. For that experience had been but a stepping stone on her path to here.

A path that had brought her through grief and heartache, yet brought her riches beyond measure in her personal life. She smiled at Bonnie's handwritten banner already pinned in the window – 'Coming soon'.

The prize for daring to dream and coming through her darkest hours.

She honestly couldn't be more proud of her crazy, impulsive friend, for whom kindness underscored every choice she made. Forged in steel.

And then Jamie ground to a halt opposite Harrison's. It

seemed like a lifetime ago that she'd fled the store, holding a bleeding Henry upright and abandoning what she was owed, buying into Nick Harrison's gaslighting through her own insecurity.

But now she was stronger, supported, and secure in her own beliefs of right and wrong.

Accountability shouldn't just apply to people like her and Indira Norton.

People like Nick Harrison and Kieran Jones deserved to answer for their actions too – people who took advantage of the disadvantaged.

People who knew, deep down, that they could get away with it.

Staring at the shopfront, watching Nick buzz around inside like the petty tyrant that he was, she realised that she herself would never be able to draw a line under the whole sorry episode until she made the effort to not only reclaim her money, but also her self-respect.

Always so ready to stand up for others, it felt like a test of character for Jamie now, to stand up for herself. To earn the faith of those people who might be trusting her insights and advice.

She thought once more of the Kintsugi vase on the window-sill in the annexe at The Old School House – damaged, yes, yet not truly broken. Was she ready to be her most vulnerable, yet strongest self in the name of her beliefs?

She stood at the side of the road, a smile illuminating her

face, looking back at the empty shopfront behind her and taking a deep breath.

She wouldn't allow herself to go back to the blinkered fool she'd once been, was now a little embarrassed to have been. And she knew that it was Ruth and Henry's altruism that had added a new perspective to her world view.

So long as she could cover her and Bo's living costs, could she truly go back, reaching for more, constantly questing for *more*, knowing that other people were still stuck?

The last few years had shaped her, emotionally, politically, and yes, to a certain extent, socially.

Turning a blind eye was no longer an option.

She pushed her shoulders back and allowed herself to slowly exhale.

She owed it to the posse of women who had given her back her sense of self, her sense of place and the confidence to look for more in life than a pay cheque to make ends meet.

She owed it to herself.

Jamie crossed the road and pushed open the door, stepping inside to the all-too-familiar smell of Parmesan and freshly baked ciabatta.

'Hi, Nick. You look surprised to see me.'

Chapter 60

Kath raised a glass. 'To me, for finally biting the proverbial bullet! And to Jamie for her indisputable—'

'If not *long* overdue,' Bonnie heckled.

'Chutzpah!' Kath concluded, punching her glass into the air until the fizzy apple cider sloshed over the side and down her wrist. She caught it from running up her sleeve by licking it dry.

'Such class, darling,' said Ruth drily, clearly delighted that they had all chosen to gather around her kitchen table to share their news.

Her home, the beating heart of their little group.

Kath stuck out her tongue in response and Jamie laughed, the expression on Bo's face an absolute treat. It confused him enormously when grown-ups didn't act the way he expected. But to his credit, he simply watched, taking it all in.

Jamie was overwhelmed in that moment with love for her wonderful, outspoken, awkward boy, who was trying so very hard to be a part of all this. Even when they both knew he would probably so much rather be somewhere quiet, somewhere predictable, somewhere he could control every variable.

'But what did you *do*?' he asked Kath.

'I took a leap of faith, Bo. And I can highly recommend it.' She turned around and picked up a huge shopping bag. 'Oh, and I brought these for you from my girls. Who have apparently decided that the craft cupboard should now become the make-up and hair-dye cupboard. I never thought I'd be sad to say goodbye to those fecking aqua-beads but there you go . . .'

She rolled her eyes, but there was also amusement in there somewhere – it was obvious to Jamie how incredibly proud Kath was of her two teenage girls. Possibly the kindest and most empathetic teenagers Jamie had ever come across and it was easy to see why, with Kath as their mother.

Jamie mouthed her thanks as Bo's face lit up like Christmas, disappearing with Amy to pore over their spoils. 'Thank you,' he said, turning, remembering. 'I really love them, but I've never had any before.'

'You're so welcome, my love,' Kath said. She dropped her voice. 'I know they're horrifically expensive, Jamie, so I thought waste not, want not. I hope I haven't stepped on toes.'

'Never,' said Jamie, the weight of her belated wages from Harrison's heavy in her back pocket. Only what she was owed. And hardly a fortune. But worth the world to her. Worth seeing the look on Nick Harrison's face when she stood her ground and demanded her own due.

'And I'm so proud of you for resigning,' Jamie said. 'It's one thing feeling underappreciated and put upon, it's a whole new ball game doing something about it.' She spoke from the heart, still basking in the warm glow of satisfaction herself. 'But what made you change your mind?'

'You. Henry. Your faith in me.' Kath shrugged. 'That, and I want a divorce.'

Jamie gave a nervous laugh. 'For a moment there, I thought you were breaking up with *me* . . .'

Kath laughed too. 'You're worth twenty of my sodding husband, Jamie, and you know it. But it struck me in the middle of the night last night, wrist deep in some arsehole – literally and metaphorically, I'm afraid to say – who'd been out on the lash with his supposed friends and wanted to "experiment", that I'm so done with men.

'All men, actually. On every level.' Her eyes sought Bonnie's, a shared look of understanding and affection passing between them.

'Being corrected, being interrupted, being made to feel less than I am, when actually it's *my* hard work and determination keeping the ship afloat. I'm just done,' Kath reaffirmed.

She leaned back against the kitchen island, as though literally deflated. 'And to walk away with nothing from this marriage, because believe me, I want nothing of his, I needed a pay rise. It's that simple.

'And if that means leaving my lovely A&E, then I can't think of nicer people to work for than Henry and Ruth.' She paused. 'It's amazing to me how much necessity can focus the mind and boost your bravery, isn't it? But then, look who I'm talking to.'

Jamie nodded. Her conversation with Indira Norton had been a game-changer.

She was still reeling from the possibilities that a little support at the right time might make to all their hopes and endeavours. Early investment was everything to a scheme like the one she was building.

And then, she stopped and corrected herself.

Intention was everything; the money was merely a means to make it happen.

It would be self-belief that carried her forward, on her quest to be the change she wanted to see in the world.

'If nothing else, it's nice to be reminded that it's good to be the lead character in your own story from time to time.'

Jamie laughed quietly. 'I think I'm long overdue a BAFTA nomination for Best Supporting.' But even as she said it, she felt that the sands were shifting beneath her feet, as though she too were on the cusp of changing lanes.

Kath yawned and stretched until her shoulders clicked. 'Right. I should probably fuck off home and make the girls some supper. God love 'em, they'll have sorted the house before I even get home, so I have big plans for some sleep.'

'Or they could join us here?' Ruth interrupted. 'Start as we mean to go on – besides, we're party planning this evening, didn't anyone tell you?'

'Whose birthday?' Kath asked.

Ruth shook her head. 'No one particular reason. Just lots of small, cheery wins to celebrate – and God only knows, you have to celebrate every single one at my age,' she smiled. 'Please call them ...'

It was obvious already that Kath joining the household would be a game-changer. Even if, by definition, Jamie's own role would be curtailed.

Yet Henry had been firm on this – the more, the merrier – they needed family around them, he'd said, at this stage in their lives. Whatever form that might take. More so now than ever, after a lifetime of choosing, of adopting, souls into their world and then investing the time, effort and love to build those relationships.

This was not a zero-sum game – they all stood to benefit.

As the chatter around the table built to a deafening crescendo, Jamie saw Bo slip away with Amy to the orangery, paints in hand, even as Kath fussed after them both, checking what they might want for supper.

Kath and Ruth. Two mothers cut from the same cloth: both outward-looking and generous. The kind of role models that stood in direct contrast to Jamie's own start in life – the kind of people who managed to make everyone around them feel valued, feel like a part of something, inspiring them to be their true selves, rather than stuck following old patterns.

Nature, nurture, Jamie sighed, thinking that, for her at least, it was never too late for a bit of nurturing.

She may be the parent these days, but the child inside her still longed for validation and unconditional love.

Being here, among the laughter and teasing, and absolute support, was the closest she had ever come to feeling at home.

And to think how easily their paths might never have crossed if her stubborn pride had had its say. She shivered at the very thought.

'Are you coming? Do you want to see?' Bo and Amy stood in the doorway to the orangery, their faces lit up with excitement. 'It's all done!'

There was nothing linear or logical about Amy's mural sweeping across the walls of the room, lit up by the deepening purple twilight outside the windows. This was magical and fantastical, capturing the light and glossy foliage of the real-life plants in clusters around the room.

It was a work of art.

And hidden among the painted branches and foliage were tiny Easter eggs, little motifs nestling to be sought out for each of them. Miniature sherry glasses catching the light as though from burnished antique glass, a pair of hairdressing scissors, small seedlings questing for sunlight and sketching pencils that seemed to come alive on the wall. Each miniature motif hidden like a personal gift, as they all crowded into the room, exclaiming and delighting in what they had all achieved.

'Bloody hell!' said Bonnie bluntly, awed by what she was seeing.

'Well, isn't this just sensational!' Henry said proudly, choked with emotion, as he studied their work closely.

Ruth simply walked around the room, as though in a daze, one hand trailing through the leaves of Willow's plants, not missing a trick. She ran her fingers over the smooth curves of polished wood of Chris's settle, refashioned from the timber of the school lectern.

'I am so very proud of all of you,' Henry said, gathering himself together and holding up his mug of tea in salute. 'We're an unlikely little group, I'll grant you. But look – just *look* what you can achieve when you come together with a common goal. I'll wager that there's always more that unites us than divides us – if only people choose to look for it.'

Ruth returned to his side and glanced up at him, her eyes milky and unfocused. 'Souls always recognise each other, love, you know that. Woven together, we're always so much stronger.' She took his hand, squeezing it tightly. 'And to think where we all started . . .'

Jamie looked over at Bo, who was wide-eyed at everyone's reaction to their project, and smiled. Ruth made a valid point.

They'd come a long way.

Even as the last of the sunlight dipped below the horizon and the orangery perceptibly darkened moment by moment, there still remained a warm glow in the room.

Ruth looked up at Henry, as though entranced. 'I'm so very lucky to have met you.' She spoke with feeling, her eyes following his every movement, his every tremor.

'The feeling, my wonderful Dotty, is entirely mutual,' he

said, leaning forward and kissing her forehead. 'We're a good team, you and I.'

'The very best,' she agreed. 'And do you remember the dress I wore, the night we got engaged – in a room almost exactly like this?'

'I do,' said Henry, gazing lovingly at his wife of forty years. 'Silver. And didn't you shine . . .'

Ruth smiled softly. 'Come and help me – I want to see if it's still in the wardrobe upstairs. I want to wear it for the party.'

And, of course, Henry being Henry didn't protest, but simply followed his wife's lead with an indulgent smile.

Jamie watched them go – knocked sideways by the simple, and yet apparently elusive, realisation that it was so very much easier to follow your dreams when you had a template – an idea, even – of just what it was that you were aiming for.

What kind of life would fill your heart.

And the choices that were required to get there.

She saw Kath and Bonnie, hand in hand, with Kath's daughters watching indulgently on. No judgement, only relief perhaps, at seeing their mum so serene and comfortable in her own skin.

Chris and Willow were snuggled in side by side on the settle, eyes only for each other. And, while their relationship would make no sense to a casual observer – Chris's bland middle age to Willow's ethereal youth – they somehow complemented each other perfectly and their happiness was evident to anyone who cared to look beyond appearances.

This room – these people – so filled with promise and potential.

Not only did it feel like a rare and wonderful thing for Jamie and Bo to feel so intrinsically a part of something, but Jamie was all too aware of the privilege of her new position. Not only her job here, but having the opportunity, with The Hub, to provide a springboard for other people – people like her – back into lives with agency and potential.

As a testament, perhaps, to the lives that had been truly lost over those few hideous years, when endurance and persistence – God yes, even survival – had been the only priority that mattered.

When love had trumped selfishness for just a short while there, even the most insensitive among them thinking of others, locking down for the greater good.

Too late for her adored Anik, of course. But God knows he would be so incredibly proud now, to see what she had achieved, to see the world she had rebuilt when their own shared dreams had died along with him. His sheer exuberance for life had become an intrinsic part of her own, igniting her quest to reach out to others wherever she could.

It was telling how many of the souls here, rebuilding and reshaping their lives, had fallen into the abyss of vulnerability for a while there.

Better times ahead, Jamie thought, taking in the work of art that this room had become. A collaboration of souls, and etched onto the very walls – as Bo would say – the art of friendship.

She felt Bo slide his small hand into hers, that instant recognition bringing happy tears to her eyes.

'Do you think they liked it?' Bo asked. Always checking, always wanting to be sure.

'I know they did,' Jamie replied. 'In fact, I think they loved it.'

And Bo simply nodded, happy to be reassured.

EPILOGUE

A few months later . . .

'Bo! Come on, you're going to be late!' Jamie hollered up the stairs. She wasn't sure who was more nervous about his first day of secondary school – her or Ruth.

Bo, as always, it seemed, danced to his own beat, taking his time, making sure everything in his backpack was perfectly aligned.

Jamie hovered by the front door, folding and refolding his new school sweatshirt, freshly laundered and removed of all tags and potential irritations, just as Bo's new advisor had instructed her. She pressed the warm softness to her face and inhaled, relishing this moment, this landmark of parenting a child like Bo, that had never once been a given.

The crest of Stoneleigh was embroidered in a bold yellow on the chest and filled her with hope that this fresh start, this leap into a new environment, would be everything that Bo needed. Or at least a giant leap in the right direction; between the art department and the learning support team, he was certainly going to have a busy schedule.

Hannah Wilmslow had made sure of it.

While politely and respectfully declining Jamie's application to join their team, and making a sizeable donation to The Hub from their charitable fund. 'Get out there and make a difference, Jamie. If you're going to help people live up to their potential, then the very least you can do is live up to yours!'

It was the most life-affirming job rejection that Jamie had ever received.

And so now, she split her time – half the week with Ruth and Henry keeping house to cover her bills, and half the week with her friends building their exciting project from scratch.

She smiled at just the thought – who knew that job satisfaction came in all shapes and sizes? Putting aside financial gain had been the most rewarding decision she'd ever made.

Ruth tapped her fancy new floral cane impatiently against the door frame. 'Now look, shall I go up there and give the lad a nudge?' she offered. 'Kath's taking me swimming in a mo and I don't want to miss the big reveal.'

Jamie shook her head. 'Nope. I've been given my orders and I'm letting him steer the ship for a bit, just while we find out what works for him.'

'I could pop up and give him a few words of wisdom, you know, man to man?' Henry offered, poking his head inside from the doorstep, where everyone had assembled to see Bo off to school.

'Stop fussing,' Bo instructed firmly, clattering down

the stairs from his bedroom. 'All of you! And, Mum, *don't* unpack all my stuff while I'm at school.'

Jamie held up her hands in surrender. 'I wouldn't dream of it,' she replied. 'But you did promise me a photo?'

Bo rolled his eyes, humouring her, but with such affection and good grace it rather undermined his newfound urge for teenage independence.

'Come on then, Mother,' he said, taking the sweatshirt from her hands and tugging it over his head, careful not to muss his carefully crafted hair. 'Let's get this over with.'

He stepped outside and laughed. 'Mu-um! You said no fuss!'

Jamie stepped out beside him, unable to restrain the beaming smile on her face. Henry and Ruth, of course, he'd known about. But perhaps she should have forewarned him about the rest.

Daniel stood at the end of their front pathway with his fancy camera, while Bonnie, Amy, Kath and her two girls all crowded outside the front door, holding daft helium balloons and grinning like loons. Even Father Bill had come along to join them. Cheering Bo on, pride writ large on all their faces. Bonnie and Kath's newly acquired engagement rings twinkling in the morning sunlight.

Thank God she'd been able to dissuade them from the party-poppers, Jamie thought – yet another good use of that eye-wateringly expensive assessment she'd organised for Bo over the summer. A little authority went a very long way when shaping people's expectations and actions, and a small part of her felt that she might yet owe Andrew Davies an apology, or acknowledgement at least, that he'd made a valid point or two. However clumsily.

All those months of worrying, of trying to always, *always,* do the right thing – and while she knew that was just part and parcel of being a parent, Jamie was also utterly determined never to let that fear eclipse the joy, the special moments together, that would be over in the blink of an eye.

Moments like this.

'Come on then,' Daniel called. 'This one's for the mantelpiece!'

'If you ever bloody unpack so you can find it—' Bonnie chimed in, as they all huddled together, with Bo centre stage for the photo, laughing as he batted away an errant balloon.

'Wait, wait,' Jamie said, turning to pull the front door closed behind them. The little yellow door of the cottage the perfect backdrop for their photo.

The perfect place for her and Bo to call home.

She smiled for the camera, feeling years younger, the weight lifting from her shoulders with each passing day. The air flowing more easily through her son's lungs as they cut out the hidden allergens that had clearly been tormenting him for years. Thank God for Kath swinging one last bat for them before she left the NHS behind.

Call it nepotism, or cronyism if one preferred – or just call it friendship.

Because Jamie was way past feeling any stubborn pride or discomfort when it came to asking for help these days;

indeed, she spent most of her days encouraging others to do the same. To reach out, to ask for help.

To recognise that doing so wasn't a sign of weakness, but of strength.

That other people might see your path more clearly than you did yourself.

Bo leaned in for one of his koala hugs. 'Thanks, Mum,' he said into her jumper, pressing his face into her shoulder and squeezing his arms tightly around her.

He didn't need to say what for – theirs was a blanket understanding these days. They worked as a team, navigating a path together through their new and ever-changing landscape.

Even a week ago, who would have thought that Chris and Willow would be off, hightailing to Scotland and the promise of a job together on some far-off Scottish estate – gardener and handyman – and the most idyllic flint cottage on the shores of a windswept loch.

Apologetic, yet filled with excitement and anticipation for their life together, they'd said their hurried goodbyes. Jamie had been somewhat shocked at first by how philosophical Ruth and Henry seemed to be at their departure – excited even, to see them go.

Until Ruth had leaned in closer and exhaled wistfully. 'It's a catch and release situation, you know. All parenting is. People come and they go – it just means we're doing something right ...'

Henry had nodded. 'This is exactly what we wanted to

do, isn't it, Dotty? Restore the natural order of things – life can't stay static forever, as we know only too well. So why not offer a springboard back into life, and just savour every soul that passes through.'

They'd been gone but half an hour when Henry had quietly approached Jamie as she emptied the dishwasher, pulling her aside and pressing Willow's housekeys into her hands. The tiny keyring of a silver egg nestling into the palm of her hand.

As though it were meant to be.

The little house with the yellow front door.

'Make yourselves a home there, Jamie. You and Bo. I know Kath, Bonnie and the girls will appreciate some more space in the annexe than they have in the main house with us, so you'd be doing them a favour too. But most importantly—'

He'd leaned in closer. 'I want you to have a five-year lease, okay? I want you to know – you and Bo – that having somewhere clean and safe to live isn't something you ever need to worry about while he's in school. So then, you – Jamie – can take all that headspace and get out there and make a difference to the world. Both of you,' he'd instructed sternly.

Jamie had blinked, completely blindsided, and she remembered mumbling something about not wanting to accept charity now she was back on her feet. He'd fobbed her off there and then, insisting that she would still be a regular rent-paying tenant.

It was only once they had moved all their stuff across, made up the sheets on Bo's bed and hung curtains to block out the early morning light that illuminated his bedroom, that Henry had given her the tenancy to sign.

A peppercorn rent didn't come close.

'Hard work and decency should be their own reward, even if that isn't always the case. But, you know, I'm convinced it's the people who *think* differently that change the world, Jamie. And we both know that the apple doesn't fall far from the tree with you two. So, pick up the reins for me, Jamie, please. Carry on the legacy that Ruth and I have worked our whole lives to leave behind. After all, what footprint do we leave behind in this life except those in the hearts of the people we have loved? And the choices we've made.'

And then he'd handed her the second document, smart and stiff in a legal folder. A document making her a trustee of the Waverly Trust – managing their legacy more literally than metaphorically. A calling rather than a job. And an absolute honour.

Theo's financial prowess had come good, it seemed, wrangling his parents' affairs into order.

A dialogue thankfully opening up between them.

Finally.

Even if it was on the only terms Theo could really comprehend – his actions speaking louder than so many words.

Henry had tapped the paperwork. 'You and Theo will need to work together on this though, Jamie. Dotty and I are choosing to invest in a future we won't be around to see, but I've never been more confident that it will be in safe hands.'

He smiled warmly. 'Keep our lad on track if you can, love. He might need a reality check from time to time.'

'For the love of God, would you all stop *talking* and look in the same direction at the same bloody time!' Daniel hollered in frustration from the end of the garden path, waving his camera in the air and trying to get their attention, the professional perfectionist in him unable to cope with framing such a chaotic family snap.

For that is what they had become, this unlikely group of souls – filled with good intentions and open hearts, supporting each other across the generations.

Not just a group of friends, but a family of sorts. A family of choice.

Guiding each other towards opportunities of their own making, only made possible by changing their perspective. Putting aside the external forces that had shaped their lives thus far, and pooling the courage of their convictions.

But of course, Daniel had not appreciated who exactly he was dealing with, as one and all instantly pulled stupid faces, looking off in every possible direction. Striking silly poses and laughing at the sheer confusion and frustration on his face, until he too saw the funny side and pressed the shutter closed.

A moment in time, captured together. Their futures duly entwined.

Anything possible.

Acknowledgements

The characters in this story arrived in my head in the middle of 2020 – the strangest and most unsettling of years – and yet their story, their friendship, and working through Jamie's evolution, brought me much comfort that there were brighter times ahead.

By the time this book is in your hands, I genuinely hope that is true for you, my lovely readers.

There's a very special sense of responsibility when crafting a story like this one – knowing that someone, somewhere, is living through these same experiences (far too many people these days, it seems) so I can only hope I have done Jamie, and Bo, and everyone at the Food Bank, justice.

Should you feel so moved, I know the team at The Trussell Trust (www.trusselltrust.org) would be only too delighted to hear from you – whether you are in need of help, or able to offer some . . .

Hard times are hard enough without facing them alone.

I would like to thank the amazingly skilled team of people who keep these pages turning, making sure the words are polished, the cover is captivating, and that each of my books finds its way onto the shelves ... For you, dear reader, to discover.

To my cracking publishing team at Simon & Schuster, and to the gorgeous Rebecca Ritchie at A.M. Heath – my deepest and most heartfelt thanks to every one of you, for your guidance, patience and ever-enthusiastic support.

To all the booksellers, librarians and book clubs – your support means more than you can possibly imagine.

And to my truly inspiring Cotswold authors' group – and indeed those lovely writing souls I only seem to 'see' online these days – all of them ever-ready with kindness, friendship and genuine kick-ass advice ... Thank you for everything – I'd be lost without you.

Lastly, but always, always first in my mind – to Sam, Rosie and Bertie, and indeed our duo of Ginger Ninjas. Thank you for riding this rollercoaster with me. The highs and lows – even the white-knuckle bits – softened, in hindsight, by the sheer joy and elation of our life together. I love you so much – and it may be the end of an era, but it's also the beginning of our next big adventure. Together.